THE LIFE OF RILEY

and his **"Troubles"**.

Rob Little

In memory of Patricia,
my loving wife of fifty years.

Special thanks to Luke Fielding for creating the cover.

All persons mentioned in this publication are fictitious and any resemblance to persons living or dead is coincidental. The guilty have had their names changed.

I will send a donation from each book sale to the
Nicola Murray Foundation, ovarian cancer charity.
Nicola Murray Foundation <info@nicola-murray-foundation.org.uk>

ISBN 1533531773

The Life of Riley and his "TROUBLES"

PART 1

The roar of an explosion jolted Big Martin Muldoony, Commander of Belfast's Hillshanks Republican Brigade, to a worrying wakefulness. He levered himself upright in bed, waited, listening for the sounds of alarms and sirens that would surely follow.

There was nothing, only the calm voices of his neighbours conversing over the fence with passersby using the pavement outside his terraced home. He relaxed. There were no sounds of panic nearby, whatever the intrusion was.

Enough light was entering the bedroom through curtain chinks for him to see clearly the face of his wife, Tracy, close to the dent in the pillow his head had just left. Her head was still. It seemed she wasn't breathing. Then in an instant her entire, obese body twitched, her lips puckered and she let rip a heroic snore.

Martin laid his head onto the headboard, took a deep breath. He had reacted to Tracy's throaty eruption directly into his ear, the way he would have to such sounds on any morning before the signing of "The Good Friday Agreement".

Once, it was Tracy's rampant sexiness as the cock crowed that had agreeably roused him. The rockets had not only fired for them then; they entered the stockade through the gun-ports, broached the doors of the armoury and blew up the barracks as well. Nowadays, he had no thoughts of mounting her.

At their local pub the night before, they had each guzzled ten pints of Guinness. The boozing hadn't ensured a peaceful night for him; too often, he had hurtled to the cludgie, emptying. Tracy's head had hit her pillow and never moved.

The bedside alarm clock said it was 8a.m. Quietly, he swung his legs from beneath the duvet, slid his feet into slippers, and shrugged on the housecoat that Tracy had knocked together from several Irish Republic tricolours.

He padded through the kitchen to the back door, then into the backyard of his terrace home. His greyhound was whining in its kennel. He let it out to roam in its adjacent chicken-wire run.

He had taken delivery of a sheep's head the night before. Too large for the fridge, he had kept it outside overnight, in a bucket, covered with a plastic bag. It had been a warm night. A swarm of bluebottles circled the bucket and he waved a hand at them.

Taking hold of an ear, he lugged the head into the kitchen, dumping it in the sink. With the knife for the job in hand, he sharpened its point. The head, stripped of skin, would make sheep's-head broth, the accelerator of racing dogs.

He placed the skinned head in a pan, added water and veg, then placed it on a gas ring of the stove standing next to the sink. In minutes, the mixture was bubbling, spitting juices, the head grinning over the rim surrounded by dancing onions, carrots and spuds. Meat was leaving the bone; eyes were popping from their sockets, ready to spill down the jowls; brains were bursting through the hole made by a slaughterman's cleaver.

Martin ignored the smell of hot mutton fat tainting the air; he was used to it. He wet a pot of tea and took a steaming mug into the bedroom for Tracy, still noisily asleep.

At 9.a.m., Martin was sitting at the small and wobbly kitchen table, smoking a roll-up, sipping tea, thinking ahead. He expected Mickey O'Rourke, a potential brigade rookie, to arrive for enlistment that night. Since the brokered peace deal in the province, recruitment to the brigade had slowed. Mickey had visited Martin's home a few times to profess his interest in the cause. He had major credentials. Ten years previously, at the height of the troubles, a Proddy paramilitary bomb had blown his parents to bits. Now, he wanted revenge.

New blood, the keener the better, was always welcome. Martin always adhered to the test required of recruits, whether they were fanatical or not.

The back door of his home opened, then closed. ''Sthat you, Sean?' he called towards the sound, his voice sounding rough. It did most mornings from booze, smoking and snore-broken sleep.

He knew without looking out the window onto the yard that a friend was calling. The greyhound had only whined for attention; it had not barked, warning of an approaching stranger.

Martin stood fully six-foot-five inches tall, angular of body, bitter of face. Brigade subordinates had often felt uneasy beneath his gaze, had their own thoughts on him, but never spoke them aloud: 'He had undertakers' eyes: hard, cold, as grey as steel and would only light up on seeing a dozen laid-out for preparation on his slab.'

'Aye, it be me, Martin, top o' the morning tae yeh,' a Derry voice, nasal and whiney, called back to him as the back door closed.

Martin rose from his chair and shuffled across to the kitchen fridge. He pulled on the door, stooped, peered in and then shoved a hand into the fridge interior. The light wasn't working and he roughly pulled out an ill-fitting plastic drawer. He said loudly, 'Where's those packets o' bacon and stuff.' He found streaky bacon, a link of sausages, two eggs and some black pudding.

He didn't like the look of the soda bread. It was soggy, tinged with blue mould, past its use-by date. Straightening, he squashed the soda bread into a ball and tossed it over his shoulder, in the direction of the kitchen sink. 'Blue-tainted crap,' he called after it.

Sean Mullroony pushed through the kitchen door. He was Martin's lieutenant; his comrade and back watcher in many skirmishes with the hated Proddy paramilitaries and the "Army of Occupation". Sean was wearing a black donkey jacket, which his scrawny frame didn't fill, black gloves and black woolly bonnet. He took off the gloves and bonnet and stuffed them into a side pocket, turned and closed the door behind him.

It was warm outside, but his attire was the uniform of the brigade and he always dressed correctly when visiting the home of his chief.

The ball was still airborne as Sean turned to face Martin. The soda-bread ball thudded into the plastic basin sitting in the sink, but some soggier bits had broken off in flight, landing on Sean, white specks appearing down the length of his donkey jacket. His droopy, Ché Guevara-style moustache, streaking across the top lip of two pursing in agitation, began twitching furiously. Pawing at the offending stodge, he brushed it from the jacket onto the floor and spread it with a kick over the kitchen carpet.

'This soda bread is manky. Streaked with blue. Proddy mould it is, tae be sure. Ah couldnae trust that wife o' mine tae keep grub for a scabby mongrel dug, Sean.'

'Away with yeh. Tae be sure Tracy keeps the place spotlessly clean and white,' Sean defended.

'So she might, but its stickin' out a mile why wimmen get married in white?'

'Tell me.'

'Well the dishwasher has tae match the fridge and the cooker and that's a cracker?' Martin roared the answer.

As Martin was in full flow, the door leading to other parts of the house was shouldered open. Tracy entered, sounding a grunted greeting, just in time to hear the conversation.

Just out of bed, she wore a matching housecoat to Martin's, tied around her middle with a leather dog lead. A faded towel wreathed her head and on her feet were ragged, dog-worried, rabbit-shaped slippers. Tracy was a big woman, bloated and blotchy of face. 'The results of too many nights down the pub drinking Guinness, too many fags and too many hours sat on her fat backside playing bingo,' Martin had often told her.

Shuffling her way towards the sink, Tracy sniffed and flapped a hand across her face; she had never got used to the pong of the dog's pot. With her hands clasped beneath her protruding belly, she reached the sink, lifted her paunch and eased it on the worktop edge. She reached for the half-pint glass tumbler, sitting on the windowsill, holding her false teeth and dental cleanser. The liquid was milky in colour, some of the soda bread outfliers having fallen into it.

She lifted the glass and bawled, 'What's this? Porridge?' She stuck two fingers into the glass, removed both top and bottom sets, washed them beneath a tap, widened her mouth then entered them in, locating them onto her gums, using fingers to seat them securely.

Martin pushed in beside Tracy and opened the window behind the sink. He picked up the soda bread from the basin and hurled it out through the gap. It didn't reach the greyhound prancing and whining for attention in its run at the rear. Instead, it fell in splodgy pieces onto the arid piece of cracked cement and uneven flagstones of the yard.

A pair of greenfinches, lurking close by, beat a blue tit to the scraps. Feathers fluttered but it was a one-sided confrontation. The blue tit, driven from the feast, fluttered up onto the perimeter wall. Settling between pieces of broken glass cemented there as a deterrent to trespassers, it waited any leftovers.

'Give that wee blue scab some stick there. Get it down yeh afore it nicks it off yeh, ma wee green darlings. Like they bluenoses did the six counties from us, so it was.' Martin bellowed out the window.

''Tis good to hear you sounding brave and staunch this morning, tae be sure, so it is,' Sean said, standing smiling in the direction of his chief.

'It's just Martin's guts rumbling again. He's a pig. They've been doing it all bloody night and me not getting a wink o' sleep because of it, so it is,' Tracy said, holding the kettle under a tap. 'I heard him in the cludgie. What a racket! Sounded thought he was passing flights o' starlings, so it did.'

'Stop yer rabbiting, woman, and get that kettle on,' Martin told her.

He turned, looked at Sean and said, 'If our wonderful leader, Big Gerry, was a greenfinch and that ridiculous excuse for a politician, yer man, Big Ian, was a blue tit, Our Man would win the soda bread wars every time…and we'd be in charge.'

Martin pointed a thumb towards his chest and a wild, faraway look came into eyes. Martin was picturing the scene. 'It'd be like "Planet o' the Apes" but a bit different, Sean, just the like. This time, we'd be the monkeys on horseback; we'd be kicking Proddy backsides for a change. We'd beat the skulking, trough-fattened swine into the ground, Sean, so we would.'

'He's always dreaming so he is,' Tracy said, looking in Martin's direction and nodding sagely. She filled the kettle, turned to the cooker and placed it on a lit gas ring, next to the bubbling pan.

Rattled by Tracy's words, Martin came to his senses. With a shake of his head he said, 'Huh, ignore her, just. She's a minger, that. Goin' tae get her toes taken off tae get her closer tae the sink.' He grinned at Sean, pleased with his gag and theatrics.

He returned to the fridge, pulled out a sealed pack of tattie scones and held them aloft. 'What about yeh? Dae yeh think yeh could pack away a bit o' scran afore we have our meeting? Martin asked Sean. 'I've found these tae go with the rest o' this stuff. They were bagged in the Irish Republic so they're dead on.'

'Aye. Dead on. I'd love some scran, just. Plenty grease and a slice of fried soda bread would go down okay dokey.'

'Sean, there's nae soda bread. They burds are packing it intae their gizzards the now,' Martin said loudly. His thumb raked the air, gesturing towards the window.

Tracy fried their breakfast next to the spitting pan.

Ten minutes later, only the sound of champing jaws broke the silence. As Martin and Sean were eating, they swiped the back of a hand across their unshaven faces, removing the runny fat and egg dribbling from their lips onto their chins.

Tracy slurped tea from a mug bearing the Celtic FC logo and peered out of the window, her paunch resting on the worktop. In her womanly way, she was looking for something else to say and upset Martin.

Martin cleaned his plate with the last of his toast then pulled his chair back. He stood up from the kitchen table, belched loudly and opened a lopsided drawer in a rickety sideboard. 'MFI crap!' he exploded. Ratching about in the jumble, he removed a tangled mess of family heirlooms, long forgotten. 'There's plenty of bits of string, rabbit snares, mousetraps, watches that don't work and put by for a rainy day... but where's the Rennies?'

Nobody answered. More searching uncovered the indigestion remedy, hidden beneath other pharmaceutical preparations stuffed into the back of the drawer: dog-wormers, flea killer and mange preparations. The washable condom, unwittingly disentangled from the jumble as he rummaged, he pushed back out of sight.

He tossed a half-open packet to Sean, closed the drawer noisily, poured another mug of tea each and then said, 'We've got a clever youngster by the name of Mickey O'Rourke wantin' tae join the brigade. He's coming round t'night for the test.'

Sean licked his plate, tongued his moustache clean and fingered the last of his tomato-sauce-spread toast into his mouth.

'I've checked out the lad and he's scrubbed up clean, but. Mind yeh, Sean, he's had his moments. Apparently, at a chapel fete, he went into the buffet tent and asked the auld nun in attendance, Sister Anna, for a quickie. The priest, called tae sort out the source of the Sister's vexation, found that our man was a bit dyslexic. He was really after a slice of quiche. Ten "Hail Marys" and a round of the stations it cost him.

He says he robbed an off-licence single-handed and got away with a few bob and some bottles. The cops still don't have a clue. That's the type of warrior we need in the brigade, don't yeh think?'

'Sounds as if he'll fit in as an ideas man on some of our bigger jobs, just, eh?' Sean said.

'Sounds as if he's got two more brains than you lot,' Tracy quipped, slipping plates into soapy water. Looking out of the window towards the dog run, she said, 'If you don't get that dog out for a walk soon, Martin, it'll never chase a hare again, just get slow and useless... like you.'

'Tracy, give my heid peace, won't yeh? We're talking brigade business here,' he growled, incensed at her interruptions. Turning to Sean he advised, 'Take nae notice o' her, but aye, we'll have tae see. Apart from his wee social indiscretion, and we can handle that, there's not a blemish on his character at all, at all, tae be sure.

'There's some encouraging signs. Apart from his parents gettin' smithereened by the Proddies, I'm told he throws stones at Orange bands on the twelfth and fingers "Big Ian" when he sees him on the box. What says yeh?'

'Yeh can get him tae walk the dog,' Tracy suggested, sliding washed plates into a rack.

Martin just sighed with exasperation, refusing to be drawn.

'Oh aye, as long as he's staunch and is dead on about the rules,' Sean said, 'especially the one about the bullet in the back o' his heid if he ballses things up. If he's dyslexic, though, will he be sound on what balls-ups are all about?'

'Oh aye, I reckon if he's sound on what's a cock-up, he'll be dead on. Yeh'll have tae be here t'night, though, tae give him the test. I'm giving you a brekk. T'night, I'm being the guinea pig.'

'Martin, you're a real pig, no imitation,' Tracy said, again joining a conversation in which she wasn't welcome.

'Keep your great gob shut, won't yeh?' Martin fired back, this time giving Tracy a surly, silencing look. 'As I said, Sean, t'night you put the black bag over my heid and tie me into the chair...'

'Yeh can leave a live bullet in the gun for me,' Tracy butted in.

'There she goes again, the brains of the Falls Road. Shut up will yeh, yeh daft wumman?

And when Mickey arrives, you give him the gun with the blanks in it. You explain tae him that he's tae go into the room where he'll find a murderous, Proddy bastard trussed up in a chair, gagged, sweating heavily and hooded. Tell him when he shoots him dead, that's when he'll get into the brigade and put on active service. Your dead on about that caper. There would be no need tae tell me auld Fenian granny how tae suck eggs now, would there?'

'Oh aye, I'm sure looking forward tae doing your bit in the recruitment drive,' Sean said.

Belfast at 11:30 p.m. that evening was warm, misty, a fine drizzle dampening the ground. In Martin's house, expectation circulated along with air pollutants.

Martin had dined earlier, now he was sitting at the kitchen table, half-asleep, belching. A supper of colcannon and fresh soda bread washed down with six cans of Guinness was bagging him up and his stomach rumbled as gastric battle ensued.

Tracy was sitting in the front room watching TV, needles flashing in her hand, knitting another black bonnet for the cause.

Some ten minutes later, Martin twitched awake on hearing the insistent banging and scraping on the back door. Sean pushed the door open, quickly closed it behind him. He entered the kitchen, looking sour. The greyhound was loose in the yard. Martin had ignored Tracy's remarks about the dog becoming unfit and he had let it roam, instead of walking it.

'No sooner had I opened the yard door than the greyhound was about me,' Sean gasped.

'The dog's had its sheep's-heid broth. It should've been up on its bunk asleep by now,' Martin commiserated.

'It was a very scary welcome in the dark. Each of the dog's front paws has landed on a shoulder, having stood in its own crap. I could tell it had sheep's heid. Its breath stank as it licked its smelly greeting.'

Martin shallow laugh turned to a gurgle. The smell from Sean's jacket was jerking tears from his eyes. 'Was its nose cold when it snuffled you?' he asked.

Sean looking down his nose at the mess on his shoulders said, 'Aye.'

Martin's body was shaking with mirth. 'Then the dog's fit. Might have been worse for you had it scoffed the stale soda bread, eh?'

'Look at me! The dog's pawed all over me. Tae be sure, there's crap on me ears and on me donkey jacket. This one's brand-new. It was stolen only yesterday. A lorry driver crossing on North Sea Ferries nicked it. Now it has two brown badges-of-rank, one on each shoulder. It's as if I've just been promoted in the field. My shoes are mingin'.'

Martin laughed loudly and then said, 'Give me those shoes here. I'll wash the crap off them in the sink. Mickey O'Rourke'll be here soon. You can hang that jacket outside in the yard, on the nail, where the dummy hare hangs. It's kind o' ripe in here.'

Martin led Sean into the room reserved for the test. It was bare, except for a sturdy wooden armchair placed in the room's centre and secured to the floor. 'I'm getting too old for this lark, but yeh deserve the brekk. Sitting in the dark with a hood over the napper can't be good for the old ticker, even when it's dead on that it's no' for real. Must have got tae you sometimes?'

'I appreciate the brekk. There's no light at all gets into that bag. It frightened the crap out o' me sometimes. The bhoys appreciate the serious nature of the vetting procedure we use. They know that every recruit that passes the test in this room is dead on,' Sean said, with conviction.

*

By midnight the trussing and hooding of Martin was complete.

At the appointed time, Sean heard a bark and a bit of a scuffle in the yard, then an urgent knocking on the back door, together with the utterance, 'Get aff me, get!'

The greyhound was still on the loose and greeting arrivals.

Sean opened the back door, prised the greyhound from Mickey and tugged him inside.

Mickey was small of stature, had a small, rat-like face with gappy teeth, a developing Ché Guevara-style moustache and wore a black baseball hat, two sizes too large. The dog's paw prints plastered the hat's crown and Mickey's shoulders.

'Bayjasus, that dog's breath smells. It's not so fresh in here either!' Mickey exclaimed. Hanging in the kitchen air was a lingering smell of dog crap, boiled sheep's head, onions, kale and an aerosol-delivered, domestic fragrance.

'Aye. I've just had a dose o' it myself. Martin's late. He's away out looking for some different grub for it. He'll be back soon. I'll take yer jacket, Mickey. Yeh'll no need it for the test.'

'It's newly stolen from P&O Ferries,' Mickey said. 'Cost me a tenner t'night in the pub.'

Tracy had heard the racket and looked into the kitchen. 'It's all right, Tracy, Mickey's just having a crap day,' Sean told her.

'Crap idea altogether,' Tracy said, sniffed derisively and drew the door shut.

Sean took Mickey's jacket and carried it towards the kitchen door. 'I'd better inspect the shoulders,' he said with a snigger. 'The dug might have given you a premature promotion.'

He found a hook and hung it up. Hanging there were donkey jackets stolen from each of the ferry companies that traded to the province and some from beyond. Sean returned to Mickey, placed an arm on his shoulder, took a revolver from a pocket and asked, 'So, yeh want tae join the Hillshanks Brigade, do yeh?'

Sean fingered the revolver. He was interested to see Mickey's reaction when told he was about to kill for the first time.

'Aye, aye, I do. I've always wanted tae join the bhoys, fight for the cause and all, get revenge for me parents,' Mickey said, wondering what was ahead for him. He eyed the revolver, breathed in slowly. Then he let it out, as silently as he could.

'Yeh'll need tae be staunch and do what yer told,' Sean told him. He screwed on a silencer, toyed again with the revolver, tossed it between hands. He watched Mickey's eyes; they might tell him something now and more when he explained to him the nature of the test.

'Aye, that's stickin' out a mile,' said Mickey, guessing the next place for the butt of the revolver was in his hand. He wiped the stickiness off both palms down the legs of his jeans.

'This gun has a hair trigger… squeeze it gently,' Sean explained, holding the gun close to Mickey's face, 'there's no need tae jerk your shot.

'Your test t'night is tae take the gun into the room at the end o' that passage opposite the back door. There, yeh'll find a hated Proddy. We captured him last night. He's hooded and trussed-up like yer proverbial chicken. We've gagged him so he can say nothing. He'll be shakin' and pissin' hissel', because he knows what he's getting, but he's secure in the chair. Shoot him dead and yeh'll be recruited into the brigade, t'night,' Sean said, his eyes were on Mickey's, never leaving them. 'It's yer one and only test, so do the job right.'

Mickey grasped the gun and weighed it in his hand, as he had seen cowboys do in films. It was the first time he had held a firearm; it felt good in his grip, making him feel strong, one of the bhoys.

'Just put the gun tae the side o' his Proddy heid and pull the trigger, like this.' Sean grabbed for the gun, his action a blur. The gun out of Mickey's grasp, he pushed the silencer nozzle against his temple, pointing the barrel inwards.

Mickey leapt backwards, feeling the coldness of the pressing steel, anxious that it might be a set-up, wondering if he was next for planting in some bog.

Sean said quietly, 'Blow his Proddy brains out! But don't be so jumpy. Yeh'll never make it in the brigade if yer jumpy. Yeh've tae get the job done right.' Then, his voice sharper and commanding, he said, 'Take the gun, now. I've already cocked it. It's ready tae shoot. Be careful. Like I said, put it tae his heid and pull the trigger once, nice…and …slow. It's all yeh'll have tae do.' He was still looked for the signs of panic, the show of doubt that he had seen in the faces of other prospects and which might show in Mickey's.

'Just show me the d,d,d, door,' Mickey said, hardly controlling a nervous stammer.

Acting brash, he threw his shoulders back, thrust out his chest, took a deep breath and started to walk towards the kitchen door, the revolver raised at the side of his head.

'In there,' Sean said, following him and pointing towards a closed door at the unlit end of the passageway.

Mickey reached the door and pushed against it. It was hard to budge, stiff and heavy with the weight of donkey jackets stolen from all the heavy engineering companies with workshops in the province. A forceful nudge with a knee opened it a crack.

He slipped through the gap sideways: as he had seen that done in films. He lowered the gun, gripped the butt with two hands, swinging it around the room. Lifting a foot, he nudged the door closed behind him.

Sean walked to the kitchen door and looked back. He heard Martin mumbling and pretending to struggle. Then some quiet talk. He made out the words, 'Proddy hardman are yeh?' Sean smiled. Mickey was taking the piss a little, winding up who he thought the victim was, before pulling the trigger.

He expected to hear the dull thud of a silenced-pistol shot, then maybe two or three more in quick succession. The number of reports sounding depended on how Mickey reacted to the situation.

Some prospects had blasted off more shots than were necessary, experiencing enhanced, maniacal delight the more they fired. Others had raced out of the room as if the devil himself was after them, after a single shot.

Sean knew it was all gut-tightening excitement; he himself had killed more than once. He quietly said, while shaking his head, 'The thought of dispatching a hated Proddy tae a wet scrape, into a deep bog, is a heady business for one of our bhoys.'

The kettle was boiling gently over a small flame. Sean filled a teapot and prepared three cups. He thought the test would be a bit of an ordeal for Mickey, and Martin. Both would be thirsty and need a cup of strong tea while they laughed over it afterwards.

Time passed. The tea had brewed and now it stewed. Sean poured a cup, added milk, sugar, and then sipped slowly.

Worries soon began to tighten his stomach muscles. He hadn't heard any muffled shots. He walked to the kitchen door and looked along the passageway. Mickey had entered the execution room a good six minutes earlier.

Sean held his breath to listen. A moment later, he breathed out and sighed, 'Bayjasus.' The door to the room was opening.

Mickey's strides were short, his shoes scuffing over the linoleum. He was gasping for air on the short walk down the passageway. His face was bright red, glowing, bubbles of sweat forcing out of his brow. He handed Sean the revolver and gasped, 'That's it done then.'

'That's definitely it done, yeh wee numpty,' Sean said harshly, standing looking hard at Mickey, confident that he had panicked, unable to go through with the test. 'I never heard any shots. You've no' blown the Proddy's brains out. You've banjaxed it. You won't get another chance tae join the brigade now.'

Mickey looked up at him, his eyes shining with a wild light. He nodded his head slowly, a thin, nervous smile creasing his face. Confident of success in the test, he prepared the words with which to tell Sean, words that would prove his suitability, his dexterity in meting out death, his usefulness to the brigade. 'Shoot the bastard, did yeh say? Shooting was too good for the Proddy so I strangled him!'

Sean spluttered. The milky tea he was about to swallow shot down both nostrils. 'Yeh... yeh...wh...what! Yeh must be joking. It was only a test of your courage and resolve for the cause... using blanks... yeh, yeh... eejit. Yeh've not followed orders, now yeh say yeh've gone and strangled Martin Mulldoony. Are yeh aff yer heid?'

Sean's words set Mickey's lips quivering, widening his eyes and tightening his buttock muscles. The full horror of his actions were kicking in, scaring him shitless.

Retribution would come quickly from the Hillshanks Brigade. Mickey gasped. He knew if he didn't get out of the house quickly, it most certainly meant the killing of the killer of their commander by members of the brigade's crack assassination squad. They would do it, no messing!

FOREWORD TO PART TWO

Ulster's County Boil stretches from the western shores of Loch Neagh to the borders of County Donegal, its landscape exhibiting some disquieting features: beech hedgerows, disturbingly high and concealing to short people; unsignposted boreens, worryingly long and winding to the lost; the carbuncular peaks of Mount Boil, which inhabitants fearing heights see as plooks on the arse of the county.

Fifty years ago, the Bishop of Ireland confirmed Arthur Whynot as Vicar of the County Boil presbytery and Whynot Hall, the family home, became his manse. During the years of his ministry, most summers were as wet as the winters were. On some July days, rain plummeted as if welding rods released by the gods.

The scarcity of dry days prompted locals to give their own weather reports, which blossomed as a public-bar art in County pubs. Arthur thought any drunken, lay futurologists proclaiming weather-wisdom from bar stools, were in cahoots with Auld Nick.

In front of crammed congregations, Arthur would stand proud in his pulpit, upright, stony-faced and loudly castigate Satan's ways. On wet Sabbaths, his flock hardly filling a single pew, he'd cast a mean eye, smile knowingly and rant bitterly and crabbedly of eejits and gullible parishioners. 'Sorcerous fools cannot claim to know nature's work. Foretelling that the common phenomena of grazing horses sheltering their rumps tight against hedges is a sign of imminent stormy weather, and a reason for not attending church, I find a bit of a worry,' was an often repeated tirade.

Arthur favoured the genuine forecasts of TV weathermen using satellite images to support their predictions. A forecaster for Friday July 13th, that year, predicting torrential rain, the blustery wind creating such a froth-speckled mist that Ulster might consider honouring it with the title of Paisley Day; that struck a raw nerve.

As well as offending Arthur, the report of more rain moved farmers to fear webbing might spontaneously sprout between their toes

Nothing in Whynot family records suggested other than that the rug of Presbyterianism had always lain unyielding beneath the feet of Arthur's ancestors. Until, and to Arthur's mortification, his only sister, possessing an easily-turned head, had fallen for left-footer charms and crossed the religious divide.

Twenty years later, his beloved niece, Dotty, the product of that union and the sole beneficiary of his estate, lugged the rug from under *him*. She had insisted that *he*, her only uncle, officiate at and bless her Catholic marriage to a young medical student, Riley Dernehen.

Arthur saw the man she was stubbornly in love with as another no-user about to become a barnacle on the arse of his family name. To his embarrassment, staunch parishioners guessed that he, like practicing left-footers, couldn't pull out. That, too, was a bit of a worry to him.

A reformist he wasn't; only reluctantly, did he accept Dotty's marriage and buy the odd-fish world in which he now preached.

Enterprising, he was. Taking a keen interest in modern technology, he invested in new-fangled gadgets as they became available. When computers were in their infancy, he purchased an early-version Apple Mac. Later, when the internet became a reality, he connected through a slow, but then state-of-the-art modem, which allowed him to download weather maps and make his own weekly weather forecast from the pulpit.

Quickly, he lost interest in the elements and he left the maps unread; he had acquired a superior word-processing package which gave thesaurus and spellchecker options. Using this useful software, he spent his time injecting additional superlatives into his sermons and saving the more forceful creations on floppy discs.

Twelve months ago, already left and right click conversant, he upgraded to a Hewlet Packard internet-ready laptop.

Arthur was aware of "search engine" potential, but wasn't yet proficient at ferreting out the reams of information available on the World Wide Web. To steepen his learning curve, he set about constructing his family tree.

Sitting in his upstairs study, during the week following the purchase of his laptop, he puffed at his pipe while booting up and logging-on to the Church Of The Latter Day Saints genealogy site. On request, he entered a family name from as far back as he knew. Eyes down for the result, he watched the download's progress. Eagerly, he waited for the genealogists lurking in cyberspace to reveal details of his ancestry.

The screen flashed, a window appeared and his eyes darted back and forth. Appraising the recorded particulars was a bit of a worry. The researchers revealed the existence, one hundred and fifty years previously, of a Theresa Maria Chastity on his mother's side.

Shock rooted Arthur to his seat, but his hands flew up from the keyboard and he cried aloud, 'Bayjasus, this is the last straw. A left-footer of a great, great, great granny I never knew I had.'

Kicking out with his right foot, he connected with the desk. Thrusting himself violently backwards, he unintentionally propelled his state-of-the-art, castor-fitted stool on a course for the door gaping open behind him. With his eyes wide, he shot across the landing. Over the top step, the pipe stem tightly clenched between his teeth, he somersaulted. As he tumbled, his billowing vestment flapped heavenwards, covering his head and blinkering him during his juddering descent to the hallway and the broken neck that caused his demise.

THE LIFE OF RILEY and his "TROUBLES"

PART 2

Chapter 1

In fields near Whynot Hall, combine harvesters roared, their mechanical blare shattering the peace. Farmers worked with haste. It hadn't rained that last Saturday afternoon in July, which was unusual for that month in Ulster. Since dawn, the sun's rays had warmed the land, flushing out the vapour wisps streaming thinly upwards from the sodden County Boil earth.

Doctor Riley Dernehen was sitting at his desk in the Hall's second-floor study. The window open, but the din, summery sounds or the earth under pressure weren't bothering him.

The doctor was concentrating deeply. Writing up his case notes, a chore he had always thought dire tedium, he had succeeded in shutting out the entire outside world. He had to; in the recent past, his mind had easily strayed.

For all of his professional life, until that springtime, his job had completely absorbed him, daydreams never interfering. Now, visions of Nursing Sister Mavis O'Rourke, in various sexy poses, drifted in, affecting his attention. They always did if he lost the will to keep them out.

He had been writing continuously for an hour when he lifted his eyes to scan a nearby notebook. He tried to make out some prescription scribble that, during the previous week, he had hurriedly penned during rounds at Ballyboil Hospital. That brief moment disrupted his focus. The fantasy that he was trying so hard to exclude was quickly in his mind's eye, troubling him. His thoughts were taking flight again… up and away… soaring aboard a sexual seesaw.

Released from its shackles, his imagination was again spawning for him a vision of the comely Mavis. He could see her plainly. She was lying naked, on her back, in the missionary position, on her nurses' home bed. Her hands were reaching out for him. Her heels were pressing deep into the mattress. Her hips were writhing, lifting upwards. Her mossy mound was beckoning. Oh how he wanted to mount her then - for real - as he had often done recently.

In the trice that his imagination had turned riotous, he threw himself back into his chair, closed his eyes and covered them with a hand. His lips puckered and he began breathing deeply, his chest leaping. Mavis' nipples were erect and he was kissing them, titillating each in turn with the tip of his tongue, then he was sliding it down into the valley between her breasts.

His knob throttled-up and throbbing strongly it lifted the bathrobe in which he sat.

Completing the writing up of important case notes hadn't been enough to quell his yearnings for Mavis. He was unable to uproot his lusting for the most kissable parts of her luscious body, at all.

Riley looked around for a distraction: something to relocate his mind to the clerical task. The intrusion had reduced his progress to a doodle.

He turned his head towards the study window and looked out through a gap in the pine trees surrounding the Hall towards Mount Boil. Once, the twin peaks of the mount were his two most treasured places on earth. Now, picturesque beneath their summer carpet of colourful wild flora, they offered him no diversion. Then he lowered his eyes towards a flowerbed within the Hall grounds.

The seesaw plummeted, crushing the yearnings so inflamed a moment ago. His wife, Dotty, was on her hands and knees, industriously grubbing weeds from the floral array with a trowel.

Dotty was dressed like a scarecrow: wellingtons, khaki trousers taut over her bony behind, sagging polo-necked jumper covering her upper body, and on her hands, tattered rubber gloves. She had tucked the curlers shaping her hair into a hairnet, though some of the devices had escaped and were hanging precariously on white ringlets. Midges were infuriating her and she was puffing strongly at a cigarette, the smoke surrounding her head in a deterrent haze.

Through it, Riley could see Dotty's face, thin and wrinkly. He knew it to be the result of years of tobacco abuse, and lately, her liking of brandy.

Riley was consultant plastic surgeon at Ballyboil Hospital, where, in springtime that year, his affair with Mavis O'Rourke had begun. Mavis was quite a bit taller than he was, but their eyes had met over the top of their theatre masks. He was performing, and she was assisting with, a minor operation.

He thought Mavis' startling, starling-egg blue and black-speckled eyes were beautiful. They had sparkled with interest when his first met hers - had jolted him back - after suffering nine years of the prohibition Dotty had put on marital sex when entering her menopause nine years previously - to sexual arousal.

During those sex-free years, until that day in the theatre, his mind had been empty of any sexual thoughts. That day it was awash with them, creating the heat in his loins, making him achingly hard, telling him that he had to have sex with Mavis.

He had handed the final procedures over to a colleague and left the theatre. Mavis had followed him. Alone in the washroom, their arms had entwined, clasping each other tight. They had kissed, he on tiptoes, she stooping slightly. When Mavis felt his erection pressing urgently against her knee, she had pulled him to her, had moaned, and wilted into his arms.

Before the theatre emptied, they had skipped off, hand-in-hand, to her nurses' home apartment. There he had performed, like a youth possessed: not like the sixty-two year-old that he was.

Mathematical calculations he had mused over following that first session of passion with Mavis, proved that he had missed many erections during those nine-years free of sexual thought.

Using the barest of assumptions that men of his age should have one erection each day, his arithmetic told him that 365 times 9 meant he had missed the pleasure of 3287 erections, there being two leap years in that period. He thought it little wonder why, that day in the theatre, he had gone so stiff.

The initial inferno in his loins was now dying a bit; no painful, iron-hard erections had returned - but that hadn't bothered Mavis. He could always guarantee a lasting stiffy for her - and his lusting for her had continued unabated throughout that wet summer.

He knew that Ballyboil Hospital, like most establishments employing local labour, was a hotbed of rumour. To get around this, he deduced he needed sneaky ways and off-duty times to meet Mavis.

Volunteering his services as Police Surgeon to the local RUC station was his "get out" card. Being on call to the RUC, he had realised, was a good excuse to leave the Hall. Dotty's fondness of a brandy or two before and during dinner completed the equation: she fell asleep, on a sofa, in the lounge, and slept from early evening until the small hours.

Riley usually awakened Dotty to go to bed proper, whether he had attended a call-out or not. It was all he required to continue the relationship with Mavis. He was sure Dotty would remain asleep during the times he was absent from the Hall of an evening, and she would never know, never find out, never suspect and, therefore, would never be hurt.

Both Riley and Dotty were sixty-two years old, married for forty of them. Riley loved Dotty dearly, since their first meeting, and still did; but he hadn't realised how much he missed sex, until that day in theatre.

The sounds coming from the fields weren't interfering with Dotty's thoughts, either; though, with her head so low and amongst lavender, carnations, gardenias and hyacinths in full bloom, the fragrances were.

As Riley was looking down on Dotty, she gave a sudden snort of disgust and sat back on her heels. A strong, scented whiff from the flower varieties had jerked her back to her awakening early one Sunday morning that springtime. Riley had pulled her to her feet from the lounge sofa, where she had been asleep since dinner. A bit befuddled, she had reeled. Falling against him, the sickly aroma of a perfume had engulfed her - wafting from his open shirtfront.

Had the RUC called him away earlier on police surgeon business, was her first thought. She could only previously recall him returning from those duties smelling slightly of surgical spirits or iodine. She expected that - but not reeking of "Jolie Madame", as he had done – the kind of perfume that she had never possessed!

Dinnertime was approaching when Riley conceded to a sort of writers' block. The feeling of thorough defeat was entirely attributable to his fixation for Mavis.

Grunting, he pulled a face, closed a folder with a thud on his desk and shoved it roughly into his briefcase. The writing-up of half of his cases was incomplete, but he had chosen to chill away any remnants of his fixation beneath the ultra-cold spray of the shower. He would need his cool at dinner to face Dotty: she always drank some brandy before then. Its influence always interfered with her thoughts, producing nonsensical notions, which often riled him.

After showering, Riley dressed. From his wardrobe he choose modest clothes that he'd wear all evening: white shirt with a red bow tie, Donegal tweed jacket with leather patches at the elbows, brown, shapeless corduroy trousers and brown brogues. His hair he centrally parted and sleeked with a bay rum gel.

*

At dinner, Riley was sitting opposite Dotty at the table. As she poured a large measure of brandy into a goblet, Riley was looking blankly into the distance over the top of her head. He had already broken his bread roll into small pieces, had buttered it, and now waited, his soupspoon poised.

He was thinking ahead to his desired visit to Mavis' nursing home apartment. Later, on her bed, there was the live chance of him acting out his wild imaginings. Escaping the Hall, staying late in her company and moderating his yearning in a wild knobbing session was the evening's goal. Dotty would sleep, surely. A quick glance at her eyes told him they were already glassing. Two large measures, he reckoned, she had sipped before dinner. The brandy glass was again full and the decanter was close to her hand.

The call would come; it had never failed to. It was Saturday; Mavis worked shifts but was always off that weeknight. Ballyboil's pubs were always riotous - the RUC always got involved, always arrested a drunk or two, never with delicacy.

Mrs Bridie O'Kane, the Hall cook, poised for culinary activities in the kitchen, had heard the Dernehens entering the dining room.

Bridie was a pocket-dynamo of a woman, sturdily built by honest toil. She had prepared tasty and wholesome fare for her employer's dinner. Now, to ensure perfect presentation of the cream-of-watercress soup, she carefully filled the pre-warmed bowls from a simmering pot on the Aga. Then she introduced the final ingredient, thick dollops of cream, spooning it into the bowls and gently spiralling it across the soup's surface with a wooden spoon.

Bridie shuffled into the dining-room with the steaming bowls balanced on a tray, set it down, and served with care.

Suddenly a loud woof rumbled and the sound of a heavy object falling came from the hallway. Cedric the St Bernard and family pet, sprawled on his rug, had tossed the bone he was worrying, frustrated that he was unable to probe its inner cavity. His ill-fitting tongue was proving useless. Even a beast with a better-equipped head wouldn't find the tasty marrow, long since boiled out to thicken the stockpot.

When they finished the soup course, the cook removed the empty bowls, gaining the expected plaudits: no one made soup quite like her. She then served the main course: battered fillet of cod, chips and fresh garden peas.

As the cook placed the plate in front of him, Riley saw the questioning look in Dotty's eyes. That gaze had been a dinnertime feature recently; the frown and the wrinkles lining her face deepening as some worry returned.

Riley wondered what uninteresting topics she would broach tonight; he knew the brandy would already be confusing her. What queries had she dreamed up while digging weeds out by the roots and despatching them to the heap? Lately, local wildlife in some of its various forms had been an issue. He didn't relish the thought of listening to any new fears she had for the survival of fieldmice in their waterlogged environment, her last concern.

Nor did he know of the suspicion nagging away inside that small head... a bit of a worry. Turning an ear towards a window in a quick movement, Dotty asked, 'Riley, listen, do you hear that awful feckin' racket?'

'Racket... what awful feckin' racket is it that's bothering you, Dotty?' Riley inhaled then sighed mournfully, drawing it out. He hoped Dotty would notice his irritation, and desist.

Combine harvesters were still working, but at a distance now, the rattle of their diesel engines hardly an annoying racket. He felt sure Dotty was about to reveal some new, troubling issues. Making a statement he thought silly, was how she started her prattle of a dinnertime. He feared the worst; he had no desire to engage in a batty, brandy-fudged conversation; he didn't want it getting off the ground at all.

Riley had always called his wife by her given name, Dorothea. It was old fashioned, but he liked it. The scatterbrained idea Dotty had of changing her name had come not long after they had moved into the Hall. After searching the building, top to bottom, they'd found no secret cache of gold, silver, money, anything of exceptional worth: a parson's stipend hadn't stretched to that. The only interesting find had been Uncle Arthur's store of vintage brandy, gifted by loyal members of his congregation who knew he enjoyed such a tipple.

Riley had been teetotal all his life, but Dotty quickly developed a taste for the smooth cognac, drinking the whole cache as aperitifs and as sippers during dinner, in only a few weeks. He regarded her brandy drinking as liver-and-brain-debilitating, *and* the reason she now insisted that everyone should call her Dotty.

'It's a nice name for an elderly, eccentric and rustic lady,' she had voiced snappily, when he had questioned her.

An inferior brandy now filled the decanter. Nightly, as the decanter lowered, so the silly chatter had increased. The brandies Dotty drank earlier that night, he blamed for her alone hearing the "awful feckin' racket". What she had sipped at since they'd sat down to dinner had just increased the sound a decibel or two, but only within her ears.

Dotty was having difficulty focusing her eyes on her plate, even through the half-spectacles perched tightly on the pinched end of her nose. Troublesome was the battered cod fillet, which she saw as having an identical neighbour. Both were sliding about, together with the peas, the chips and the thin red line of tomato ketchup. Prodding the fish with her fork, she rocked a little and occasionally jerked her head. Pinning the fish to the plate, her knife sliced through the crisp batter, opening up the fillet to reveal the thick flesh.

'It's a bit of a worry, and an issue that we should confront,' she said, as she secured a piece of fish to the tines of her fork, along with a crinkle-cut chip, lifted it from her plate and held it in midair. 'County Boil blacksmiths, forging ploughshares in their smithies, are thumping and grinding out a grating, unmelodic air. The noise blots out the plaintive sounds we used to hear of expectant mother hares, in labour, straining to whelp their leverets in the lush meadows that surround Whynot Hall.'

Riley shuddered and jerked back in his chair. Dotty's slurred, inane prattling had begun. Like the other times, it seemed he had no chance of ignoring her. Eating his meal in silence, his own thoughts uppermost and pertinent to the evening ahead, just wasn't going to happen.

Head down, his gaze low, in the direction of his plate, he followed the movements of his own knife and fork closely until his irritation finally got the better of him. The mouthful of cod he was finding quite pleasing to the palate he quickly swallowed, let out a laboured sigh, and reacted, 'Ach, damn, catch yourself on, will you?'

He constructed another layered forkful of food: a chunk of fish, a chip, a topping of peas and placed the lot carefully into his mouth. That masticated and swallowed, he thought he'd try again and retorted sharply, 'It's because it's August tomorrow.'

Dotty chewed rapidly and emptied her mouth, having thought of a suitable repost. 'That matters?' She snapped.

'Ach, we're surrounded by fields around which combine harvesters are roaring,' Riley said, sounding vexed; common sense wasn't working, 'cutting corn and harvesting the grain, night and day and in haste.

'Haven't you seen the weather reports? Clouds will again billow in from the Atlantic. Rain is never far away in Ulster. The harvest should be in by now and it isn't. Farmers will be concerned that the weather will change for the worse before they're finished.

'It's combine harvesters that you're hearing clattering. As for hares, they get *their* oats and do *their* jig thing in March, dancing the night away on frost-silvered earth, beneath a dazzling moon. All eligible hares get rid of *their* craziness then. Even Harry the Hare will have run around with a dose of the horn. That's when he'd have had *his* leg over!'

'It's leg up, Riley, surely not leg over?' Dotty interrupted shrilly, sawing away at another part of the itinerant fillet with the crispy coating.

'It's a distant memory, Dotty,' he sighed, 'but when we last had sex, I recall it was leg over.'

'And a treatment called the horn?' Dotty said, actively loading a fork and not spotting the suggestion.

'I believe it can be painful.' Riley said. He recalled his first erection for nine years and the one that afternoon, put his knife down and adjusted his trousers.

'I suppose it's peculiar to hares, is it?' Dotty asked, cleaning her plate with a bread crust.

'Ach, bayjasus, don't be silly. Listen, can't you?' Riley asked and stuck his head out over his plate, staring purposefully across at Dotty. 'The mum of the species will have dropped her young eight weeks or so after conception. If you've had your ear to the ground at this time of year, then you'd have been listening to Bigwig the Rabbit at it, getting *his* leg over. Bigwigs have several choices and hump willy-nilly all year round.

'As for bambies, no eligible doe is safe from any rampant Rudolph, without a red nose, but with a burning passion for the opposite sex. Eavesdropping on a summer rutting will include listening to stags bellowing their feckin' heads off.'

His explanation finished, he threw his head back and guffawed at the thought.

Mahogany panelling lined the interior walls of the dining-room. A window looked out over the lawn and the mature monkey-puzzle tree at its centre. Riley's eyes lifted towards the fireplace. Either side of it sat small bureaus. One held the late Reverend Arthur Whynot's King James Bible - well thumbed, dog-eared and as thick as a doorstep. The other held his Psalter - as tattered but a shade thinner.

Above the fireplace hung a head-and-shoulders portrait of the Reverend in his dour, black vestments. Riley shuddered seeing again the twisted, brandy-pickled face looking down on him with a bit of a leer; that gaze had always been a bit of a worry to him.

'You must also have noticed that owls' hoots no longer precede their hunt for voles,' Dotty said, her head bobbing. 'And I cannot detect the plopping sounds rounded balls of regurgitated mouse bones make when hitting the ground beneath their roosts, high in the trees surrounding Whynot Hall.'

'For the love of Jasus, aye.' Riley sniffed. How the feck did anyone hear mouse-bone balls hitting the ground, he asked himself? He said, resignedly, 'It's not like you to give a hoot about, or show any fondness for any sort of rounded balls.'

'But, Riley…,' Dotty shrilled, sitting back, looking at him piercingly now. She had correctly guessed his insinuation – which caused her to recall again, with disgust, the perfume-wafting incident. She continued, 'Even the cops have scant regard for our wildlife. They use our country lanes as if they were practising for the Monaco Grand Prix.

'I've heard their bells dinging and tyres squealing as they speed dangerously around every bend. I do not know how they keep control of their vehicles. The squashed bodies of hedgehogs, with the tread patterns of tyres imprinted upon them, and left lying in cop cars' wakes, are a bit of a worry. Firestone, Pirelli, Dunlop. I have seen them all, I'm sure.'

Riley lifted his head and rolled his eyes. 'Mercy me… Aye… aye, it's true. The cops are responsible for most of the prickly-beast carnage seen on our roads. It's their high-speed chases in substandard vehicles pursuing poachers' Land Rovers filled with Harrys, Bigwigs, Rudolphs and Bambis that are incapable of giving a hoot.'

He gasped, took a breath and rattled his knife and fork down onto the table by the side of his plate. 'And the hedgehog stickers plastered onto the doors of police vehicles are the proud badges which show the cops' successes. They indicate the number of flattening jobs they've done using both-barrel front wheels.' Picking up his knife and fork, he resumed his dinner. Deftly, with expert flicks of his knife and clamping with his fork, he succeeded in removing an overlooked bone from his fillet.

*

Minor operations such as the removal of a length of bone from a human being - no matter how miniscule, inaccessible or delicate - were never a worry for Doctor Dernehen. He had become renowned as a plastic surgeon during the twenty years he held the important title at the Royal Dilbert Hospital, Belfast; or as Ulster-dwellers knew it, "The Kneecap County Hospital". There, his patients had the utmost confidence that his skills would soon have them on their feet again. He would say to them, while grinning hugely, 'I'll have you running around like a feckin' eejit in no time at all, at all.' This amusement delighted them, as did his fantastic stories and ribald jokes.

Children awaiting operations with him went under the anaesthetic with less fear. His promised visit from a leprechaun or other such rib-tickling little person, who'd spirit away their pain while they slept or restore their beauty before they awakened, giving them great comfort.

Many of his adult patients considered that only his aftercare and bedside manner had "pulled them through" to a full recovery. A jokesmith amongst those reconstructed souls made the comment: 'He laced his needles with heavenly thread and, like his tales, they had us in stitches.'

It had become Riley's way to extract some humour by mocking Dotty's silly, alcohol-fuelled prattle and to allow smart remarks to slip off his tongue, her annoyance at his replies only encouraging him.

'It wouldn't surprise me that the brandy you've drunk tonight is dulling and pounding your head like the inside of a Lambeg drum, banged to a hellish, unmelodic rhythm on the twelfth of July,' Riley said. He clattered his cutlery down and pretended to swing drumsticks at a large drum.

Dotty gave a derisive sniff, showing she hadn't taken kindly to his rebuke. Her face became stern. With her lips slowly forming a pout, she reached for the decanter, rattling its lip with that of the goblet and pouring another large measure.

'And why do you have to dress so dowdily for dinner?' Riley asked. 'Have you no pride in your appearance? Your choice of clothing makes you look beggarly. It swamps you.'

'You know I've been weeding for Freddie our gardener all afternoon. He's too old to single-handedly tend all the flowerbeds surrounding the Hall.' Dotty said, her voice rising at the censure.

'But those Wellington boots you've worn. You've traipsed into the Hall in them, kicked them off next to Cedric. There's earth spattered everywhere.'

'Oh, it will clean,' Dotty said and then sighed. 'But since our move back to the tranquil backwater of County Boil, where we have few visitors, I didn't think it mattered that much.'

'Well, aye,' Riley said, nodding his agreement forcibly. 'Since the brokered peace in the province, and the opportunity to step back from the front line, I too have shed much of the cloak of responsibility I once had; indeed, I have relaxed considerably here at Whynot Hall.'

Bang! Riley's remark caused Dotty swiftly to turn her head. Now she was eyeing him doubtfully over the top of the goblet. What he had said had her thinking… Riley had become a bit of a worry. Bringing muck into the Hall and relaxing. *I'll* give *him* muck and relaxing. He has me thinking that he's been doing a bit more than relaxing…thinking he's been mucking around with some woman who lashes on too much perfume.

'It's also true, Dotty; if your Uncle hadn't left you the Hall, I don't know where we'd be relaxing today,' Riley said. 'His death certainly provided an escape route from the workload the "Troubles" brought me. I'll always be grateful to him for that.

'But I am also correct, Dotty; most of the time you dress worse than the tinkers' mingers that knock at our door. They're a bunch of scruffy, smelly ingrates. If they don't sell us clothes pegs, sprigs of lucky white heather and other useless trappings, and aren't allowed to tell our fortunes for a fiver - for a silver coin isn't enough anymore - they lay a feckin' curse on us for our trouble. You washed your hair last Tuesday; since then a shower bonnet has covered it and the curlers…even in bed…'

'That wasn't very nice,' Dotty cut in, her voice raised, lips tightening, eyes narrowing. 'No one sees me at the Hall. I just potter around the gardens when it's dry. I seldom go into town…and when I do I'm always presentable.'

'But it's most eccentric of you,' Riley said. 'And you're hardly an appealing or rousing sight for a husband to see, especially over dinner. It upsets me greatly that the cigarettes hanging from your bottom lip, for most of the day, create nicotine-laden smoke that rises and stains the front of your otherwise snow-white hair. None of it turns me on at all to be sure; and smoking has been proven a bit of a worry.'

Dotty looked at him over the half-spectacles. Of course, she recognised the situation; she had started it. Riley would have the last word in any verbal exchanges - he always did. She was silent for some time. Then she lowered her head and screwed-up her eyes, focusing on the goblet, turning its stem with her fingers. She whirled the last mouthful around the bottom, saw it was spinning like her head. Through the swirl of the golden liquid, she saw colourful recollections flashing before her…………

*

Dotty met Riley at a local barn dance. She had seen him standing, hiding his shyness behind some taller pals. All were out on a talent-spotting mission; ogling the girls lined up along the opposite wall, she was sure. At first, Dotty only got a sight of his head and he hadn't shown that too often. His pals were barging into each other, throwing themselves about, he peeping between them as he could.

Dotty wouldn't have associated herself with any of the drunken youths standing with Riley. In those days, she hardly drank alcohol, a shandy being the strongest she had tried. She had walked around the barn to get a better look at him, to see if there was anything about him to like, and there was. They were the same height and he wasn't bad looking. Later, she asked him for a dance when the band announced a "lady's choice".

Riley was smartly dressed and he hadn't yet danced, wasn't overheating like the rest of the dancers. His intense, yet sympathetic eyes never left hers as they glided in step around the barn floor, dodging sweaty farmer types dancing in heavy brogues. Later that evening, they stood together, their eyes locked; it was love at first sight for both of them.

Dotty was excited when she discovered that Riley was a medical student about to qualify, finishing his internship at Ballyboil hospital. Her friends said he was "a bit of a catch".

She remembered the slopes of Mount Boil being so beautiful on that summer's day of their first walk together, though its terrain had been difficult to cross.

That day, Dotty and Riley tasted the purity of the water from a spring on the mount, drinking it from each other's cupped hands. Dotty breathed in deeply the mingled fragrances of gorse, bluebells and foxgloves blooming there in abundance, making her giggly.

She heard the sudden, frantic flapping of wings and saw winging away the partridge brood disturbed as she steered Riley towards a clump of white heather. She felt his body tense when she tapped him unexpectedly and hard behind one knee with hers and pulled him down onto the ground.

They lay together, kissing long and passionately. She clasped his trembling hand tightly to her firm breasts as she began to breathe heavily. Coming up for air, she eased her clothing, encouraging him to explore with a hand her secret places - places on a woman that he had only ever touched professionally.

They both tore at and removed his trousers. She had heard the term "small man all knob" and had thought it rumour. Riley's knob was so upright, so hard, so large…a feckin' wheeker. She wondered how someone so small in stature could possibly fill it with blood. Then, she considered Riley was an even greater catch.

She held his slim, firm, matador's bum in both hands, while he positioned himself, rather inexpertly, in the missionary position. His knob should have hurt her, but she was so moist and he was so immature and overeager. He hardly entered her; with two strokes, he was finished, completing prematurely his vinegar stroke.

They lay together after that first, short sexual encounter and laughed hysterically. It was there that Dotty told Riley that in her job she had seen enough bulls' knobs to put a handrail around the Titanic. They thought they would die laughing; such was the affect of her unrefined work description.

She explained that she was training as a veterinary nurse at Ballyboil Veterinary College; she didn't tell him that her colleagues there had given her the tongue-in-cheek title of Dumbro - short for Dummy Bell-Ringer Operative. Part of her training included farm visits and extracting bull semen for artificial insemination using a dummy cow.

*

Sitting facing Riley at the dinner table, her interest in knobs were as far gone as the Titanic's rusting metalwork. Any importance she might now place on them would be a bit of a worry to her. She might have taken Riley's cherry - but now he could have it back!

Although they never had children, they did have a sex life after they were married.Immersed so deeply in his work, Riley often needed Dotty's support, and got it: she was there for him; through all those long days and longer nights that he spent in the theatre during Belfast's "Troubles".

The "Troubles" affected Riley deeply. Sometimes, in bed at night, he would jump at the crump of a bomb detonating in the distance. Dotty would hold him, caress him, sure that she was preventing him from becoming "doolally".

She knew that the stresses involved with working on so many mutilated victims could have that affect on him; it had on some of his contemporaries. On many nights, she cooled his fevered brow with a damp cloth and held him tightly, as he fought the demons plaguing his sleep.

Often, Dotty could do nothing but listen to Riley crying out in his nightmares, anguishing at the horrors he relived. It was a lot for her to bear, but she had always been pliant to his every sexual whim; taking all of him, trying to tire him into peaceful sleep with her favours, painful though it sometimes was, until the menopause, when she told him that she no longer wished sex.

Dotty had never thought that taking a step back from those traumas, relaxing, living at the Hall, would cause *her* any despair. Riley began to sleep soundly quite quickly, but she would jerk awake on many nights, a terrifying cry rattling her head. She found a glass or two of brandy helped her sleep, kept those demons at bay. Her lips closing with the brandy goblet a little too often wasn't good for her health, she knew, but it was her way of blotting out those memories. Being there for Riley during the "Troubles" had had that price tag.

Since Dotty began drinking at dinner, she had fallen asleep every night on the sitting-room sofa, and always seemed to be there when Riley roused her to go to bed.

Her suspicions that spring morning, when Riley had returned from his police-surgeon duties and she had caught the whiff of the perfume, haunted her still. It was as much of worry now, as it was then: did an ulterior motive exist for Riley's interest in those duties. She had said nothing, just waited to see if there would be a reoccurrence.

Suspicious also was the sorry excuse of a pencil-line moustache that he had grown. With the gap between his two front teeth, Dotty wondered if he thought it made him look like the caddish Terry Thomas, who, she believed, in private life, was one for the ladies!

That Riley might be finagling (Dotty's word for the sex act, adulterous or otherwise) perplexed Dotty. She had wondered what she'd do if she ever did confirm her suspicions.

Crossing her mind often was a tale she had heard during her training days at the Veterinary College. A farmer's wife had devised her own method of correction, on finding her husband, 'With his trousers down,' they said. The farmer, himself, had made a whip from a bull's knob, having cut the thing out complete from the carcass. After stretching it, shaping it, curing and stiffening it, he had then lacquered it. Sometime later, the farmer's wife had caught the farmer with the milkmaid. The storyteller had exaggerated the tale, Dotty knew. "On the job", "laying pipe", "knobbing", "shagging the arse off the girl", he had said, when 'finagling' would have sufficed.

The farmer's wife had watched and waited for the opportune moment. When it came, she surprised the pair in the hayshed. She saw her husband's arse, bucking and thrusting, spotlighted in shafts of sunlight piercing the building through cracks in the wrinkly-tin roof. Sneaking up behind him, she had tramlined his arse with his own whip. The farmer had squealed loudly, hopped from the hayshed, like a kid in a sack race, his trousers around his ankles.

Word was that the treatment had worked perfectly, the farmer never again looking at another woman.

Dotty was certain that if she were to catch Riley in similar circumstances, the wheals she would leave on his arse would be deep, painful, unforgettable… branding him forever as no one else's but hers.

Chapter 2

Dotty raised her head. Her mental imagery was fading, though she was aware what her thoughts were. She gave Riley a quick, waspish look; tried to detect in his face any pleasure that a call from the RUC station for his services might bring. As usual, his face was impassive, telling her nothing.

Suddenly she blurted in a strained voice, 'Riley, I love you dearly. Since first we met, throughout the "Troubles", and I always have.'

Riley looked into Dotty's eyes. Her voice had strangled to a squeak; he heard the anguish and saw her eyes moisten. He had never doubted her love for him, though Dotty had often trotted out the "Troubles", quoting the same stories: how they had affected him, how that had affected her; having to cope with them, why she drank so much brandy.

Dotty's eyes crossed a little. Shaking her head, she again turned her gaze towards Riley. This time she was looking for some appreciation for her preserving his sanity during those hellish times. She saw none.

Since Dotty began to tipple, Riley had watched her closely. Upon seeing any drift towards alcoholism, he had pledged to step in, to give and, if need be, to get help for her. She only ever drank at dinnertime, never at any other time of the day; he hadn't thought that a bit of a worry. Not one little bit - the tipple made her sleepy.

'You're on call as police-surgeon this weekend in Ballyboil, aren't you?' Dotty pried. Taking the mouthful of liquor left in the goblet, she spun it around her mouth and allowed it to spill slowly over her throat.

'Aye,' Riley replied. 'I'm on call this evening. When the cops at Rippington Avenue RUC station begin intervening in Saturday-night-drinker's pleasures, they'll run in a few unfortunates. They never fail to arrest a drunk, a drunken driver or injure a yob or two while pulling them in, creating the need for my presence.

'The youths of today are a stroppy lot. They drink too much, get drunk too easily and want to fight authority physically. The town cops usually draw blood while making an arrest. If they don't, they'll use a sly nudge or trip on the way to the cells. That makes them feel hard, in control, authoritative. During my duties at Rippington Avenue I've noted several cops with a brutal side to their nature.'

The call had to come later, for sure. It *was* Saturday night.

Dotty's face was aglow, the brandy doing its job rosily. She realised that her powers of reasoning were now slowing and took a deep breath, tried to fend off the approaching fogginess and pry a little further on the subject before that happened.

'Riley, you're a notable surgeon. Few equal you in your specialisation. I thought you'd be happy with your NHS contract and trousering the extra fees you're now making from your private work.

'Since the Good Friday Agreement, Ulster is booming. There are plenty of pounds in pockets. Cosmetic surgery, body augmentation, boob jobs, tucks and lifts cannot come cheaply. You say we can afford a brand-new Jaguar motor car without overstretching the Hall budget or touching our nest egg. So I don't see why you have to run after the few quid the cops toss your way.'

In one respect, Dotty was correct. At the Royal Dilbert Hospital, Doctor Riley Dernehen had learned intricate skills and perfected them. He had become an expert in restructuring skin, flesh and bone; fixing the human messes the "Troubles" delivered to the operating theatre. During his years there, he had reconstructed an endless stream of burned, bomb-blasted and gun-wounded patients to passable likenesses of their former selves.

The paramilitaries' sadistic practice of putting a bullet through a victim's knee as a punishment was a common injury on which Riley operated. The grotesque six-pack, where the victim's elbows, ankles and knees received the same treatment, was an even eviler abomination that he dealt with. The bullet in the back of the head, however, was outwith his remit for repairs and a job for the undertaker.

Not interested in religious divides, it had never occurred to him to differentiate between his patients. Damaged legs, upon which the owner would never again be able to stand properly, from up the Falls or the Shankill Roads, he treated the same.

'I've specialised for years. I need to keep my hand in at general practice,' was the answer with which Riley quickly fended her off.

'Hmm.' The answer didn't satisfy Dotty. Another topic crossed her mind. It would change the subject, but it intrigued her how Riley might reply? 'Another thing I ponder is spare part surgery. Within your specialisation, what are they?' Dotty asked.

Riley was, initially, glad of the change of tack. He knew that knob talk disgusted Dotty. He would grab the moment and give her a daft answer: one he thought she deserved, wouldn't like, an answer that might stop her from prying into his police-surgeon activities. 'At the moment, I only have an intromittent organ.'

Even if Dotty's brandy intake had ravaging her memories of their most recent dinnertime conversations, she had at least grasped one thing. Since Riley became police-surgeon, his answers had become offhand, contemptuous… as feckin' unbelievable as his stories were and now he was acting downright arrogant! During all of their married life, until he began those duties, he had treated her lovingly, courteously. Their discussions had been sensible, he explaining sympathetically the things she might not know, but not know! She knew of the term he was trying to fox her with, rarely if ever used these days, and wondered just how far he would stretch this story; how much more of a fool he thought her. 'An intromittent organ, what the feck is that?' she erupted.

'It's what we Irish doctors call a knob.'

'Knob! Dotty exploded, for effect. 'Please don't dwell on that horrid subject. When I was pre-menstrual, my mammy called them tiddleypushes. Daddy called his The Old Fella. Mammy told me to steer well clear of them. Keep them at arm's length. They'd only get me into trouble was the essence of the lesson.

'A time ago, we had our share of fun with yours... We're older now, too old. Thankfully, sex has drifted out of our lives and we ought to call them tiddleypushes again. A much nicer, less offensive word that is, to be sure.' Dotty finished her tirade and looked at Riley. With what nonsensical tale would he follow that?

Riley chortled behind his deadpan face. It seemed his words were having the desired result. He thought he'd shock her again and said airily, 'That's an old-fashioned word, a bit like Polyphemus, the one-eyed snake. Today, a knob is a knob. I intend collecting a selection of them. They come in various shapes and sizes. Currently, I only have a black one in storage at the hospital. A feckin' beauty it is to be sure. It's fully eighteen inches long, coiled up like a black mamba and ready for phalloplasty.

'Men wishing something a little bigger to handle and present to their ladies will find it very attractive. Some will find it contemporary, I'm sure.'

'Oh... how repulsive. What is the world coming to?' Dotty asked, clenching her eyes shut, trying to kid him. When she opened them wide she leaned forward and looked at him with what she hoped was an incredulous gaze. 'But how did you get your hands on something like that?'

'I've never had my hands on it,' Riley snapped. He twisted in his chair, wishing he hadn't begun the farce, but a fabrication was nearing completion. 'The paramedics removed it from a piece of twisted and jagged metal surrounding the windscreen of a crashed car, where it was hanging by a few bloody slivers of flesh.

'The previous owner, a holidaying American athlete, had a head-on collision with an oncoming carthorse. His passage through the windscreen, at terrifying speed, ripped it off, his lunchbox plundered. He died at the scene, clutching his bloody testicles in his hand.'

'Oh the poor man,' Dotty said, 'it must have been a dreadful experience for him. It must have been simply hellish having it pulled off in that manner. It must have come off so quickly...and was gone...flown.' Dotty put a hand to her heart and lifted her eyes towards the ceiling, showing anguish at the thought of it.

'I'm sure someone had pulled it off more pleasurably and slower on many occasions before it came off in that manner,' Riley said, grinning behind the napkin he had put up to wipe his lips.

Showing no seeds of doubt, Dotty asked, 'But how do you keep a thing like that fresh?'

'Fresh!' Riley answered rattily, looking at her as if shocked at her not knowing. 'We don't just keep things like that fresh, in a fridge, along with the passion fruit and the courgettes. We keep them frozen solid, rock-hard in a cryogenic chamber, as good as the day they were last used.'

'Of course, I'd forgotten the practice,' Dotty said. She stifled a hiccup and asked, 'Are they then not a little hard to work with if they're frozen?'

'Aye, they are, but we do thaw them out first, you know. They do become hard again after transplantation,' Riley answered disdainfully, a smug grin forming. 'Indeed, now that you ask, in each phalloplasty I've performed, all necessary functions have remained in place. I take pride that in each case I've never once lost a vinegar stroke.' He was sure that phrase ought to have her guessing.

Only that evening Dotty had thought of vinegar strokes. During her bull-semen collecting days, she had often heard the term. Then, it served as an instruction to her. Hearing it meant she had to quickly position the bottle (or the long cruet, as it was known to her team) through the dummy cow's side door, ready to collect the deposit the duped, bulbous-eyed bull was about to make. Riley never knew of that task, so she asked, 'What to feck's a vinegar stroke?'

'It's the colloquial term for the strokes immediately preceding ejaculation; shooting one's load at the conclusion of coitus. It's also experienced by wankers going solo, letting one fly over their wrists,' Riley said, shaking a half-closed fist.

Dotty exploded with disgust, giving the impression that she was truly upset at his demonstration. 'Ach…that stuff…I saw enough of that when I was at the veterinary college.' She shook her head, but stopped on realising the motion was making her feel giddy. Her focus returned. 'But don't they fall off with the rejection thing?' she asked.

'We use drugs. The Americans have come up with a wonder drug that makes transplants stick better,' Riley said.

'A kind of super-glue pill, is it?' Dotty thought that a suitably daft question.

'Aye, it's something like that.' Riley tidied his plate, pushed his chair back and yawned, letting her know he was tired of her questioning.

Dotty didn't bite. 'Surely, that type of work is more interesting than taking blood and urine samples from drunk drivers in smelly, inhospitable police cells,' she proposed.

'Aye, you're correct,' Riley said. 'Drunk drivers are usually faffing around, acting the goat. They all have enough puff to blow into the breathalyser tube, but they don't take matters seriously. Sometimes it's quite difficult to get any cooperation from them.'

Dotty probed deeper, wanting to hang on in there, but she could feel her concentration wavering…perhaps she should give up the brandy. 'You bandage and stick plasters on the drunks, work in their vomit and listen to their incoherent ravings. How do you stomach that?'

'Sometimes I send the worst to hospital without treating them. It's usually because they need their stomachs pumped,' Riley answered.

'Obviously, you don't mind treating these prisoners,' Dotty enquired.

'Treating broken ribs, contusions, bumps, gashes, cuts, dislocations, the black and blue testicles, the gouged eyes that prisoners allegedly suffer in cop stations is all good experience,' Riley said.

'You like telling lies for the cops?' Dotty asked, her eyes searching his face. Would he answer that question truthfully?

'No, I don't! But it's true I've been turning a blind eye,' Riley said. 'That's an effort to convey the message to the miscreants residing in Ballyboil that zero tolerance is in operation. If it's effective in cutting crime and loutish behaviour, then I'm all for it. I'm sure it all adds up to a safer town. Aye, Dotty, working at Rippington Avenue police station is a bit like "The Bill", the cop soap you've been watching on TV.'

Riley hadn't told Dotty that often cops with sniffles or pains approached him for an instant diagnosis to their ailment; that earlier that summer, Constable Gabriel O'Hicks had taken him to one side and self-consciously whispered a confession that he was "Pissing fishhooks". The cop was too embarrassed to tell his wife about his problem, it being a bit of a worry, and asked if Doctor Dernehen could covertly prescribe something for him.

To tell Dotty that he had prescribed a course of antibiotics to take the edge off the barbs of the cop's problem, would have caused her a bit of a worry and him some earache.

The cook served the sweet course, homemade rhubarb tart and creamy custard, and then poured the coffee.

Dotty's eyes began rolling as she stirred brown sugar into the cup, which she then pushed to one side without tasting. She realised the brandy's affects were finally overwhelming her. Her head drooped, but almost immediately, she jerked it upright.

Riley was waiting for this; he had seen it happen so often. Unsteadily she rose from the chair, screeched the legs over the floor as she moved it back from the table. Lurching for the wall, she felt her way; hand over hand, out into the hall, towards the sitting-room door.

The sofa was in the centre of the sitting-room; with two unsteady strides, she reached it. Gingerly, she felt her way to its front. Collapsing onto it, she laid back. Her head rolled for a time, then settled. Quickly she was snoring, rasping resonantly from narrowing air passages.

Once her head rocked back and her eyelids closed, Riley knew the "all clear" had sounded. He had played the "get out" card successfully. If Rippington Avenue RUC station called, he could visit Mavis and make unhurried love.

*

Neither the snores nor the crash of a toyed bone drowned out the hall telephone that began ringing some time later. Riley had reclined himself on a chaise longue awaiting the call. The sparks and flames roaring up the stone chimney from the blazing logs in the open hearth took his interest, while he sipped tonic water over ice.

In the changing colours of the fire's dancing flames, he had perceived the toing and froing of a sea battle. Square-riggers, with sails set to luff, had exchanged broadsides in heaving, angry waters. The fleet's barrage had battered into many Spanish galleons, putting the armada to flight.

Riley could handle that. It was the sight of the bosoms on the figurehead of the flagship, as proud and as firm as Mavis', ramming into an enemy vessel's side that had stirred him from those musings and jerked him back to reality the instant the phone began ringing.

Riley walked into the hallway, picked up the handset and placed it to his ear. He groaned. For the first time that evening, he saw Cedric had his jaws clamped around a marrowbone. 'Feck,' he mouthed as Cedric wagged his tail and tossed the bone, thinking there might be a game on, 'I should have spotted this earlier,' he said to himself, 'I told the cook and Dotty never again to give him a boiled bone from the stockpot.'

Cedric retrieved the bone and gnawed noisily at it. All the while, his eyes, languishing in drooping and inflamed sockets, were on Riley. Tiredly, Cedric gave up his thoughts of play and stilled his tail.

Cedric's progress at devouring the bone was minimal, but Riley knew that digestion problems and constipation would be the upshot of the bony feast. Reluctantly, in the past, he had treated the problem and Cedric would require treatment again - the sooner the better. Now, he happened to be smartly dressed and had no desire to dishevel himself wrestling the dog for the prize of the bone, even if it would save it some pain.

Riley answered the phone, said his 'Hello,' and then 'yes, sergeant, I'm on my way. I'll be at the station shortly.' Whynot Hall was a fifteen-minute drive from the RUC station in Rippington Avenue, Ballyboil. With a grin spreading, he walked into the sitting-room, collected his case and glanced at Dotty, lying awkwardly and comatose on the couch. Realising his goodbyes would go unheard he left her undisturbed.

Muttering to himself, he walked towards the hallway, 'Sounding like a braying donkey playing a fractured kazoo again, my dear. I'll be out for a few hours I would say.'

Facing the hall mirror, Riley checked his attire and brushed his hair. Now in the ranks of Jaguar owners, he was sure his garb was acceptable wear for professionals sitting behind the steering wheels of top marques.

On the steps of the Hall, he stood for a few moments listening to the breeze rustle the branches of the monkey-puzzle tree. Looking north, he saw clouds racing overhead. The moon shining over the roof of the Hall, laid spiky shadows on the lawn. Snores escaping the sitting-room and the sounds of teeth attempted to shatter bone in the hall, were the only sounds robbing the night of its stillness.

'But where are the sounds that Dotty said were missing from the countryside?' he said, raising his arms skywards. 'Can I hear the dinging of bells, the wailing of sirens, or the splat of hedgehogs being compacted to tarmacadamed roads? No. Do I hear the demented hoots of owls incapable of regurgitating balls of mouse bones? No. Do I hear the concerned cries of mother hares? No. Then I must be a silly sod for listening for a feckin' compendium of nonsensical noises.'

Chapter 3

At 5:45, that same Saturday evening, the constables parading at Ballyboil's Rippington Avenue RUC station for the difficult 6p.m. to 2a.m. shift, awaited the arrival of Sergeant Billy Liptrott. He would allot them foot-beat duties or comfortable motorised patrols.

The sergeant limped into the parade room, head down, looking glum. A muffled voice said, 'Some woman's dumped him.' Low moans and audibly declared 'Nice ones,' followed, as the sergeant instructed constables either to take up a walking beat or to man a motorised patrol.

The sergeant had no qualms regarding working the 6 to 2 on Saturdays. If the shift followed its usual pattern, many miscreants would fall beneath the gaze of the constables, and he always incited them to "keep their numbers up". There should be many arrests: that afternoon, Glasgow Celtic had beaten their old rivals Glasgow Rangers in their first match of the season. Many fights would break out between the opposing supporters drinking in the town and he would deal with the arrested.

The beat duties assigned, Sergeant Liptrott sat down on a short-legged stool. He hadn't yet dismissed the parade, but sat facing the constables lounging around the parade room in disinterested poses. Removing one boot and then the sock, he exposed his blue-veined foot, which was showing the results of many years incarceration in footwear with synthetic soles.

The constables were looking on in mock horror when the sergeant quipped, 'To be sure now, I'm only about to howk the dead skin from this corn. It's been playing me up for weeks.' He took a Stanley knife from a side pocket, slid out the blade and wiped it on his trousers.

The constables', their horror quickly turning from mock to the real, shielded their eyes as the sergeant probed deeply into his corn with the blade point.

The sergeant was in his thirties, his face ruddy and podgy and he stood six foot two in height when erect. Thin of build, he wielded a pronounced beer belly that lurked half-hidden beneath his uniform tunic.

Paring off some dead skin, his face twisted in agony and he began rotating the blade, digging it into it the corn.

'Pay particular attention to the vicinity of O'Reardon's Bar at throwing-out time,' he told the constables between lengthy grimaces and anguished utterances. He withdrew the knife, shuddered and breathed in deeply. He looked at the yellowy matter on the blade, held it out for the constables to inspect, and said, 'There'll be undue celebrations at O'Reardon's. Don't let any partying there get out of hand.'

The sergeant dipped a hand into a side pocket and found a plaster. Removing the protective strip, he placed the plaster over the bleeding hole. 'We shouldn't let them become carried away with themselves, should we now? Throw a few into the paddy wagon. If that doesn't keep the rest quiet, haul them all back. Bring a yob or two for me to smack around the head and lock up for the night. It'll look good having reams of charge sheets and full cells when the inspector calls.

Wincing, the sergeant began pulling his boot back onto his foot. 'What else is there? Oh, I almost forgot. They never publicise their events, but the grapevine tells me the bunch of rotten meatheads, the Unlanced Boils Motorcycle Club, is holding a bash at their regular, hillside site. Bikers will pour into the area, toting drugs in large quantities. I'll be doing stops and searches on one or two of that fraternity. I'll be looking to locate and confiscate their stashes and lock a few of the shitheads up. Constable O'Hicks, you'll accompany me in a patrol car. First, though, you can nip down to the pie cart in Market Square and fetch me a hotdog. Double up on onions and mustard, will you?'

Constable O'Hicks wrote down the order on a pad and then held out a hand towards the sergeant, expecting some cash to change hands.

The sergeant stood up and waved the constable's hand away. 'Get it for nothing, can't yeh.' He then pounded his boot onto the cement floor, each stamp of his foot distorting his face.

Constable O'Hicks said to anyone interested, as his shift colleagues left the parade room for their duties, and he headed in the direction of the pie cart, 'Sarge's pain bodes ill for some poor sods. It could be a brave old night for the rest of us if the corn keeps on playing him up.'

*

The "Unlanced Boils" bikers chose well the location for their bashes: a concealed hollow, a natural amphitheatre, situated beneath Mount Boil's smaller peak. It was also far enough out of town to remain free from complaints of drug use and noise. Locals knew the place as "The Stye".

In daylight, the hollow's rim gave an uninterrupted view of anyone approaching with intent to disrupt tranquil, drug-induced dispositions and the fall-about-laughing games that bikers played. During the night, bikers, taking turns as guards, provided security.

Traditionally, a stratospheric-sounding rock band entertained, playing their cover versions of bikers' favourite tracks at eardrum-damaging levels and dulling the hearing of perhaps four hundred bikers from Ireland and beyond.

The bikers experienced no problems in retaining the use of their venue. They always left the site spotless. The following day, only crumpled grass betrayed their presence there.

Sergeant Liptrott, though, didn't only suspect the bikers were up to no good, he knew they were.

He munched away at his hotdog as he drove to the boreen leading up to the site. Finishing the sausage, he threw some remnant bread and the wrapping paper out the car window. He turned his head and said to Constable O'Hicks, sitting beside him, 'They erect a huge marquee up there. Right now, it will be filled with blootered bikers, high with the "black stuff", poteen and the best locally-grown skunk grass.

'I know this from reports and my own observations over a number of years. It has never best pleased me, either. Stopping a solitary and unsupported biker was always my best chance of nicking one. The "high heid yins" aren't keen to send in reinforcements for a raid. We've never been called upon to sort out any trouble up there, though, surprisingly enough.'

Parked up at a junction, he watched despondently, muttering 'bastards', mainly, as the lines of bearded bikers and their machines, some with a "lady" on the pillion, converged on the hilltop site. Being badass bikers and always wary of cops, they arrived in groups of six and sometimes as many as twenty. Many leered at the sergeant as they passed, angering him.

As 8 p.m. approached, he'd sighted no solo biker whom he could stop. From more than one biker, his knowledge of the type suggested he would receive a rough reception if he did. This would lead to blows being struck, likely to lead to his injury and not theirs', so he thought better of it.

'The "ladies'" knickers will be wringing wet already. Screwed to the ground tighter than the guy ropes of their marquee as soon as they get to the site, they'll be,' the sergeant erupted, breathing in deeply, then exhaling slowly.

'Do you think so, but?' Constable O'Hicks asked.

'Randy bloody lot them bikers' "ladies",' the sergeant said. 'I've heard it said most need a good knobbing early on in the bash to calm them down. Probably stops them from straying to other horny bikers. That's what keeps any fighting to a minimum, I suppose.'

'Has no one tried to infiltrate the bash and get evidence of drug offences?' the constable asked, showing keenness.

The sergeant noted the constable's sudden interest in police work, looked at his innocent face, thought him gullible and a likely candidate for a spot of piss taking. He said, 'A couple of years back, two men in plain clothes tried a clandestine operation. The bikers cottoned on to them quickly though, saw them for what they were.'

'Oh, what happened?' the constable asked, all ears.

'They fell off the moped in front of the bash guards,' the sergeant said.

'You're having me on,' the constable retorted, 'don't believe you.'

'They were country cops and not very bright,' the sergeant said. 'Daft as "Old Barneys" we said of them.'

'Didn't the bikers piss them off?' the constable asked.

'No. The bikers' "ladies" got a hold of them', the sergeant said. 'A lot of filthy-minded bitches must have attended that year.' The sergeant noted a change: the constable was showing keen interest in his tale. He had him hooked. He would lay the nonsense on thick.

'Tell me then?' The constable blurted.

'They were stripped naked and tied to a tree,' the sergeant said.

'And then?' the constable quickly asked.

'The bitches stuffed a couple of one-hundred-milligram Viagra tablet over their throats,' the sergeant said, 'then they left them for a couple of hours until each of them had a rock-hard hard-on. The women then teased them, played with them, had them screaming, their knob-ends painful and bulging.'

'The women knobbed the two cops against the tree, clapped on by the bikers,' the constable ventured, took several short breaths and shifted in his seat.

'Not quite,' the sergeant said and smiled, 'the women heavily laced a yogurt with hash and spooned it into them. An hour later, they released them. The two cops ran back down the hill. Screaming their bloody heads off and laughing their bollocks off at the same time, they were.'

'Piss off, sergeant, pull the other one,' the constable said, tiredly, knowing the sergeant's bawdry story had duped him.

The sergeant shook with laughter. 'Well, you can go up the hill now and find out for yourself. Otherwise, when it gets to 9 o'clock, and no solitary arsehole biker has come along, we'll go. I'm desperate for another hot dog for when its grub time, but.'

The constable settled down, reclined his seat and drew his cap down over his eyes. 'Right on, sergeant,' he answered and let out a yawn.

At 9 p.m. prompt, Sergeant Liptrott left the junction and pulled onto the bypass.

*

Seth Mulligan, President of the "Unlanced Boils" Motorcycle Club, had few admirers outside the bike club. He, too, had a "lady": a farmer's daughter, who had spent most of that Saturday sitting on a John Deere tractor, moving trailer-loads of wet grain from the fields to the driers.

Listening to the roar of the tractor's engine for twelve hours had deafened her, drove her nuts. The heavy rock and blues music she was expecting to hear later, after her father called time and the tractors stilled for the night, would send her crazy much more pleasantly.

At 9 p.m., Seth clambered behind the wheel of his trike and left the site. He expected to collect his "lady" and two of her friends from the end of a track leading to the farm.

Seth sped down the boreen leading from "the stye" with a silly, whacked-out grin spread across his face. The journey was short and he worried not that his Master-at-Arms, pie-eyed on skunk grass and the black stuff, was too blootered to accompany him. Giggling merrily and unperturbed about journeying along police-infected roads alone, Seth drove onto the bypass and made for the pick-up point.

*

Flannigan's pie cart, a converted ambulance, had a permanent pitch in Ballyboil's Market Square. As Sergeant Liptrott drove there, his stomach was rumbling. He looked directly ahead, miscreants were not a priority when he needed food fast.

Pulling alongside the cart, he stepped out, a wry grin spreading. No customers waited service and the cart operative wasn't in sight. The sergeant ambled up and rapped on the counter with a coin until he heard some movement. A red-faced boy appeared from the cab, carrying a soft-porn magazine, which he tried to hide when he saw the sergeant.

'Dirty young muppet. Wash your hands and give me a hotdog with plenty of extras,' the sergeant ordered. Sniffing his disgust, he began looking around the cart, paying particular attention to the tyres. 'The treads are poor. There's not two-mil left on any of them,' he voiced loudly and pointed out the offence to the boy. The sergeant was after a free hotdog and it worked.

'Bayjasus, sergeant, I'll tell me Da to get them changed,' the boy said, his face a touch redder. 'You'll have this on the house, won't you?'

The sergeant walked back to the car licking his lips, carrying his grub in a newspaper-wrapped polystyrene container. 'Look at the feast I mumped from that dafty. I got more than the usual portions of onions and mustard,' he was saying as he opened his door. 'Take this, constable,' he said and held out the package to the constable, still lolling in the front passenger seat. Seeing there was no hand held out to take it from him, he eased himself into the car and placed the container on the back seat.

The sergeant was heading back along the bypass and about to turn off for Rippington Avenue, when he checked traffic flow and scanned across to the other lane. Sighting Seth Mulligan on his trike, he erupted, 'Gotcha! The bloody' hotdog can wait.'

The passengers on the back seats of the trike wore their hair long, untethered, the tresses billowing in the air rushing past them, along with the sparks blasted from the large joint they were sharing. 'Whew, more "ladies" being transported to the bash,' he said quietly.

As he watched, the trike began swaying; "ladies'" hands grabbing for the framework to hang to on as the trike zigzagged. Seth Mulligan was wearing dark, wraparound spectacles, his ponytail flowing out behind him. Grinning hugely, he spun the trike wheel maniacally. Pulling out, he overtook other vehicles. Then he quickly pulled in front of them, causing their drivers to brake sharply.

The sergeant pressed the accelerator pedal flat to the floor. With a growl, the police car picked up, carrying him and the constable towards an exit onto the other carriageway. At the exit, he turned and with the blue light flashing, he pulled out in front of on-coming traffic. In pursuit of the trike and confident of an arrest, he pressed the accelerator hard to the floor and roared down the outer lane.

Constable O'Hicks, shaken from his catnapping by the increase in engine noise and the police car swerving, sat up, righted his seat and began to take notice. Immediately, he realised the sergeant's hunger to wolf the hotdog wasn't causing him to speed.

The trike in sight, the sergeant changed down a gear. Ahead of it, he pulled in front, the car engine racing. The constable, fully alert now, wiped his eyes with the back of a hand and pulled on his hat.

With the bells ringing loudly, the sergeant slowed, causing the trike to stop.

Looking evil and eager to feel collar, the sergeant turned to the constable and said, 'Bloody-well gottim! Mulligan's already had a good day at the bash on the hash by the looks of him. He has no hope! He won't be heading back there to toke some more and mess with all that tasty pussy sitting there in the back.'

The constable looked through the rear window towards the trike. Sounding vexed, he said, 'Surely you're not going to ruin the night for the girls, sergeant?'

'The girls can go grab a taxi. I'm going to mess up Mulligan's night. Be prepared to drive the trike back to the station, once I have him cuffed and his arse is safely on this back seat. I'm going to do him for going through the last set of traffic lights and anything else I can think of. I'm sure he'll test positive for drugs, too!'

Chapter 4

Taking a deep breath, Riley stepped lightly down the steps to the pink, crunchy stone chips of the driveway and walked briskly to the Jaguar. A flick of his key fob opened the boot lid for it to rise automatically. A light illuminated the interior and he placed his doctor's case inside, alongside some splints, emergency medicines and other equipment.

Three strides later, he opened the driver's door and sat behind the steering wheel. He didn't yet have the hang of the seat adjustment procedure, but he flicked at a switch he thought was the right one. An electric motor hummed into life and his seat rose to a position giving him better forward vision. He felt good. Excited with his new marquee, he sniffed at the newness of the leather seats. He was sure that someone would ask him how it performed before the day was over.

As Riley was fiddling with the ignition key, he was mimicking Dotty. 'I must hold on tightly to the purse strings. There's not much left of the bequest. Your NHS income goes on the upkeep of the Hall, the gardener's and the cook's wages and keeping us both well provided in a beautiful, commodious home.' I do not understand why you need a boy's toy, a Jag, of all things. He gave a loud chortle. Then he said in a deep voice: 'I've got a feckin' Jag now and I'm going to enjoy it,' and thumped his hands onto the wheel.

The Jaguar engine kicked over and purred into life. Riley moved off. Out on the open road, the 4-litre S-type swept along, quickly reaching the speed limit for country roads. Just as quickly, his mind went into sexual overdrive. Mavis was in for a good seeing-too, to be sure. Tonight he would attempt the big two: a double visit to Mavis' mound of perpetual delight. Throwing his leg over again after a short rest and giving it to her another time would prove he still had the stamina.

He toed the accelerator feeling a little less like "Riley the doctor", more like "Riley the Ballyboil ram".

On his drive towards Rippington Avenue RUC station, Riley looked in the rear-view mirror and saw the twin peaks of Mount Boil looming behind him. He sighed; it seemed so long ago now that Dotty had seduced him in the hollow between the peaks.

The short section of bypass behind him, he entered the town's suburbs, taking the road running parallel to the River Boil. The river had lost its depth quickly after the recent rains. Rank smells were returning, assaulting his nostrils, making him wrinkle his nose. A quick dip into his bag of erotic daydreams had him concentrating on something much pleasanter: another vision of Mavis. They were jauntily walking, hand-in-hand, on the Mount, both looking for tufts of bouncy heather.

In a giddy mood, Riley switched on the radio, wanting to hear a love song. Instead, fevered, bass-reinforced, Saturday night music blared from the four speakers of the technologically-advanced, quadraphonic sound system. He hadn't yet worked out how the gizmos or the auto-tune worked. His jabbing of a finger at buttons or tweaking sliders and turning rotary controls hadn't controlled the volume. It still played far too loud for his pleasure.

He sat back; back to reality, listening to the raucous guitar sounds of Thin Lizzie playing "The boys are back in town". He smiled as the number ended. He was back in town, driving a Jag. He'd flaunt the Jag in the station yard to any interested cop. The younger cops, he was sure, would also enthuse at the sounds the radio kicked out.

Before taking delivery of the Jag, Riley had driven a vintage Mazda with a whirring rotary engine. It was their second car now, which Dotty drove.

He was proud of the Mazda and had maintained it well. Oil leaked from the sump, but he had entered it into vintage shows and had won prizes. At the shows, RUC traffic-division cops stopped by and spoke with him about the pros and cons of the engines. Each of them offered some suggestion as to what the manufacturers could do to improve oil seals.

The traffic cops cracked jokes, swapped the addresses of spare-part suppliers, bonhomie existing between them. When they saw him driving the Mazda on local roads, they always poked a friendly hand out the car and waved to him.

When he had driven the Mazda to the RUC station, few of the cops there had shown any interest in it - but he had heard many complaints from them regarding the inadequacies of their police cars. It seemed cops openly mourned the days when they were fast, sleek, criminal-catching machines with street cred. They longed for the return of cars with a bit of acceleration, a high top speed, impeccable on corners. The present fleet of Mondeos, Cavaliers and tank-like Land Rover Discoveries, seemingly left them unmoved.

He had also heard words of hate and resentment towards Jag drivers, belligerently mouthed by RUC cops. They considered that none other than their ilk possessed the relevant skills to keep one on the road at speed. Riley didn't believe he was included in that category; after all, wasn't he their police-surgeon and deserving of their respect.

Not feeling any unease, Riley let the thought slip from his mind. He was sure, though, on pulling into the yard, that the sight of his brand-new, personalised-number-plated and blood-red-painted Jag guaranteed that cops on duty would gag for a gander beneath the bonnet at the power unit. A chat with him about its spec, or a demonstration spin in it at speed he thought would definitely be on the cards, too. His imagination remained revved up until he completed the journey to the station.

His early arrival at the RUC station hadn't always meant his police-surgeon tasks began immediately or finished quickly. Often, it took him a while to patch up a prisoner in receipt of physical abuse for being unruly. He also found the conduct of certain cops towards their prisoners was anything but considerate.

Riley swung the Jag into the station-yard entrance, a gap in the high, wire-mesh fencing around the building's exterior, a part of the bomb defences. The station had remained free of any bomb-lobbing occurrences during the "troubles" and he was driving a car that not all cops were used to seeing him in. He didn't want them to confuse him with any potential bomber; driving slowly up to the yard gate would give them plenty of time to identify him as Doctor Dernehen.

To announce his arrival, he pressed the button with the long arrow pointing to it, when the pillar supporting it came within his reach. The creaking sound he heard outside was the car-window-level video camera panning around to focus in on his face. The gate clicked open, moved back and a voice said, 'Good evening, doctor.' He didn't mind not receiving his full title, but chuntered inwardly when all he got was Doc.

Revving the engine a little more than necessary, he pulled the Jag inside and drove across the yard to a parking place away from the main building. On Saturday nights, the station yard could become a lively place, truncheons as well as fists flying.

The doctor eased himself out of the Jag and retrieved his case from the boot. He moved to the bonnet and stood still, swinging the case in a nonchalant pose, waiting for his eyes to adjust to the glare of the yard's floodlights. As shapes became clearer, he scanned the area keenly.

A succession of overweight cops passed by one another on the external staircase leading up to the canteen, situated on the second floor of an out-building. The doctor mused: a diet of canteen chips, baked beans on potato scones or soda bread, and swilling down endless cups of tea has a lot to answer for. I wouldn't like to haul a gut like any of those around an extensive foot beat.

Other activities in the yard caused him to pull back his top lip and stretch his pencil-line-thin moustache. It was hardly noticeable in the floodlights' glare, but Mavis liked it when it tickled.

The doctor clenched his eyebrows and furrowed his brow as he watched. The business of policing Ballyboil manor was under way. Cops were already proving zero tolerance alive and well; keeping numbers up, the count of crimes solved and arrests made, was occurring in front of his eyes.

Indeed, the apprehension of a selection of Ballyboil's Saturday night miscreants was off to a bloody good start.

A paddy wagon had pulled into the yard behind him, the two burly cops in the cab rocking back and forward as it braked. It lurched to a stop and then reversed to within two yards of the charge room door. The van's back doors crashed open, banging against its sides.

The person eager to flee the van interior was recognisable as a male youth, a pulled-up Guinness T-shirt covering his head.

The doctor saw the youth's legs flailing air in an effort to regain equilibrium, then crumple as his feet made contact with the ground, his pinned-back arms straining against handcuffs.

Two cops followed the prisoner from the wagon, their bodies launched, their hands reaching to regain control of him. Landing on the prisoner's spread-eagled body, they held him down on the yard concrete until he stopped struggling. When he had stilled, they took an arm each, pulled him onto his feet, then marched him towards the charge room steps. 'Monkey bastard,' one cop shouted. The other kneed the prisoner in the back.

It is unusual to see one's work materialise in front of one's eyes, the doctor mused, sighting blood pulsing from the prisoner's damaged nose.

'C'mon chummy, into the charge room with you,' one manhandling cop shouted. The prisoner fought against the steps, back-heeling unprotected shins. Both cops yanked on his arms. Howling in agony, the prisoner was bundled through the charge room door.

The doctor followed the two cops, skipping up the steps behind them. Sergeant Liptrott was sitting behind the charge desk, watching the youth's arrival and displaying a twisted grin of pleasure.

A man waiting charging for a drunkenness offence was already swaying in front of the desk. 'Okay, so I'm pished. It'sh no big deal, sharge,' he was saying, spraying saliva.

The sergeant shifted his gaze back towards him, presenting a face that was both bitter and brutal. Curling his top lip back, he showed his teeth, slightly apart. 'Shut t'fock up,' he hissed.

The doctor recognised the sergeant as a bit of a bully. He hadn't taken to the man, or his brutish demeanour. On occasions, he had witnessed the sergeant chastising his constables as roughly as he had the prisoners.

The charge-room was rectangular-shaped. At one end stood the charge desk, behind which was the door that led to the cells. At the other end of the charge-room was a seated area where arresting officers kept their prisoners, until they were charged. Drunken singing was issuing from cells. A shout of, 'Feckin' bastard cops stitched me up again,' from one miscreant already incarcerated there, rose above the unmelodious bedlam made by others.

The youth who had crashed to the station yard with such force, sat on a bench seat. He moaned continuously, his face colourless, apart from smeared blood, scrapes and bruises. His eyes darted fearfully around the charge-room, over the bundle of tissues he held to his skinned and bleeding nose. His other hand he clasped to a sore spot on his ribcage.

A cop with one foot placed on the bench seat, created a barrier between the prisoner and escape. In that position, he used a knee to rest his pocket book and wrote up the offence details.

The other cop responsible for manhandling the youth left the reporting to his colleague. Passing by the doctor on his way out of the back door, heading towards the canteen for some tea, he smiled and tossed his head in the direction of the youth. Addressing the doctor he said, 'Chummy thinks he's a funny focker, Doc. He's just a piss-taker and obnoxious with it. Nicked him for being drunk and disorderly, we did. See if you can fix him up a bit. Make him look presentable for his court appearance on Monday morning, will you? While you're doing your bit, I'll get you a tea from the canteen. Will yours be sugar and milk?'

From what the doctor knew, Rippington Avenue RUC station had seen many similar Saturday nights during the course of the summer.

The sergeant began to read details of the charge to the drunk. 'You're not obliged to say anything…'

Suddenly, the drunk's legs crumbled. With an audible whump, his head thudded against the side of the desk on its route to the floor, his nose touching first, blood splattering.

'That's him. Fock reading him the charge.' With a pointed finger, the sergeant instructed the arresting officer and one of his colleagues to carry the drunk to a bench seat. 'That's two bloody noses tonight already, Doc,' the sergeant said, with a snigger. 'Pity you're not on a bonus for plugging them. Now you've a choice of arseholes to work on. Which do you want to perform on first?'

The doctor grimaced at the use of "Doc" whilst placing his case on a window ledge. He clicked the case open, pulled out a pair of prophylactics, dragged them over his hands and rummaged around until he found some cotton wool. Forming it into four suitable bungs, he approached the prisoners and manipulated one up each bleeding nostril, stemming flows.

Finished with that task, he trod on the lever of a waste bin and dropped the bloodied gloves inside. Then, he looked around, trying to spot the subject of his original call-out. No one else was lying about looking forlorn and abused. All the injuries requiring attention had occurred in his presence; someone previously apprehended had to be waiting his attention in one of the cells.

The back door opened. The cop leaving for tea walked in carrying a tray of plastic cups. He had been wearing a grin when he left for the canteen, but now he had twisted his face into a sneer. For the first time, the doctor noticed that some cops as well as the sergeant used these nasty grimaces. He wondered whether they'd become compulsory at this RUC station. Quickly, he found out the reason why the tea-bearing cop was wearing his.

'Who's the lucky chummy with the new focken' Jag, then?' the tea-bearing cop asked. He had said it loudly, so that everyone could hear him. He looked down at the doctor from a great height as he picked up a plastic cup from the tray. Squeezing the cup in the act of passing the tea, he deliberately spilled some over the doctor's fingers.

'A new Jag! who's got a new focken' Jag?' Sergeant Liptrott bellowed, sniffed and pulled a face. The outburst and facial contortion indicated to the doctor that the sergeant had no nice feelings towards Jag drivers, either. Glowering, the sergeant rose to his feet, kicking his chair back against the wall as he straightened.

His eyes, and those of the other cops loitering in the charge room, seemed to turn in an instant and lock onto the doctor, and all from a great height.

'Aye, aye, I've a new Jag. They're ten-a-penny these days. I obtained a good deal on a lease. Cannot afford to buy one outright on my salary.' the doctor fibbed. He made an effort to appear annoyed as he shook the hot tea from his fingers. 'It's no big deal anymore for anyone wanting to lease a Jag.'

Trying to play Jaguar ownership down, he ignored the cops' stares. O'Hicks, the cop for whom he had prescribed treatment for the fishhook-pissing knob-infliction, walked into the charge room. Realising the issue he had walked into, he looked towards the floor, wanting to keep out of it, it seemed.

The doctor walked to the window ledge, put the tea down and fussed with the contents of his case. Now he knew it: these cops harboured some animosity towards Jaguar owners.

Nothing had previously crossed his mind that he, a police-surgeon, after all, and compliant to cop wishes in the past, was in that grouping. Now, his confidence that a cop might ask for the car keys so the lads could inspect the power unit had completely disappeared. Such was the effect of the sneering; all the cops present, bar O'Hicks, seemed to be staring at him.

The doctor snapped his case shut, sipped some tea from the half-full cup, and turned. 'You have someone else for me to see?' he asked firmly, facing the sergeant. The doctor's head turned, his gaze sweeping the charge room. He noted several sets of eyes still glaring at him.

More eyes than in a sack of spuds, he mused.

The sergeant walked from behind the charge desk and stood directly in front of the doctor, shaking a bunch of keys. 'Aye, we've done a biker by the name of Seth Mulligan. He went through a red traffic signal. We suspect while driving his trike he was under the influence of drink and drugs. He's refused the breathalyser. We think he possessed cannabis, but he's gubbed it before we were able to search him.'

'Gubbed it? That's not an expression I'm acquainted with,' the doctor said.

'It means we suspect he's swallowed the shit, which means we can expect he'll be in the throes of a whitey soon,' the sergeant said.

'A whitey, that's another new one on me.'

'Ingesting too much cannabis can cause the skin to go pale, bring on fits of giggling, and later, cold sweating. You ought to know that, Doc.'

'We doctors would know the condition by its medical term, "faeces de facia".' The words he had thought up in a trice to bullshit the sergeant with.

The sergeant looked blank, giving the doctor the impression he mightn't think it could mean "Shit-faced".

'Okay. I don't understand your medical guff,' the sergeant admitted, 'but we're holding him in a cell. He's an "Unlanced Boil". The "Boils" are a local badass bikers' club. They're an evil, unbalanced bunch of villainous, druggy, piss-artist bastards, to be sure. We've been pressing to put the squeeze on some of their number for a long time. Especially their heads, if you get my drift?'

'You're not expecting a visit from his villainous mates if they're such dreadful people?' the doctor asked.

'We reckon his muckers will all be fucked in the head with drugs by now. That's their game: drug taking and drug running. Another little sideline is the fencing of stolen motorbikes. Many a decent biker has woken up in the morning to find his treasured wheels gone. With friends like them, who needs enemas, eh doc?'

'Very droll, sergeant. Is he the one I can hear hollering about being stitched up?'

'No, but to be sure he's a bit pissed off. We stopped him on his way back to the bash with three tasty "ladies" aboard his trike,' the sergeant said. 'Sitting happily in the back, they were. Silly bitches had toked up. Sparks were flying everywhere. They threw the joint over a hedge when we stopped them. Carried on to the bash in a taxi, so they did. Some shouting and swearing came back from the taxi window, I can tell you. Me being a cop born out of wedlock and all that, would you believe? But Mulligan's certainly whacked out on something, whatever he's taken.'

'I see. It sounds as if he could be a handful,' the doctor suggested.

'To be sure, sometimes he's shouting, "I'm coming on strong." But mostly, he's taking it easy and slow. These are strong symptoms of cannabis ingestion. You can smell he's been drinking heavily, too. His beery breath is vile. He's been raving on about missing the rock band, "Dumpy and his Rusty Nuts", or something like that.'

'Did you find any evidence of Class-A drug possession?' the doctor asked.

'No, but his long greasy hair smells like a shit factory in full production. You'll smell the pungency of burnt cannabis quickly. Any other drug flushing through his veins, and there could be all sorts, will be down to you to discover,' the sergeant said. 'That's if you can get a sample from him.

'A good night's screwing we've focked up for him, that's for sure. The only thing stopping him from already having gone a bit apeshit over that loss is the impending whitey. When the affects of the cannabis ingestion wears off, he'll be dead cross. Only then will he grasp that we've prevented him having an all-night pussy-dipping session under canvas.'

'I don't suppose you mean he was going to hang a cat from a piece of twine and lower it repeatedly from a bridge into the River Boil for a bit of fun?' the doctor asked.

'No. I meant the other type of pussy,' the sergeant said, smiling slyly, his lips quivering, becoming wet with saliva as he licked them, relishing the thought.

'Ah, the vaginal pussy, the one all we men crave for. He's going to miss a real, all-night, pussy-dipping session, poor man. Seth Mulligan will be cursing you, sergeant,' the doctor said, raising his eyes.

'He can curse all he wants. We know him well. He refused the breathalyser the last time we nicked him. He was already on a driving ban then. We'll book him again for drug-related offences, for the red light and for driving without tax and insurance.' The sergeant gave a half-smile. It was the look of pleasure he kept for the occasions when he had swung one on someone.

'Do you think he'll agree to give samples?' the doctor asked.

'No. I told you he had refused before. Then we did him for failing to provide samples. Your substantiation of his drunkenness and drug ingestion will be crucial for his trial if he refuses again. Give me the goods. Guild the lily for me and I'll swing one on him. Get a proper result this time.' The sergeant's face then reverted to the look of hatred he reserved for all miscreants and he gave out three guttural, 'heh-hehs.'

'Which cell is he in?' the doctor asked.

'I'll take you to see him. You can question him yourself, but I'll station a constable outside the cell door. Press him. Get him to admit as much as you can. Get him to tell you what he's on. It's the sample that will best prove his drug guilt, but.'

The doctor thought Seth Mulligan faced a list of potentially serious charges, if the sergeant got his way, though the sergeant would have greater difficulty proving the drug ingestion. His evidence would be more than helpful to the sergeant in confirming that.

The doctor thought he had mused enough. Now he must proceed with haste. The talk of pussy-dipping sessions had whetted his appetite. The one he had planned with Mavis O'Rourke wasn't fanciful; it was real and couldn't come quickly enough. The quicker he took body fluids from the whacked-out biker, or not, as the case may be, the sooner he might be able to dip the pussy, as the sergeant had so eloquently put it.

As the sergeant opened the cell door, the doctor reeled backwards. He had always recoiled from the smell of old urine and even older vomit that lingered within Rippington Avenue police station cells.

He entered the cell. Seth Mulligan was sitting passively, on the bed, looking down towards the cell floor. Seth didn't look up. Had he done so, above his head he'd have seen moths and leggier insects flitting around the fluorescent fitting, shining down from the high ceiling and safely out of any prisoners' reach.

Seth Mulligan's unkempt hair was hanging loose, released from the ponytail. His scuffed leathers bore evidence of many sliding contacts with road surfaces. The doctor's first impressions of Seth was that he smelled a bit like Cedric did, the last time he fell asleep in the rain close to his tree-side lavatory, and later had entered Whynot Hall, steaming and wet.

The cloth patch on the biker's jacket-back featured, in red and yellow metallic-thread embroidery, an aggravated, suppurating boil. The legend above the patch said: "Unlanced Boils M.C.", beneath: "Filled with Pus".

Seth Mulligan's face was the white of a sickly Laplander in winter. He was swinging his legs idly over the side of the bed, his eyes now staring straight ahead, his pupils dilated and apparently fixed on a spot on the opposite wall of the cell.

The doctor placed his case by the biker's side and opened it. Seth didn't budge or take notice. The doctor caught a whiff of pungent cannabis rising from Seth's hair, its sweetness perceptible above the residual smells of the cell.

He took a slim-line torch from his case, stepped back, and flashed the torch beam from one to the other of the biker's staring eyes.

'What t'fock you doing that for, man?' Seth snapped, reacting with annoyance. He lifted a hand to cover his eyes. The doctor clicked the torch off. 'Don't you see I'm concentrating on that fly having a shit on t'focken' wall opposite, but?' Seth complained, without changing his stare.

'I'm Doctor Dernehen. You must listen carefully to everything I say,' he said clearly. 'Will you provide me with samples of your urine and blood, Mr Mulligan?'

'Doctor Dernehen, you'll get nuffink out of me for t'focken' cop bastards,' Seth said, his voice rising.

'I'll have to report that as a refusal, Mr Mulligan. Can you tell me why you think you're here?'

'It's the pussy, Doc, man. T'focken' cops don't like seeing us bikers getting all the stunnin' pussy, when they're getting nothing, but. They try hard. The ugly bastards are always chasing the pussy, but the pussy never takes any notice and who can blame them? It's a well-known fact in these parts that the cops are never on the job, heh, heh. You know what I mean? Get it, Doc?' he asked, not lifting his head, not expecting an answer.

'Mr Mulligan, the sergeant says you went through a red light without stopping.'

'There were no lights, Doc. T'focken' cop bastards they're telling lies, stitching me up again.' Seth's eyes began to swirl slowly about in their sockets, like dumpling bags in a simmering pot.

'Mr Mulligan, what colour of light did you see?'

'Okay, Doc, have it your way. The light I saw was blue.' Seth's eyes lost their motion and stilled. Pop-eyed, he looked up at the doctor.

'Mr Mulligan, are you sure it was a blue light you saw?'

'Doc, I've told you, there were no lights, but seeing you're insisting, the light I saw was definitely blue and as far as I know, I don't have to stop at a light that's blue.' He stared down at the word "Hate" tattooed in blue onto the knuckles he held up close to the front of his face.

'Mr Mulligan, you're sure the light you saw wasn't red?'

'It was blue. Normally the ones I stop at are red, but tonight they were blue. I thinks t'focken' cops has invented lights and changed the colours just so they can rob me of a night in the tent at the bash with the pussy.

'They've made me miss hearing Dumpy and his great band, that's what they've done.' He pressed his hands onto his thighs, took three deep breaths, let out three mournful sighs, and seemed resigned to staying in the cell until the court bailed him on Monday morning.

The doctor carried his case from the cells into the charge-room. He found Sergeant Liptrott sitting at the desk, writing up a charge sheet. Constable O'Hicks was sipping tea.

A look of fury showed on Sergeant Liptrott's face, immediately he noticed the absence of samples.

'I was unable to persuade Mr Mulligan into sparing a splash of urine or a spurt of blood to corroborate the offences you wish to charge him with,' the doctor said. 'Though I'm reasonably sure that Mr Mulligan will have other drugs coursing through his system, he was with-it enough to refuse giving me samples.'

Sergeant Liptrott curled his top lip back, clenched his teeth and breathed in through them with a urinal-plunging, sucking noise, showing his annoyance at the lack of results. 'You did your best, Doc, I'm sure,' he said, shaking his head and rolling his eyes. 'Mulligan's a bastard to deal with, we know. Rest assured, though, his charge sheet *will* read well when we've finished beefing it up. 'Constable O'Hicks,' he said, sharply, 'let's have a look at your pocket-book. We'll see what we have and haven't got him for.'

Sergeant Liptrott anchored an armpit over the chair back. Sniffing, he turned over pages of the pocket-book and read the list of offences penned in against Seth Mulligan. Slapping the book down on his desk, he said, 'It's not enough. Get it in here,' he said, ramming a finger into the page, 'that he failed to give a sample and we'll fit the bastard up with something serious as well. I think you should go along with an assault on police. He thumped you while resisting arrest, didn't he?'

'Well aye, I suppose so, sergeant, if you say so and think we ought to,' Constable O'Hicks replied hesitantly, as if fearful of saying no.

'Well then, start writing. Get it in here that he resisted arrest and hit you in the guts with his clenched fist.'

'Okay, sergeant, if that's what you want, but,' Constable O'Hicks said.

'It's what I want, constable,' Sergeant Liptrott growled at him, 'and I'll corroborate it.'

Turning to Doctor Dernehen, the sergeant said, 'Okay, state in your report there's visible bruising on the constable's abdomen. That's you about finished for tonight, but. I think we can dispense with your services now, it's quieting down in the town.'

'Zero tolerance policing has been effectively applied this evening, by officers serving at Rippington Avenue RUC station, I take it, sergeant?' the doctor asked.

'You have it in one. We don't mess about with chummies at this nick.'

The sergeant began to rub his chin. A thought had crossed his mind. Then he stood up, kicked his chair back and peered down his nose at the doctor. 'Before you slide off, Doc, I'd like to take a gander at your new Jag.'

The sergeant stepped alongside the doctor, placed a matey hand on his shoulders and gently guided him towards the charge-room door and the yard.

Suspicion had plagued the sergeant's mind since the mention of Jags earlier that evening and he'd be happier with that bit of a worry put to rest.

It was half-past midnight, the station yard empty of cops. Approaching the Jag side by side, the doctor pointed his key fob towards it and pressed the button. With a click, the sidelights flashed and the doors unlocked. 'Spectacular are they not, sergeant, the gizmos of today?' he said, sounding pleased.

Sergeant Liptrott raised a hand, scratched his head and walked forward. His face waxed quickly into the distortions it assumed when he was angered.

Close to the Jag he stopped, thudded his studded boots onto the ground without a hint of a wince. He raised a boot and scratched the sole backwards along the ground, much like an angry bull. Reaching forward with the toe of a boot, he touched the personalised front number plate, rattling it with a succession of quick taps.

Turning, the sergeant lifted his shoulders, spread his arms and took a pace towards the doctor. Looming over him, the sergeant blocked out a floodlight and cast him in shadow. The sergeant's cheeks ballooned, his top lip curled back towards his nose, he clenched his teeth tight. His teeth were grinding and air whistled through the gaps as he sucked in a long, slow breath. In a rush, he exhaled and hissed, 'It'ssss… you… you.'

The sickly-sweet, disgusting aroma of mustard, soused onions and canteen tea wafted up the doctor's nostrils. He turned his head; everything nasty seemed to be heading his way.

The sergeant's arm had lost all of its mateyness now and he threw a hand out, shoved the doctor out of his way and pushed past him. Striding out, he reached the charge room steps, leapt up them and swung a boot, striking the door a kick. His shoulder banged the door wider and once inside, he back-heeled it closed behind him with a crash.

'Strange cove,' Riley murmured, 'the man is fast becoming a bit of a worry.'

Feeling warm, Riley removed his jacket and bowtie, rolled up his shirtsleeves, before settling behind the steering wheel of the Jag,

.

Chapter 5

Passing through the station gates, Riley opened his side window and laid his elbow on the window edge. Pulling away, he felt the breeze jiggle his arm hairs, sending a tingling through him, making him shiver. To his left as he drove towards Ballyboil by-pass, the River Boil flowed luminous beneath a rare shaft of moonlight.

Local pubs should have stopped serving, but passing the Boil Arms, he noticed chinks of light escaping badly-drawn curtains. 'Aha, a lock-in in progress,' he said aloud.

He chuckled while he mused over a rumour that he had heard: cops had a fondness for mumping food and drink. It made him wonder if Sergeant Liptrott would join them later for sneaky, on-the-house slurps of the "black stuff". From the size of his potbelly and rampant halitosis, he looked guilty of poor eating habits, and well suited to a beery, after-hours bingeing.

The car radio was playing music for lovers. Pat Boone was singing "Young Love". Riley remembered the number from his youth and crooned along with it, word perfect.

He was reassured to find the streets on the edge of town free from traffic: nothing to delay him. In the distance, he saw the lights of combine harvesters still working in distant fields. Some farmers were taking advantage of a dry night, harvesting with urgency lest the weather change.

Entering the bypass, he turned in the direction of the nurse's home. With the side window down, he could hear the clip of the tyres and smell the warm tar. Tarry smells, he liked; they had a soothing quality.

In the distance, he saw the narrow clump of trees and bushes on the hillside, which obscured incompletely Ballyboil hospital from the bypass: outside lighting flickered through gaps in the less-dense foliage like twinkling stars did through broken clouds. The nurses' home lay to the east of the hospital and was mainly in darkness.

In daytime, he often used the nurses' car park, in favour of his official spot at the hospital main entrance; it was handier for him to reach his office. He had reasoned that his car parked there at night would not look odd to any hospital staff that saw it.

Riley knew the route ahead well: take the next left turn off the bypass, drive the half-mile-long tree-lined avenue, through one set of traffic lights at the pedestrian crossing. Take the next left turn beyond the crossing, drive one hundred yards to the front gates of the nursing home, which were always open, welcoming him.

Suddenly, the thought of the treat awaiting him, the nearness to a sexual coupling with Mavis, was exciting him, as it had each clandestine visit. Heat was rising from his loins, and his knob, already nestling springy, was halfway prepared for action. He breathed in deeply as his pulse began to race.

Into his mind's eye shot images of Mavis' apartment patio door, and he walking towards it, the toes of his shoes flying out at comic angles. Then a vision of Mavis, her black hair cascading over her generous, milky-white body, as she lay on her bed. Her ripple of applause for the bustling way, the clown-like actions, the shuffling feet of his bedroom entrance, and her greeting, 'Come to me, my darling Riley, we mustn't waste a second,' he heard above the radio.

He let out the bellowing, bull-like roar that those words had often encouraged from him, while he quickly undressed, before lofting his short, naked body onto the bed in a spectacular dive over the bed-end.

Plumbing his memory bank of pleasurable moments with Mavis again, he saw her starling-egg-blue eyes widening with incredulity at his actions, heard her shriek of laughter as he landed beside her, and her saying, in her smooth, Belfast drawl, 'You're an Olympic springboard diving champion,' while she held up six of her fingers, indicating his top mark.

The thought excited him further: the award had always qualified him for that special number following the six in their own Kama Sutra of positions, and the treat that she said would only ever be for him. He took a firmer grip on the steering wheel. The end of his nose was nearing Mavis' belly button and she was encouraging him to tickle it with his moustache...

Unexpectedly, there was an intrusion into those recent memories. His thoughts had returned to that first time he had sex with Mavis, how then she had massaged his ego. 'Nothing,' she had said, 'will make me believe you're over sixty years of age. Your performances in bed are those of a young stud.'

He had believed Mavis was only being nice to him. Henpecked at home and not getting his rations were the problems he thought that she saw in him. From that moment, he had thought the relationship could not last... how many young studs did she know?

The pedestrian-crossing lights were straight ahead. 'Stay green,' Riley said quietly and let out a little chuckle at something Seth Mulligan had said earlier in the evening. It amused him now. In response, he sang out, 'Please don't change to blue and I will be through.' But this set of lights had annoyed him in the past, generating curses; they seemed to change on a whim whenever *he* was about to pass through.

Speed within the law was essential to Riley. Making sure of this, or that he wasted no time, he changed down a gear, revved up, and kept his speed steady at 30.

With his eyes close to the windscreen, and still some yards yet to go, he shouted 'Feck!' and pounded a hand on the steering wheel in frustration. The green light had changed to amber, which he knew meant stop unless it was unsafe to do so. All was clear, not another vehicle or pedestrian was in sight; time was on his side so he toed the accelerator. The car leapt a little in speed and he drove straight through the lights.

Riley relaxed; the lights were still at amber when he drove through the crossing. He never liked taking risks on the roads, only ever exceeding speed limits accidentally; the victims of the many tragic, messy accidents ambulanced to his theatre was still clear in his mind.

He checked his rear mirror after turning left beyond the crossing. A vehicle was catching him up fast, its headlights blazing on high beam. He didn't identify the car until he saw the blue light begin whirling on its roof and heard the fast ringing of bells. Different thoughts were now uppermost in his mind. Was the police driver just trying to get past him? Were his services required again and would that prevent him visiting Mavis? Why, if they had his mobile number, had they not called?

Riley pressed the brake pedal, began to slow down. He turned left, the police car followed. Ten yards from the open gates to the nurses' home, he pulled up. The excitement in his loins was quickly dying; becoming as flat as the battered cod he had earlier enjoyed for dinner.

The police car swished past him, brakes squealing. The driver controlled the skid expertly, pulled in front of him, then reversed tight to his front bumper.

Sergeant Liptrott stepped out of the driver's door, hatless, his face already fixed in a wicked grin. Flicking nonchalantly at his uniform jacket with a finger, he removed some adherent bun crumbs.

Riley recognised Constable O'Hicks clambering from the other door. He turned, spread his feet, leant on the car roof, looked into the distance, taking no interest in him, or the sergeant, walking purposefully towards the Jag. The doctor thought he could be wrong, but the constable seemed embarrassed at being in the sergeant's company!

'You were going a speed,' Riley said and chuckled through the open window. 'I thought you might be on a call and continue through those gates ahead, such was your haste. Or do you have a prisoner I missed at the station and in need of treatment?' he asked, looking up at the sergeant and smiling.

'You are not obliged to say anything…' the words were spat venomously by the sergeant, his bottom lip quivering like a sliver of raw, bloody liver tossed into a pan of smoking fat.

The sergeant undid a button, opened a pocket on his tunic and removed his pocket-book.

The doctor saw this as worrying, as was the brutality etching the sergeant's face, which had reddened greatly since he last saw it at the station.

Whilst snarling the first words of "Judges Rules", the sergeant was showing all the menace of an armed Klu Klux clansman finding a black man in his chicken coop at midnight, with two of the coop's plumpest and best layers already gutted and stuffed with walnuts from his favourite tree and oven-ready.

Finishing his warning, the sergeant boomed, 'Have you anything to say?' Grabbing the driver's door handle, he pulled on it savagely and frenziedly whilst gesturing with a raised thumb, 'Please step out of the car, Doctor Dernehen,' he said as he drew the door wide.

Riley stepped out of the Jag, his mind buzzing, having little idea what he had done to deserve such a demented display from the sergeant. He drove carefully at all times, never took liberties with road signs. The traffic lights had shown amber when he drove through them and that wasn't an offence. He was certain they hadn't showed red, weren't even close to showing red, and he hadn't exceeded the speed limit, either.

In fact, he drove as he always did: careful not to commit any traffic offences. Although the sergeant's initial words suggest that he definitely had.

Whatever charge the sergeant was trumping up, it was a bit of a worry.

The doctor's mind began working overtime; looking for reasons why the sergeant should accuse him of any offence, especially after giving the cops sterling service as police-surgeon, during the summer and up to ten minutes previously. Had the patching-up of injured prisoners for the cops done him no favours, he wondered? Had the owning of a Jaguar motorcar initiated the sergeant's persecution of him?

Quickly, the words 'It's you,' spat at him by the sergeant as they stood together looking at his Jag, back in the station yard, struck Riley as having significant relevance to the predicament he was now in.

Turning towards the nurses' home, the doctor saw the dull glow of a bedside light coming from one ground-floor apartment's partly open, patio door. In the otherwise darkened block, he recognised it as Mavis'. A small breeze ruffled the curtains making the light flicker, as if a signal.

The sergeant nodded his head, as if reading the doctor's mind, rolled his top lip back and turned to stare deliberately at Mavis' patio door. The doctor sussed it. It could be nothing else. This was all about the sergeant fancying nursing-sister O'Rourke, too. Now the sergeant was trying his best to warn him off, telling this birddog to keep well away from his quail.

During the early hours of the previous Wednesday morning, following a surprise mid-week call for his services from the RUC station the night before, Mavis had awarded him a six followed by a nine. They'd dispensed with the special treat, made passionate love, then had lain entwined, recovering from their frenetic efforts. Their breathing had been noisy and rain had pattered hard against a window, but that hadn't drowned out the sounds of a car moving slowly around the nurses' car park.

He had propped himself up on an elbow, looked over the expanse of bosom he loved so much, towards the bedroom window. He had watched as the car pulled up close to the building, its headlight beam changing rapidly from low to high. For a time, they'd stayed on high beam and shone through the lightweight curtains.

It had intrigued him who might be prowling around at that hour and had slid off the bed to find out. Moving the curtain a touch, he was able to see a police car facing him. Whoever sat behind the wheel had made no effort to get out. It seemed the driver had given his signal, then waited for some recognition in return.

To park up and come on in was the response Riley had thought that someone awaited.

The signal hadn't come… because he was there!

No signal of encouragement received, the driver had swung the police car around and drove up to Riley's brand-new Jaguar, which he had taken delivery of only that day. A cop of a rank he could not tell had left the police vehicle and walked around his. Moments later, the police car had exited the car park, its wheels spinning, kicking up clouds of dust.

Now an excellent reason existed for believing that the visit wasn't police diligence, them checking the security of the car park.

With his pocket-book in hand and Biro poised, the sergeant took a deep breath and said gruffly, 'You're being done for going through a red light. Now I know you've had duty calls this evening, Doctor Dernehen, but did you drink alcohol at any time during the last twenty-four hours?'

The sergeant's voice still had a nasty edge to it. The doctor gave his answer some consideration; keeping his anger under control and not bouncing up and down on the balls of his feet, as he felt like doing. 'Nothing for forty-eight hours, sergeant,' he replied at length. He was teetotal, but didn't feel like telling the sergeant anything. He asked, 'Can you tell me why, after working as police-surgeon at your station last evening, you're booking me on a trumped-up charge?'

'Trumped-up… trumped-up,' the sergeant boomed. 'You think that do you? Well, I'll have you know this. Since the inception of Operation Roadsafe, the RUC's initiative is to cut down on road accidents. Our instructions are to prosecute all offenders. Verbal warnings are out.'

The sergeant was giving him a load of unnecessary guff. Still he felt helpless: could do nothing but stand and listen.

'Me, Constable O'Hicks and the rest of the strength at Rippington Avenue, have done our level best to keep the roads in Ballyboil accident-free. Pedestrians might have been using the crossing when you crossed on the red signal.

'You saw Doctor Dernehen going through the traffic lights when they showed red, didn't you, constable? We must act without fear or favour, mustn't we, constable?' He didn't look in the constable's direction once, just tapped his Biro onto his pocket-book, whilst staring purposefully towards the dull light shining from Mavis O'Rourke's patio door.

'Aye, sergeant,' replied Constable O'Hicks, his gaze fixed on the stones he was now kicking along the ground.

'Constable, bring the breathalyser here and test Doctor Dernehen anyway,' the sergeant said, smothering a snigger. He knew that he had the doctor where he wanted him: on the spot and perhaps warned off the spot he wanted solely for himself.

The doctor fumed. No doubt now existed; the sergeant was persecuting him because he, too, fancied Mavis. He, being the driver of the police car that had snooped around the nurses' home car park that Wednesday morning, had seen the brand-new Jag, and had confirmed ownership of it earlier, in the police-station yard.

In Riley's mind, the entire ghastly affair amounted to the sergeant also having an affair with Mavis. Clearly, his presence in Mavis' apartment the early hours of the previous Wednesday had prevented the Sergeant from getting an invite into her boudoir. Perhaps on this Sunday morning, too, the sergeant had thought his way clear. The charge that he had failed to comply with a signal given by a set of traffic lights, witnessed by Constable O'Hicks, was the sergeant's revenge for his own pussy-dipping sessions with Mavis going unfulfilled.

The doctor felt humiliated blowing into the breathalyser beneath the sergeant's gaze, and just a few yards from the hospital where he was of some renown.

More worrying to him, alarming even, was the thought that Mavis might be sharing her favours with others; including a man who worked alongside the "fishhooks pissing" Constable O'Hicks, who had received unofficial treatment from him for the pox! That infection could quickly spread! All of the cops at Rippington Avenue could be knobbing the same women and spreading the problem around, willy-nilly!

The breathalyser reading proved negative. Sergeant Liptrott said to him, 'You're being reported for the offence of failing to comply with a signal given by a road traffic sign. Do you wish to say anything in your defence?' Entirely fed up with the sergeant's charade, the doctor replied, 'I think the light you're talking about showed blue when I crossed, sergeant.'

Riley felt weary and anxious after his encounter with the sergeant. The musky whiff he got of Mavis' "Jolie Madame" French perfume didn't uplift him either, as he entered her apartment through the patio door. It was an uncommon perfume for a young woman to use, stimulating him at other times, but its fragrance didn't send his pulse racing, didn't have him eager to launch himself directly onto her bed.

Mavis saw his dejected state, laughed out loudly, and as he flopped into a chair, pointed mockingly at him.

'Bloody man's crazy,' Riley said. Slowly he began to slip off his shoes and clothes. Clambering cheerlessly onto the bed, he lay on his back beside Mavis, his head falling heavily onto a pillow.

She held a finger out, toyed with his knob and giggled hysterically at its flaccid state. 'To be sure, your knob's like a dollop of new putty straight from the tin,' she said with great difficulty, tears streaming. 'For sure, I can only give you a two for one that won't be able to give one, one.' She howled and condescendingly propped his knob up with the finger.

It didn't please Riley either to view his flaccidity. He remained glum and didn't respond to the mirth Mavis saw in his uneasiness.

'There's a problem tonight with my perfect-six man?' Mavis asked him, soothingly now. Calming herself, she reached out for him and pulled him close to her.

Riley shifted his position, lifted his head above her breasts, leaned across her and kissed both nipples in turn. As his head moved from one nipple to the other he said, 'I've just had an encounter with that dreadful Sergeant Liptrott. He's reporting me, *feckin' wrongly*, I may add, for going through a red light at the crossing outside the gates of the home.'

Mavis frowned, but said nothing.

How could he tell Mavis that he suspected Sergeant Liptrott had charged him for the reasons that he had thought of earlier? If he told her that, she would be livid and he could be out of her life, permanently. How else did he expect her to react if he confronted her with his suspicions that the brutish sergeant was knobbing her?

He was unhappy with his thoughts, but he wouldn't upset her. No. He'd rather go on enjoying her company and for as long as it was available to him.

Settled in his intent, he hauled himself onto Mavis' body. He lay quietly in her comforting embrace, his face resting on the side of one breast, the nipple of the other in his ear, his elbows taking a bit of his weight, as he listened to the beating of her heart, wondering.

Riley's body rose then fell erratically as he lay, his rapid breathing easing, his knob beginning to display some rigidity. Mavis felt his arousal and without a word, shifted her position. Stretching an arm down between his legs, she found his knob. A slow massage with her soft fingers soon had him hard. Feeling the firmness in her hand, she had him enter her. The way she breathed hotly into his ear, the gasps of passion as he thrust, the nails dragged lightly and teasingly down his back and across his buttocks, had him believing that she was eager for him.

Riley speeded up his rhythm, as if he was going for a quickie. Then he slowed and began teasing her, grunting into a shoulder blade, not able reach her earlobes and nibble at them.

Both their bodies were sweaty, sticky, her thighs lathering as he smacked his against hers.

Riley lowered his head into her cleavage. There, in what he had always thought a wonderful valley, a hair, solitary and wiry, waited, spiralling, ready to spring with latent menace. Unaware of the dangers present and unable to keep control any longer, the vinegar-strokes imminent, he began to buck fiercely. With his eyes closed and his face screwed-up, intent, experiencing joy, his crotch banged against Mavis' mound. Mavis screamed, 'Yes... yes... yes!' and Riley ejaculated with several short, wobbly bursts of energy.

Riley's breathing had normalised when he lowered his face into her cleavage. The hair lurking there jiggled its way up into a nostril and his head rocketed back. A colossal sneeze followed. Before he had time to raise a hand and stifle the nasal irritation, he sneezed three times in rapid succession. Unable to control the arching of his back, he felt sharp pain from his sciatic nerve and spasm grip his sacroiliac.

Riley rolled from Mavis onto the bed then laboriously swung his legs over the side to stand on the floor. He forced himself upright with a grimace and placed a hand in the small of his back. In some pain, he said sharply, 'Remind me to have that feckin' hair removed, permanently.'

Mavis quickly moved from the bed. Standing close to Riley, she put her arms about him, hugging him close. 'Thank you for making wonderful love,' she said, and then stooped to kiss him on the temple. Feeling for his hand, she grabbed it and tugged him towards her small shower cubicle. When the spray ran warm, she pulled him in alongside her and ran the curtain around.

Acting like children, they giggled. Like adults, they applied body-gel and frothed each other up, cleansing each other's most intimate places.

The showering complete, Mavis towelled Riley down. When he was dry, she led him by the hand back to the bed, where she had him lay face down.

Mavis straddled him and began massaging his lower back. When he had relaxed, the spasm abating, she hurried to a cabinet and found a tube of Fiery Jack. Applying a liberal quantity to the painful area, she pressed deeply with fingers, thumbs and the heels of her hands until it was all absorbed into his skin.

*

At 5 o'clock that morning, Riley eased the Jaguar into the drive at Whynot Hall and drove slowly up to the front steps. Leaving his case to collect later, he locked the car and trudged wearily up the stairs to the front door. At night, leaving the front door of the Hall ajar allowed Cedric to wander off in search of the monkey-puzzle tree or any other vertical objects against which to find doggy relief.

Pushing the door wider, he saw that the position Cedric was adopting as a bit of a worry, but more to Cedric than to himself. Cedric's front paws were working like dual metronomes, pad, pad, padding to a steady beat. His back paws were off the floor, lifted high, and he was dragging his backside slowly over the hallway carpet. With his tongue lolling, his mouth frothing, he greeted Riley with a loud, resonating yowl of distress. Coming to a halt, Cedric extended his claws, sought to grip the carpet and attempted to rise onto four paws.

'Feckin' bones, I keep on telling Dotty and the cook never to give him feckin' bones from the stock pot,' Riley said aloud. Finding Cedric in such a wretched state prompted him to wish the dog already interred in the pissy patch chosen by Dotty's uncle for its grave.

While Riley looked with pity towards Cedric, he himself began to wince, shifting his footing, opening and closing his buttocks and scratching there. A Fiery Jack flare-up in that region called for some mutual sympathy towards Cedric. The embrocating was running down Riley's back fixed in a river of sweat, trickling into his crevice and superheating a tender spot.

Riley had never liked working with animals. However, the only way he knew of avoiding a vet's huge night-call bill was for him to prescribe for Cedric and deliver, as kindly as he could, a significant dose of castor oil.

After the dosing, he would tie Cedric to one end of a short chain, secure the other end a distance from the Hall, the dog enduring alone the painful outcome of the treatment, whilst howling at the moon during the night and passing stools containing significant amounts of indigestible bone.

A walk-in cupboard between the doors to the dining and sitting-rooms was the safe repository for his medical supplies. Cedric cast a wary eye over Riley as he walked towards it. Then he began to rotate his backside on the carpet.

Inside the cupboard, Riley moved bottles around on shelves until he found a two-pint bottle marked "CASTOR OIL". 'Yuck, feckin' horrid stuff,' he muttered, picking it up. Moving other bottles, he was disgruntled not to find a suitable castor oil delivery system for the treatment of dogs.

He stepped into the hall and muttered, 'Must have forgotten to get something after the last episode. Nothing for it. Here we go again, Cedric, daddy's coming.'

A much louder yowling greeted him as he approached Cedric with the bottle visible. No daft dog, he recalled the previous treatment - he didn't need to call on his elephantine memory, just his painful one.

Cedric's front paws lifted. Turning on the carpet, he began dragging his backside across the hallway, away from Riley, closing with his dosage. Cedric was panting and saliva dripped from his tongue, hanging limply from his head. His eyes had sunk deeper into their sockets, making him look a lot sadder than usual.

Cedric was intent on escaping to the Hall grounds and started to rise. His legs were unsteady as he lurched towards the door. Stepping quickly forward, Riley blocked off his escape route. Reaching with his empty hand in the direction of Cedric's head, he grabbed and held firmly the slack skin hanging around his throat. Then sliding the crook of his arm down Cedric's neck, he squeezed tight, hung onto his shoulders, wrestled him to the carpet and held him there.

Sitting down on the carpet alongside Cedric, Riley made a face and brought the neck of the bottle up to his mouth. Gripping the cork between his teeth, he tugged it out and spat it away. He took a brave swig of castor oil and tried hard not to gag: the oil tasted just as foul as he recalled.

Cedric, restrained and immobile, looked up miserably. Riley placed the bottle on the carpet and turned. Grabbing for Cedric's jaws, he pulled them around, forcing fingers in first, then both hands into his mouth. The jaws were stubborn and they frothed. With a jerk, Riley opened them, pulled them upwards and spat a stream of the vile-tasting liquid over Cedric's lurching throat.

Cedric's eyes seemed lost within his head and his legs began to kick. 'Humans are unwilling recipients of the treatment too, Cedric,' Riley said sympathetically as he lifted the bottle to repeat the dose. Gargling sounds, hardly of joy, gurgled from Cedric's throat. Reluctantly, he had swallowed the lot.

Slipping and slithering, Cedric crossed painfully to the front door. Both his elephantine and painful memories had kicked-in together, prodding him to expect that the remedy would once again work speedily and painfully at some distance from the Hall. He knew the route. Riley followed and chained him up behind an outhouse. From there, his previous yowlings had gone unheard in the Hall.

His canine treatment over, his hands washed, Riley pushed gently on the sitting-room door, opening it a tad, looked in and noted that Dotty's position had changed little since he left the Hall some hours before. His wrestling match with Cedric hadn't disturbed her. Resting half on and half off the sofa, her head lay awkwardly, her mouth agape. 'Feckin' hair curlers are hanging down beneath your shower hat like the guts of a hedgehog sliced open by a Pirelli tyre,' he said quietly. Dotty snorted, strangling snores before they began.

'Come, my dear,' Riley said quietly. Taking hold of Dotty's hands, he pulled on them and straightening her into a sitting position. An eyelid flickered. He shook her again, making her head rock. Quickly, she opened her eyes, sat bolt upright and blinked beadily towards him, all the while flexing her jaw.

Miraculously, her glasses had remained perched on the end of her nose all evening. When her eyes focused properly, she peered over the lenses, looking him over, quizzically.

'How long have I been here?' she asked hoarsely and removed her hands from Riley's to brush down her clothing.

'Since dinner. You fell asleep soon after. I returned from Rippington Avenue RUC station just before midnight. I've been asleep on the chaise-longue. Cedric woke me up and I've been seeing to him. He needed some medicine, but I can explain later. Now I think it's time to retire to bed. Don't you think so? The light of a brand-new day is already streaming in.'

In the act of standing up, Dotty inhaled through her nostrils, sniffing, slowly and deliberately. At full height, she feigned to stagger and threw her arms out towards Riley's shoulders, using them as a support. In that position, she checked his neck for marks and took a longer, controlled sniff while she was up close to him.

She was alert enough to seek traces of any suspicious perfumes. The "Jolie Madame" perfume that wafted from him that early morning during springtime was no cheap, doorstep-purchased brand. It's musky, lingering fragrance was one that a mature women might consider using before leaving home for a night out on the town…looking to attract a man.

She had never used that perfume. Finding traces of it on Riley had been and still was a bit of a worry.

Tonight's sniff test had Dotty wondering--could she have imagined it all? She thought she had been discreet, but had Riley detected her sniff tests and now showered before returning home? His body felt quite warm. He perspired, but nothing remotely like perfume wafted her way this time. No, the smell welling up from him now was horrible, camphor certainly and traces of an oil. What could that be?

If Riley was taking a shower at her place, was he cleaning himself after his finagling using carbolic-type soap? Could that be it? His lips were shiny and oily. Could that be lip-gloss left behind from him having a necking session with some tart? Had he been visiting one of those massage parlours, those places of ill-repute springing up in Ballyboil, set up by Albanian pimps with imported whores? Had he been with a bloody oily, foreign hooker? Yes, finagling with a hooker, that could be it. Why else did have black bags beneath his eyes and they look glassy? And if he hasn't caught something, why is he continually reaching behind himself to scratch at his arse?

Chapter 6

Riley awoke late on Sunday morning. His eyes, sticky with sleep, began blinking rapidly, reacting to the sun's rays beating through the bedroom window. He had slept peacefully his head remaining on the pillow, exactly where he had placed it some six hours earlier.

Dotty had opened the curtains and was standing fussing with them, twirling her spectacles, turning her head from side to side, cocking an ear, listening.

Riley pushed himself up into a sitting position, rubbed his eyes and quickly glanced at the bedside radio-alarm clock. It was half-past eleven.

'Listen, Riley,' Dotty said, on hearing him stir.

'What will I hear, Dotty?' Riley asked somewhat crabbedly. It was always too early to appreciate her nonsense.

'Listen, will you? It's strange, I know, but I can hear owls hooting in daylight. It's coming from the thicket. Isn't that wonderful? I wonder if they've regurgitated any rounded b…'

Abruptly, Dolly stopped talking, turned and put on her spectacles. Slightly hung-over, she had a hazy recollection that Riley hadn't welcomed her remarks on that subject at dinner the previous evening. Perhaps it was a tad early in the day to annoy him with them again.

Riley had listened, instantly recognising the sounds. They weren't owl hoots and his crabbedness doubled. He voiced loudly, 'You're becoming so silly. My ears have not yet tuned into the new day, but I can tell that it's Cedric you're hearing yowling his head off. Not feckin' owls! I had a terrible task dosing him with castor oil when I returned home last night. I tied him up behind the outhouse after the treatment. He's yowling a hell of a lot louder this time than last and, I fear, it's all because you and our cook keep on feeding him boiled bones from the stockpot.'

'Are you sure? Dotty asked, a trace of incredibility tingeing her voice. 'Teeny bits of boiled bones passing through his guts have caused that woeful sound?'

'You know damned well that's so,' Riley answered. 'It's happened before and you heard Cedric then. You do the dog no favours. The pain and the throbbing in his anus will cause him to yowl stridently. It's a dog thing to attract our attention.' The notion reminded Riley to take a shower. The Fiery Jack was still troubling him; he'd have to ease the burning in his buttocks before sitting down to breakfast.

'At first, I thought someone with a loud ghetto blaster was playing an "Enya" track in the woods. A Banshee can't sound worse when it has locked-on to the scent of death, I'm sure,' Dotty said, sounding shrill now, just like Cedric.

Riley was now fully awake and began teasing Dotty, exaggerating Cedric's condition. 'Aye, it's a shame. Poor old Cedric will be unhappy with his lot. If you were to visit him now, you wouldn't find any rounded balls of regurgitated bones. Neither would you find anything sitting upright on the ground in the shape of an overripe conference pear. Instead, laid there will be a perfectly formed, extruded length of indigestible marrowbone…'

'Oh, poor dog, he will be suffering so,' Dotty interrupted, feigning a shudder, knowing that intestinal problems of that magnitude would kill Cedric.

'It will have passed painfully through his intestinal tract like a fast-moving glacier dragging flint-hard moraine with it, having gouged a fissure and removed portions of his colon,' Riley continued. 'Prunes, syrup of figs and paraffin oil have their uses, but the castor oil I dosed him with is *the* class-one aperient. He needed something that effective to shift the blockage. It will not have greased his passage, just speeded the indigestible bone through it.'

'His bottom must look like a bee hole excavated deep through the pith into the flesh of a pomegranate,' Dotty said, appearing gulled.

'It's more likely that Cedric's bottom will resemble a handful of king prawns marinating in a deep-red, tandoori sauce and buzzing with attendant wasps,' Riley said.

'Oh…oh, how graphic,' Dotty gulped. 'I can see it vividly, a circular hole, blood red with the surrounds as shiny as a baboon's bottom. Can we do anything for the poor wretch?'

'If he's passed all the bone, I'll give him a sedative. That will make him groggy for a day and quieten him down. I have no balms in my medicine cupboard to apply and soothe his pain. I doubt his flexibility to contort himself, get his tongue around there and lick it better.

'This afternoon, when I take my report to Rippington Avenue police station, I'll get a prescription prepared at the duty pharmacy in town. You have delicate, sensitive fingers, Dotty. You're concerned for poor Cedric. When I arrive back at the Hall, you can be vet and apply the unguent to his arse this time,' Riley said, tongue in cheek, expecting Dotty to voice objections.

Dotty noticed the implications in Riley's suggestion, picking out the word prescription. Was Riley mad? 'A prescription for a dog, Riley, from a chemist?' she asked.

Riley's intention was to purchase a suitable anal coolant. Determined to continue his teasing he said, 'Aye, I will make the prescription out in your name. You're more than sixty years old now and get them free of charge.'

Dotty hadn't expected that reply from Riley. Really, he was becoming quite insulting towards her. 'Oh! Riley. What will the pharmacist think of me?' Dotty howled, feigning deep hurt.

'That you have piles. It's not unusual in a woman of your age,' Riley said.

'Tut,' Dotty voiced loudly enough for him to hear and pulled a face so that he could see his remarks had hurt her. Then she watched him stalk off for a shower, aloof, seemingly thinking it a great laugh.

The cook had hung around the kitchen since nine o'clock that morning, waiting to begin cooking breakfast, as the first signs of life emerged from the Dernehen's bedroom. The fresh-laid farm eggs, the Ballyboil pork sausage, the sliced rashers of Ballyboil bacon directly from the ham hanging from a hook in the ceiling, and the wild mushrooms that had sprouted overnight in a farmer's field, were already prepared.

Other ingredients for Sunday's breakfast were two slices of Riley's favourite soda bread and Crosse and Blackwell baked beans. Stiffening above the electric toaster slots were four slices of whole-meal bread waiting further browning.

The cook thought it unusual that Cedric hadn't already lurched into the kitchen for his breakfast of Bonio soaked in milk. Strangely, she recalled, Cedric hadn't appeared the morning after the previous occasion she had cleaned out the stockpot and tossed him a boiled-useless marrowbone.

That time, Cedric had loped off happily, the bone securely locked in his jaws. That time, he had missed his breakfast the next day. That time she had heard the owl hoots during daylight hours. That time, like this, she had wondered at the wisdom of feeding dogs boiled bones. The last episode had upset Riley. He had instructed her and the missis never again to give one to the dog.

When she cleaned out the stockpot yesterday, she had seen Cedric's pleading eyes looking up at her and she had relented. It now occurred to her that, if this bout of awful hooting was coming from Cedric, perhaps she should never give him another such bone, unless specifically instructed to do so by her employers.

Riley knew he had to tell Dotty of his encounter with Sergeant Liptrott and did so at the breakfast table, changing the time of the occurrence in his account. 'I had done my bit for the cops and left the station. Then, didn't they just turn nasty on me for no good reason that I could see. I *could...not...believe* what was happening to me. It occurred after I got a call on my mobile at about eleven-thirty, asking me to visit a patient causing the hospital's nightshift intern some concern.'

'Whatever happened?'

'Sergeant Feckin' Liptrott was the cop in charge of affairs at Rippington Avenue last night. Not a nice person. The deranged feckin' man pulled me over after I'd crossed through those traffic lights close by the hospital. Feckin' grinning like a loony he was when he accused me of going through a red light.

I knew I hadn't. Definitely hadn't. He feckin' booked me anyway, even after all I'd done for the cops.

'The faces he pulls at other times are strange indeed, bitter, like that of a dumped woman. Most of the cops attached to Rippington Avenue have learned to mimic the look. I gathered from my visit to the station that he and the rest of the cops resent the fact that I drive a Jaguar. The whole, tawdry stitch-up stems from them not having Jaguars in which to speed around local roads. It's sheer, bloody-minded envy.'

'Liptrott, that sounds an English name. I have never heard of an O'Liptrott or a Fitzliptrott around here. I wouldn't trust an English cop, either,' Dotty said.

'I don't care who his parents are or if he ever had any,' Riley said. 'He's a bastard either way. I suppose I'll have my morning in court with him and the constable. Two cops in cahoots and telling lies, ugh. What chance do I have of proving my innocence?'

'You'll have to listen carefully to what they tell the Magistrates. He doesn't sound too bright. Perhaps they'll be too sure of themselves and won't corroborate each other's story perfectly. It's occurred before in court cases and the accused has escaped a fine. If it happens in your case, you'll be able to catch them out.'

'When Liptrott reads my report on Seth Mulligan, a biker taken prisoner and whom I had to attend last evening, they will know just how unhappy I am over the charge,' Riley said. 'Of course, the upshot of giving them my report, which will exonerate Seth Mulligan, is that I will have to watch my rear-view mirror for the presence of cop cars, permanently. Driving on local roads could turn out hazardous, whether I'm found guilty of the traffic-light thing or not,' he said, deep in thought.

Dotty had put away a good-sized breakfast and now buttered some toast. 'Seth Mulligan. I knew a Seth Mulligan once,' she said, 'but that was a long time ago. He was an old man then. Perhaps he was your man's Papa, though he must be dead now. All the folks attending his wake thought he was dead when I met him.'

Riley had just savoured the last mouthful of mushroom and bacon. 'Come, come, you're talking in riddles again,'

'It's true. I attended a Seth Mulligan's wake. It was what you did years ago. All the women of the village and the family were called to the Mulligan house.'

Prising the lid from the marmalade jar, Riley said, 'Why was that?'

'Old Seth had a Yankee up on the horses. Apparently, he was a bit of a wit and had told everyone he had picked the four horses using a fork instead of a pin.

'His winnings were quite substantial. He had bought several jugs of poteen from "Phil the Still" and supped most of it in less than a week. Then one morning, he didn't awaken. I saw him laid out on his deathbed. He certainly looked dead to me. Some said they had seen more signs of life in a tin of corned beef. His false teeth had fallen down his throat and we had to fish for them. His face was the colour of a blown-up pig's bladder. His tongue was the colour of bruised corn and his eyes were blank. The whites were yellow and the things looked up into his head.'

Riley spooned some double cream into his coffee. 'The look you describe is about dead right for anyone being deceased.'

Dotty sat upright and focused her eyes on some distant spot, trying to remember the details exactly. 'It was the custom of the village for the women to bathe the dead body and prepare it for the box, before the doctor came to issue the death certificate. A woman, I can't remember whom, but experienced in such delicate matters, stuffed each of old Seth's orifices with cotton wool and tied his tiddleypush around the end tightly with a piece of binder twine.'

'I'm sure a qualified undertaker couldn't have handled a stiff better,' Riley said, zestfully.

Dotty sipped tea while she thought. 'Seth was laid out nice in a clean pair of pyjamas. I thought he looked at peace when we retired to the living-room. We all sat around the fire commiserating with poor Teresa, his wife, and drinking the last of Seth's poteen, diluted with lemonade, of course. Teresa gave us quite a rundown on Seth's life. He had been good to her, but I had my doubts.

'Twelve children, I ask you, and forty-eight grandchildren she had. The children would all miss him she tried to convince us. She made us all laugh. Seth had forgotten how long he had been out of work. Apparently, he had lost his birth certificate. The older women cackled a lot when they heard that, but I didn't get the joke then. I was too young, I suppose. The one about making Seth work harder in death than he had ever done in life, by having him cremated and putting his ashes into an egg timer, I'd heard before. We all screeched with laughter, I recall.

'Then Seth stumbled into the room, naked apart from his pyjama jacket, complaining that his hearing sounded muffled, that he couldn't breathe through his nose, pee with the "old fella", and asked why someone had stuffed a bale of cotton up his arse. His foreskin was bulbous with urine, very painful too, no doubt. It was hideous. Most of us averted our eyes. It looked like a plucked turkey's neck with the head still attached....'

Riley interrupted. 'You had a good look and it wasn't like an earplug, then?'

'Ach, there you go again,' Dotty said angrily, looking squarely at him. 'Can't resist upsetting me, can you, Riley?' But Dotty was going to finish her say. 'Then Teresa fainted and fell into the fireplace, tipping over a boiling kettle and scalding her feet. We all let out screams, crossed ourselves and shouted, "Hail Mary, save us from the departed".

'Thankfully, at that moment, the door opened and the doctor walked into the room. He was as amused at old Seth's predicament as old Seth was shocked, to be sure. Mrs Mulligan recovered and said it was a good job Seth lived, because with her scalded feet, she couldn't have walked behind his funeral cortège.'

'A sorry state of affairs by the sound of it,' Riley opined.

'Bad news travelled fast in the village. Just after that, a sleazy-looking rep for the Ballyboil Insurance Company arrived. He gave forth to the assembled women on the advantages of having insurance for all eventualities. He rumbled on about sickness, health and death. Tried to sign a few of them up, he did, using encouraging mumbo-jumbo and mentioning how kind his company was and the considerable amounts of money they'd get back for a few pence given. We'd never heard the likes…'

'It wasn't cold calling, then.'

'What do you mean it wasn't cold calling?'

'Well, old Seth wasn't dead.'

Dotty gave Riley a steely look and continued: 'If their kids were sick, they'd afford beef dinners for them. The old ones could afford lashings of the best Irish whiskey. On death, his insurance company would bury them the best, giving them the finest funerals that folks watching from the sidewalk would ever have seen. Quality care the company promised and a nice payout to provide for the widows and children of the insured.'

'Did he flog any, then?' Riley asked.

'No. Old Seth recovered enough to tell him to feck off because he'd never need it.'

Chapter 7

Sitting in his study later that afternoon at his typewriter, Riley wrote,

To whom it may concern,

On Saturday, 31st July, at 22.30 hours, Sergeant Liptrott, attached to Rippington Avenue RUC station, telephoned requesting my services there as police-surgeon. At 23.00 hours, in a cell at Rippington Avenue RUC Station, I saw a Mr Seth Mulligan. Sergeant Liptrott stated that he had seen Mr Mulligan ingesting cannabis resin.

In my professional opinion, Mr Seth Mulligan was ill. His symptoms were synonymous with those of an impending attack of influenza. I saw nothing to indicate that Mr Mulligan abused drugs and, although he had refused to take the breathalyser test, it is my opinion that he had not ingested alcohol or drugs during the previous twenty-four hours.

I examined Constable Gabriel O'Hicks who complained of stomach pains after an alleged assault by Mr Mulligan, during his arrest. I noted no bruising or any other indication, which led me to believe this constable had not suffered any injury, whatsoever.

Riley signed the statement and placed it in an envelope, addressing it to the Duty Inspector at Rippington Avenue RUC station, thus ensuring its receipt by an officer senior to the sergeant.

'That ought to get this Seth out of one or two of his most recent difficulties,' Riley said aloud.

Dotty's head appeared around the doorjamb. She shouted into the study, 'The phone. It's an emergency. Riley, come quickly!'

Riley rose to his feet and followed her down the stairs to the hallway.

'It's the intern at the hospital. He sounds frantic and so pleased you're at home,' Dotty told him, handing him the phone.

'What is it?' Riley asked snappily, putting on a show for Dotty, though he never liked being disturbed on Sundays.

'Thank heavens you're available, Riley,' began the intern. 'A farmer by the name of Ryan O'Toole has had an accident and is being ambulanced in. The paramedics have radioed ahead, advising us that we need a surgeon to attend. A thumb, partly severed, apparently, but the details can wait until you get here.'

'What's that all about?' Dotty asked, appearing at his side holding a goblet of brandy. Since breakfast, she had been thinking what she might do: her suspicions that he might be finagling when he stayed out late hadn't gone away. Now, she wondered, would Riley believe she was tippling during in the day and would he take advantage of it. Would he be reckless, give her the opportunity change his ways with a few lashes of a whip?

Riley was quick to see some mileage in her earlier-than-usual visit to the brandy decanter and he used it. 'I've just found a use for that black knob I told you about,' he said, gathering his jacket. At the door, he turned and said airily, 'A farmer by the name of Ryan O'Toole has also been harvesting in earnest. He has had his knob torn off in an accident with a combine harvester and is in need of an intromittent organ transplant.'

'Ripped off? Oh…how terrible,' Dotty cried. Frowning, she turned and walked into the kitchen.

Chapter 8

The cook's shoulders looked broader than a Charolais bull as she leant over the sink, soapsuds up to her elbows, washing the breakfast dishes with a dish mop.

Kitchen chores and the preparation of "Haute cuisine Irlande" was only a part of Bridie's mastery. She had won prizes in rabbit-gutting competitions held at village fêtes. Using the corner of an antiquated Gillette razor, she could remove the innards of a bunny within five seconds. Twenty seconds later, the skinned carcass, its head and its lucky feet hacked off, would be stuffed with a mixture of breadcrumbs, sausage meat, parsley and thyme, and oven-ready for roasting.

As Dotty hurried through the kitchen door, Bridie turned her head, saw the stern look on Dotty's face and asked, 'What troubles you, missis?'

'Riley's slipping, Bridie. He's becoming a bit of a worry. Among other things, he's fallen foul of a cop sergeant by the name of Liptrott, if I can believe a word that he's telling me. Lately, he's become a feckin' fanny-spinner, a right "seanchai", as they'd say in the Gaelic. His tales are so implausible that he reminds me of the legendary Tom Pepper. He got thrown out of hell for telling lies.'

'He's away in the head, missis.'

'My Riley, do you mean? I can believe that.' Dotty put the brandy to one side, switched on the coffee percolator, took a pack of cigarettes from her trousers, lit one and inhaled deeply.

'Of course not, not Doctor Dernehen. That eejit Liptrott, I, I, I, mean. He's always clattering his prisoners, giving them black eyes and the likes when they're blootered.'

'Riley thinks Liptrott has swung one over on him.'

'I, I, I, away on. Doctor Dernehen won't be the first if I know that one. His Mammy's waters burst at the height of a full moon and you know what some fools from around here think about that. Fearful, buy-a-pig-in-a-poke folks and all they are. The dafter, pregnant women from around here will suffer agonies through the full phase of the moon. They think they're supposed to keep their legs crossed lest their wean is born blighted. They believe that the merest of moonbeams must never be seen in the sky at the bursting of the waters. If one does, they'll try to hang on to the wean.'

'I hadn't heard that story,' Dotty said, 'but you're correct in asserting that there are some loonies living around here.'

'That one in particular was always tainted with lunacy, but. I, I, I, he… he… he… hasn't been the same since the day he was supposed to get married, but didn't. Had something against the world and its brother since then, but.'

Dotty was standing on her tiptoes, moving jars about in a cupboard, looking for brown sugar, 'You seem to know a bit about him.' she prompted.

'He was a bit of a firebrand when he was young, was Billy Liptrott. He should have turned out a broth of a boy, all the same. He was from a good home and all, even if his mammy wasn't all there. A rugby player of some repute he was, too. We reckoned he'd get a cap for Ulster, but. His nickname was "Billy the Miller" and he was as fast as a greyhound over a short distance.'

While Bridie was talking ten to the dozen, she was also drying the plates. Dotty looked at her questioningly, 'Billy the Miller?'

'Even around here you'd never call a Billy Mick, but. The story goes that Billy was playing on the wing in a cup final for the "Ballyboil Squeeze" rugby team. They needed one point to secure victory with a minute to go, they did. The ref gave a scrum down and the Squeeze won the ball against the head, whatever that means…'

Bridie moved towards the sink, leant forward, put her shoulder to it and pretended to field a ball from under her skirt and between her legs.

'Billy Liptrott, covered in mud, as black as the Earl of Hell's waistcoat, caught the ball and sped down the blind side. Brave he was.'

Dotty stood grinning and shaking her head in disbelief at Bridie's actions.

'And the way folks tell it, he was never seen again, but. The truth of the matter was, however, he ran so fast he was nothing but a blur. No opposing player got near him and he touched down at speed, winning the game, he did.

'But running on uncontrollably, he tripped up on a divot and sped headlong, deep into the crowd. The crowd surrounded him and patted him on the back as he careered through them. At the back of the crowd, a party of blootered hillbilly types from the Donegal Mountains, with jugs of poteen to spare, insisted he take a slug of the cratur.

'Instead of returning to the changing-rooms and the victory celebration that followed, he headed for the hills with them. The hillbilly lot kept him filled with poteen and threw plenty of finagling women under him. He wasn't seen again for weeks, he wasn't. He would have taken a bit of wringing-out after boozing with that lot, but.

'The next we heard was of him in hospital with perforated guts and peritonitis. The doctors saved his life, obviously. He had a colostomy bag for months after that, but. When he was all connected up again, he walked funny. Folks said the doctors had stitched up his arsehole tighter than the folds of a new bud on a lemon tree.

'Then, he…he…he had a big problem at his wedding. Met a cracking young piece at an away game, he had. Not a minger her, a bit of class she was. A real cracker she was. All for calling the wedding off, she was.

He had a slippery tongue even then had Billy. Some said his tongue was as long and as wide as a duckbilled platypus' tail. Whatever uses a woman would have for something that long and that shape I'll never know. He still managed to sweet-talk her into the church only two days after the doctors removed the stitches and his arse hadn't yet started passing solids.'

'It sounds as if he was taking a chance on marrying so soon after his reconnection. I mean, he could have burst his stitches finagling on his wedding night,' said Dotty.

'I, I, I'm sure he was, missis. Folks talk of the wedding service to this day. Every time they pass a dung heap, the smell reminds them of Billy Liptrott.

'He stood in front of the parson. You know the one, him with the bleak, religious face that's as hard as slate… that had peeled a thousand chips. Folks say he puts the fear of Christ up them. Anyway, standing in the church, Billy held her hand. All the time he was looking into her eyes and waiting for the words that would bind him to her forever.

'Then a throaty hiss came from his arse. Quickly increased in volume, it did. That's the best I can explain it, missis, but then the sound changed. It came rolling out sounding like a bald tractor-tyre rippling across soft tar. To be sure, it was the brave Billy. He…he…he… hadn't passed wind since his arse was reconnected and he was letting an almighty one rip. He…he…he…didn't have the normal restraints in place. He hadn't recovered the art of sphincter control to the same extent as those folks whose arses had always been fully functional. You know what I mean, missis. He never had a hope in hell of holding it back, had he?

'I, I, I'm told the smell was so horrid guests spewed over the pews. The parson turned green and him in the Black Perceptory of the Orange Order and all. A bat fell from the rafters and hit the font with a splash. The poor bride, she turned and ran, never seen in the area again, she was.'

Dotty nodded away and sipped at her coffee. 'And you think Sergeant Liptrott has a mean enough streak to swing one on Riley?' she asked.

'He…he…he's mean all right,' Bridie said. 'He'll do you as soon as look at you. They say he doesn't even like himself, but.'

Dotty returned to the dining-room and tipped the brandy from her goblet back into the decanter.

Chapter 9

Riley drove to the hospital, keeping his speed just under the limit. On his arrival, he went directly to A & E. Sundays were usually quiet and some staff sat near a coffee machine, in conversation.

Ryan O'Toole was the sole case waiting and he lay on a stretcher, his face taut and white. A medic had applied a tourniquet and fitted a morphine drip. Even that amount of painkiller hadn't removed all the pain from his mangled thumb, hanging by a sliver of flesh and a sinew.

'Around noon, Ryan O'Toole caught his thumb between chain and cogwheel,' the intern explained, 'whilst attempting to clear an obstruction on a combine harvester.'

It was clear to Riley that emergency microsurgery was necessary to save the thumb. He foresaw spending the rest of the afternoon, at least, in the theatre. 'Who's all on emergency theatre duty this weekend?' he asked the intern.

'Sister Mavis O'Rourke is theatre sister, according to my list,' said the intern, consulting his clipboard. 'We have a duty anaesthetist. I was able to assemble a theatre team quickly, Doctor Dernehen.'

Riley's heart skipped a beat. He hadn't looked into Mavis' eyes for twelve hours, not since she was shouting 'yes' in rhythm with his thrusting earlier that morning. His nose wrinkled slightly, thinking of his nearly abortive efforts to satisfy her desires. He suppressed a grunt of annoyance, recalling how the malicious intervention of Sergeant Liptrott, with his trumped-up charges, had scuppered, for a time, his lustfulness.

He cheered up. Dotty had boarded the brandy train very early. Sleep would come as sure as rain. Thumbs up, he thought; certainly a poorly looking one had provided him with another opportunity to dally with Mavis.

By 8 p.m. that evening, Riley had successfully reattached Ryan O'Toole's thumb. He had sweated profusely in the theatre, his buttocks nipping but he hadn't clawed at them, which was what he felt like doing for most of the operation. Back in his office, he was scratching and easing his underpants and considering how to tell Dotty of his proposed delay in returning home. 'A complication,' he said aloud, 'I need a complication,' and picked up the telephone handset.

The cook was waiting for instructions to prepare a late dinner, because of Riley's call to the hospital. Dotty sipped slowly at a snifter of brandy, deciding to have just the one, remain awake and eat when Riley returned home - keep a sober eye on him.

'I still have to reattach Ryan O'Toole's thumbnail. The machinery pulled both his knob and his nail off,' Riley said quickly, without giving Dotty time to say 'Hello.' He was sure that by now she would have drained most of the decanter.

'How devilishly awful,' Dotty said, feigning the slur that Riley expected to hear.

'He was holding onto his knob at the time, having a pee. This will take a little time and will prevent my early return home.'

From Dotty's shuddered 'Ooooohhhhhh,' Riley guessed that she had drained the brandy decanter fully and was about to hit the couch.

'Don't expect me too early. I've had a quick coffee and a snack. Have the cook leave me out a cold-meat salad.'

Dotty had the cook make up the dishes and let her leave early.

Riley met Mavis at the side door. The car park was quiet and together they sauntered across to her apartment. They forewent any preliminaries but made love twice in an hour. His stamina following an afternoon in the theatre surprised him and pleased Mavis. She praised him and kissed him all over. Then they slept peacefully for an hour.

When they awoke, they enjoyed a shower together. Mavis' hands were everywhere attempting to arouse him. 'Just one more time,' she pleaded. She was unsuccessful and by 10 p.m., he was heading for home. He was feeling great, in much better fettle, well satisfied with all aspects of his day's work. Even the Fiery Jack nipped a little less, after Mavis had rubbed in some Nivea cream.

Riley stood by the side of the Jaguar at the foot of the Hall's steps. Cedric's yowling had ceased. The dog hadn't needed any unction for Dotty to rub in or the sedative he forgot to administer, before he left that day for the hospital.

He went directly to the dining-room. The cook had left some cold Ballyboil ham and a salad of local produce between two plates. Dotty hadn't touched hers so he picked up her glass of fresh orange juice and carried it into the sitting-room. Dotty sat on the couch, her head resting on a cushion, her eyes closed. A shake of a shoulder aroused her. Popeyed, as she looked, was the state in which he expected to find her. Riley handed her the juice, which she swigged back at once. 'Come, dinner awaits us,' Riley reminded her lightly.

'I'm a bit peckish now,' she said. Rising shakily from the couch, she shuffled her way into the dining-room in her oversize slippers. Things bothered her; questions needed asking about Riley's emergency, but she needed to be coy and not seem quite sober, yet.

'Was I mistaken, but did you say something about some poor farmer by the name of O'Toole having an accident?' Dotty asked, squeaking back her chair and sitting down.

'You surely did. A farmer by the name of Ryan O'Toole had his knob ripped off, completely detached, caught in cogwheel and chain of a combine harvester.'

Dotty eyed him over the top of her glasses. 'You're having me on now,' she said, raising her voice a touch and throwing in a hiccup for good measure.

Riley pared fat from a slice of ham. 'No, seriously, he was in a dreadful state to be sure,' he replied.

Slicing the salad greenery and tomato into manageable portions, Dotty loaded some pieces onto her fork, then spilled them back onto her plate while en-route to her mouth. 'Do you know how the accident happened?' she said as she recovered the dropped mouthful with her fork. 'Mrs O'Toole attended the hospital and told me quite a bit of the occurrence. The woman went on and on about the work she did on the farm and how poor the profits were...'

Dotty interrupted. 'Farmer's wives are hard-working women, Riley. At least that's how I remember it from the days when I visited farms.' Dotty salted a portion of tomato, picked it up with her fingers, dropped it, picked it up, then forced it into her mouth, Riley noting her bungling attempts.

'She did look a doughty woman,' Riley agreed. I'm sure she was a great help with that sort of work. The muscles on her arms and legs had me believe she could clear a cowshed knee-deep in dung, after having just done the morning milking, all on her own.'

Dotty finished chewing and said, 'I've known a farmer's wife of a morning having to milk the cow, feed the calves, milk the goat and feed the pigs, then go on and muck out the byre. After which she fed the chickens and gathered the eggs. The previous night she'd have driven the ducks from the pond into their run in case a fox got at them. She'd have let them out and gathered their eggs. If there were no vegetables for supper, she'd raise some from the garden. If nobody had thought to gut and skin the rabbit for supper, she would do that too and put it in the oven on the timer...'

Riley interrupted. 'Gutting rabbits can be quite a messy affair. Not a job for a woman, especially if she nicks the intestines with her knife and gets stinking faeces over her fingers... pass me the brown sauce please, Dotty.'

'She would probably wash that off when she peeled the potatoes and skinned the vegetables,' Dotty said, shuddering. 'And if the washer had gone through its cycle, she would have removed the wet washing to put in the drier. The dried clothes she would put out on a line to air. By then it would be seven o'clock in the morning and she would be knackered already.

'She would probably need the toilet and, with a bit of luck, she'd have enough time to wipe her arse before her screaming, slave-driving husband bawled for her to work in the fields.'

Riley had heard what Dotty was saying and asked her, 'This woman had no kids?'

'She had eight kids, Riley. We wondered when she ever found the feckin' time to lie down to conceive them, let alone have them. We reckoned that the farmer was at it with her while she did the milking.'

'The woman sounds like a hardy creature to me,' Riley said.

'Did Mrs O'Toole see the accident happen?' Dotty asked.

'No, she said she was away with a load of corn to the grain-drier and stayed awhile to do some chores around the farmhouse. A bit like your woman, I suppose,' Riley said. 'Mrs O'Toole told me she was earmarking some of the profits for home improvements. She had worked hard to get the harvesting finished and that there would be no new tractor for her husband to replace the one she thought still capable of doing the work.

'O'Toole is a tall, angular man with a severe, rough-hewn, part-shaven face and not the type of man to take fools gladly. I doubt, though, if he ever argued or disagreed with his wife. She was definitely the boss.'

'The farmer had no other help?' Dotty asked.

'His son was with his mother at the hospital. Apparently, the boy's a bit of an idiot. To me he looked wayward, callow and perhaps only fifteen years old,' Riley said. 'I also thought he suffered a deep-seated, spiritual deformity. He definitely displayed a dire poverty of intellect. He had walked behind the harvester all day with a cleft stick, felling rabbits when they appeared from beneath the machine. He brought with him a collection of rabbit and hare ears cut off by the reaper. He caused the accident to happen in the first place.'

'How could he have done that when he was walking behind the machine?' Dotty asked.

'Oh, O'Toole had stopped the machine for a drop of tea. It seemed the ache in his bladder had reminded him he hadn't passed water since breakfast either and he thought he had earned a pee. He was peeing alongside the harvester when the idiot boy started it up again.'

'Farm workers relieving themselves in a field in full view of the road?' Dotty asked, raising a guffaw, faking incredulity. 'Come, come, Riley, you and I know that farmers don't piddle in the middle of a field if there's a hedge. Years ago, you couldn't miss a farmer's arse or his tiddleypush sticking through the foliage when out for an afternoon walk down a boreen.'

Riley was enjoying himself. The patter was flowing. 'Well, I spoke at length to O'Toole,' he said. 'I thought him a shy, modest man. He told me he abhorred life's crudities and that he himself never ever considered appearing crude. It was his way; he was desperate, and thought that close by the side of the harvester facing away from the road was the very place to find relief.

'If he had flashed his knob towards Mount Boil, he would still have it. I'm sure he was having flow problems, prostate trouble, no doubt. He said he waited some time, his knob firmly held in one hand, expectant of the sustained gush that would signal his bladder had begun to empty properly.

'He said that the moving parts of the harvester had come to rest. The harsh, white-sound caused by sitting for a whole morning in close proximity to the roaring diesel engine was subsiding in his ears. When, suddenly, unexpectedly, dragging him back to his senses, the harvester had burst into life, started up by his son. Imbecile, I'd call him.'

Riley clasped his hands together over the table and, in a jerking motion in front of Dotty, demonstrated how the accident happened. 'But before O'Toole could move away,' Riley said, 'he felt a sudden, sickening, clawing and grabbing at his knob and the rotation of the machinery tugging it from his hand.'

Riley's plate had a little cheese left on it. Leaving his story, he said. 'Pass me a couple of pickled onions and a gherkin please.' Continuing, he said, 'Then, the rotating cogwheels and link-chain drew him in.' He demonstrated that movement with a sharp twist of his wrist that had Dotty gasping, 'O'Toole said he felt excruciating pain and the elevation of his whole body. Then he staggered back, on the verge of collapse and close to unconsciousness.

'The shock of seeing his knob orbiting in isolation around a cogwheel must have been devastating and brought that on. I'm surprised he didn't die then. Seeing one's knob transfer slickly to a smaller cogwheel higher up the chain would have that effect on most men. The smaller cogwheel would have been rotating faster. O'Toole saw his knob catapulting off it with a flourish. I said to him, "I suppose it had a distraught eye and seemed to be saying to you, oops, why tear us apart as it looped at speed towards the primary entrance of the harvester?" But he didn't see the funny side of that remark.'

Dotty had come to expect a load of tommyrot in every tale Riley told. Now he was excelling himself: a knob in orbit, of all things. Whom did Riley think he was kidding with that nonsensical tale?

Riley was too preoccupied to notice her sly look; she intended keeping up the pretence of believing him; to see how far he would stretch it; to see how stupid he thought her. 'Ryan O'Toole was in some state when his tiddleypush disappeared into the machine's inner workings, was he?' she asked, the question derived to hint that she had not sussed him out.

'Aye, I saw him an hour after his accident, on a hospital trolley,' Riley answered. He was sniffing and moaning in agony. His nose had a dewdrop that kept disappearing up a nostril as he breathed. I can say he looked far from happy. The morphine drip piercing his arm gave him little in the way of relief. The frame keeping the weight of the bedding from his painful area only pointed to the root of his problem.

'I noticed he was a shade paler than white, facially, his skin damp and tacky. His ears ought to have surgery to remove some ugly chilblain calluses. Cutting kale for cattle on frosty mornings gets you them and feckin' painful they can be, too.'

'You couldn't save Ryan's private, yet you had no words of comfort, no compassion for the poor man?' Dotty said sharply.

'I thought my chances better of saving that filmed soldier, Private Ryan, in the heat of battle. All I could tell Ryan O'Toole was the good news that we'd stripped down the combine harvester and found his knob; the bad news was that it was now, sadly, mince!'

'Mince! Riley! Oh, how could you be so callous?'

'Of course, I quickly told him not to worry. With the miracles of microsurgery and my techniques, I could stitch him on a new knob, personally selected by me, which I had kept perfect, in cryonic suspension, to offer men suffering such accidents...'

Dotty interrupted loudly. '*Mince*! I do not believe it, you told him *mince*!' Dotty hoped her head shaking showed her disbelief at his insensitivity and not his yarn.

Riley didn't notice; he was in full flow. 'I told him that the donor's family gave me permission for its transplantation. I also tried to convince him that it would make a suitable and ample replacement for him, with all necessary functions remaining in place. I'd hooked him on the idea I was sure. Especially when I told him I took pride that in all transplants of that nature, I had never once lost a vinegar stroke...'

Dotty interrupted again. 'There you go again with your funnies on the seed of life. You're a real trier.' She was sure Riley would expect her to be outraged at that, whether under the influence or not.

'Honestly, I fetched my cryogenic briefcase along to his bedside and together we viewed the sample. I told him the replacement once belonged to a young athlete who had died tragically. I thought a good sales pitch was that the donor hadn't used it much. I could see he was excited when I told him its length was a full eighteen inches with a large, traditional head, with more than two woman's handfuls around the base.

'But he was visibly upset when I told him they only ever came in black and a little expensive at twelve thousand pounds. Of course, I tried to impress upon him that if the harvest was exceptionally good this year, he might consider investing some of his profits in the replacement.

'The hospital records showed that his blood type was compatible with the knob. With limited medication, it wouldn't drop off. The idea stunned him and I thought he was beginning to swank a bit. I'm sure he could picture himself toying with it. I tried to convince him he should go for it. I told him he suited the contemporary look. How can you refuse this opportunity to please your wife with the double-handful I'm offering you? I cajoled.

'We began haggling over the costs of the procedure. Farmers are never keen to part with their money, as you well know, but eventually we agreed a price for the transplant work.

'Then I left the ward. I guessed O'Toole needed time to mull over the idea that he might spend the rest of his life with an eighteen-inch, black, transplanted knob. '

'So when are you doing it, then?' Dotty asked him brightly, making out that she was a believer right to the end.

'I'm not.'

'You're not?' Dotty asked, feigning incredulity, her eyebrows raised.

'No. When his wife turned up she told him they were spending the harvest profits on a new, fitted kitchen, instead.'

Dotty was looking at Riley, sitting behind his smug façade, seeing him now in a much brighter light. He might have improved his patients' recovery times and entertained friends with his wild tales, but now he had just gone beyond a joke. Now he was making up mind-boggling fables to make her look silly. For sure, he must have an ulterior motive for telling them. It was a bit of a worry.

Chapter 10

At 08:45 on Monday, Riley left Whynot Hall for Ballyboil hospital. It had rained overnight; now scudding, black clouds repeatedly blocked out the sun. One shaft of sunlight, briefly finding a rare gap in the cloud-cover as he drove through the Hall gates, had him blinking. He pulled the sun-visor down and sat forward for a better view of the road ahead. The seated position took some weight off his buttocks. Fiery Jack's burning was fading but it still a needed a calming scratch.

Adhering to the tarmacadam, according to Dotty's predictions, he'd find tyre-printed, splattered and flattened hedgehog cadavers. The tall, beech hedging lining the road taking him from the Hall towards Ballyboil bypass was prime habitat for such beasts. He saw no small, prickly, comical, recklessly scurrying beasts, and none squashed into misshapen splodges.

What a silly bleeder for checking that one out, he thought.

The road ahead was about to become the bit of a worry. It would take his mind totally from the Fiery Jack's irritation. As the troubling occurrence unfolded, it crossed Riley's mind that he should be thankful that the unction's remnant presence was sufficient to cause him to sit forward in his seat and alert.

On a long straight, where he had always observed the speed limit for that class of road, a cop stepped out from the cover of the beech hedge. He was holding a speed-detector gun steady, with the business end pointing towards the approaching Jag. Flashing past, Riley saw that the tall figure was Constable O'Hicks; the field's adjacent gated opening in the beech hedge was hiding police car. The cop had made no effort to stop him, but waved to him in what seemed a friendly gesture, whilst wearing the broadest of smiles.

Had it been Sergeant Liptrott standing holding the thing, Riley had no doubt that he'd have been pulled over, the odious man then penning into his pocket-book bogus details of a speeding offence.

'That bastard Liptrott is behind this,' Riley muttered. He was convinced that the sergeant had ordered the cop to report him, or even trump-up a motoring offence he might have committed on his way to work. It was guesswork, of course, but Riley knew of one good reason why that particular cop hadn't carried out those instructions fully.

Riley completed the rest of the journey to the hospital nervously. In every hedgerow gap, he looked for the sergeant, parked up, unobtrusive, his lips curled back in a grimace of pleasure, waiting and ready to pounce on him.

At 9:05 a.m., he arrived in his consulting room. Bright and modern, it contained the items of hospital paraphernalia patients would expect: an examination bed with an encircling screen, a filing cabinet, a sink with towel rail, wall charts showing human skeletons with different layers of dermis peeled back, and a desk.

To the front of the desk were two comfortable chairs. Prior to seeing his patients in the theatre, and as professional etiquette demanded, he would interview them seated there. Explaining the surgery he would perform and stress the dangers of going under anaesthetic and the risk of post-operative infections was a part of his job.

When he consulted at the Royal Dilbert, he generally first met up with his patients in the operating theatre, their arrival there urgent, without the benefit of a prior appointment.

Like at the Royal Dilbert, the expertise he had shown at the Ballyboil hospital had brought him flattering acclamation from the many patients benefitting from his skills: an incision with his scalpel; a carefully placed new layer of skin, a hole strategically placed with his drill or a precise chip with a chisel.

Riley sat down behind his desk, tapping his fingers rapidly on its top, pondering. Sergeant Liptrott's trumped-up charges had made it impossible for him to continue in the role of police-surgeon. If he took the decision to cease those duties, it brought complications. As he sat, they seemed unsolvable. Continuing to meet secretly with Mavis was a bit of a worry.

Unable to think of some other Hall-escaping contrivance, but convinced one would materialize in time, he picked up his phone, pressed a button, and when his secretary answered, uttered a muted, 'Ahum. Cynthia, before you bring in my diary, please telephone Rippington Avenue RUC station. Have them remove my name from the police-surgeon's call-out roster. If they ask why, just tell them I'm much too busy for any further duties.'

At 9.20 a.m., Cynthia appeared with his diary and a tray with coffee, milk, sugar and a digestive biscuit.

'Who do we have this morning?' he asked her, brightly. Cynthia poured a coffee for him, tore the top from a sugar sachet and trickled the correct amount into the cup. 'We have a Miss Ophelia O'Rooney, at nine-thirty. She's coming up from Limerick to see you. Apparently, she's opted to see you rather than a Dublin surgeon.'

'Limerick's quite a way for her to come. What do we know of her?'

'Not one thing. She was quite talkative on the phone, but gave little away, insisting only on an early appointment.'

Miss Ophelia O'Rooney arrived promptly, Cynthia showing her directly into his consulting room. Riley noticed immediately her light-brown skin and that she was of mixed race. She walked liquidly, her pelvis rotating loosely. That impressed him, for never had he seen a woman's legs pass one another so sexily. He shook her hand in welcome and noticed that her clothes were classy. The body-hugging cotton outfit was so low-cut that it exposed a good eyeful of her ample, coffee-coloured bosom.

His professional eye told him her breasts might once have undergone surgical augmentation.

He ushered Ophelia to a chair into which she settled, sitting back seductively and crossing her legs.

He found it a wrench to drag his eyes away from them.

Her flattened nose also drew him. It was wide at the base and the nostrils flared. He visualised scalding steam snorting down them, dragon-like, when she threw a tantrum, and thought that some reconstruction work wouldn't go amiss there.

He also thought her thick, African lips must continually remind her of one parent.

Looking up from a page of his diary he said, 'Miss O'Rooney, I see you have come quite a distance to see me. Dublin is closer to Limerick than Ballyboil. Didn't you consider seeking surgery there?'

'Well, not really. I heard you were the best in the business so I flew over to Limerick from Gatwick yesterday. I lived in London for many years and I've come to dislike city life,' she said in a London accent still laced with a trace of the brogue. As she spoke, her eyes sparkled from sockets ringed with a sprinkling of a cosmetic lustre.

'I imagine properties are very expensive in London,' Riley said.

Assessing a prospective private patient's wealth, experience had told him, was a good point to begin appointments.

'Too true, doctor,' Ophelia said, 'but I've retired to one of the southern Home Counties. There were plenty of properties on the market from which to choose. After many escorted tours by bloodsucking estate agents, I chose the bungalow in Balls Green over a semi-detached in Balls Cross.

'Balls Cross I ditched because it would have reminded me too much of my past. I find it quite expensive living in Balls Green, but I can easily afford it, having made a mint during the years I was on the game,' Ophelia said, tapping the gold-threaded purse she held in her lap.

'"On the game", Miss O'Rooney?'

'I was a Brass, a Tom. I hawked my mutton for forty years back there in the smoke,' she said, pointing over her shoulder with a finger.

'A Brass, a Tom, Miss O'Rooney? I haven't....'

'A prostitute, doctor,' she prompted.

'Interesting, hmm, aye,' he said, 'your life must have been quite fascinating.' He shuffled his feet and cast his eyes down towards a notepad onto which he would jot down her requirements. Then he pushed it to one side, feeling it wasn't required yet.

'My forty-year career on the game began on the streets of London's Kings Cross, towards the end of the nineteen-fifties. Then, I was a slight, sixteen-year-old girl. Mostly, I worked on my own, but later, as my services became more popular, I took a flat in Soho, London's notorious red-light district.

'There, I had a pimp to bring in the business. I was lucky to find him. He was good to me and a good pimp is a rare commodity. Business was brisk and I threw myself beneath twenty men nightly. For an extra twenty quid, I did the business on top. To others, I gave relief in their preferred ways.' Ophelia stopped speaking and looked at Riley coyly, through large, brown eyes.

Riley looked for one ounce of shame, but none showed.

'The dangers existing for a prostitute, Ophelia, must have been a bit of a worry. You do not mind if I call you Ophelia?'

'Suit yourself, doctor. It's my proper name, though I never much liked it. Yes, I suppose I experienced some rough moments. Most streetwalkers I knew had threatening, unprovoked hassle. Mind you, we all learned quickly. I never expected any favours from or gave any to my punters.

'Often, I took them up darkened alleyways. In that situation, if their tenner didn't swiftly appear from a pocket or wallet and disappear into my purse, then the wank, which is all they would get for that fee, wasn't what they got.

'Streetwalking had made me adept at kicking men up the bollocks with a pointed shoe. I found it not one bit of a worry to give them that treatment, free of charge.'

'My, my, my,' Riley exclaimed. 'You dispensed instant, open-air justice in instances like that?' he asked.

'Yes, I did. Some punters, I learned, were fascinated with pain and punishment. It's known as S&M in the trade. Although I found the practise strange, I was willing to provide pain if the readies were right. Sometimes men paid me to tie them up and kick them hard on their bollocks with the instep of a bare foot.

'Initially, they all squealed, raised their feat and hung by their wrists in the special harness I had made. I thought they all must have enjoyed it. They all walked away doubled-up, but they were grinning insanely. Some even demanded I repeat the treatment. Exiting my place, those punters had sets of painful bollocks as red and as large as Edam cheeses, resting tenderly in their Y-fronts. I offered other personal services, too, but they cost more.

'My half-caste appearance attracted different sorts. Punters requiring THH, traumatic head-humping to the uninitiated, made great demands on my time. THH was an exotic extra, provided exclusive by me, which I advertised as Cannibal Roulette on the cards I had pasted-up in most of the telephone boxes situated around Kings Cross, Euston and Soho.'

Riley thumped the palm of a hand onto his desk and erupted, 'Traumatic head-humping! Oh, dearie me… and cannibal roulette! You amaze me, Ophelia.

I have never heard of such goings-on. Whatever can that practice be?'

He pushed his chair back, stretched his legs and thrust his hands deep into his trouser pockets. A lengthy and absorbing listen seemed in store. He would draw more revelations from her. Ophelia seemed intent on relating her full, sordid past to him. That he show interest was important: the other two consultations that day for private surgery didn't fill his diary. A show of considerate and patient listening might secure this private work.

'When THH punters stuck their knob in my gob, they didn't know the state of my appetite until I'd satisfactorily completed the blowjob and wiped my chin,' Ophelia answered.

'During a blowjob…er… you gave them a traumatic head-humping, Ophelia?' Riley asked, incredulously, not believing his ears. Mavis was always doing little tricks like that for him, but tenderly. Perhaps the revised version according to Ophelia O'Rooney might interest her experimentally. He shuddered at the thought, perhaps not; it would be a bit of a worry.

'Well, chewed them mainly,' Ophelia said. 'Nibbling with my incisors and inflicting pain, I scared them into believing that, with one swift and sharp clenching of my jaws, I would bite off their bell-ends. Men will take little risks like that, even if it does make them shudder and they think it a bit of a worry. It's a game of chance to them. I never suffered from tackle-hunger, but it paid well and business is business, you know.'

'Tackle-hunger sounds like it could be one of Bob Geldof's charities to me. Your definition of a little risk varies greatly from mine, and I do consider that a bit of a worry' Riley said, shaking his head, 'I'm sure my fears will be shared by many men. However, I'm just beginning to understand better the nature of the services you provided.'

'Well, if that's what the punter wanted, it's what he got,' Ophelia answered offhandedly, not thinking it an issue.

'You would have seen quite an array of weaponry in your time?' Riley asked, and chuckled.

'I never really looked, didn't care. I never had a lot of interest in the end. Punters, standing proud, flashing their lengthy knobs at me and expecting me to be impressed, I charged the same as punters with thimble-like excuses and the ones who couldn't get it up at all. Whatever their bit of a worry, I always had a go at pumping out their bollocks for them.'

The lurid explanations were shaking Riley. For each question he asked, Ophelia offered a more shocking answer. He hadn't expected to hear her full working history. That's what he was getting, though, and it sure was interesting. 'You say most men like kinky sex?'

'It's a fact, doctor. Men are into any sort of sex. I had some punters who would leap onto a toad's back readily if it stopped hopping in front of them. However, my ability to satisfy punters was legendary. Cottoning-on to their preferences early in my career, earned me plenty. To get shot of any punter quickly, and increase turnover, I perfected a method of rapidly ridding their bellies of dirty water.'

'Dirty water... Ophelia... what in heaven's name is that fluid?' Riley erupted with a snort, not having heard that expression before, either.

'I don't know what you medical fellows call it, but it's what shoots out the end at the end, if you know what I mean.'

'I know what you mean now,' Riley said, showing slight embarrassment at not having known. 'And what was the rapid method?' He had spoken before thinking. Bayjasus, I shouldn't have asked that he thought.

'I grew an extra-long fingernail on the index finger of my right hand...'

'An extra-long fingernail!' Riley erupted. He now knew for definite that he shouldn't have asked.

'That did the trick every time. I had grown the nail so long that it curled back on itself in a double helix, a bit like a helter skelter. It was the weirdest of talons. It frightened me even,' she said, giving a mock shiver. 'It's spade-shaped end I occasionally loaded up with an illegal or eroticising substance. That part held just the correct amount that I could vacuum into my head through one nostril.' She opened her handbag, rummaged and found a clear-plastic paperweight, which she handed to Riley.

'My word, what a devilish-looking object,' Riley said, squirming in his chair and looking at the nail encapsulated within the clear plastic.

'I could use it in anger or if I felt threatened. On the job, I'd use it just as punters were about to mount me. Wafting the nail in front of their eyes usually had their peepers crossing and them thinking it a bit of a worry. When they began thrusting, I'd grip the cheeks of their backsides with both hands, letting them know its position. As soon as I saw fear and apprehension showing, I would skirt the periphery of their ring-piece with it, using a circular movement. That let them know how close I was to using it.

'It never failed to promote instant ejaculation either by fear or by the notorious "anal stimulus effect by proxy" method.'

'I'm not surprised!' Riley said, squirming, 'though I'm unaware of the method or its title.' He could have told her that a finger smeared with Fiery Jack, timely and strategically inserted, might have saved her the trouble of growing the nail.

'A nail the likes of this would be a shocking discovery, a bit of a worry to any man finding it close to such a sensitive area of his anatomy, I guarantee,' he said, paused and then asked, 'Why exactly did you retire from the streets, Ophelia?'

'The omens were not good. Gay bars were opening on every street corner. Talk in the trade was that men wanted to try something different. The notion abhorred me. In all the years I'd been on the game I'd had never allowed anyone to violate my tradesman's entrance. I wasn't about to start that obscenity.

'It annoyed me too, and it didn't seem fair, that men would forsake women, preferring to seek out that form of sex in those abysmal places. Before I moved from Soho, I sought the locations of several gay bars. I would stand outside their doors. Once I had the attention of the mincers flouncing inside, I'd vent advice in the form of an insult. "You're a bunch of cock-sucking bastards and the shit's going to fall out of your slackened-off arseholes," I'd shout. The prophecy contained in my insult, they ought to have seen as the dire consequence of their filthy practices.'

'Indeed!' Riley said, loudly. Then he asked, 'Did you retire then because of the proliferation of gay bars?'

'No, I made a career move, a few years before I retired. I moved from Soho to a private flat in Mayfair. There, I entertained wealthier, more prestigious clients. My standard of living and the quality of my customers increased greatly. Eventually, only Arab millionaires could afford the massive increase in my charges.'

'You enjoyed the company of Arab men?' Riley asked, without the waver in his voice that might indicate his disapproval.

'Arabs are very generous people. Their knobs are no different. However, I did insist on the complete removal of any traces of the Sahara from beneath their foreskins, before allowing them sex with me. At the end of an evening of giving head to desert princes, sand and toothpaste made for a gritty clean. I only let that happen once, but I was spitting sand for weeks after. It was a bit of a worry.'

'You're quite graphic in your narrative. Did you earn a great deal of money?' Riley asked.

'Cash poured in. I did very well. Inevitably, wear and tear of my main working area became more noticeable, a bit of a worry. I found I could no longer contract my vaginal-wall muscles, grip knobs and create the sound beloved of all men, and for which punters willingly paid extra to hear. It's the fanny fart, doctor.'

'Ophelia, it is certainly a long time since I, too, heard any whisper from the lips of love,' he said, rocking gently and tittering. 'The hiccup from the love pump, the sonorant bass-beat from the tunnel of love. A wonderful, satisfying sound, whatever a man may call it.'

'Retirement was inevitable, doctor. That's when I began seeking a retreat in a lovely, idyllic, rural backwater of southern England. I was able to furnish my bungalow with the best. My contacts within the furniture trade, from whom I purchased many sturdy beds and firm, but well-sprung mattresses, were notable. The deliveries of furnishings arrived incognito. I didn't want any old acquaintances to find my new whereabouts, nor my new neighbours to know of my past.'

Riley thought he detected a hidden question there, and said, 'Your confidentiality is ensured within these walls, Ophelia.' He leaned forward and gave her a meaningful stare. He was looking at a few bob for this job and he wanted to dispel any bits of worry she might have. She still didn't given him a clue to what surgical enhancement she might require, just rambled on: 'Then, during this present springtime, I decided that the large front garden, the lawn, the orchard and my vegetable plot to the rear of my home, ought to look the best in the hamlet. That's when I employed Oliver.'

'Oliver?'

'Oliver Balls is a local man. He's handsome, thickset, muscular and thoroughly conversant in countryside ways. The availability of a load of manure for the vegetable plot or a setting of delicious Golden Wonder potatoes is but a part of his rustic knowledge.

'He was an experienced gardener and I was pleased to employ him part-time. Oliver proved very good and clipped my hedges into a fantastic landscape of shapes, subtle and tasteful. My borders were aflame with a profusion of blooms. A sheet of white blossom covered my mature orchard in springtime. When it became windblown and strewn over the surrounding lawns, it looked like a sea of field daisies.'

'A very picturesque setting you were creating in your garden, Ophelia,' Riley enthused. Then he asked, 'Do you enjoy gardening?'

'Yes, I do. My lawns I neatly trim and flat-roll, doctor. I do the mowing sitting upon a motorised mower. I dress in jeans, a floppy sweater and wellies, tuck my hair beneath a headscarf and dig up the weeds plaguing the garden. I look and feel as if I'm a countrified woman.'

A lot prettier looking than Dotty does doing the same chore, Riley mused.

'Twice a week, Oliver called and attended to my horticultural needs. Within weeks, I found I was looking forward to his arrival. My heart had first fluttered one evening when he arrived later than usual during a prolonged dry spell we were having in June. The sound of his bicycle clattering against the garden shed alerted me to his presence.

'I had been sitting relaxing, dressed in a silk housecoat and a pair of light, slip-on shoes. On hearing the noise, I glided silently through the back door into the garden. A gush of clear water arcing out over my vegetable plot caught my eye. It surprised me that it originated from a position that approximated to the fly area of Oliver's overalls.

'What manner of bladder and ancillary equipment did a man need to project a stream of piss over such a great distance? I asked myself. Even with my extensive experience of knobs, nothing, I was sure, had matched this.

'However, as I drew closer I realised how wrong I was. It became clear to me that Oliver was handling a hose.' Ophelia demonstrated how he held the hose using two half-closed hands placed together in her lap.

'I felt quite foolish not to have heard the power-pump humming away in the garden shed. Oliver caught me eyeing him. Quite surprised he was to see my interest. My housecoat hung loosely over my body and he saw my shapely bumps.' Ophelia lifted up her breasts in cupped hands as she spoke.

'Oliver desisted in his efforts to irrigate the parched soil and entered the shed to switch off the pump. As he strode out, I noted, with a fascinated eye, that he did indeed have a large bulge in his manly area. I was surprised that Oliver's knob interested me. Arousal at the close proximity of a man was something that hadn't happened for some tens of years and I hadn't considered it a problem.

'Doctor, from that moment, our relationship experienced a headlong rush. Oliver was of a shy disposition, but seized the opportunity. Though wary, I encouraged him, but remained physically at a distance. We were attracted to one another, had compassionate hearts and loved the countryside. We began to hold hands on outings to a cinema on the outskirts of London. Marriage or at least a time when Oliver might want to tumble into bed with me appears close. Being plain Mrs. Ophelia Balls, sounds good to me. It gives me a nice feeling, it does.'

'It's a nice-sounding handful, Ophelia,' Riley quipped, smiling benignly.

'Being unable to produce the much-sought-after fanny fart, doctor, is the nature of my difficulty and it requires attention. My old box needs some repair work, before I could ever consider tumbling into bed with Oliver.' She moved forward in her seat, placed her hands on his desk, looked straight at Riley and began to speak earnestly, with a passion.

'Doctor, any young man falling in love with an older woman would find it a bit of a worry if she has a worn-out old box.' She sat back to let the words sink in.

'Because of my past, my old box has lost its elasticity. No longer is it as tight as a drinking straw. No longer can it grip a knob and administer vaginal massage. A box ought to be capable of ridding a man of all carnal desires in one mind-shuddering moment of great joy, and mine has become too dog-eared, so to speak, ever again to provide that sensation. Doctor, friends have told me that you're the best in the business at restructuring human flesh. I want you to renovate my box; tighten it up and make it as if it were little used.'

The request shocked Riley, had him rocking back in his chair. Reconstruction work on that area of a woman's anatomy was new to him. He would need the assistance of an obstetrician but he knew for definite it was possible and, of course, he ought to agree to do the job. Why sidestep an interesting and lucrative challenge?

He said, rather hesitantly, 'We're not a clinic specialising in "box restoration work", as you put it. However, I am a plastic surgeon. As such, I sometimes perform minor miracles reconstructing and reshaping human flesh.

'With the assistance of a surgeon skilled in obstetrics, it is possible that I will be able to neaten things up a bit for you. First, though, I will have to conduct an examination to ascertain the amount of reconstruction work necessary.'

Sitting for a moment musing, his mind conjured up what, to him, seemed the ultimate box refurbishment credential. 'Have you considered that if I restore your box to its original state, successfully, I'll be able to add F.F.F.R.S after my name?'

'And what might that new title be, doctor?' Ophelia asked and gave a short giggle.

'It means I'll be a Fellow of the Fanny Fart Restoration Society.' He stood up, smiling, pleased that his wit was up to scratch.

Ophelia laughed loudly as he took hold of her arm and led her to the examination bed. Pulling a curtain to one side with a swish, he showed her where to undress and the foot stirrups, pointing out they were standard on examination beds.

In an undignified position, but one that she knew well, and stripped from the waist down, Ophelia waited.

Riley pulled on prophylactics and approached Ophelia. Standing between her raised knees, he placed one hand on each, ready to push them gently apart. Ophelia said, 'The last time a doctor examined me this way, he told me I had acute angina.'

The old joke registered with Riley. He replied, 'I doubt he would say that now.'

The moment he uttered the words, he had an instant flashback. It took him to the living-room of his parent's home on the morning his A-level results had dropped through the letterbox onto the carpet.

His father had snatched up the envelope, opening it in haste. His wish was for his son to follow him into the medical profession. Viewing the results, his father had cried out, "Eureka! Riley might not be tall enough to consider ever becoming a brain surgeon, but now he has all the qualifications needed for him to qualify as an obstetrician."

Riley's training had taken him in a different direction. He had no obstetric skills; he was prepared to view the main working area of a retired "Lady of the Night", but he didn't know what to expect. Certainly not the "Fingal's Cave" sculpted out of flesh she presented to him for examination.

Riley was aghast and cried out in disbelief. Not only was his cry audible, it received a false echo for effect: 'Ophelia, Ophelia, Ophelia, Ophelia. What have we here, here, here, here?'

Forty years of screwing for a living had left well-defined wear and tear. The sight amazed Riley. He scratched his head; had a disbelieving look on his face as he conjured up an image of Countdown presenter Richard Whitley's face: it was Friday; the final game of the day, and a T hadn't appeared on any show for the series. The contestant requested a consonant, then a vowel, then another consonant. Carol had placed CUN on the board. Then the contestant had asked for another consonant....

In his career, reconstructing flesh and bone had never taxed his ingenuity and to constrict a vagina of such circumference as Ophelia's, he thought a bit of a worry and difficult to achieve. However, the opportunity of trousering a few bob was well worth considering and that thought settled his mind on what he must do.

He began by explaining to Ophelia the vaginal shape he hoped to achieve, demonstrating the shape using his hands cupped together. 'This enhancement procedure will make you maidenly again,' he predicted, 'with a giggle-pin proud and eager for titillation. This ought to delight Oliver. If my memory serves me well, what the obstetrician will tell you is this: your epigynum will look a great deal better for the procedure. Vaginisimus will still be achievable during intercourse and you will suffer no chronic dyspereunia.

'I will not have created a virgin, Ophelia, but to your partner your internal architecture will look quite secure and feel little used. The tightening and neatening up will fool any young man. What I'm saying is that your Oliver ought to be deceived into believing you are a lady hardly used to the sexual act.'

Ophelia was looking at him with her mouth open and slightly askew, the medical terminology going over her head.

With a professional smile, he invited her to dress.

Ophelia dressed, composed herself in the toilet and then sat opposite him again. He offered her a cup of coffee, which she accepted. Relaxing her while he broached the subject of cost, he thought a good idea. Ophelia O'Rooney looked moneyed. A bank-account-inflating and Dotty pleasing figure looked achievable.

An agreement on the figure came quickly, without quibble, Ophelia simply enquiring, 'What will the damage be?'

'I will need a team of six in the theatre. The operation will take approximately two hours. Then there is the cost of the bed and the rehabilitation. He punched some figures into a calculator and told her the total cost.

'I think it will be cash well spent, doctor. Oliver will love me and will never know of the leap my body is about to take back into the past,' she said, nodding her acceptance.

Riley looked pleased with the outcome and smiled reassuringly.

'The costs are not exorbitant for the best fingers in the business,' Ophelia said. 'I thought I'd have to pay a lot more. I also needed the guarantee of complete anonymity you promised.'

'No one will know you're here.'

'Okay. Can I book a bed in the private ward for this week?'

'Well, my diary is empty on Wednesday and a theatre is free. Putting a surgical team together won't be a problem.'

Ophelia sat stroking her chin, deep in thought, before looking up at Riley and saying, 'I wondered earlier, what was that medical gobbledegook you were spouting about my new box?'

'Well, Ophelia, now that you ask, to layperson it means this: when I've tightened your box up, you will be able to shag Oliver's rocks off quite painlessly, most effectively, with all the enthusiasm of youth, to the sound of fanny farts trumpeting a renewed reveille.'

Chapter 11

'What kind of day have you had, Riley?' Dotty asked. It was now Monday evening and they had just sat down to dinner. A bowl of thick, creamy lentil soup steamed on each of their tablemats. The meat from a pig killed and cured in the cook's village had just gone on sale and the rich aroma of smoked ham rose from the bowls. A bacon chop, sausage, egg and colcannon waited them as the main course.

Riley quickly noticed the topped-up brandy goblet and the decanter standing close to Dotty's right hand.

'I interviewed one prospective patient. He was a strange man called Henry, aged about forty, who had never been married and his parents were dead.'

'He told you all this?'

'And some intimate details about a failed love affair at school. Then he went into a lengthy rigmarole of the events leading up to his self-disfigurement.'

'I see,' Dotty said, slowly, suspicious that Riley was about to embark on another of his dinnertime horror stories.

'Apparently, he fished for carp each weekend throughout spring and summer at a country pond, situated on the other side of Ballyboil. Such marvellous and vivid descriptions he painted of the flora and fauna of the place. Even I could picture it in my mind's eye. He talked of the first thrusts of springtime, gusting winds, fragrant hawthorn-blossom blowing hither and thither, the frost-hard ground alive with its wispy, frantic fling.

'So carried away was he with his tale, his eyes were continuously looking up into the roof of his head. A right feckin' eejit I thought him when he talked of the raucous cackling of crows and the squawks of seagulls as they followed ploughs. I thought to myself what a generous listener I must be, but I couldn't bring myself to stop his flow. Henry was so hideously self-mutilated.'

'This sounds a much nicer story,' Dotty said, staring at him earnestly, looking suitably gulled into believing that the tale wasn't one of his fabrications.

The cook bustled in, whisked away the soup bowls and served the main course.

'He told me that for many weekends he sat by the pond, on a small stool, fishing rod at his side, hook baited, fish breaking the pond's surface, newts and water rats popping up and testing for spring.

'Occasionally he'd throw fistfuls of wriggling maggots towards favoured lies, to tempt the small fish that he'd throw back before the end of day. That proved to me the man was a loser. A monster pike, as long as two arms-lengths, concerned him. It lurked hidden beneath telltale ripples but it had never taken his bait. Need I say more?

'Apparently a drake, known as Sir Francis to the anglers, a tough old bird with a puffed-out crop, filled with mooched food and his own importance, ruled the roost. He was domineering, bullying, wild-eyed and sex-mad, apparently, a mongrel of the species who lorded it over his drakedom…'

'What to feck's a drakedom?' Dotty boomed.

'I thought at the time it was a word he had made up himself. His use of glorious racket stirring the air to describe duck noises, the squawking, the treading of water during breast-to-breast skirmishes, the contesting for food and territory, was sheer verbosity, too, in my opinion.'

'Then last May, he fell in love with a duckling…'

'What did he mean by that?' Dotty interrupted sharply, a portion of bacon-steak speared on her fork. Was the story veering towards a bestial liaison?

'This one duckling was bright, mysterious and inquisitive, just a bundle of white fluff. His eyes never left it. He thought it might be in peril, you see. Apparently, the monster pike took ducklings, ate the feckin' things.

'Anyhow, one day, the duck, fully-grown by now, spread its wings and fluttered from the water to his side, took a liking to his maggots and helped itself. That day he named the duck Henrietta.'

'Henrietta?' Dotty erupted, wondering where this tale was going.

'Lovely name, I thought. Quite animated he was about her when he told me that Sir Francis tried to muscle in, move her on, precociously tried getting his own way with her. Evidently, Henry repulsed the drake by deftly directing a plimsoll beneath its tail, which sent it skedaddling across the pond, performing tantrums and gyrations and in a bit of a paddy.'

'An Irish duck, obviously, if it demonstrated a bit of a paddy,' Dotty suggested, lifting an eyebrow, wryly.

'Ducks of all European breeds and some exotic varieties are commonly seen on our waterways. I know there's no species of duck exclusive to Ireland,' he said, nodding his head knowledgably.

'Anyway, where was I? Oh yes, during a summer squall, and we know plenty about them, rain deluged, thunder roared overhead and lightning split an adjacent tree asunder, sending deserted crow nests flying. The storm frightened Henrietta so much that she leapt into his lap, burying her body deep beneath his waterproofs.

'Perhaps the bird felt warmth, flutters from his heart, or recognised a safe repose, who knows?

'Then he said he killed Henrietta.'

'He wrung the poor soul's neck?' Dotty asked, raising an eyebrow, questioningly.

'There's even more rigmarole. Henrietta had become quite tame and as the fishing season was about to end, he took her home with him. He lived alone and he had intended to keep her comfortable and warm all winter, nestled in a basket by the fire. He's obviously a bit of a romantic, too.

'However, earlier this spring, sense eventually got the better of him and he took Henrietta back to the pond…'

Dotty was speechless for a moment and then cried out. 'A duck indoors all winter…by the hearth! What in heaven's name was he thinking of?'

'Duck droppings everywhere, perhaps,' Riley rattled on, enjoying his invention, 'I'm not sure they're house-trainable. I'm sure it was nothing to do with my patient's hormones. The rampant Sir Francis, however, he seemed to have dredged up a sexual urge. Henry plunged Henrietta back into the pond and the drake quickly paddled up to her, fussed around noisily and bullied her away from the shore. Nudging her like a tug against an ocean liner, Sir Francis soon had her out in deep waters, beyond Henry's reach.

'Then they flighted together. Wheeling sharply, Henrietta would try to escape the drake's attention. Several times, that day, she attempted this manoeuvre but the drake always had the upper hand. Then night fell. Confronting Henry now was *its* menaces as well as those of Sir Francis, whom he thought treacherous.

'Henry said the evening star winked into life as he stood alone and bereft in the twilight. The moon, rising and lying just above the land, cast a wan light over the pond and sent spiky shadows streaking. Then he saw Henrietta's whiteness loft into the night sky, her silhouette stark and black against the moon, Sir Francis, her fussy escort, in close attendance.

'Henry heard their wings whapping as they winged towards a copse. Then he saw the flashes from the shotguns, heard the gunshots booming then echoing through the woods. He feared the worst on hearing those dreadful reports. Birds flighting in confusion filled the sky and he couldn't pick out Henrietta, but he knew the poachers must have thought her whiteness a splendid target.

'The sound of frantically-beating wings receded into the distance as birds struck out for safer feeding grounds. Just as suddenly as the turmoil began, Henry felt the night go still. The fusillade had stunned his hearing and he didn't hear Henrietta's laboured approach or see her injured, pained body in flight.

'The first indications he had that she was nearing was an audible rush of air. Then the feather-light kiss of her dead body, violated by poacher's lead, glanced against his face as it whizzed past his head, to strike the ground at his feet with a sickening whump. When he looked, Henrietta was lying there, dead.

'The snapping of briar and thorn brought him to his senses. Bulky figures pushed through the hedge, their game bags stuffed with poacher's fare. The poachers had him stand in their midst. Henry was shell-shocked and a source of amusement to them. He said a voice, gruff and countrified, uttered mind-changing words that, on reflection, whetted his appetite for Henrietta. The poachers asked him if his preference was for duck cooked crispy or sautéed and served with noodles.'

'The poachers were a rough, unscrupulous, shotgun-festooned bunch who sold the wild ducks to Chinese restaurants, the owners preferring them to our domestic breeds. Knowing Henry, and that he was a soft touch, they bundled him into their Land Rover and drove him into town to a Chinese restaurant.

'In my opinion, Henry is a slate short of a roof...'

'With the under-felt in disrepair, too, if you were to ask me,' Dotty butted in while dragging a crust over her plate.

'Exactly. The poachers took Henry into the restaurant and forced him to drink strong liquor. Henry said he wasn't used to alcohol and that they kept him there for nearly two hours, drinking copiously.

Then the Chinese chef pushed a "hostess trolley" from the kitchen into the restaurant. 'He had caressed Henrietta's plucked, gutted and lead-pellet-shattered carcass with fine oils. Then he had rubbed in oriental spices until her skin relaxed and assumed the reddish hue that guaranteed a succulent finish. Then he had cooked her to the poachers' suggestions, crispy, on his spit.

'The Chinese are famous for duck cuisine and Henry said Henrietta looked so tempting the way the chef presented her on the sizzling platter, her hissing juices releasing final, aromatic reminders of her wildness. The chef carved her up and served her to Henry and the poachers with pancakes and plum sauce...'

'Oh, dearie me... Poor man. I could never eat an animal or bird that I'd known,' Dotty erupted.

'He said that he was giddy with alcohol and had tucked in, enjoying the feast. Only duck bones remained when the poachers, drunk and boisterous by this time, rose from their seats and left the restaurant. That's when poor Henry's problems began.'

'Acting like an eejit, do you mean? Was he that drunk?' Dotty asked, concern edging her voice.

'He said he was tiddly, but went doolally when the restaurant manager presented him with the bill.'

'I see,' Dotty said. 'The poachers left without paying the bill. It would have been quite large and Henry objected to paying it all himself.'

'No, the manager presented him with Henrietta's bill, still attached to the head!'

Dotty began to stare unblinkingly over her spectacles at Riley. 'Unfeckin'believable, Riley! Poor, poor man,' she said and grimaced.

Riley was once again pleased with his delivery of a fanciful fabrication and looked up from his plate. 'I thought it far-fetched, too,' he said, but continued in the same vein. 'When he saw the bill he dashed past the manager, entered the kitchen, picked up a cleaver, slashed the end off his nose and threw it into the chip fryer. That's what disfigures him so horribly. That's why he came to see me. I just hope he doesn't do anything so silly when I invoice him!'

Chapter 12

Most motorcycle clubs of "Unlanced Boils" ilk boast of their abilities to outwit cops; they also break most laws, thinking it makes them hard. Ballyboil cops had never attempted to tackle the "Unlanced Boils" as a gang, seeing it as too much hassle, offering only bruises, pain and little reward for waging war against this club of badass bikers.

When the Irish Fusiliers abandoned their base on the outskirts of Ballyboil, they left behind many serviceable Nissan huts. Some now house blacksmiths' shops, agricultural engineering firms and mushroom production units.

The clubhouse, of the not-to-be-meddled-with "Unlanced Boils" Motorcycle Club stands alone on the old base. Scrounged or stolen armchairs, settees and empty upturned fifty-gallon oil drums, serve as club furniture. The hut reeks like a garage when it's not in use; the aromas of toked cannabis and skunk grass are raging when they hold their meetings.

Motorbikes parts hang from the roof on hooks, décor a la biker. Festooning the walls are articles stolen from other, weaker, bike clubs. They include club-name patches, ripped from leathers, a particular insult to the dispossessed biker, but trophies and testimonials to the "Unlanced Boils" daring deeds.

The hut doubled as a shebeen, an illicit drinking den, where the bikers put away pots of poteen in safety, when it's available. Hill-dwellers, often the target of Customs Officers who scour these hilly areas for any telltale signs, distil the potent brew in places where winds blow upwards the telltale smell of a production.

These efforts have little impact on the supply lines. Poteen is rarely unavailable. Not all drinkers can handle its strength, sending some fighting crazy, which was another reason why cops had no stomach for messing with the "Unlanced Boils".

On the Monday evening following President Seth Mulligan's arrest, the thirty or so bikers in attendance in the clubhouse were in an in-between mood: fired up with strong alcohol, but mellowed-out on toked skunk grass. The bikers were about to discuss Doctor Dernehen's examination of Seth in the police cell, the subsequent dropping of the drug and assault-on-police charges, because Doctor Dernehen hadn't substantiated them, and Seth's release from the RUC station.

Seth Mulligan, sitting back with his feet up on an old, leather-covered recliner, called the meeting to order and opened it with the words, 'Brethren,

Doctor Riley Dernehen is a true friend of bikers. I think we ought to do something for the man.'

'I don't know the man,' Roddy O'Dowd, their resident horticulturist and grower of the skunk grass now blueing the air, said. 'But I suppose he'll be handy treating the "whiteys" you guys suffer toking my good gear.'

The good-natured banter over the quality of Roddy's grass settled down. Joe Reardon, Sergeant-at-Arms and security-adviser to the club said, 'I know him. I see him most days at work.'

'Get on with yer. You see him there?' Seth asked.

'I'm a trolley pusher at the hospital. I push trolleys all day,' Joe said, 'and I see him leaving the operating theatre often when I'm pushing a trolley.'

'What's the "craic" with him?' Seth asked.

'He's a well-got doctor, renowned for his plastic surgery work. Not a sliver of gossip of any indiscretions at all that I'm aware of. There again, though, I'm only a trolley pusher. I wouldn't be told of any scandalous goings-on involving a doctor. I hear plenty about the nurses and the cleaning staff, but I don't go around pushing my nose in and asking. I'm only there to push a trolley all day for my pay.'

'He's a bit short in the arse,' Seth replied, holding a hand out about five-foot six inches from the floor, 'when I got my eyes focused at the cop shop, he looked a decent wee guy right enough. I'm sure we'll all find that to be true. I can't say the same for that big skinny, beer-gutted twat of a sergeant.'

'When I'm not pushing trolleys on night shift,' Joe said, 'I'm knobbing a wee honey of a nurse that lives in the nurses' home. To be sure, I've seen the sergeant floating about and in and out of there of a night. He has no preferred day. Sometimes he's in his uniform and obviously on duty.'

'Some nights he's there into the early hours. Sometimes he comes in the police car. Other times he comes in his own. He always sticks to the shadows after parking up. You can tell the pig's rolling gait anywhere. He's knobbing one of the sisters that lives there, a Mavis O'Rourke.'

'I know her,' Roddy O'Dowd said. 'She likes a toke. Giggles like fock when she's high on it, does Mavis, but she likes the old knob better. Giggled on the end of mine many a time, has Mavis.'

'You've been knobbing there?' Seth asked.

'You bet. I've made a slide for her on many a cold winter's night, I have. Couldn't get enough of me old knob, could Mavis. I first met her at a disco in the town a while back.'

'Don't you have a dose of the pox?' Seth asked, sounding scandalised, and held up two fingers as a cross, as if to ward off a visitation.

'I got that from a dirty minger a month back. It was after the last time I'd been with Mavis. I can't get it sorted out until I see the quack. You know how long it takes to see one in these parts. There's no Pox Clinic at the hospital that

I could use,' Roddy said.

'So you've got an untreated dose of the pox. Mavis O'Rourke likes the old knob. That evil bastard Liptrott is knobbing her. Does this not seem a good opportunity to deliver him some pain, get some of our club's pus streaming with attendant fishhooks from his old bobby's helmet?' Seth asked, brightly.

'But that's not the only reason why we ought to consider payback,' upped Joe. 'Word going around the hospital says that later on Saturday night he also did Doctor Dernehen for going through a red light.'

'That bastard loves his red lights,' Seth said. 'And you should to have seen his face when he thought he had me for drugs. Brighter and redder than a baboon's arse it was and his lips were folding back like one of those grinning, Typhoo chimps at a tea party.'

'Word has it that Doctor Dernehen is no longer on the police-surgeon's roster,' Joe said.

'Okay, Roddy, what do you say about sniffing around knob-mad Mavis O'Rourke and leaving the calling card for the sergeant?'

'I'd be pleased to do the sergeant that favour.'

'Okay then, go for it. Next Sunday, when we go out for a bike ride, we'll go around Doctor Dernehen's place and invite him to join our motorcycle club. He'll make a good boil. We'll ask him if he'll become bikers' surgeon. If he needs a little coaxing, we'll tell him we'll get someone to go witness for him at his court case and try to get him off, not guilty. That'll prove we have good intentions towards him.'

'What'll he do for a bike?' Roddy asked.

'Ach, to be sure I never thought of that. Maybe he'll have to content himself with a ride on my trike. Once he gets his arse onto my *man's* machine, though, I'll have him hooked. He won't be able to raise a cheek when he sees my backseats,' Seth said, laughing. Casting his eyes over the brethren, he asked, 'Do we all say aye?'

'Aye.'

'Well let's get on to other business.'

Chapter 13

Five days after the operation, Ophelia O'Rooney left hospital slowly, pushing a wheeled Zimmer frame, to begin her recuperation back in England.

The following Friday morning, Dotty was removing some dead plants from flowerbeds when she heard a Post Office van on its parcel-delivery round rattling into the Hall grounds. She turned on hearing Seamus O'Reilly, the district postie, tooting his usual welcome on the van's horn.

'Special delivery for you, missis,' Seamus called. 'The roads are bumpy around here to be sure and I think both my deliveries are looking a bit funny. Food and water is slopping with their droppings in the bottom of the cage, it is.'

'What in heaven's name have you got for us now, Seamus?' Dotty chaffed.

'To be sure, is it not a pair of parrots in a rare, big cage, missis? I'll have to give you a hand into the Hall with it.'

As Seamus opened wide the rear doors of the van, Dotty said, 'To be sure, they do look a trifle travelsick and doleful. I don't know why they're here, but look at them. I don't think they could ever have belonged to a pirate.'

Dotty spotted an envelope Sellotaped to the side of the cage. 'Ah, we might know the answer once we've opened this,' she said, and removed the envelope. With the letter unfolded and open in her hands she said, 'Their names are Milly and Molly, they're African Greys. It looks like an Ophelia O'Rooney sent them.'

'They look alike to me, missis, you're going to find it hard to tell them apart,' Seamus said.

Dotty read on:

Dear Doctor,

I have made a wonderful recovery from the operation. The Zimmer frame, I discarded yesterday. I can walk liquidly and my hips gyrate without pain. I also believe my thighs are passing one another a little closer together when I walk.

It seems the tightening and reconstruction job has been a success and, like my winter kale, I can expect to be rooting soon.

I am sending you the gift of two valuable, extraordinary and very intelligent parrots. They have lived with me for twenty years, in a corner of my working bedroom, and can reliably spot a small prick at twenty paces. My husband-to-be, Oliver, sneezes continually in their presence and can't abide them in the house. I am sure they will find a very good home in yours.

Please be kind to them and thank you again.

Ophelia.

'This other letter is for Doctor Dernehen, from the courts,' Seamus said and looked on sympathetically as he handed it over.

'He's expecting it,' Dotty said, smiling weakly. 'He's had an unpleasant encounter with that scoundrel, Sergeant Liptrott.'

'Not a nice man at all at all,' Seamus agreed.

'Riley has to appear in front of Ballyboil magistrates on Monday morning, at ten o'clock, if he doesn't want to plead guilty by letter,' Dotty read aloud, 'and they haven't given him much notice.'

'Get him a good lawyer. One that's good at tripping them up. 'Tis said that some of them cops are as daft as a brush,' Seamus advised.

Between them, they negotiated the cage into the hallway and onto a table.

'You know,' Seamus said, 'the Liptrott family be a funny lot to be sure.'

'You're telling me!'

'The grandfather, old Darius Liptrott, he was a police sergeant in the days of the "Old Barneys" and a mean feckin' man. Rumour had it at the time he was responsible for the first act of bestiality that would have ever been seen in these parts, but wasn't.'

'Away with you. Nothing the likes of that ever happened around here.'

''Tis true, but it never happened,' Seamus said, 'but if Darius had his way, it would have. A circus was in town. It came the same time every year from over the border. Many strange acts it had, I can tell you. The kids, though, liked the chimps, and the cleverest one, the main attraction, had come into season and was rampaging around its cage screaming for a mate.'

'Darius was walking around the circus one Saturday, so the story goes, when he saw this chimp, in its cage, doing back-flips and scratching its arse. He stopped for a gander, thinking it was a part of the act. The circus owner came along and stood with Darius. "Needs a mate to do the business otherwise it'll not calm and the show cannot go on," he told Darius, "There are no males with us this year and I'll have to wait until the show goes back to Dublin".'

'I've seen the dirty beasts doing all sorts of despicable things at Belfast zoo. Wouldn't go there again,' Dotty said, shuddering.

'Well, Darius wasn't adverse to making a shilling or two on the side and suggested using the local drunk, O'Hooligan, him sleeping off a huge hangover down at the jail.'

'O glory be! I don't believe it,' Dotty said, shaking her head slightly.

'Well it came to nothing anyway. When they got O'Hooligan out of his slumbers and put the question to him, he refused and made a great deal of fuss.'

'Not enough money for drink for him to blot out the memory of the act, I suppose.' Dotty said, screwing her face up.

'No, nothing the likes of that.'

'What then?'

'O'Hooligan wanted any offspring brought up good Catholics.'

Dotty erupted. 'You'd better watch out. You're becoming funnier than Riley with his unseemly tales.'

Seamus tittered, lurched into the van and drove off.

*

On his way home that afternoon, Riley became suspicious that a police car was tailing the Jag. He first saw it as he left the hospital, keeping several vehicles behind him, but then it turned off bypass.

A mile further along the bypass, he saw a trike in his rear-view mirror. Behind the trike was a line of bearded, fearsome-faced bikers, riding Harley Davidsons and other impressive motorbikes. The procession kept pace with him and then drew alongside.

Riley kept glancing out the side window at the bikers, wondering what their interest was in him. The trike rider wore goggles but no headgear, which enabled him to identify Seth Mulligan behind the wheel. The remainder were unidentifiable in their wraparound dark-visored helmets and black leathers. Seth Mulligan eased the trike back from the front of the pack to come alongside him and gave him the thumbs-up sign. That, too, had been a bit of a worry.

As each biker came level with him, they nodded in his direction. In that manner, they escorted him along the bypass, before roaring off at high speed on nearing the next roundabout.

At the roundabout, he saw that the leading bikers were using their machines to block the traffic approaching from the right. This procedure, adopted by many motorbike clubs out for a run, allowed their muckers quick and safe passage. Their practice, this time, also impeded the progress of a police car driven by a scowling Sergeant Liptrott. He was pounding his hands on the steering wheel of the car, his enraged look saying all: he wouldn't have allowed Riley unimpeded progress.

Riley breathed a sigh of relief when he pulled up at the front door of the Hall, glad at not having had any more dealings with the sergeant. A very busy NHS-dedicated day at the hospital had drained him. He had wondered if he was beginning to feel his age, if the examining of cauliflower ears and facial moles had really been that taxing.

True, he had missed Mavis's company and had walked awkwardly most of the day, tugging at his stiffness. He had thought her mean-spirited, though, when she chastised him, during the brief moment they had spent time together, for not being available on the previous Saturday night.

All that evening, Riley had sat in the sitting-room, in Dotty's company, in a state of abject misery, pretending to be engrossed in articles in the Belfast telegraph and in some medical journals. Often he had thought of Mavis. Each time he conjured up images of being with her in her nurses' home apartment he experienced arousal.

It concerned him that Dotty might notice any one of the spate of bulges affecting his trousers, or his sly looks up at the wall clock. Casually, he had glanced Dotty's way as she read a book and saw her flick her tongue over her lips, obviously desperate for a brandy.

As he had tried to explain to Mavis, Dotty, unaccountably, had not taken a drink during dinner on Saturday. When she poured a small one later that evening, she had sipped at it slowly and remained awake and alert until they had gone to bed.

His prayers that she might pour herself a large brandy take a good slug of it, then another and another and for sleep to come quickly, had gone unanswered. No excuse to escape the Hall had arisen.

As midnight approached, it aggrieved him that the sergeant's ugly frame might be crushing and soiling the sheets on his side of Mavis' bed. These worries convinced him that he'd have to set his mind to creating some other, unarguable reasons for leaving the Hall.

*

Cedric was sprawled on the top step at the entrance to the hallway when Riley pulled-up. He whistled for him to come and greet him. Cedric had eyed him warily during recent days, but he stretched himself then obediently loped sideways down the steps to him, slavers flying from his jaws, like holy water splashing at a double exorcism. Riley ruffled his ears playfully and encouraged him to walk by his side back up the steps.

Dotty appeared at the door, hands on hips, in an aggressive pose, her face screwed up, showing more vexation than usual. Shrilling loudly, she fired the question in his direction, 'Ophelia O'Rooney, how do you know this woman, Riley? And what, bayjasus, is a tightening operation?' She looked at him squarely, expecting an instant and believable answer.

Riley groaned. What in heaven's name was affecting the woman now?

'Ach, Ophelia O'Rooney,' he said, hand to brow, acting a little. He made the show of recalling, just for Dotty's benefit. 'I operated on her more than a week ago. Not a major reconstruction job, I recall, more of a tightening of the wing nut on her artificial hip which had loosened off.' It was an offhand response, he knew. He couldn't discuss his real patients with Dotty and he walked quickly past her towards the coat cupboard, coat in hand, saying, 'Why do you ask?'

'She has sent you a couple of gifts. Extras for your services, I believe,' she said, eyeing him as he turned to walk back towards her. 'And what may I ask is a working bedroom?'

The question flummoxed Riley for a moment. Unable to think up an instant answer, he scratched his head. He saw the fraying ends of Dotty's gardening pinafore. It gave him an idea.

'I'm sure Ophelia O'Rooney said she was a seamstress working from home...'

Riley noticed Dotty's hair. She had been into town and had had it washed and set. He thought he ought to mention how nice it looked, but he'd do that later if the opportunity arose.

'And gifts you say? She paid me well for my work. She needn't have sent gifts.' He didn't notice the cage until he saw Dotty pointing towards it.

'Well, she must have been pleased with your work for she has sent you a pair of African Grey parrots. They're pretty birds and quite suited to one another, I'm sure. They've been very quiet, eyeing me up and down mostly. I think they're concerned about the size of Cedric. They keep turning their backs to him, poor dog. I don't know if they can talk, but I believe we can catch a disease from them, psitta... I could never pronounce the word. It's some sort of bird plague.'

'Psittacosis is the word you're looking for. It is a contagious, viral disease of birds such as parrots, parakeets and chickens. Ducks and pigeons can contract it too. It is communicable to humans, with symptoms of fever, headache and nausea, but it is hardly serious,' he said.

'I recall now, but psittacosis is such a funny-sounding word.'

'Aye, the p is silent as in bath.'

'But there is no p in bath, Riley.'

'It is only a joke,' Riley groaned. 'But my word, the cage is big enough,' he said, walking towards it. It sat safely on a hallway table, in front of the small effigy of the Virgin Mary and Child hanging on the wall.

The parrots were just doing what parrots do when he looked in on them. Their heads bobbed up and down, viewing him inquisitively. Each trained one eye on him, treating him cagily, circling on its perch and continually changed its position.

He was having a playful poke at the side of one's head with his finger when Dotty said, 'Ophelia O'Rooney, I remember an Ophelia O'Rooney. An uncommon name, Ophelia, don't you think?'

'Uncommon woman, as I recall.'

'I was at convent school with a girl of that name. She was an unusual type of person. She was from Dublin, a trollop and a bit of a flirt. Destined for trouble, we girls always thought. She was of mixed race, with quite flared nostrils. We used to look up them for a laugh. Thought we could see into the top of her head.

'She got herself in trouble and blamed one of the priests teaching us. I was sure he was the dirty swine who did the awful deed. Always rubbing against us and trying to see down the tops of our gymslips. Always leering at us, he was. Mammy converted to Catholicism, as you know, and she said never to trust any of the narrow-eyed cassock-lifters.

'I was passing through the convent chapel to the confessionary when I heard from the sacristy the Bishop of Dublin confronting the priest over the allegations. "I beseech you in the bowels of Christ, Holy Father," the priest wailed, "to think it possible you may be mistaken. The dusky she-devil knocked me to the ground... made me hard... rode me like a horse... flames shooting from her nostrils like bolts of lightning fired by the devil himself. She pulled my cassock up over my head so I couldn't see the face of the demon doing it to me. She didn't get off me until she sucked me dry of all the Lord's sacred juices. Forgive me, Holy Father," he was bleating.

'I thought it was an unlikely story. The Bishop, though, he bought the swine's tale. They always do from one of their own. Kept everything quiet, they did, and sent the brute to one of the islands to cool off his tiddleypush in the sea, I think.'

'From the tone of the letter, it seems likely she's the woman I operated on. Now it seems she's settling down to a sedentary lifestyle.'

'She's been a seamstress all these years?'

'A very good and professional one with a nice property in the Home Counties, I believe.'

'Her note says the birds can spot a small prick at twenty paces.'

'There you are then. Where else but in a seamstresses workshop would you experience a small prick these days?'

'Doctor's su...'

'I know, I know, but that's only a part of our job. To a seamstress, it's painful. The parrots probably heard a curse or two when a sharp needle pierced a finger. They'd remember and repeat them,' Riley said. They invented thimbles to avert such eventualities, but they don't remove them all.

'I wonder how the parrots got over here, then.'

'They probably flew in.'

'But they were in the cage, Riley.'

'I meant by airmail, Dotty. Probably Aer Lingus freight.'

'I bought some parrot feed at the pet shop in Ballyboil and had my hair done while I was in town.'

'It's very nice, Dotty.'

'The parrot feed is full of nuts,' she chided.

'I can see there are many different types of nuts. I meant your hair looks very nice.'

'It wasn't all that expensive.'

'It looks too nice not to have cost you dear, Dotty.'

'No, Riley, the parrot feed was inexpensive.'

Riley gave up the conversation; the cook was ringing the gong, which usually meant they weren't in the dining-room for the serving of dinner.

On their way into the dining-room, Dotty pulled a face. Riley's off-hand remarks were continuing and becoming increasingly hurtful.

Riley had eaten half of his entrée of smoked salmon when he heard a whistle. It seemed to originate in the hallway, was long, warbling, and identical to the one he used to encourage Cedric to greet him on his return home that evening.

Cedric, faithful to his master's command, loped into the dining-room. He ought to have known better; the dining-room was out of bounds to him while the Dernehen's ate. Drooling, slavering, panting jaws made up a good part of a St Bernard's head. Both Riley and Dotty found the sight of Cedric watching them while they ate, quite off-putting.

'Daft dog. Out, out, out!' Riley shouted. Cedric slithered to a stop on the wooden floor, looked at them with gloomy eyes, threw his body around, legs slithering, and made a wobbling retreat.

'Whatever possesses him? The dog's not been the same since you dosed him with castor oil,' Dotty said crossly.

'I heard a whistle, didn't you?' Riley replied, irately.

The phone rang. Riley was sitting closer to the door; he pushed his chair back to go and answer it. The parrots were sharing a perch, their heads cocked to one side, each with an eye trained on him, watching him enter the hallway and pick up the handset. The ringing stopped, the earpiece just burring as it neared his ear. Back in his chair, he said, 'Strange, there was no one on the other end.'

The phone rang again as Riley was pouring plum sauce over his roast breast of duck. Dotty pushed her chair back and looked at him. Thoughts of a finagling woman on the phone looking for him were foremost. 'I will get it this time!' she snapped.

She put her cutlery down with a bang and frumpishly squeaked her slippered feet across the floor towards the offending ringing. The parrots watched her pick up the handset then turned around on the perch, billing their beaks together. The ringing stopped. Before she could utter 'Yes,' into the mouthpiece, she heard the burring in her ear. She looked at the parrots perched and watching her over their shoulders. Nothing has been quite the same since your delivery, either, she mused.

Chapter 14

Standing shivering and week at the knees in Martin Muldoony's kitchen, on the night that he had stupidly murdered him, Mickey saw Sean's eyes suddenly narrow. Shock and fear was showing in his, he was sure, for he couldn't stop them darting insanely to all parts of the kitchen. His mouth was opening and closing, taking in air in quick gulps, goldfish-like. His lips were twisting, his body wilting, his anus slackening, fluttering, unable to hold in a succession of short, sharp farts.

'Yeh never told me it was him,' he spluttered, but. Yeh just said it was a captured Proddy, so yeh did.'

Sean pushed past Mickey and sprinted the short distance along the passageway to the room. Mickey followed. His heart was leaping. Was Sean wrong? Was he only setting him up again? Was this a further test? But if Sean wasn't testing him further, what would he do? He'd have to make a getaway, not hang around here, nowhere near Belfast…where could he go and be safe? Hanging around now, assured his death! Pronto!

Martin was sitting in the chair, the black bag as askew as his head with dribbles of saliva dampening the front. Sean grabbed Martin's head, untied and pulled off the black bag. Mickey gasped. It *was* Martin. His eyes were lifeless and his tongue was hanging from the corner of his mouth, already turning blue.

Mickey acted quickly. Stepping closer, he landed a savage kick behind Sean's knee. Sean crumbled. Turning towards Mickey as he fell, his legs splayed wide. Mickey kicked him between them, bang on his testicles.

Sean cursed, not knowing which injury to comfort first.

Mickey grabbed him by the neck and rammed his face against the stub-ended wooden arm of Martin's chair, the force of the contact breaking Sean's nose, knocking him groggy. Then with both hands around Sean's throat, Mickey rammed his head back against a wall. Frenziedly, he repeated the battering.

Sean was out cold, maybe dead, too. Mickey didn't care, wasn't waiting to find out. He turned towards the door and ran. Heavy with the donkey jackets it might have been, but with fear gripping him, he pulled it open with a bang. Throwing open the kitchen door, he grabbed at a clean jacket from a hook and lifted it onto his shoulders. Across the yard, he raced his heart pumping hard.

At the gate out into the street, his hand landed on the makeshift latch. He lifted it and pulled the door towards him. Then something landed on each shoulder, something cold pressed against his neck. 'Bayjasus,' he cried, shuddering and gasping. Then he noticed the something cold was reeking with bad breath. The greyhound was saying its goodbyes. 'Fock, that could have been a barrel of cold steel,' he said quietly and threw the dog's paws from his back.

Mickey pulled open the yard door and ran into the drizzly night. For a few paces, the greyhound skipped alongside him, sniffing at his hand with its cold nose. Looking for more grub, its warm tongue licked at Martin's slavers and Sean's blood congealing on his fingers.

In Fahey Street, and walking fast, he considered his next move. Getting out of Belfast and soon was seriously important; otherwise, both his and Martin's temperatures would be cooling at a similar rate. The street was quiet, but the greyhound, seeing a flash of ginger that might just be a cat slinking from an alleyway onto the opposite pavement, raced across the wet road after it, dodging traffic, until a bus knocked it over like a skittle.

Mickey recognised the danger in going to his bedsit to collect any belongings. Seeking shelter and comfort in a chapel, with a priest for company and him saying he should give himself up to the RUC, wasn't for him. Trying to catch a plane or a ferry to the mainland or to anywhere on earth occurred to him. Even if he managed to get to a port or an airport, he was sure the Brigade would have sympathisers working in these places and on the lookout for him. Others would be watching the ports and airports on the other side of the Irish Sea. He would have to change radically his appearance to get away.

Nearing a bus station, he stopped to regain his breath. He knew the terminal housed a row of public phones. He walked smartly and calmly in, his breathing rate settling a bit. The few people sheltering from the drizzle or waiting for buses paid no attention to him. He picked up the handset in an out-of-the-way booth, took a handful of change from his jeans and dialled his sister Mavis' number in the town of Ballyboil. There was no answer.

He set off walking towards the west. When he reached the western edge of Belfast he took to the fields, ditches and woods giving him cover.

He'd get to his sister somehow, no matter how long it took him.

*

In the lounge, Tracy's eyes were tiring and the clacking of her knitting needles slowing. A political programme started on the television, just about the time she heard a door banging and somebody leaving in a hurry. 'Shite,' she said aloud and checked the time on the wall clock. 'Quarter to twelve already! It sounds as if those boys have finished with their silly caper and they've frightened the life out of the new recruit, it does. Eejit for getting involved.'

She pushed herself out of the armchair and bustled into the kitchen. 'Smell of shite in here,' she bawled, throwing her nose upwards. She heard a loud groan and the cry of 'Bayjasus,' coming from the room along the passageway. She felt concerned enough to take a quick look.

She padded her slippered feet to the room and pushed open the door. 'Suffering Christ! What's been going on in here?' she exploded. Sean was wobbling and lurching and hadn't yet regained control of his balance. He tried to stand upright, pawing his way up a wall. Erect, he spun around, faced Martin in the chair and then reached out for a chair arm. He grabbed hold, held on, steadied himself, then began a tentative exploration of his broken nose and bloodied face.

Tracy took another two paces into the room. Next to Sean, she saw Martin sitting in the chair, his head lolling, dead! 'What have yeh done to my Martin,' she yelled hysterically.

'Sorry, Tracy. He's dead. The test backfired. That eejit, O'Rourke, he strangled him. Instead, o' performing the test with the blanks, he thought he'd be clever. Did his own thing, he did. What a mess. We'll be after wiping him out for this,' Sean said, a little more erect now and dabbing blood from his face with a handkerchief.

Tracy sniffed. Her eyes were watery, tears trickled down her cheeks. She took a handkerchief from her pinafore pocket, wiped her eyes and took a stride closer to Martin, took hold of his chin and pushed his head back. 'Are yeh sure he's dead?' she asked Sean, her throat tightening, anguish straining her voice.

'He's going blue already.'

'Martin wouldn't have liked the thought o' that,' she struggled to say.

'There's no pulse.'

'Yeh great eejit, Martin,' she said up to his face, tears streaming down hers. 'Ah knew nothing good would come of this daft carry-on.'

'It was a gigantic balls-up. Perhaps the greatest balls-up ever,' Sean said. 'I can't see any members of the brigade wanting what happened here tae get out. The laughing stock of the entire terrorist world, so we'd be. Fred Carno's Army we'd be called. Proddies would have a field day and say we were so much shite, so they would.'

'Yeh mean we can't report this tae the cops?'

'That's the last thing Martin would want.'

'What are ye going tae dae about it, then?'

'When a member of the brigade died accidentally in the past, shot his self by accident, those sort o' things, Martin and I dumped the body so it was easily found. Then we put it around that it was a successful Proddy hit job. That always got the brigade members' paddy up. Always a great bit o' retaliation followed. One or two Proddy paramilitaries croaked because of it. We always took out more men than we lost.'

'So that's it then. All I've to look forward to now is being asked to identify a stinking, bloated corpse some day, a delayed funeral while they bastards at the coroner's office cut him up, and the rest o' my life on ma ain.'

'The brigade will look after you.'

'I think I've had enough o' brigades. Come on. I'll wet a pot o' tea. I'll need a wee nip o' the cratur to settle me after this.'

On the way to the kitchen, Tracy pushed opened the back door. 'I just want to see if the dog's alright,' she said.

The door from the yard to the street was swinging open, as was the door to the dog run. 'Bayjasus, the dog's got out,' she erupted and shuffled quickly towards the yard door, from where she looked out into the street. 'There's a cop car stopped in front of a bus along the street a bit,' she said to Sean, as he approached slowly and joined her. 'And that looks suspiciously like the body of a dog that the cop's just put into a black bag and is now dumping in the car boot.'

'Bayjasus, so it is. What run it down has severed its head. Two different bits they've stuck in the bag,' Sean said, peering around her now.

'I'll have to go out after and mop up any splattered guts,' Tracy said, weepily.

'Those noisy seagull shitehawks will have cleaned up the lot by morning, Tracy.'

'That's something else that this O'Rourke has to pay for. Martin was a pig of a man. Even though I loved him, I loved that dog more.'

'He'll be well on his way out of town by now, for sure. He'll be running scared. He'll have to watch his back wherever he goes, but we'll get him.'

'Any ideas?' Tracy asked her mind already on revenge of her own doing.

'I'll let you know what I find out. I'm in command now, brigade leader. I'm away to get a van, a couple of the bhoys and get Martin's body dumped.'

*

It had taken two weeks hard, cross-country slog for Mickey to reach the hillside overlooking Ballyboil Hospital and its adjacent nurses' home. During the two days and nights hidden there beneath bracken, observing, he was getting hungrier and smellier; his clothing was sodden and he was cold, looking like a tramp with the two weeks growth on his face. He needed a hot bath, some dry gear. Hot food had not passed his lips on the entire trek. Plenty of raw turnips, spuds and eggs stolen at the dead of night from farmers' coops had. Mavis was a great cook. She would soon have his belly filled with some hot scran, tucked up in bed, warm.

He had made out the outline of the hospital, its grounds and had worked out which was Mavis' address at the nursing home from her visits there.

He saw he could reach the home using tree cover, without venturing onto any roads. He reckoned if the Hillshanks Brigade knew of his sister's whereabouts, they would have members, sitting up in lay-bys, patrolling all roads, just waiting for him to appear. His hopes had surged on seeing nothing suspicious.

When it was dark, he would make his way down the hillside and make for the nursing home. He had waited long enough.

Chapter 15

On Saturday morning, just after awakening, Riley's thoughts turned to the tricky hours ahead, particularly those between dinner and bedtime. If events were unchanged this Saturday evening, he might not escape the Hall for a dalliance with Mavis. He hadn't regretted quitting the police-surgeon roster, he was just distressed at his inability to find another way to replace innocently the uses he made of it.

After breakfast, he did nothing but laze on the chaise-longue, reading the daily paper. As lunchtime approached, his mind still hadn't come up with a feasible escape plan. Nothing at all had germinated; nothing as good as the unfortunate Ryan O'Toole's injury had been.

At midday, the cook served up a toasty with a side salad. The toasty eaten, Riley was mopping up the remains of the coleslaw from his plate when the hallway phone began to ring. Cottoning on to the tricks the parrots were playing on them soon after their arrival, both he and Dotty were wary for more avian hoaxes.

Both of them heard the phone, but Dotty was first on her feet, collecting Riley's plate and carrying it with hers towards the hall. It could have been the parrots' mimicking or any of Dotty's friends on the other end of the line and Riley thought little of it.

The phone stopped ringing and almost at once, Dotty poked her head around the door and said, 'There's some woman calling herself Mavis on the phone for you. I've not heard you mention her before, but by the sounds of her she's from the hospital.'

Riley leapt from his chair. He was shocked. Mavis should have known better than to call him at home.

'Who is she?' Dotty asked pointedly, looking at him piercingly over her spectacles. He stretched out a hand and took the handset from her.

'It must be Sister O'Rourke. Perhaps there's an emergency,' he told her, hoping that would satisfy her curiosity, 'but the duty doctor should pass on such messages.'

'Yes, sister,' he said authoritatively into the mouthpiece as Dotty walked sluggishly towards the kitchen, an ear cocked.

'Can I talk freely, Riley?' Mavis asked quickly.

'You can, but quickly. I've told you not to call me here,' he hissed quietly behind his hand into the mouthpiece.

'A personal emergency has come up.'

'How can I help?'

'My brother is here. He has walked all the way from Belfast. He's been on his way, hiding up in woods, for two weeks.'

'So?'

'He's in trouble.'

'So, how can I help?'

'There's a Republican brigade that wants him dead. He's told me he's murdered their leader. It was a terrible mistake. I've told him you might change his appearance so he can live here undetected or give him time to safely flee the country.' Riley heard the concern in her voice.

He also felt his temperature and pulse rising quickly and his breathing becoming shallow. He considered paramilitaries, from either side of the divide, odious characters. Nothing had ever prompted him to aid these people. The implications in Mavis' request made him stutter and he said, 'Er... er, I'm thinking sister, er... er I think I'd better pay the patient a visit now, before anyone messes the case up any further. I'll be at my office in about half an hour, have the case notes there ready for me to read.'

He put the handset down. The shock of Mavis' request hit him and he grabbed the phone table to steady himself. He needed to get to her, to hear her story, to ensure that she did nothing silly, like implicating herself in her brother's crime.

The parrots eyed him through the bars of their cage; each held a nut in their claws, ready to deliver it to their beaks for cracking. He was thinking he knew what cracked nuts must feel like when Dotty reappeared and asked in a rising voice, 'What was that all about?'

He walked away from her quickly, picked up the car keys from a hallway table and headed towards the front door. He took the steps down two at a time, his mind in turmoil. He reached the car. Fussing over the key selection gave him time to think. If bullshit baffles brains, now is the time to test the theory, he thought.

He looked up the stairs towards Dotty, standing on the top step, her arms folded across her chest, her jaw slightly dropped. He said, 'Sister O'Rourke passed on a message from that old fool, Doctor O'Brodie. Apparently, he operated on a patient this morning and now finds he can't close the wound, stitch his patient up. He wants me to transfer muscle from elsewhere and without the patient's knowledge, which will enable him to close the hiatus.

'I wouldn't do anything like that, of course, but I must give him the benefit of my experience. It's the least I can do. If I don't, they'll sue him and the hospital to hell and back. I can't let the hospital get that sort of publicity. It might not have private patients so keen to seek me out, either. I also feel duty bound to help a colleague. Correcting O'Brodie's faux pas could be a lengthy procedure. Don't expect me back until late tonight.'

Riley had no intention whatsoever of helping Mavis' brother. The last sentence he spoke to Dotty, however, reminded him that whatever the outcome of his meeting with Mavis, he had at least created another opportunity to bed her.

Riley drove off and Dotty walked back into the Hall. Tripping past the parrots on the way to the sitting-room, they seemed to eye her with a sympathetic mien, their heads together, touching lovingly. She was downcast assessing the strangeness of Riley's hasty departure: why had he not changed out of the dressing gown and pyjamas he had loafed around in all morning.

She heard the croaky strains of, 'I can hear the mavis singing,' and slowed. The words were coming from the parrots' cage. Then she heard repeated, 'Mavis gives great head. Mavis gives great head,' followed by a raucous chuckle.

Bang! The parrots' canting suddenly struck a chord. Dotty stopped and turned, thoughtful now, turning her head to one side, much like the parrots were doing. What could the parrots know? She wondered.

Had this Mavis, who ever she was, sung her siren song to Riley? Did the birds have such good hearing that they heard this Mavis offer Riley "head", over the phone? Did it take the offer of "head" for Riley to react in the manner he had, to race off? Was it to see her? To place his tid...she couldn't say the word.....surely not... how could the parrots possibly know of this abhorrent, perverted practice or that this, this Mavis, this Sister O'Rourke, gave it to Riley?

Recently, though, hadn't she read an article in the Daily Mail confirming the mind-reading abilities of parrots and their talent for learning and remembering a vocabulary of nearly six hundred words? I know people who haven't a vocabulary that large, she thought.

Dotty pondered, her suspicions doubling now, for suddenly she recalled again the times unfamiliar fragrances had lingered on Riley on his return from police-surgeon duties. Were the parrots singing to point her in the direction of Riley's indiscretions? Was this Mavis singing to Riley? If so, and Riley were finagling with this, this harlot, she would have to do something about it, get her own back for his deceptions and the tales he would have her believe. She was sure of that.

She mulled over several alternative options. The tale of the farmer's wife, from the past, still seemed the best one to consider using, bringing an adulterous husband to heel. She lit a cigarette, inhaled deeply and walked into the kitchen.

Dotty saw the cook as a wonderfully reliable and robust woman. Her bull-like shoulders heaved with emotion when she discussed the problems that beset her or her own family. She also delivered up any pertinent gossip doing the rounds of the village in which she lived. Dotty usually listened to the gossip while they discussed the daily menus.

They did the shopping together too, calling on farmers who sold fresh produce from their back doors. When the fishmonger called by the Hall with his donkey and cart, she allowed Bridie to do the selecting. She always selected the freshest fish, discarding the rest, much to the monger's vexation, as cat food.

She also advised on purchases from the small shops in the surrounding villages, which supplied fresh goods. Often she would surprise the Dernehen's with an unusual tea variety, obtained from some tucked-away shop in Ballyboil.

Because of her brandy-dulled palate, Dotty hadn't noticed any differences in the tea Bridie served up... but she was willing to try now.

'Bridie, I've decided to sign the pledge,' she said to the cook, standing at the sink, peeling potatoes.

'That sounds serious... brave. What...what's brought this about?' Bridie asked, sounding shocked. She put down the potato peeler and turned from the sink.

'Riley is acting strange. Very leery indeed, he's become. I think he's finagling with another feckin' woman.'

'Surely feckin' not. Surely not...not Doctor Dernehen,' said the cook, her face hidden by the pinafore she had pulled up over it. 'Surely, doctors don't finagle, they being pillars of the community and all that.'

'Harold Shipman was a pillar in his community, I suppose.'

'He was a man who'd a different kind of prick for a woman.'

'Doctors are human. A fair share of foul-minded, fornicating little men will frequent the profession, I'm sure.'

'I see what you mean now. If I found my Charlie finagling with another woman I'd, I'd, I'd have his goolies whipped off. I'd have a vet to do the deed, if I could get no one else, to be sure I, I, I, would.'

'You'd treat it as serious as that?'

'Feckin' right!' Bridie roared. 'After all the years that I've thrown myself beneath him, put up with his grunting, his fallin' asleep on the job an' all, his beery breath...and had his weans. I'd...I'd have the job done with a pair of brave and rusty sheep-shearing clippers. The whole shooting match, the whole feckin' works right off,' Bridie said, swinging her hand in a scything motion. 'He'd have to sit down for a piss. Then...then... he would know what women's work is all about, I'm sure,' Bridie said with relish, a glow on her face and a maniacal sparkle in her eyes.

'I don't know if I could be that cruel to Riley, even if I did think he deserved it. You might have seen the TV programme shown one Sunday morning. A vet gelded a horse as the nation watched. The vet was at pains to point out it was a painless procedure, but I know differently. I don't like talking about it, but vets inject Novocain into the base of the scrotal sac, then they wait...'

'The ballbag. Aye...aye...aye, it's sad for the poor beast, but...but there'd be no painkiller for Charlie. Of that I'm sure.'

'It's usual for a vet to tie up a front leg so the horse can't move about at all. I've seen it before, assisted often when I worked with vets. Just seeing the blades on the mechanical contraption they wrap around the base of the scrotal sac before racking it up tight, would, would bring tears to your eyes, I can tell you. A savage and clean cut takes the sac off and crimps the skin at the same time.

'Cauterising by pressure, it's known as, and no stitches are required. Then, plummeting, speeding hopelessly, disconnected, untethered and with a resounding thump, the sac would hit the bottom of the plastic bucket that most vets place between the back legs of the beast. I'm sure I saw a muscle quiver on a horse's withers once, a reflex action to a pain elsewhere. Apart from that, it didn't budge a hair, just nonchalantly munched away at some hay.'

'Horses don't always have their minds on that area of their anatomies, unless they're hanging it out for a pee on a frosty morning,' Bridie said. 'To be sure, it'd be serious and brave business to consider, but. So what makes you suspect Doctor Dernehen is finagling?'

'I'm sure I caught the whiff of another woman's perfume wafting from him one morning he arrived home in the spring. More recently, a nasty, sweet and sickly oily smell was apparent. I know it was the weekend of Cedric's bone problem, and Riley had dosed him with castor oil, but he reeked of camphor too. I couldn't place that. I thought…I thought he might be finagling with an oily-skinned, foreign tart from Belfast.'

'Oh no… not Doctor Dernehen, surely he would never stoop that low,' Bridie said, 'surely feckin' not. Some of those Belfast tarts have arses on them that look like the Ballyboil end of a Belfast-bound bus… He's not out finagling every feckin' night, is he, for heaven's sake?'

'I'm sure this call today, from a hospital sister, is a ruse to get away from the Hall. He's missed getting out at nights since he finished the police-surgeon work. Last Saturday night, I could see he was feckin' desperate. I didn't take a drink until midnight nor fall asleep like I usually do. I sat watching him sweating, waiting for me to take the stopper out of the decanter. He watched the clock too and wasn't happy, I can tell you.'

'Missis, I think I once recognised a name for a man like that in the letters that make up Scunthorpe.'

'And the four letters you're thinking of run consecutively, Bridie.'

'I, I, I, right on, but are you sure it's just not the time of life Doctor Dernehen's going through?'

'Maybe, but he's lost any respect he had for me to be sure.'

'He never has?'

'One case was when Cedric had his problem. Without considering my dignity at all at all to be sure, he told me he was making out a prescription for feckin' arse ointment in my name,' Dotty said. 'Going to get it from the chemists in Ballyboil, he was. What do you think the chemist might have thought of me wanting arse ointment? And he said I had to spread the horrid stuff onto Cedric's feckin' inflamed arsehole, too.'

'He...you? You never feckin' did?'

'He didn't get any last time. The dog just recovered without help, but he did the time before,' Dotty said. 'I feckin' well did it then. I wasn't feckin' well happy about it. It was a ghastly experience keeping Cedric's tail up out of the way and plastering the stuff onto his inflamed hole with my fingers. Cedric wasn't too feckin' happy about me interfering with his arse, either. Tried to stick his teeth in my arm, he did.

'And some of the outlandish stories Riley tells me to be sure are unadulterated feckin' nonsense. Told me a farmer by the name of Ryan O'Toole had his knob... I, I, I don't much like that word. I, I, I mean tiddleypush pulled off in an accident with a combine harvester...'

'For the love of Jasus, did Doctor Dernehen fix it up for him?'

'He said he tried. He thought I'd bought the tale he did. There's only one O'Toole farming around here, though, and I telephoned their farm. It's a long story that I won't go into but I asked Mrs O'Toole if she required any new kitchen furniture and she told me to feck off.'

'She never did?'

'Aye she did, but I'm getting wise to Riley. Always mentioning the knob word in any conversation we have for he knows it upsets me.'

'My Charlie was sex mad when he was younger, I'm sure. We had a rabbit visit our garden one summer. It ate all the heads from his carrots. Called it Knobby he did because it was always in and out it was. I, I, I've...I've closed up shop to him too and all. He said he was going to the surgery in the village to get this Viagra. Said he would skip the weekdays and perform on the weekends.

'I told him if he skipped that much he'd die of a heart attack. He doesn't like it but I've had enough knob in my time to say good riddance to it once and for all. Tried to slip it...'

'I don't want to hear about it, Bridie,' Dotty snapped.

'But...but what are we going to do about Doctor Dernehen's problem, missis?'

'First, I want you to stop using the knob word. Never mention it again in my presence. Brew a large pot of tea. Then you can drain the brandy from the decanter into the cooking-brandy bottle. When you've brewed the tea, and it has a colour that's passable for brandy, cool it off and refill the decanter with the tea. Make sure it goes through a filter and there are no lees.

'In future, Riley might think I'm drunk and twittering after I've downed a few brandies over dinner, but it won't be the case. That will be enough subterfuge for a start. It will get me on his case and I'll be compos mentis whilst I'm watching him.'

'There might be a problem buying tea in my village,' Bridie said.

'Why's that?'

'You recall that old McGrottie from the shop was rendered wifeless last year when his missis died?'

'Aye.'

'He couldn't do without sex, the beast. Apparently, he took up with a shameless minger from Ballyboil so he did and now he has nothing.'

'How come?' Dotty asked, quizzically.

'Well, she's supposed to have told him his performances in bed were below par. It'd be his age and all that, I think. Anyway, the minger brings him two pills, so the story goes. She says to him, "These are Viagra, take them both now, go to bed and I'll be around in two hours for the kno...kno...finagling session when the pills start kicking in."

'So the daft gowk takes them both and goes straight to bed, doesn't he. Only they were strong sleeping pills. When he woke up two days later, the safe was empty, the stock had gone and she was in Benidorm with another bloke.'

Dotty didn't give a fig for the village shopkeeper. As she walked out of the kitchen into the hallway, she felt a trifle happier within herself: Bridie was on her side and had promised not to mention knobs again.

The parrots watched her light a cigarette then inhale the smoke. 'Plenty O'Toole,' she thought she heard one say and 'Inflamed arsehole,' the other. The parrots had not given her the courtesy of looking up from their food trays.

Dotty was beginning to enjoy the parrots' company, even if they were sometimes a trifle rude. It shocked her, though, that their hearing was also good enough to make out any of the conversation she just had in the kitchen. Staring at them, she wondered: 'How could they put together such bizarre language and where had they heard it before? Mavis gives good "head". How could they know such phrases? And did they know its meaning?

The sound of a car speeding along the drive tore her away from her thoughts.

Dotty walked towards the door and watched Riley pull up outside the Hall. He looked flustered. His face was red and he kept his head lowered as he charged indoors, heading for the bedroom, there to change out of his dressing gown into clothing more suitable to attend an emergency call.

Chapter 16

'Feck the speed limit,' Riley mouthed as he was turning the Jag out of the drive, five minutes after his bout of forgetfulness had caused him to return to the Hall.

Spinning it onto a clear road, he scattered loose stones into the air. He corrected the over steer and pressed down on the accelerator. Quickly, the speedometer showed 70.

He turned into the beech-hedged road that led towards Ballyboil bypass, his thoughts again turning to the obscured entrance up ahead and the radar gun incident. There was no cop presence there when he passed by minutes earlier, but he was still nervous. He was seriously exceeding the speed limit for the first time since he began driving and realised he could be done if there was a police trap there again.

He mumbled, 'The RUC will have more important duties to perform on Saturday afternoons, than those of persecuting a humble doctor,' and accelerated.

He was wrong. The hidden gate loomed no more than one hundred yards ahead when Sergeant Liptrott and Constable O'Hicks took one quick step into view and stood on the verge. The sergeant was holding the radar gun this time. It was steady and pointing towards the Jag.

Riley pressed down sharply on the brake pedal and slowed, but it wasn't enough to adjust his speed down to the limit set for that road.

The sergeant made no effort to stop him and Riley drove on past. In his rear view mirror, he viewed a scene that was anything but reassuring. The sergeant's face was red and gleeful and his body lifted up and down with mirth as he opened his pocket-book.

'Feck you, sergeant!' Riley said, drumming the fingers of both hands on the steering wheel. 'The bastard has taken my number and he looks feckin' pleased about it!'

He was angered that he had looked a fool in front of Dotty for driving off in a rush, still wearing his nightclothes. Now, with a radar gun pointing at him, the loathsome Sergeant Liptrott in attendance, he had broken the speed limit.

When Dotty learned this, she would comment acidly about his haste and no doubt ask more awkward questions. If he wasn't careful in his dealing with Mavis, he could find himself caught up aiding a fleeing, paramilitary murderer.

Apprehensive, his thoughts in a jumble, his stomach muscles tight, he pulled into a space in the nurse's car park.

Mavis was watching out for him from a window of an upstairs ward. To meet him quickly, she had wedged open an adjacent lift door. When she saw him pull into the car park, she descended two floors and walked quickly to his office. She was on duty and in uniform.

Riley stood and waited outside his office door. He was sure Mavis would have looked out for his arrival and would soon appear. When he saw her coming along the passage, he quickly glanced in each direction, ensuring no one else was around. When she was next to him, he touched her lightly on the hips without speaking and guided her into the office in front of him.

When the door closed behind him he caught her around the waist, spun her around to face him. Shuffling close to her, he stood on tiptoes, pulled her down and placed a fleeting kiss on her lips. Clearly, she was agitated. Dark worry bags puffed her eyes and light perspiration dampened her brow.

'It has cost me dear to come here today and it's all a bit of a worry.' He spoke to Mavis earnestly and sharply, letting the tone of his voice convey his displeasure at the situation. 'My wife isn't happy with me. On my way here, I had another run in with that bastard of a sergeant.'

'Your luck is as good as mine is. I never asked for this,' Mavis said holding his hands and looking into his eyes like a lost puppy.

'I can see you're worried. You've asked for my help. Tell me all about it,' he said, easing off slightly and patting the back of her hand.

'Mickey is in my room.' She gulped, breathing heavily, 'he came to me late last night. He was manky, smelly and unshaven. He walked here. Took him two weeks. Some silly game that paramilitaries play went wrong. He wanted to join the Hillshanks Republican Brigade. Senior members tested his resolve. The-second-in-command sent him into a room, a gun in his hand. They'd filled it with blanks. He was to shoot the fake Proddy, hooded and tied up in a chair. Only then could Mickey join them.

'They must have told him a convincing story about the Proddy in the chair for Mickey thought shooting was too good for him. The man in the chair was Martin Mulldoony… the Hillshanks Brigade Commander… a leading Republican figure…and Mickey strangled him. It was all a huge and terrible mistake. Now, Mickey is crapping himself.'

'I bet the boy is, but I've heard nothing on the news.'

'You won't,' Mavis said. 'The stupidity of it happening at all is a slap in the face for the brigade. They'll want to sort it out for themselves. They'll never report it to the cops as a murder, especially one like this.

'The cops will find Martin's body dumped somewhere out in the provinces. The Proddies will get the blame. All of the active brigades will be on the lookout for Mickey. It won't take them long to find out about me and that I'm working here, if they haven't done so already. They'll find me first, then Mickey if he doesn't move on soon. You know what will happen to him then and there's no guarantee that I'll be safe.'

'I'm not going to get drawn into this. In fact, you shouldn't have involved me at all,' Riley said, moving behind his desk and sitting down with a sigh. 'You can ask me to do anything within reason for you, but I'm certainly doing nothing for your brother.'

'Nothing, Riley…nothing? Couldn't you change his looks or something?' she said, desperation in her voice. 'He just wants to make his way to Scotland. From there, he'll get a lorry to the continent and disappear,' her voice was strained and she began to sob.

'Change his looks? Next thing, he'll want to look like Elvis did,' Riley cried, his moustache twitching furiously. 'You must be feckin' joking.' He was surprised at his ruthlessness, but he could be no other way. 'It's against all of my principles, anyway, to help paramilitaries, unless it's in the line of duty as a doctor. I'm sorry, nothing doing is my answer, and that's the way it will stay.'

'But it's for me as much as for Mickey,' she said. She had sat in a chair in front of his desk, looked down, sobbing pitifully, holding her head in both hands.

'I'm sorry, but that's the way it is,' Riley said, drumming his fingers on the desktop.

'He's in my room. You know you won't be able to visit me as usual,' Mavis said, sniffing, without looking up at him.

'That's not what I expected from you,' Riley said, sternly, and pushed his chair back noisily. 'This is a serious business and you sound as if you're trying to blackmail me. It's just not on… not on.'

'I could never do that to you, Riley, but I'm so scared. I just don't know what to do,' Mavis said. Tears were falling heavily and she dabbed at them with a tissue.

He felt sorry for Mavis. She didn't deserve the position she found herself in, but neither did he warrant any part of it. Now the intrusion had totally messed up their relationship. Certainly, nookie, right now in the nurses' home, was out of the question. Thoughts on that subject hadn't gone away and he mused: Sergeant Liptrott's welcome into the room for the duration of her brother's stay is even further out of the window than mine is. 'We'll think of something, I'm sure,' he said.

Riley moved from behind his desk, helped her from the chair and took her in his arms, snuggling his head into the valley of her breasts.

He breathed in deeply of her odour, a mixture of recent sweat and expensive perfume, and squeezed her reassuringly to him. He felt her sobbing, her body heave, and the twinge of arousal in his loins.

He thought he'd clear the route to her bed anyway and said, 'Until something does turn up, you must get him out of your room. It's for your own safety. Tonight, after dark, hide him in the hospital. Put him in the emergency generator room with plenty of blankets, some bottled water and some biscuits. No one goes in there over a weekend. The electricians are off until Monday. By then, *you* might have thought up a bright idea and *you'll* be able to sort something out for him.'

Chapter 17

Riley thought it imperative that he take his normal route back to the Hall that afternoon. Taking any detour posed a bit of a quandary. Any deviation would take him miles out of his way. Sergeant Liptrott could be lurking on any road he took and in the mood again to "fit him up", and possibly in radio contact with undercover cops watching his progress. Another episode with the sergeant, on a road different from normal, would only lead to Dotty further questioning him why he had used it.

Returning home earlier than expected from the hospital, ensured her probing him robustly why, anyway. He didn't relish the idea, but he stuck to the bypass, drove carefully, his eyes continually flicking from the road ahead to the speedometer to the rear view mirror as he went.

Passing by the entrance that had earlier concealed the police car, he breathed a sigh of relief. It was empty; there would be no repeat of the previous unsettling encounter.

The sun was shining brightly at 3 p.m. when Riley pulled up at the front door of the Hall. Steam was rising from behind the monkey-puzzle tree. With a leap, Cedric sprang into view, danced on the spot, began scraping at the grass, his back paws throwing tufts skywards. 'Ah, doggy excitement at a jobby well done and pain free, Cedric,' Riley called, gleefully.

Cedric broke into a lope, bounding up to him, sliding on the stones as he stopped. Snuffling his nose into the hand Riley had outstretched to tug at an ear, Cedric left behind lines of dribbles on it. Pulling out a handkerchief, Riley wiped them away and skipped up the steps to the Hall, Cedric romping alongside him.

He could hear the cook singing in the kitchen. The parrots looked out of their cage towards him, their eyes just above the seed-saver, their beaks busy. One tossed a piece of mango about, the other cracked nuts. 'Looking out from beyond the barricades, aye, girls,' he said in their direction.

'Lover boy,' he heard for his trouble. Each inspected him from a single eye, their heads cocked.

'My, we are talkative today,' he said back to them.

Riley stopped in his tracks when he heard, 'Fifty quid for head.'

They certainly learned some interesting phrases in Ophelia's working bedroom, he mused. He gave a little shudder at the thought of explaining them to Dotty. He moved away quickly, wondering where she might be.

Riley slipped off his jacket. In the cloakroom and about to sort out a peg for it, he heard a car pull up outside. He strode from the cloakroom to the front door, reaching it as Sergeant Liptrott's bulk blocked out the light. The parrots screeched and flapped in the bottom of the cage, fluttering and generally getting in each other's way. In their haste to climb up the cage side onto a perch, they scattered seed and shell husks over the top of the seed saver. Riley heard coming from the cage, 'It's a raid,' then 'It's the fucking fuzz,'

Riley had no idea which one was saying what. Settled on a perch, their heads bobbing up and down, they eyed the sergeant. 'Get your knickers off girls,' and 'I'm not sucking that,' both men heard.

Riley noted that both parrots seemed to have similar views on police visits. Did the parrots really understand the goings-on in a prostitute's working bedroom, he mused.

'Oh, it's you,' Riley said, offhandedly. 'What do you want now, sergeant?' he asked snappily as they came face to face. The sergeant might have looked bemused at what he was hearing from the parrots, but Riley knew what was heading his way. The prospect peeved him, freezing him inside.

'I just happened to be in the vicinity, doctor,' the sergeant said with a smirk, 'and I'm saving the RUC some cash and me some time reporting you for exceeding the speed limit earlier today. I thought I'd call by to "stick you on" and see your documents.' Quietly heh, heh-ing, he opened his pocket-book.

Riley could see Constable O'Hicks walking around the police car. He was staring into the treetops this time, showing the same amount of interest as he did when the sergeant "stuck him on" outside the gates of the nursing home.

Then a parrot spoke. Both Riley and the sergeant heard it. 'Give the cops their dropsy... and fuck them off.' It was said loudly, perfectly enunciated and with only a slight, Irish inflection.

'Who said that?' the sergeant shouted. Lunging forward, he roughly pushing Riley to one side, causing him to stumble and fall to the hallway floor. The suggestion that he was "bent" hadn't sat well with the sergeant and he stepped inside to scan the hallway, his face bitter.

'Don't push me around just because the parrots have you taped, sergeant,' Riley said, curtly, getting to his feet, wishing he had a witness to the sergeant's push.

'Your documents, Doctor Dernehen,' the sergeant said, looking evilly in the direction of the cage.

Thinking that it was worth a try, Riley held onto the doorframe, rammed a hand into the small of his back and shouted down towards Constable O'Hicks, 'Did you see your sergeant assault me, constable?'

'Bastard,' came from the cage.

'I saw what the bastard did,' said the cook, standing in the kitchen doorway, toying with a rolling pin.

'And so did I,' said Dotty. She had walked from the garden and was standing close to Constable O'Hicks. Holding a garden fork and wearing a pinafore, its pockets stuffed with weeds, she was looking over her glasses up the steps at them. 'And he did too,' she said, jabbing a finger at the constable, 'so don't get on your high horse, sergeant, and think you can come around here to persecute my husband. There are no chummies here for you to mess with and fit up. You assaulted my husband. We all saw it. So you can feck off with your trumped-up charges.'

Cedric snuffled about the sergeant's boots, leaving a trail of dribbles over the polished toecaps. Leaving the boots, he sniffed at and dragged his slavering jowls over the pocket-book clasped in the sergeant's hand.

The sergeant breathed in through his clenched teeth, then uttered threateningly, whilst drilling into Riley's eyes with his, 'Keep your back covered, Doc. I'll be watching it.' Grimfaced, he then turned and walked down the steps. Without giving anyone a second look, he ushered Constable O'Hicks into the police car, eased himself in and sped off.

'What have you been up to now,' Dotty asked acidly as she came up the steps.

'I've been up to nothing,' Riley quickly answered, 'but the sergeant thinks I have. He was going to do me for speeding on the road towards the bypass.'

'Wet a pot of tea for two for us,' Dotty instructed the cook.

In the sitting-room, Dotty sat facing Riley, over a low table, her hands grubby with soil, smoke rising from the cigarette she held in front of her. 'Sergeant Liptrott certainly has something against you, dearie. Whatever could it be?' she asked, her eyes darting, trying to make contact with his, which were anywhere but looking directly at hers.

Avoiding her stare, he said, 'It's the Jaguar-owning thing all over again.' He was hoping to appease her with the view he held. 'They just can't stand to see one on the road in the hands of a member of the public, I'm sure. It's in their mentality to prosecute the driver and on any charge they can think up.' Quickly he looked around for the tea that hadn't yet arrived. 'It can't be anything else.'

'To what lengths will Liptrott go to persecute a Jag driver?' Dotty asked.

'Until someone shoots him, I suppose.'

'Why don't you complain to his superior?'

'They might all be the feckin' same. When you wrestle with a pig, both parties get dirty, but the pig enjoys it. What could be worse than to give them more reason to act obnoxiously?'

The cook brought in the teapot, milk and sugar, and two cups on a tray. Dotty poured. Rising from the table, she lifted the brandy decanter from the sideboard and carried it to the table. Removing the top, she began topping up her cup with the golden liquid.

'You're home early from the hospital. What happened to Doctor O'Brodie's patient?'

'Oh, he died on the operating table,' Riley said, eyeing the decanter and the large measure Dotty was pouring into her cup.

Chapter 18

In the early hours of the Sunday morning following Martin Muldoony's demise, Sean moved the body in the boot of a van, far out into the sticks, dumping it in a pool near the headwaters of the River Boil.

The following day, in the kitchen of Martin's home, senior brigade members voted Sean their new Commander, once he had briefed them on Martin's demise, and Mickey O'Rourke's stupid bungling of the test, which had caused the death. At the meeting, Sean gave his lieutenants firm instructions: to alert all brigade members, find the wee gobshite, quietly remove him to a remote location, torture him, "six-pack" him, cut his knackers off, shoot him dead and leave him to rot.

Two weeks later, and it seemed that Mickey had disappeared into thin air. He had no family left whom they could threaten for information, or so they thought, until enquiries flagged up a sister and her whereabouts.

'Where the bayjasus is that?' Tracy had erupted when she first heard of the Ballyboil connection. On the map, it was in the middle of nowhere, the other side of Loch Neagh and deep in rural Ulster. Trains from Belfast didn't call anywhere near.

A short walk took her to the nearby bus station: womanly intuition led her to believe that a devoted sister would go to extreme lengths to hide a brother whose life was in danger.

A private bus company, known by most dwellers in the province as the Portavogie Safari, ran a service using ancient, rickety buses from Portavogie to Glasgow, via the Larne-Stranraer Ferry link. It called at some small towns on the route, twice weekly, including Ballyboil.

During its formative years, the firm had been more than doubly profitable. Outside the Larne ferry terminal, an employee of the ferry company would leave an office to count the number of heads he could see through the bus windows. The clerk never entered the coaches to make sure, and charged the owner accordingly.

Sadly for the Safari operators, a ferry company employee, whether he suspected the swindle or not isn't known, one day decided to check the buses interiors and found as many passengers again hiding beneath seats. Consequently, the cost of travel from Portavogie to Glasgow had now doubled.

Tracy was intent to wreak some vengeance for the greyhound's demise as well as Martin's. Sean wasn't enthusiastic about her involvement, insisting that it was brigade business. She won the day, arguing convincingly, 'If your boys put in an appearance in a wee town like Ballyboil, the world and its aunt will ken about it. It's better that I find the gobshite. No one will suspect a woman booking in at a B&B for a couple of days R&R. If I find him there, then you can move in quickly, spirit him out and dispose of him somewhere else, with me there cheering you on.'

The following morning, Tracy had joined the Portavogie Safari on its return journey from Larne to Portavogie. She would leave he bus at Ballyboil.

Chapter 19

It was gone 10a.m. when Riley awoke on Sunday morning. The sun was splitting the trees surrounding the hall, bathing the province with warmth and flooding the bedroom with light. From beyond the door, he could hear the drone of Dotty and the cook gabbing merrily away. Probably sharing some gossip, he thought.

Sleep had come flittingly for him. For most of the night, he was restless, not drifting away until after he had noticed the first hints of dawn penetrating the edges of the curtains. He would have slept on, he was sure, but for Dotty's fussing around in the bedroom when she arose. She had drawn the curtains wide, tied them back, noisily opened a window to allow in some fresh air, opened and closed drawers and draped his clean clothes over a chair.

Riley slipped out of bed and took a shower. By 10:30 a.m., he was sitting in front of a full Ulster breakfast, all local produce and fried.

At mid-day, he was recumbent on the chaise-longue, ploughing through a selection of Sunday newspapers. He had read most of a lengthy Belfast Telegraph editorial when the doorbell rang. Dotty answered it. He heard her greeting of 'Great to see you, Father.'

Then he heard the bluff response of 'Top of the afternoon to you, Dotty.' Riley rose to go to the hallway: he knew the voice of the male visitor.

Father Mack, the priest at St Furuncles Chapel in the town, was standing in the hallway, holding Dotty's hands in his. 'To be sure now you're looking in top order, Dotty,' he was saying to her.

Father Mack had a benign and saintly manner. Well into his seventies, he still served a doting flock. White-headed for many years and now permanently stooped, he took the weight of his parish problems on his shoulders. His name had never been associated with any of the various scandals befalling the Roman Catholic Church in Ireland.

He wasn't like some of the other narrow-eyed cassock-lifters prowling chapels and eying up the talent, Dotty had once sniffingly said of him. To her mind, he had never had the pleasure of supporting his bulk on his elbows whilst making love to a woman or had ever lusted after the deed.

Father Mack let go of Dotty's hands and stepped past her. Smiling broadly, he faced Riley, took hold of his hand and shook it firmly, Father Mack said, in his lilting, West-of-Ireland brogue, 'What about you, then? To be sure have

I not come to wish you well for the court case tomorrow against that eejit Liptrott. I had dealings with him some years ago, you know. Be very wary of him,' Father Mack said in a rush. He continued: 'I opened my bedroom curtains one morning, and there, on the lawn in front of me, a dead donkey lay, legs in the air, belly all bloated. My first thoughts were to telephone the RUC. Liptrott came on the phone and I said to him, "Top of the morning to you sergeant, this is Father Mack from St Furuncles church in the town. There's a Donkey lying dead in middle of my lawn."

'He spoke to me in a condescending way when he realised who I was. You get to know a staunch Proddy voice, to be sure. "Well now, Father," 'he said,' '"it was always my impression that you people took care of the last rites!"'

'I thought quietly for a moment before I made my response. I said to him, in as dignified way as I could without laughing aloud: "Ah, to be sure, that is true; but we are also obliged to notify the next of kin."'

'In my case, I fear bad news has travelled fast, Father,' Riley said, forcing a smile.

'How's it hanging, Father?' sounded distinctly from the parrot's cage.

'Bayjasus, what was that I just heard?' Father Mack asked, the parrot's words causing him to sway on his feet. Turning slowly on one foot, he peered into the cage.

Dotty was startled at the parrot's choice of words and moved quickly, steadying the Father, stepping in between him and the cage. As an extra precaution, she turned him so he faced away from it, saying, 'It's the parrots having a little laugh at your expense, Father,'

'Father like a little head today,' sounded from the cage, followed by a mucky laugh and the sounds of a nutshell splitting, the fragments hitting the cage sides.

Dotty turned to the parrots and admonished them as she would a rude child, 'Father's quite happy with the head he already has, girls, if you don't mind.'

The parrots were in their tactical position for pursuing mocking observations: on the cage floor, behind the seed saver, with one eye of their bobbing heads scrutinizing their victims from over the top.

Father Mack had flushed and become pink around the collar. Seeing his embarrassment, Dotty took him by the arm. 'Come away with you into the sitting-room, Father. Our cook will wet us a pot of tea.' Quickly, she guided him away from the hallway.

'An interesting pair, those birds you have there, Riley. Where did you pick them up from?' Father Mack asked. He chose to sit on a low chair behind a coffee table.

The cook, prepared for such occasions, had a tray waiting. After Dotty poured the tea, Father Mack sipped at a cup and sucked intermittently and nervously on a Garibaldi biscuit.

'A satisfied English patient of mine, apparently more than happy with the quality of my expertise, she sent them over,' Riley replied.

'A weird and ungodly choice of language the parrots have, to be sure. I've never heard the likes of it at all in all my life,' Father Mack said. 'It's agricultural talk. Talk of the yokels and the farmyard, to be sure, and most probably of the bordello as well. Certainly, they're words I have seldom encountered. In fact, the last time I bumped into such words were in written form. They were in the pornographic books I confiscated from some would-be priests attending the saintly-named school at which I once taught. Before expelling them, I recall, in a manner of speaking, my monastic boot connected with each of their arses.

'Nor are they words I'd normally expect to hear in the home of one of my more refined parishioners. In Genesis, there is never a mention of parrots joining The Ark along with Noah and his missis. I wonder why? But being birds, I suppose their foulness is forgivable, but no less understandable for all that.'

Dotty was beginning to wonder about Father Mack's squeaky-clean reputation. If, as she feared, the parrots had sussed Riley out as a finagler, had they used their intuition and sussed the Father out too, as someone with a fondness for "head"?

Dotty was also interested to find out what Father Mack might know of Riley's patient, he having been a teacher at Catholic schools. 'A woman called Ophelia O'Rooney presented them to Riley,' she chipped in. 'I think she was at convent school with me in Dublin, Father. Riley performed corrective surgery on her slackened hip. He says she's now working as a seamstress in southern England.'

'Interesting,' Father Mack said, rubbing his chin. 'I wonder. Could that possibly be the Ophelia O'Rooney who prostrated herself on the floor of a Dublin convent, offered her wares to a poor unfortunate and sex-mad priest serving there at the time?'

'There can be none other to be sure,' said Dotty, her head nodding, confident that Father Mack had identified the sinner.

'Some twenty years ago,' Father Mack said, 'I heard she was a prostitute working the streets of London.'

'Don't look at me like that,' Riley addressed Dotty, noting the bitter grimace she was directing at him. 'She told me she was a seamstress. I believed her. I'd never heard of her before the appointment.'

'It's perhaps no wonder, then, how the birds have picked up their vile prattle,' Father Mack observed. 'If they've been educated while perched in that environment, and with that sort of person.'

'Twenty years in the working bedroom of a prostitute. Work that one out, Father and tell me what *you* come up with?' Dotty asked.

'My word, what manner of language would they have heard caged within that place of ill repute?' Father Mack asked. 'Perhaps there's no limit at all to their filthy talk, for that's all it is, to be sure.' Taking a rosary from a trouser pocket, he began circling the beads between fingers and thumb.

Riley fizzed. He was dying to tell Father Mack to catch himself on. Tell him that he must have come up the River Boil in a soapy bubble; if he thought what the parrots said had any meaning. 'Bayjasus, aren't they just feckin' mimics?' he asked, placing upturned hands out in front of him, pleadingly.

'Language, Riley, and in front of Father Mack,' Dotty snapped.

'Bayjasus, why are we getting ourselves so worked up over the ravings of a couple of mimicking birds?' Riley asked. 'They never learnt the foul words they often repeat, here at the Hall. That's all that matters.'

Father Mack had heard enough. Sipping the remainder of his tea, he put his cup down, eased himself up from the chair and walked slowly away. 'Keep me informed of any other interesting observations they make,' he said over his shoulder to Dotty, following closely behind him.

In the hallway, he looked towards the cage and made the sign of the cross. Each bird had a single eye focused on him. 'Father like the full treatment today,' rattled the Father's ears. With an audible and shuddering 'Ohhhhh,' he left the Hall, his stride lengthening.

*

Dotty went weeding as soon as Father Mack left the Hall that afternoon. She finished about 4p.m. and then went for a shower. The cook was in the kitchen as she passed by, waiting for the precise moment to pop the roast of beef into the oven, for carving pink at 7 p.m. She was humming a verse of "Paddy McGinty's Goat". Since she believed the missis' suspicions about Riley finagling, the goat now belonged to Riley McGinty in the song.

The parrots had settled down and were preening each other on a perch. Cedric lay sprawled on his blanket beneath the stairs, slobbering noisily. A light breeze was blowing through the open hallway door, bringing with it delicate, summery fragrances. The countryside was basking in the tranquillity of the warm, late August afternoon.

Riley was again reclining on the chaise-longue, his hands linked on his forehead, shading his eyes. He was attempting to relax, but his mind wouldn't let him; churning over his problems and not finding any answers to them.

Any thoughts he had were lost when he heard the racket that forty or so motorbikes were making as they entered the Hall grounds.

The noise sent Riley striding into the hallway, rubbing his eyes as he went. The parrots had moved to the pit of the cage and were looking warily over the seed saver. A squawked 'Shiiiiit...Hells Angels,' he just made out above the popping of the last motorbike engine to cut out.

Riley arrived at the doorway, shading his eyes to view better the arrivals. Cedric lumbered to his feet and joined him. Together they looked down at the group of hairy, scruffy, mainly straggly-bearded, leather-clad bikers, straddling their machines.

Seth Mulligan had parked his trike at the foot of the steps. He was sitting upright, both hands resting on the steering wheel, grinning up at Riley. After a quick wave of acknowledgement, he began to remove his driving gloves. Cedric lowered his shoulders, stretched out his front legs in readiness for an attack and let out a wavering woof. Cowardice prevailing and frightened by hairy creatures as ugly as he was, he returned to the safety of his blanket.

The parrots fluttered frenziedly, feathers, food and husks scattering from the cage. Shrill cries of 'Evil bastards,' were repeated.

Riley walked down the steps to meet the bikers, the parrots' chatter not registering with him.

'Afternoon, Doc,' Seth said, grinning continuously. He moved his goggles onto his forehead and tipped Riley a wink. 'It sounds like some parrots are doing a spot of raging in there. Like the birds know one or two things about us biker types, but.'

'The parrots are gibbering a bit. It's likely the bikes have upset them,' Riley said.

'Hearing language like that, it sounded like a couple of bikers' "ladies" bellyaching, Doc. You sure you're not hiding any away in there?' Seth chided.

The other bikers dismounted from their machines, placed their safety helmets on bike seats and sauntered over to surround Riley, and Seth, who remained seated on the trike.

The rear end of Volkswagen Beetle motorcar, the engine still in place, formed the main part of the trike. Fixed behind Seth's single front seat were three wooden toilet seats, with hand-painted inscriptions running around the inner rims in Day-Glo orange. The inscription on one was "Born to be Wild", on another, "Instant Satisfaction". "Cranked Up" graced the centre seat. Painted above the backrests was the inscription: "Pus to the People".

Riley wondered if the trike also provided a potty service on lengthy journeys. Some bikes were Harley Davidsons, customised with high handlebars and transcendental-artwork-decorated petrol tanks - all highly polished, they glinted in the sunlight.

Others were classics, veteran Indians and Nortons. Some seemed purposely burned to imitate those used in the Mad Max movies: Electra Glides in smoke and rust.

Standing close to the bikers, all wearing sweaty leathers, Riley could smell some rancidity rising from them, and high-temperature exhaust fumes, petrol and toked cannabis. He hoped none of the bikes leaked oil. Dotty would sound off if Cedric stood in a pool of it and padded oily paw-prints around the wooden floors of the Hall.

'You look a better colour than the time I last saw you, Mr Mulligan,' Riley began, his moustache twitching during the quick, professional once-over he gave Seth. 'But to what do I owe the privilege of the visit?'

'Thanks, Doc,' Seth said, tipping him another quick wink. 'We thought we'd call to wish you all the best for your court case tomorrow morning and offer you the services of a witness for the defence, but,' Seth said cheerily. Loudly spoken ripples of agreement came from the assembled bikers, mainly in the form of, 'Too feckin' right.'

'I don't understand,' Riley said, shuffling his feet and taking a quick squint at the array of hairy faces watching him.

'You know I was in the nick that night, so I can't help, but most of my muckers will say they saw you go through the lights when they showed green. In fact, some of them are prepared to say you were nowhere near any lights, but,' Seth said.

'I don't buy that. Saying that in a court of law is perjury and I wouldn't expect anyone to lie for me,' Riley said, sounding shocked.

'It's no worse than what that feckin' Liptrott's done to you. Remember, we owe him one too, for what he tried to swing on me,' Seth said.

'Right feckin' bastard,' most of the assembly seemed to agree.

'Right on,' rippled from others.

'I'm supposed to be up in front of the beak tomorrow,' Seth continued. 'But I won't be appearing. They'll lock me up for non-payment of fines and add on a couple of weeks inside for this latest load of bollocks. I've been sending the court letters pleading guilty, but I mention mitigating circumstances that suggests I'm not guilty at all.

Neither the court nor the cops like what I do, but they can stuff it. I don't give a shoite. It delays judgement day and keeps me out of the pokey until the rally season finishes next month.'

'Feckin' well take their help, Riley. Don't let that feckin' sergeant get away with anything,' He heard Dotty say from behind him.

Riley looked around. Dotty was standing in the doorway listening. Straight from the shower, her dressing gown hung daringly open, showing breast, her curlers stuck up under a plastic shower cap. She twirled her glasses in front of her and smoke curled from the cigarette hanging from her bottom lip.

No quality image there, Riley thought. He hadn't ever seen a biker's lady, but Dotty might fit the bill, appearing like that.

Riley turned back towards Seth and said, 'Liptrott has a witness in Constable O'Hicks. The Magistrates will take the word of two cops, no matter how twisted it might be, before anything a biker might say in my defence. The magistrates will cotton on to you right away. None of them will have come up the River Boil in a soapy bubble, you know. I'll have to take my chances with the Bench.'

'Well, if we can't help you, then maybe you'll help us. Our motorcycle club wishes for you to become its honorary bikers' surgeon.'

'Feckin' right,' was the unanimous feelings muttered by the assembly, some pulling on beards, others nodding.

'What?' Riley asked, not believing his ears. How could he possibly consider that? He knew of other doctors who had joined bike clubs, but they were respectable clubs... a lot tamer than this one. This one, by all accounts, had a bit of a reputation. There were initiation ceremonies that could be a bit of a worry. "Unlanced Boils" initiation probably meant sucking the head from a boil, using a length of glass tube, like street medics did in India. Maybe it meant biting the head from a live toad. Most bike clubs of this ilk had a particular dare, which a prospect had to complete satisfactorily before their acceptance into the club.

'Come to the bike rallies with us, Doc. We rally all over Ireland and venture regularly to the mainland. During the summer, we're away every weekend. The season's about to end so come with us before it's too late. Have some fun, eh?' Seth tipped him another wink, 'Get a trike. Enjoy your free time. Get a life.'

'Feckin' right on. You'd be guaranteed a great time,' he heard from someone in the crowd. Turning towards them, he saw they all were in the process of joining up cigarette papers along the glued edge.

'Going to have a toke with us?' one grinning biker asked Riley.

There were no signs of threat from any of them, but Riley suspected there might be a few large, incriminating dog-ends to pick up after they left. Ashtrays on motorbikes were rare commodities.

'Not for me, boys,' he answered.

'I wouldn't mind going for a ride,' Dotty said, from her stance in the Hall doorway.

Bayjasus! No! Riley had a quick, terrifying flash of himself at the wheel of a trike, Dotty, the cook and Cedric sitting upright on the toilet seats behind, all wearing goggles, while he tore along country lanes looking for squashed hedgehogs.

'Come for a ride on the trike, Mrs Dernehen,' Seth said and beckoned to Dotty to come down the steps.

The cook poked her head out next to Dotty's, holding a tureen she was polishing.

'You're game too, then?' Seth asked Riley.

'I hate being a spoilsport, but not today, though I might take a short jaunt with you in the future. When did you say your next rally was?' A germ of an idea had flashed into Riley's mind.

Seth removed a wallet from his back pocket, selected a card and held it out towards Riley. 'My mobile number is on that. Get me on it anytime, you can. Next weekend, it's the "Big Blue and Cuckoo" bash over in Scotland. We're going over in the early hours of Thursday morning, by ferry from Larne, for a long weekend. It's on a block booking.

'There'll be no hassle. We just turn up, hand our tickets over and drive straight onto the ferry. The cuckoo crowd are putting on a Doctor Feelgood tribute band. You'll be into them, eh?'

'I will get in touch if I feel good enough to take a ride with you to Larne. You can take Mrs Dernehen and Bridie for a spin, if you wish. I'll look after the Hall,' Riley said. He needed to order his thoughts. For a moment, the idea that he could escape the Hall acting as biker's surgeon breezed around in his mind. He dismissed that as absurd, but saw that an opportunity had presented itself to dispatch Mavis' brother to the mainland, thus uncluttering the pathway to her bedroom, when chances arose?

On hearing the offer of a trike ride, Dotty turned and ran into the Hall to change. The cook returned the sparkling tureen to the kitchen, then took off her apron and put on a head square.

Riley assisted the women onto the trike, helped fit their goggles and settled them onto their seats. He looked for seatbelts to strap around them, but there were none. He thought them inadequately dressed for a trip, even through leafy glades on a warm August afternoon, and reckoned they wouldn't stay away too long.

From the top step, Riley watched the bikers ride away, then turned and entered the hallway.

He was sure he'd never be alone when Molly and Milly were close by; they were still watching him closely. Still not believing the intuitive qualities attributed to them by Dotty, he picked up the telephone and dialled Mavis' number.

'How tall is your brother?' he asked immediately she had answered. 'You say five foot six. Interesting. Tell me: facially does he look anything like me? A Ché Guvera-style moustache and gappy teeth, you say. With a makeover, the moustache trimmed until it's as pencil-thin as mine, a crash-helmet with visor attached to his head and a muffler around his neck, could he'd possibly look a little like me?'

He then told her how Mickey might escape, disguised as him, on the backseat of a trike bound for the mainland.

Chapter 20

At 11 p.m. that Sunday evening, Riley slipped beneath the sheets knowing that sleeping soundly, if at all, would prove difficult. It was the night before his court appearance.

He tossed and turned, lashed out with his arms, scratched at his body, kicked out and raised the duvet from the bed with his feet to let some air circulate around them. In none of the positions he periodically assumed, could he settle. His mind just couldn't stop working out how he might answer the trumped-up motoring offence in court the following day.

He did drift off for a while but woke at 5 a.m. Though still tired, he decided to rise and slipped his overheating feet out of the bed.

Dotty, too, had had a restless night. She put it down to her not having consumed any mind-mugging brandy. That afternoon, the bikers had returned both her and Bridie, all rosy of cheek, to the Hall. After spending two hours in their company, both women were giggling hysterically. Riley didn't understand this uncommon bout of risibility until Dotty had garbled an explanation. The bikers had stopped in a lay-by near Mount Boil, had toked up and had allowed them to sniff at the fragrant-smelling smoke the joints gave off.

What the bikers had blown in Dotty's direction, hadn't summoned an efficient sandman, just made her restless, and alert to all of Riley's twists and turns. She rose soon after him, put on dressing gowns and joined him in the sitting-room, where they sat, sharing a pot of tea.

'You had a shocking night. I recall nightmares were never far beneath the surface of your sleep during the "troubles",' Dotty said sympathetically, as she poured a cup. 'It's been a stuffy night, but it's only a lightweight duvet; it didn't seem warm enough to cause the degree of agitation you were experiencing. I watched you for a time. You were performing like someone who's still prone to "wee boys"' tendencies,' she said scornfully.

'How do you mean?' Riley railed.

'You're hands was never far away your tiddleypush all night, tugging at it, stretching it, repeatedly.'

Riley thought quickly and countered the accusation. 'I must have been protecting it. I dreamt vividly during the only period I slept. Afterwards, I was in and out of the dream in flashbacks.'

'Some dream! I'll have to check your sheets for nocturnal emissions.'

'The dream possessed moments of interest, but nothing to cause that. Sergeant Liptrott featured chiefly in it.'

'Oh, what was he up to this time?' Dotty asked, doubtfully.

'He was trying to get me involved with a woman.'

Dotty eyed Riley squarely, but he was staring directly ahead. 'I see,' she said, the words forming slowly.

'Dreams are often difficult to recall.'

'But this one was vivid, you say.'

'Very much so. I'm sure it held special significance for my court appearance today.'

'In your dream, Liptrott was after you again, then?'

'In the dream,' Riley said, 'everyone seemed black, Negroid, Liptrott even, and so was I. The blackness, the entire hellish affair, could have represented the Judge's gown, I suppose. I was somewhere in the Mississippi delta, I think. It was very warm and a wide river flowed close by.

'My mother was black and she continually lambasted me for ejaculating on my sheets. I remember that much. It seems I was young, fit, my hormones were flowing freely and my knob hung pendulously; any slight whim would harden it.'

'Riley!' Dotty reproached and raised her eyes.

'It's true. I saw mother wrestling with my sheets, trying to break them across her knee. She gave up and stood them up in a corner. Stiff, rock-solid they were. I haven't worked out any underlying reason for that. I think you were correct in thinking my knob was involved...but only in the dream.'

'Some dream! Wet, if you ask me,' Dotty retorted, stridently.

'Well, you asked. Liptrott's lips were huge and vibrated silently. He performed like a peacock, a strutting braggart, always crowing and making false statements. He said he was going to have me cut. From that, I thought he meant he'd castrate me if I didn't accompany him to a crinkly-tin-roofed shack, situated at the rough end of town, along a yellow road built from hardened, brick-shaped, cow dung.'

Oh...oh, beware, thought Dotty as she eyed Riley. From his earlier account, she only suspected his dream recollection was another of his fanciful fabrications. With the "Yellow Brick Road" built from cow-dung entering the equation, she now knew for definite that it was.

'In my dream I did go to the shack with Liptrott,' Riley said, looking into the distance. 'A covered veranda sheltered the front. Some skinny, flea-bitten donkeys, tethered by long halters to a hitching rail, and roaming cattle, chewed at the sparse grass. In the everglades, alligators lashed out and snapped at prey.

'I could hear great jaws crunching and some poor animal screaming. Trout leapt from the river, devouring flies and water boatmen in great quantities. Larger bugs buzzed, dived at and bit people.

'Several black women sat on the veranda in colourful dresses. They were sucking meat from boiled pig's trotters and tucking into plates of fried soda bread. A dog with flapping jaws, looking a lot like Cedric, but darker of coat, was also hunkered there.

'Occasionally, the dog lurched into life and hoovered the veranda, much as Cedric does the hallway carpet following a bout of boiled-bone syndrome. I even heard rounded balls, owl regurgitations, all those mouse and vole bones, rattling past the fan, vacuumed up and flying into the hoover bag. The sound effects were convincing enough. Mind you, there were two grey parrots patrolling the veranda railing. The hoovering noises could have been coming from them. Our two are quite mischievous with their mimicry.'

'You're trying too hard,' Dotty said, derision tingeing her voice.

'Come, come, I'm not. It's everything as I remember it and in chronological order. Listen. One woman, old and wrinkly with snow-white hair, was sitting in a rocking chair. She lurched back and forth with a pair of pince-nez, a bit like yours, perched on the end of her nose. She smoked a short-stemmed clay pipe and blew out clouds of exotic-smelling smoke. It was possibly to do with the dispersal of flesh-eating bugs. Copious tea drinking had blackened her lips. I guessed.'

Dotty frowned. Copious tea drinking: surely, Riley couldn't be that perceptive of *her* increased intake.

Riley continued: 'Another woman was knitting a gigantic sock, though I suppose it might have been a knob warmer, using three-feet-long needles. A young black woman, dressed in a low-cut dress, was showing off her ample breasts.

'Liptrott tried desperately to get me interested in her. She was pretty, round of face, had a pair of voluptuous lips, a generous mouth and a full set of ultra-white teeth. Her black, silky hair flowed all the way down her back and covered her buttocks. It wasn't stubbly and fuzzy with tracks cut in it, making her head look like a hand grenade, like some black women have.'

'And you fell for these charms?' Dotty asked.

'That's the part I cannot recall. I ended up in court. For what reason I don't know, don't remember. The magistrate had a fearsome persona, grey and grave and wore a wig with a square of black material sitting on top of it. His lips kept rolling back and he snickered.

'It seemed that Liptrott had metamorphosed into a hanging judge. He looked daggers at me. I knew the look, but this time its portent frightened me. It's a wonder my dream didn't turn into a nightmare then. No wonder I was restless. The young black woman was standing in the witness box and kept pointing at me while she spoke to the judge. "It was like this, Judge," she kept on saying to him, followed by, "he took his knob out, Judge" and the Judge sounded-off "Laudy, laudy, I'm going to send this Riley down." Her voice screamed to a crescendo and she took the pince-nez glasses from a pocket and said, "Then he put these on the end of his knob, Judge," and he said, "You look around, son, make sure you ain't missed anybody."'

'Sex played a large part in your dream, then?' Dotty felt stung to ask.

'No evidence of any sexual activity exists when you look deeply into the dream's message. My mind was obviously playing games, tricking me. Can't you see that's the case? It was my estimation that Liptrott is a prick and the prick was looking to get me into bother.'

'A prick! Riley?'

'A prick, a knobend, is a term of abuse used by countless Ulsterfolk to describe a person they dislike or think an imbecile, Dotty.'

'I'll keep on dousing my brain with brandy and sleep in sweet oblivion. Dreams like that you can have for yourself,' Dotty said, looking around for the decanter, carrying on the deceit that seemed to be working well for her.

Chapter 21

'It should take no more than thirty minutes for *me* to get to the Magistrate's Courthouse, as it's only on the other side of town.'

It was now 08:30 a.m., Monday morning. Riley and Dotty were sitting facing each other at breakfast. Riley was stressing to Dotty that he would prefer to go to the court alone. She was yet to reply. Dressed sombrely in a striped, charcoal-grey suit, which he thought apt for the occasion, he was dressed, if not ready in mind, to face Sergeant Liptrott from the dock.

Riley poured milk onto his muesli and mixed it in with his spoon. The tail of a drab tie he stuffed between two buttons of his shirt, preventing it from dipping into the bowl. The delicious aroma of fried bacon and mushrooms wafting from the kitchen usually made his nostrils twitch in anticipation. He could smell nothing appetising.

Though he had dreamt during the night, he could tell that Dotty doubted he'd had a dream at all. True, the dream was vague and what he couldn't remember he had embellished in his telling of it to her. It worried him, though, that the threads he did recall contained premonition of his inability to prove his innocence to Sergeant Liptrott's charge, to the bench of magistrates.

As he was eating, he kept thinking ahead to his court appearance, mulling over his options. Perhaps he should have pleaded guilty by letter. He would have, had he not thought it a coward's way out. Would the trauma of facing the sergeant from the dock prove too much? Should he plead his guilt from the dock, take a reduced fine? Minimum fuss, pay up, leave his licence behind for endorsement and depart the court was the easy option?

The prospect of having to listen to the sergeant telling his lies to the magistrates, and they believing them, galled him more. He just wished he could provide the evidence proving that he was not guilty; he had no witnesses and doubted mitigation that he was a doctor on call would aid him.

'*Me, me,*' Dotty was saying loudly, whilst frowning at him over the top of her spectacles. Backcombing her hair had taken twenty minutes before breakfast. It sat tidier than usual and matched the rather frumpish, peaty-brown trouser suit of Donegal tweed she was wearing.

Dotty had assumed that Riley would want her tidily dressed and ready to accompany him; to show him support in court. 'Don't you mean *we, we* should take no more than thirty minutes to reach the court. After your performance during the night, I think someone who's still prone to "wee boys'" night-time games will need rock-solid company.'

'Oh come, come,' he said loudly, shaking his head and looking away from her. 'I'm sure you're exaggerating the situation. Once, I awoke jerkingly. It was quite itchy down there. I was having a good old scratch around, that's all. There's absolutely no need for you to accompany me to court.'

He concentrated again on chewing his muesli and didn't look up. 'You obviously haven't thought how embarrassing my case will be for you. You really don't want to see your husband quivering in the dock, do you? I can tell you all the gory details tonight. It'll be over quick. I'll make a guilty plea, pay the fifty quid fine, accept the endorsement on my licence and that'll be that.'

Mavis might be at the court too. He didn't need her to greet him there, to make as if they knew each other. Later he would need to discuss her brother's problem with her. He finished his muesli and put his spoon down. Mavis would need to know of his plan, urgently.

Dotty looked at him sternly. She could see his preoccupation and his lack of attention. He just wasn't listening. 'I'm coming and that's all there is to it,' she said. 'If you don't take me in your car, I'll follow you in mine. I'm going to support you, whether you want me there or not.'

'Drat!' Riley said under his breath. Dotty was proving obstinate on the subject.

The cook carried in a heaped and smoking breakfast plate using a tea towel and stood sniffing to one side of him. She leant over and lifted his empty bowl with one hand; with the other, she placed the breakfast plate on his tablemat with a clatter. She said sharply, aware of Missis Dernehen's suspicions, 'Mind you don't burn your fingers, doctor... the plate's red-hot.'

Riley hardly noticed the cook's presence and sighed, 'Aye.' Resignedly, he said to Dotty, 'Have it your way. I'll drop you off in the town after if you like and pick you up when I've finished work. I've arranged today so that I haven't much on. I should be through by 3 o'clock.'

'That's a better idea. I need more parrot food and tropical fruits. They're nearly out. I also need some brandy.' Dotty cut the porridge into shapes with the edge of her spoon, spun it around in the milk in her bowl and watched his reaction over the end of her spectacles.

'The parrots. Do you think it's wise to keep them?' Riley asked, while cutting soda bread into bite-size chunks. 'They seem to have picked up some awful crudities that don't make a lot of sense.'

'They're lovely birds. In fact, I'm growing fonder of them every day,' Dotty said cheerily. 'I believe they're bright, watchful and intuitive. Only the other day I heard one of them reciting Hickory Dickory Dock. Word-perfect it was. It was so lovely and childish. That revealed their innocence to me, even if they have been subjected to rough language at some time in their past!'

Riley smiled to himself. If they were innocents, why were the parrots keeping their tastier observations for him? Hickory Dickory, feck the Doc they might have chimed, if it were he within their sight. 'Have it your way,' he said, 'but they're only birds. You can't put much faith in their mimickings.'

'I'm expecting many more blockbusting revelations from them,' Dotty said as she left the table, her eyes glued to his face.

In the hallway, on their way out to the car, Dotty trilled at the parrots, 'Goodbye Milly, goodbye Molly.' To the cook rattling plates in the kitchen, she said, 'That's us away, Bridie.' The cook left the kitchen to see them off, only to catch part of a recital by a parrot, of the poem Nick, Nack, Paddy, Wack give the dog a bone. 'Give the dog a bone,' was the only line of the poem the cook heard and it sounded just like Mrs Dernehen calling from outside the Hall.

The cook didn't doubt her ears. A verbal order from her employer was one she obeyed implicitly. She returned to the kitchen and fished a bone out of the stockpot for the dog.

In the hallway with the bone, the cook initiated a playful tussle with Cedric over the immediate ownership of it. While teasing the dog, the cook heard a parrot say 'Baby cheeses.'

'Baby cheeses! My wee darlings, how sweet,' she said. She gave in to Cedric and went to the door on the off chance that her employers might still be there. They had left. She returned to the kitchen and the fridge from where she selected two chunks of cheddar. Returning to the hallway, she fitted them in-between bars of the cage. 'There you are, my darlings,' she warbled. 'We won't get any baby cheeses in stock until the next shopping trip.'

*

As Riley and Dotty were travelling towards Ballyboil, several plovers flew through a gap in the beech-hedge lined road and over the car. Riley eyed the bonnet of the Jag, which still had its showroom sheen. Looking upwards through the windscreen, he said, 'Birds can drop great dollops of faeces, which are acidic and not good for paintwork.'

Pointing to the gap where the cops had lain in wait for him when it came into view, he said accusingly, 'That's where they hid, waiting with the radar gun.'

Dotty looked towards the gate and said, 'Minging swine!'

Dotty's head had been free of any debilitating alcoholic mists since her self-imposed pledge. She had kept some nonsense talk going, of course. If she were still drinking, Riley would expect that of her. Which is why she said: 'Keep your eyes peeled for any Tiggy-winkles on the way,' and sat forward, looking into the distance for them.

'Ach,' Riley grouched, not interested in listening to her nonsense, 'you're more likely to see a magpie or a jackdaw feeding off the squashed and bloody remains of one in the middle of the road,' He sighed. Since the arrival of the parrots, birds seemed in fashion. To show his disinterest he looked up at his rear view mirror and adjusted it a trifle.

It didn't put Dotty off offering more annoyance. 'Were the magpie and the jackdaw named after famous people?' she asked.

'Bayjasus, how the feck would I know?'

'Well, I suppose a Margaret Pie could have given her name to the magpie and a Jack Daw to the jackdaw. It sounds quite a convincing assumption to me.'

'I've never heard anything so silly,' Riley snapped. 'I've never heard of any famous people with those names.'

'Mag Pie. She could have been a famous baker, the Fanny Craddock of her day, a constructor of meaty, avian pasties. You can get crow pie. She might have baked the first magpie-filled pie. I wonder what it would have tasted like? Jack Daw; he might have been a man in at the dawning of motor-vehicle jacks. The jack bit will have come from the act of jacking up. Daw, old dictionaries will tell you, comes from the intransitive verb, to dawn. What do we have when we conjoin them..., Jackdaw.'

Riley shook his head: 'Silly, silly, I have never heard anything so silly. I suppose, using your analogy, that long-beaked, marshland bird the curlew, which is also known as the whaup, was named after a mongrel dog called Lewis?'

Their conversation ended long before the courthouse came into view. Riley pulled into the half-full car park in silence. He recognised a few of Seth Mulligan's biker friends sitting on their machines, waving a welcome.

'Seth's not among them,' Dotty said.

'He said they'd arrest him for non-payment of fines if he showed his face. His muckers are probably up to answer some non-arrestable charges, though.'

Riley parked in a space to the side of the court. While easing his way out of the car, Constable O'Hicks drove into the space next to him and called, 'Doc' from behind the wheel and through the open passenger window. Riley lowered his head towards the window. 'Doc, that stupid bastard wants you all to himself,' the constable said. 'He doesn't want me to corroborate him. So remember this and use it for it will surely get you off. Travelling for two seconds at thirty miles per hour will take you eighty-eight feet. He'll give the speed and time bit as evidence. Get your head around the maths, it won't be difficult, savvy what he says about the car lengths and you'll be able to work out the rest.' He closed the window, pulled the car out and drove to a space further along.

'What did he say?' Dotty asked.

'A little tip for in court, I think.'

Several cops were loafing about, some sucking on polystyrene cups steaming with tea when, hand-in-hand, Riley and Dotty entered the courthouse foyer. The police inspector in charge at the court had a cheery reddish face. He prowled, clipboard in hand, asking arriving civilians their names and ticking their presences off on his list, if they were up for trial. He approached and asked Riley courteously, 'Your name please?'

'Riley Dernehen.'

The inspector looked at his case list and said, 'You're on first, Mr Dernehen. You'd better get yourself into courtroom 2.'

Sergeant Liptrott took to the steps of the courthouse, grinning from ear to ear, his stomach lurching beneath his tunic. Surveying the scene inside from the doorway, he spotted Riley and smirked towards him, as was ushering Dotty into the courtroom.

With Dotty walking in front of him, Riley seized a moment to look around. Mavis was sitting by herself in the back row, looking downcast, a darkness beneath her eyes. She wasn't looking in his direction or letting on that she knew him.

The sergeant had followed close behind them and was standing at the back. Riley noticed the coy wave and the suggestive leer with which he tried to attract Mavis' attention.

The courtroom was typical of all Magistrates' Courts in the province. The public area faced a raised bench with a door to each side of it. The clerk-of-court sat at a desk to the front of the bench and just beneath it. The bench of magistrates, when they entered moments later, consisted of two men and a woman chairperson.

They'd be local Justices, Riley was sure of that, but he didn't recognise any of them. None of them looked like the judge in his dream and he cheered up briefly.

The weedy, lank-haired, anaemic-faced clerk, wearing a black suit, dandruff speckling the shoulders, rose shakily to his feet and called, 'Riley Dernehen.'

'He'd look more realistic as a judge at a hearse of the year show,' Riley whispered to Dotty as he left his seat to step into the dock.

'Good luck, Riley,' Dotty said quietly and squeezed his arm. Riley entered the dock positively, buttoned up his jacket and stood facing the witness stand. The clerk read him the charge and asked how he pleaded.

In receipt of the snippet of information from Constable O'Hicks, and searching his knowledge for the fact that a body travelling horizontally at 30 mph covers a distance of forty-four feet per second, he said, 'Not guilty,' loudly and confidently though he knew not what arithmetic he might yet have to work out.

Sergeant Liptrott took the stand. For effect, he rattled his boots to attention. He read aloud the oath then said, 'Your Honours, this was on Sunday, the first of August, at 00:50 hours. I was driving along Ballyboil bypass in a marked police vehicle, in company with Constable O'Hicks.

'I saw a motor vehicle in front of me, driven by the accused. It approached the traffic lights ahead, travelling at a steady 30 miles per hour. The traffic lights changed from green to amber when the motor vehicle in front was 10 car lengths from the traffic lights. The time gap between the amber light changing to the red is 2 seconds. The motor vehicle did not slow down but passed through the lights after they had turned to red. I stopped the motor vehicle and pointed out the offence to the driver, the accused, Mr Riley Dernehen. When cautioned and asked if he wanted to say anything, he replied, in a belligerent manner, your Honours, "The light was blue, officer."'

Murmurs, snorts and sniggers circulated the court. Riley looked around. Dotty was wrinkling her face with distaste and looking unhappily up at him.

She had remembered him telling her that he had returned home before midnight on the night of his offence.

'Do you wish to question the sergeant?' the clerk asked.

'Yes,' Riley said loudly and confidently towards the bench. He was sure of his facts now. The sergeant's evidence might just have the flaw to which Constable O'Hicks alluded. With his first question, he would try to bring out that discrepancy.

Riley repeated the oath. The clerk said to him, 'Put your questions to the sergeant.'

'You say ten car lengths, sergeant. Can you be more specific please and tell the court the number of feet in ten car lengths?'

The sergeant lifted his eyes and said without hesitation, sure of his facts, 'It's 75 feet, your Honours.'

Riley did a swift calculation based on Constable O'Hick's suggestion.

'Your Honours,' he said. Then he began laying it on thickly. 'The sergeant has damned himself from his own mouth. The sergeant said, and I quote, the car in front was travelling at 30 miles per hour. That being the case, the car I was driving would be travelling at forty-four feet per second. During the two seconds in which he stated the light remained at amber, the car would have travelled eighty-eight feet. The sergeant said, and I quote, the car in front was seventy-five feet from the lights when they changed from green to amber.

'It is my calculation, then, that two seconds later, the car would have been thirteen feet beyond the lights when they changed to red.'

The sergeant's face looked murderous and his lips had rolled back, showing his thoughts at that moment. The magistrates looked at each other concernedly. The chief magistrate beckoned her associates into a huddle. Close together, lips to ears, wearing frowns that meant a bit of a worry had developed, the bench discussed Riley's demolition of the sergeant's evidence.

Reading the signs, the clerk turned towards the bench. Without asking if there were any other witnesses, he rose sluggishly to his feet and said, 'There will be a recess.'

The bench left through a side door, but 3 minutes later, they shuffled back in. 'The case has not been proven,' the clerk piped up. 'Mr Dernehen will be awarded £50 expenses.'

The chief justice addressed the sergeant, whose ears were beginning to glow as red as his face had already gone, 'A report on your evidence will be sent to the local RUC authority. It will set out our thoughts on what you have told us on oath today, with which you have attempted to prove the commitment of an offence by a road user.'

It wasn't a great moment in judicial history, but on his way from the courtroom, those bikers in court during the proceedings rushed forward and pounded Riley's shoulders heartily, to the cries of, 'Feckin' well done, Doc.'

Dotty tried to look pleased, but couldn't. Riley might have got off with the charge, but he had fouled up with his times. How could he have been in the house since before midnight that night and on that crossing at the stated time? Something didn't fit. Whom that young woman was who brushed past him as she left the courtroom? That, too, puzzled her. Why did she fit her hand into his and squeeze it? Was *she* the fragrant woman of her suspicions? Was this Mavis O'Rourke… the woman with whom she had reason to suspect Riley was finagling?

The sergeant was standing on the steps of the court, watching the Dernehens depart, when suddenly his inflamed lips began to vibrate. Turning, he began to berate Constable O'Hicks, standing close by, who was looking suitably shocked at the sergeant's outburst. 'That was a bloody useless idea of yours to use ten car lengths. You're a blithering idiot,' he screamed at him. 'Thinking of it, ten bloody go-carts would measure longer than that.'

'At training school, they tell us to use examples that the bench can relate to,' the constable said whingeingly. 'It was you who kept on insisting that 10 car lengths were 75 feet, but I couldn't convince you it was closer to 100 feet.'

'It's different when you're out on the street, you feckin' eejit. To get a conviction, you never tell the truth if a lie fits chummy up better.'

*

'If you drop me off at the pet shop in Boiler Street, at what time will you pick me up from outside there? Dotty asked Riley as they left the car park.

'I'll meet you just after 3 o'clock at the drop-off point, if you agree,' Riley said. 'But isn't that a rough area? And are you sure that's where you want set down?'

'Most of the shops there are closed due to the smell from the River Boil, but the only decent pet shop in town is on that street.'

*

From a depression on each summit of Mount Boil, spring water bubbles from geological faults. The water irrigates the swathes of moss, scarlet and white heathers, bracken and gorse, and ploughs furrows down the slopes.

The Simmer Burn forms where several infant tributaries merge on the plateau between the peaks. Locals laugh at the choice of name for the burn: the simmer coming before the boil. From there, the burn picks up speed as it tumbles. Becoming a torrent, it twists and surges deep. Eons ago, it scoured out the earth from the rock-strewn fissure that today scars the hillside and along which it now flows.

It reaches the ragged outcrop of Boil Scarp in spate, flecked with foam. There it plummets vertically for two hundred feet as Boil Falls, seething and roaring into Boil Pool.

The pool empties in tumult, squeezing into Boil Gorge Narrows, forming a tributary of the River Boil proper. Leaving the high ground, the arm sweeps along towards the leveller plains of County Boil in a succession of doglegs and switchbacks.

Arcing like a great bow on its passage through flat farmland, the river widens and provides irrigation for popular potato varieties and other crops. Its energy dissipated, the river eases gently along.

Reaching Ballyboil town, the once-pristine waters of the river are flush with insecticides, herbicides and manmade fertilisers and reeking of stinking, tear-jerking, nostril-clearing slurry washed from many fields.

Untreated sewage, replete with a floating and frowned upon abundance of colourful and knotted condoms, swells the foul mix on its meander west, before dumping the lot into Loch Neagh.

For a time, the river flows parallel with Boiler Street, then on through the town centre where it laps walls in Rippington Avenue. Townsfolk seldom venture there without hankies held close to their noses, so eye-dampening is the odour it gives off.

For reasons not apparent, many inhabitants know the thoroughfare as "The Split". In olden days, it housed the mistresses of wealthy seed and cattle merchants and racehorse trainers. Today it boasts of nothing but run-down properties with chipboard sheets covering the many broken windows.

*

'We will share the fifty quid when it comes,' Riley said. 'In the meantime, buy something nice for yourself. I'll see you at 3 o'clock, on-the-dot.'

Riley found the Pet Shop in Boiler Street. It was the only business stacking sacks of dog food and dog biscuits outside. After dropping Dotty off, it took him five minutes to reach the hospital.

Success in the court should really have cheered Riley, made him feel buoyant, but misgivings filled his mind. The time the sergeant stated in court for when the offence occurred, was troubling him. Dotty must have heard what the sergeant had said; she was listening avidly to everything. It would just be his bad luck if she recalled him saying he had arrived home before midnight that Saturday night. She might require a convincing answer from him and not take too kindly to him pooh-poohing that portion of the sergeant's evidence. Had she been far enough under the influence? Would she also assume that the sergeant lied about the time and think it not significant? Aye, it was all a bit of a worry.

In his office, Riley refused Cynthia's offer of coffee. He still felt tetchy and he had to read up the notes on the patients he was about to see. Ten minutes later, a thick folder of notes beneath an arm, he walked from his office towards the wards.

Mavis was waiting for him to leave his consulting room. She walked briskly from a side passage wearing the same clothes she had worn in court. Quickly they were in step.

'Your brother's okay?' Riley asked as they walked along.

'Aye, he's fine, but I've had a visit from an evil-faced, Belfast woman. She's looking for Mickey. Owes her for a greyhound, she says, and wants to know his whereabouts. I didn't believe that. I haven't seen him for months and I didn't know he was into greyhounds, I told her. I didn't ask her anything. She told me she had booked into the Boil Arms for B&B and if my memory improved, to contact her there. Feckin' cheek of her.'

'No one else is looking for him, then?'

'No, she's the only one. I'm not telling Mickey about her. He'd go apeshit and might take up and leave. I think he's safe here for now, but you wouldn't know with that woman about. She had intense eyes and looked at me with hate. She could have been on drugs or something.

'I went into the Boil Arms the other night with a friend for a drink. She was there, sitting with a bunch of bikers, exchanging ribald jokes, laughing like a drain and toking cannabis. She might hang around. Keep your eyes peeled for her. She's a big hulk of a woman.'

'You'd have a better chance of getting your brother out of here if you prepare him as I said to you on the phone.'

'I've trimmed his moustache until it's as thin on his top lip as yours is. I've cut his hair and blackened it. It's just his clothes now. Once I get those sorted out, he'll be a passable resemblance of you, but only in the dark. No one looks quite like you, though.'

Mavis turned her eyes seductively towards Riley. He was deep in thought and missed the glance. Changing direction, he guided her into the staff cafeteria. 'Coffee?' he asked and reached for a tray.

'Aye, with milk and sugar, please.'

They sat near a window. 'You can't keep him in that generator room for much longer,' Riley said. 'You'd better get him into a bed in the private ward, one you're in charge of. Keep his face bandaged, give him a false name and show him as another doctor's patient, preferably one that's away on holiday. Make him out a sheet as having had cranial surgery.

'You'll have to make sure he doesn't starve. You'll have to ensure he remains there until Wednesday night. I won't be going near him so I won't be involved. If anyone discovers he shouldn't be there, then the deception will be off and you'll have to come up with an idea of your own.'

'Won't the bikers realise it's not you?'

'They've not seen me all that often. They're taking an early morning ferry to the mainland so it will be dark for most of the time Mickey will be with them. I suspect it'll be a bit of a rabble and most of them will be high on drugs and pissed. There's about forty of them crossing on a block booking. I'll organise the pick-up from the back door of the hospital, the one nearest your apartment. Wearing a crash helmet, a visor covering his eyes, a muffler wrapped around his neck and sitting on the backseat of a trike, he'll look little different to me.

I'll tell Seth that I'll accompany them to the ferry terminal in Larne, that I'll do the crossing, there and back, then take a train back to Belfast. Tell Mickey to answer to Doc. He must board the ferry as a biker; then, he must hide. Locking himself into a toilet for the crossing will keep him out of sight. On the other side, he must retain his disguise but mingle with the other passengers leaving the ferry.'

'You've done really well for me. There's only one way I can repay you. With whom will you be spending Wednesday night?' Mavis asked, smiling at him seductively.

'I hadn't thought about it,' Riley said, 'but I must admit to a little twinge of interest. If I stay in your room, you'll have to keep me especially happy, and for most of the night.'

Riley returned to his office as soon as he had completed visiting his patients. He sat behind his desk, took Seth's card from his wallet and dialled the number given, getting through to Seth immediately. Seth was overjoyed that Riley was taking the ride with the club and agreed on the time and place of pick up.

Riley knew that the plan had to work without any hitches. "Unlanced Boils" bikers would exact revenge on anyone messing with or duping them.

The journey back to the Hall was uneventful, except for Dotty rabbiting on about the new food mix with extra nuts that she had bought for the parrots.

On the journey, Riley told Dotty of his plans to please the bikers by taking a short run with them to Larne. She raised no objections, indeed she suggest that he went for it. 'You never know, you might get to like the life,' she cajoled and made vrooming sounds.

On pulling up outside the Hall, some activity in the hallway drew Riley's eyes: the sight of Cedric transporting himself past the open door and in a position suggesting that the dog had yet again been gnawing at a boiled-useless bone.

'That feckin' dog's hoovering the carpet again,' he said to no one in particular on stepping out of the car.

Riley loped up the steps two at a time. Approaching the door, he heard the unmistakeable hum of a carpet cleaner. In the hallway, however, it was clear to him that the sound was coming from the parrot's cage.

Dotty struggled in behind him laden with the shopping. The humming from the cage stopped, 'Change the dust bag,' were the squawked words then heard.

In a bit of a flap and drying her hands on a towel, the cook appeared at the kitchen door. 'It's a bit of a worry, I, I, I couldn't get the feckin' bo…bo…bone back off him,' she shrilled.

'Which one of you dafties gave him the feckin' bone anyway?' Riley snapped.

'I, I, I distinctly heard Mrs Dernehen say, "Give… give… give the dog a bone," doctor,' the cook blubbered. 'Her voice came as clear as day through the open door as yourself and Mrs Dernehen left the Hall this morning. I didn't realise how, how, how much of a worry it was until Cedric assumed his… his… his hoo… hoo… hoovering position and was dragging his ar…ar…arse across the hall… hall… hallway carpet.'

'Nick, Nack, Paddy, Wack,' said a parrot. Both of the birds' heads were moving from side to side. An eye of each in turn gave the bereft cook and the Dernehens the once over, then their heads ducked down behind the seed-saver. The chunks of cheddar cheese remained untouched.

'Each time I went to the cludgie this afternoon,' the cook said with a sob, 'and while I was trying to pot, if it wasn't the telephone ringing or me hearing 'Stick em up' in a cowboy drawl it was someone rapping on the door. Each time I was smartishly pulling up my drawers. Once I had myself settled and I heard the feckin' bells of a cop car ringing. Those feckin' birds really had me going until I cottoned on it was them.'

'The birds have been at it, mimicking. I ought to ring their feckin' necks,' Riley fumed.

The sound of two hard-shelled nuts splitting open almost together, then the crunching of the contents, made Riley turn towards the cage.

Cedric's perambulations differed little from the previous times Riley had encountered them, but this time the dog's doleful eyes were sadder, redder and more watery.

Dotty took the shopping bags into the kitchen and returned. 'What are we going to do with him? I'm only asking because I'm informing you that if his arse needs any smearing done to it this time, then it's all yours.'

'I'm so glad you have considered that *we* might do something for Cedric,' Riley said harshly. 'Look in the medicine-cupboard. Find the castor oil, fetch it to me and I'll allow you to assist me in administering this ancient Irish remedy for greasing the intestinal track of a dog about to suffer dire constipation.'

Riley removed his coat, slung it over a chair and moved in on Cedric. Dotty appeared at the medicine-cupboard door, shaking the two-pint bottle.

'Don't just stand there. Take the top off and be ready when I say so,' Riley instructed.

'Oaaah,' Dotty uttered, looking suitably disgusted, having guessed what Riley expected of her.

Riley rounded on Cedric and grabbed hold of him. Lurching together, they collided with the table supporting the parrot cage. Moving it with a creaking sound a short distance across the floor, it hit the wall and rattled the figure of Virgin with Child from its hook onto the floor.

The parrots screeched and clung with talons and beaks to the side of their cage. Outstretching their wings, they fluttered to restore their balance.

Cedric dug his claws into the carpet and moved off with Riley's arms wrapped about his neck, dragging him across the pile. Riley's knees were warming up fast, close to receiving friction-burns, until he finally halted Cedric's progress, boxing him in behind the outer door. Easing his position, Riley took a fresh grip on Cedric's shoulders, forcing him onto his back, turning his slobbering face upwards and presenting it to Dotty. With Cedric's head steady, Riley placed his two hands over Cedric's nose, forcing fingers into his mouth and prising it open.

'Come on, be quick, get over here with the bottle,' Riley shouted at Dotty, dog dribbles beginning to course over his hands and down his wrists onto his shirt cuffs.

Dotty shuffled forward. With a gulp, she removed the bottle cap.

'Quick, take a brave swig and spit it in here,' Riley said, holding Cedric's jaws open.

'Oaaah, I can't do that, I'll be sick,' Dotty groaned, turning her head away.

'Of course you can do it. You come from a brave line of Whynots, remember?'

'Bridie, over here, hold the bottle for me,' Dotty called to the cook.

Dotty slugged a mouthful. The cook rushed forward and grabbed the bottle from her.

'That's brilliant, wonderful. What a natural dispenser you are,' Riley said, as Dotty bent over and spat a jet of the oil over Cedric's steaming throat. 'Now another one, be quick and just as accurate.' Riley was smiling, enjoying Dotty's discomfort.

Riley released Cedric. The dog floundered for a time, but his elephantine memory remained intact. Without instruction, he headed for the door and his usual tethering site.

Dotty rushed into the kitchen. At the sink, she filled a cup of warm water with which to rinse her mouth. The cook slouched up behind her. 'Salted water is best,' she advised in a shrill voice, 'then suck a peppermint.'

Sucking a peppermint, Dotty walked back into the hallway and straightened the carpet with her foot. She saw the figure of Virgin with Child lying on the floor. Stooping behind the parrot's cage, she picked it up and wiped it over with a hand.

The parrots seemed to take an interest in this recovery and fluttered onto the cage side. 'Baby cheeses,' one of them said in a croaky voice.

'There you are then,' Riley said. He was standing behind Dotty, having just returned from tethering Cedric. 'The parrots are more likely to have heard about Baby Jesus in the working bedroom of an elderly seamstress, not in the environment you suggest they came from.

'Father Mack and you might just be wrong. If he had heard what they have just said, he'd be right on the phone to the Vatican, proclaiming to have witnessed a miracle, claiming the Parrots as RC's and putting them up for sainthood. Sillily so, may I add. Much like in the case of Paddy whose toast fell from the table to the floor and landed buttered side up, which *he* proclaimed a miracle.'

At dinner that evening, Riley wondered why the cook had placed an entree of Atlantic mussels in front of him, liberally laced with garlic sauce. A favourite dish of his at one time, the mussels had remained in the kitchen freezer since he began his relationship with Mavis, having instructed the cook never ever to present him with garlic dishes again.

He had fobbed Dotty off with tales of stomach problems unbecoming of a doctor. In reality, bedding Mavis with raging halitosis was the event to which he didn't look forward.

Dotty knew the dish would leave a lasting, repugnant and repelling halitosis, only dwindling over days with the use of a strong mouthwash, which is why *she* planned the meal. If Riley refused them, it would be added evidence that he expected to be finagling again soon and wanted to keep his breath fresh.

Dotty watched him sniff at the mussels, turn towards the cook and rage loudly, 'I thought I told you I wouldn't eat this dish again.' He picked the plate up and thrust it towards the cook, standing looking suitably chastised and thinking that the missis' assumptions were correct.

Riley had no objections to the main course of fillet steak garnished with fried mushrooms, onion rings, pepper sauce and chunky chips, which both he and Dotty sat and savoured in silence.

After the main course and the dishes cleared away, the cook fetched a steamed brandy goblet from the kitchen and dried it at the table. Dotty poured a large measure from the decanter, spun it around the goblet, looked through it and sniffed at the bouquet.

'I spent a little extra and bought a nice drop of Metaxa in Ballyboil today,' Dotty said, looking at Riley over the top of the goblet.

It pleased him that Dotty found the Greek brandy to her liking; its level in the decanter indicated it should give her many hours of uninterrupted sleep. 'I'm so glad you're enjoying it,' he said, feigning indifference.

Chapter 22

Late that Monday evening, Sergeant Liptrott felt his world was crumbling. He was disconsolate, miserable: as sick as an Orangeman discovering that his life-saving blood transfusion had pulsed from the veins of a Knight of St Columbus.

Sitting alone on a settee in his one-bedroom apartment, the whites of his eyes were a crazy paving of lines, red and wriggly: like maps represent roads radiating from the centre of a large city. His feet were bare, save for a corn plaster, and he was wearing his uniform trousers and an open-necked shirt.

Since leaving court that morning, his mind had churned over his disastrous choice of evidence in his case against the doctor. The delaying of his expected promotion to inspector, even though his record showed that he had never lost any of his previous five-hundred motoring cases, he saw as the upshot of that blunder. With truth, or lie, whatever it took, chummy had always gone down, guilty as charged.

Infuriating him further was the stalling of his ongoing persecution of Doctor Dernehen.

Sneaky asides, the painful ribbings from colleagues, were also becoming unbearable. As soon as news of the court fiasco leaked, mockery and mimicry seemed to flow at his expense, from every nick in the province. 'Was that light you saw true-blue, before you crossed through, sergeant?' and 'How many cars make seventy-five?' he had heard countless times.

Back at the station, his telephone had bleeped continuously. Answering, disjointed voices, from some anonymous nick, asked him the same stupid questions. Then the barrage of loud, braying laughter followed. Every cop in Ulster seemed to know he had dropped a clanger!

Sitting, sniffing sorrowfully, he occasionally blew blobs of snot into a damp handkerchief from his reddening nose. An empty Bushmills Whiskey bottle, his favourite tipple, lay on the floor, together with remnants of a "Cantonese Style Set Meal for Five". A Chinese takeaway, at whose kitchen door he had often mumped food, had delivered it to his apartment. Bingeing thus, he attempted to forget his shame.

Thundering out yawns, he headed towards sleep. His eyes had blurred earlier; now double vision affected him when he sneaked both eyes open. He pivoted on his backside, turning himself ninety degrees. His feet settled onto a settee arm, his head slowly falling back onto a cushion. He blubbered, 'Focken' stupid bastard that O'Hicks. Shouldn't have focken' listened to him. Fock the training school and their new-fangled method of presenting evidence.'

He clenched his eyes tightly shut, but still the room spun, star-shaped lights projecting a psychodelia of colours onto the insides of his eyelids. The oriental food, lying heavy and undigested, kept leaping into his throat. Lifting his head and turning, he burped and spat some lumpy regurgitation into an empty food container.

His head resting on the cushion again, a black cloud descended. Unconsciousness quickly enveloping him, he sank into a deep, impenetrable sleep.

Surfacing from a deeper level of sleep as the morning light penetrated the room, he became restless, dreamt.....

The antique shop, in the street that led towards the river, had an unmistakeable, rickety "Olde Worlde" quality about it. Old porcelain figures, marine and metal artefacts and heroes' medals lay behind the glass of the shop's windows. Out on foot patrol, he had often stopped and looked in on them. The adjoining properties looked similar, though some businesses had closed permanently, boards shuttering shop windows and doors.

The antique shop traded in the past glories of country and empire, and he suspected the shelves inside held many more curios worthy of a browse: relics with portholes looking out into some peoples' interesting pasts.

The shop's shiny, black-painted door with its brass knocker and hinges set in crooked styles, appealed in a quaint, crazy manner. It was set down two feet into a sunken pavement, where the street level might once have been. At any moment, a Dickensian character, wearing a tall, black hat, might push the door open, slip out into the street and glide away in wraithlike, without anyone thinking it odd.

He pushed on the door. Inside the shop, he stood below the low ceiling beamed with gnarled-oak spars salvaged from a wooden-hulled sailing ship. The shop atmosphere was an eerie, swirling blueness, tinged with the aromatic whiff of burning pipe tobacco. It wrinkled his nose pleasantly, putting him at ease.

In his restlessness, he inhaled deeply, blubbered loudly, 'Cannabis shite.'

The pipe smoker, a man with a pallid, wispily-bearded phizog, was standing behind the counter to the rear of the shop. Insolently, he was blowing smoke rings in his direction. Placing the pipe stem back in his mouth, he took another, longer, deeper draw, before firing more rings in his direction. Dressed in a biker's outfit of black leathers, he sported sideburns, long, bushy; like his hair, tied back in a pony's tail. He lay down the pipe and picked a shiny object from his counter, holding it tightly. Perhaps it was a new purchase. The pipe smoker diligently polished the thing, occasionally perusing it through the eyeglass clenched tightly to one eye.

He had no idea what he hoped to buy. He had no wife. No beloved's anniversary loomed. Perhaps Mavis, whom he was unwillingly sharing with the Devious Doctor, might have a birthday soon. Pleasing Mavis with a gift might encourage her to ease the doctor from his patch: the patch he visited when he ought to have been out patrolling, keeping the streets of Ballyboil free of crime; the patch that he sneaked onto often, which Mavis kept warm for him.

The surface of sleep not yet punctured, he blubbered some more. 'I gave you it all, you insatiable colleen. Never were you happy. I kept on giving you more, more, more…then the doc…strayed…patch.'

He turned towards the shelves. He would look for some small object of interest. The weather was fine and warm, the streets peaceful. He saw no reason at all for haste. He could browse at length and, if he lingered long enough, the pipe smoker might offer him a cuppa: tea, the fuel that kept top cops going for that little bit longer.

'Have a good gander. Pick things up and turn them around. Inspect them fully and weigh up your options. If there's anything with which I can help you, do not be afraid to ask, but,' the pipe-smoker said, using the vernacular of the area.

He thought the man's face familiar: knew the cut of the smoker's jib.

He grimaced. Spotting a genuine antique was an ability he didn't possess. From the dusty, jumble-stacked shelves, a treasured, priceless relic of significance would need to leap out at him, immediately be apparent as a worthwhile purchase.

A selection of bronze statuettes drew his eyes. Amongst them, he saw the replica of a slinky cat, complete with impenetrable, sphinx-like smile. It reminded him of Mavis, when he brought her to shuddering orgasm, she looking happily up at him, her head sunk deep into a soft pillow.

The cat had no whiskers on one side of its face, just small, dark holes where they should be. The other side fared better, lengths of curly piano-wire sprouting. The face was unbalanced, a little pockmarked and lopsided. It was repairable and somehow appealing, ripe for inspection. In the days of peat and log fires, it could have beautified a hearth in the home of someone rich and famous. The price tag said £10, o.n.o.

He picked up the statuette and although it was heavy, passed it easily from hand to hand. He turned it over and looked beneath the teakwood plinth for some word of the bronze founder. He shuddered as he read the words on metal plate pinned there: "Dernehen and Company. This pussy was first dipped in 1848."

He turned over the price tag, glancing briefly at it. Exaggerating a disbelieving shake of his head, he let out a loud and derisory sniff: the same sniff and shake of the head from which his prisoners gathered he knew they were telling him lies. Quickly, he replaced the statuette.

The pipe smoker, now a vague outline in the thickening smoke billowing upwards from behind the counter, voiced boomingly, 'The price you see is the price you pay.'

He noted a need to recoup some expenditure existed in the timbre of the pipe smoker's voice and offered £8, with a smirk. The offer accepted instantly, he tendered a £10 note. The pipe smoker fished in a purse for change, handing it to him through the haze.

The statuette hugged to his solar plexus, he staggered from the shop. The cat's remaining whiskers were sharp, pressing into his skin, the pressure of his embrace pushing bile up into his throat.

He was wobbling along a riverside pathway. His mirror-like toecaps were reflecting the morning sunlight, sending daggers of brilliance skimming over the adjacent buildings, awakening blissfully-purring, basking pussies.

A gloriously-coloured pussy left its warm refuge, slithered down a gutter to a drainpipe leading to the ground. Scampering, its tail high and circling, it swanked towards him. Giving a muted meow, it began rubbing itself against his leg.

Twitching, his head rocking back and forth, he burst forth with a song remembered from his rugby-playing days.

'Pussies on rooftops,

Pussies on tiles,

Pussies with syphilis,

Pussies with piles,

Pussies with arseholes wreathed with smiles,

Revelling in the joys of fornication.'

He laughed loudly, but slept on.

He was nearing a bridge, but he laboured in his progress towards it. About his feet, hundreds of other colourful pussies mingled, tails high and circling, all arseholes wreathed, smiling pertly at him. Immediately, he delivered the second verse...

'Pussies on rooftops,

Pussies on rocks,

Pussies with syphilis,

Pussies with pox,

Pussies with great big swollen knobs,

Revelling in the joys of fornication.'

The river and the path he followed passed beneath the bridge. Looking up towards a parapet, he saw his archenemy, the doctor, looking down at him. He was dangling a length of string, a three-pronged hook fastened to the end, dipping it towards him, fishing to snag his treasured pussy.

In a flash, the hook caught in the pussy's remaining whiskers. The doctor began reeling in, wresting the pussy from his grasp. Lifting jerkily beyond his reach, the founder's name became clearly legible as it soared higher. Without warning, the whiskers parted from the lopsided face, the pussy hurtling down towards him, aiming for his head, wording on the base becoming larger and brightly legible as it fell: dipped by Dernehen and Co....

He threw himself from the settee, landing in the mess of empty food containers. Awaking immediately and sitting up, he brushed away the remnants of a sweet and sour dip trickling down his face.

Chapter 23

There was an interesting agenda waiting attending members at the "Unlanced Boils" meeting that Monday night. Seth was sitting in his usual position of authority, on the recliner. The attending bikers sprawled on the other furnishings, in their leathers, toking skunk grass, slugging at the cratur, alert and listening.

Seth brought the meeting to order, giving the gathering a summary of recent events, which included details passed on to him of Doctor Dernehen's court appearance.

He called for three cheers for Doctor Dernehen and then quickly turned to Roddy O'Dowd, with a question. 'I know it's been done, but so the rest of your muckers can hear. Your task of spreading a dose of the pox to infect Sergeant Liptrott, Roddy, how did it go?'

''Tis done,' Roddy said. 'To be sure I gave Mavis a good goosing and all. Loved it, she did.'

'For sure you're a boasting focker. Though I'm sure it's agreed that the payback to that bastard should be painful.'

It was agreed by all.

'I think I've said goodbye to a woman who knobs reasonably well, though,' Roddy said, shaking his head in sorrow.

'Perhaps you have. It won't be forgotten that you did it for the club,' Seth said. 'At the next bash, the first unescorted lady to arrive is yours, but get your problem sorted out first, we wouldn't want to get the club a bad name.'

'No focken chance of that,' each attending member joined in.

'She'd better be focken' pretty,' Roddy said, smiling roundly.

'You've no focken' chance of that,' the thundered response.

'I've an idea how we can really put the sergeant in the shit, deep in it,' Joe Reardon, the Sergeant-at-Arms, said.

'Explain,' Seth commanded.

'Have any of you noticed the number of hedgehogs killed and squashed down the side roads in these parts?'

'Not really,' someone mumbled.

'Well, it's gen. Guess who I've seen haring around the side roads in a cop car, his face broken out into a huge, rotten grin and purposely steering for anything on four legs he sees moving in front of him, eh?'

'That description fits only one focker,' Seth said.

'You're right. What would you say then, if I were to make up a dummy hedgehog from one of those prickly, whalebone boot-cleaners you see about farms? Then I mix up a spot of homemade explosive, stuff it into the dummy and connect it to a pressure detonator? Then I leave it in a place where the focker will run it over?'

An eruption of noise confirmed the total support for the idea.

'Have you a spot in mind, Joe?' Seth asked.

'I... I have, to be sure, and an idea how to lure the evil bastard to the place.'

The meeting closed with Joe tasked to prepare the exploding hedgehog.

Chapter 24

On many days during August, rain-bearing clouds had piled up over County Boil. Skimming in from the Atlantic at high altitudes, they shed their load, darkening the sky for a time, then slipping over the horizon to deluge elsewhere.

It was now Tuesday morning and Riley arose early, feeling a touch liverish. Thunder and lightning had disturbed his night's sleep. Setting in around midnight, the claps and flashes had continued until daybreak. His thinking, whilst laid awake during the rumbling disturbance, centred on stomach rumblings and the embarrassing bouts of flatulence the eating of too many garlicky mussels at dinner that night might have caused him.

At breakfast, the onions he ate with the steak at dinner were enough to bring about a lengthy belch.

On his way out of the Hall, Riley thought the parrots a touch subdued as he passed them. The thunder has cooled their vocal abilities were his thoughts until he heard from the cage: 'Where's Cedric?' He surprised himself when he answered: 'Sorry, girls, I'll go and fetch him.'

On route to the hospital, he stopped at a filling station to buy some Rennies, needing to calm his stomach before he saw any patients.

Seeing an Army patrol in the area was a rare occurrence; County Boil had been one of the more harmonious parts of the province during the troubles. Being quite a distance from, and on no direct route to the Irish Republic, it was never a hotbed of paramilitary activity. The population was a hard-working religious mix, dwellers never expressing many sympathies for one side or the other.

The appearance of the Army patrol took Riley by surprise. As he approached the junction with the bypass, members of a patrol scrambled from a ditch, to take up a position in the road some fifty yards in front of him, and begin signalling that he should stop. Quickly, they turned their weapons in his direction; he was happy to note they pointed downwards.

Twigs, ferns and heather were stuck in the soldiers' hats and their faces were smeared brown and green. Other soldiers of the patrol were laying flat on the ditch banking, weaponry resting on sods; some stood blending in with the vegetation, automatics across their chests, ready to cover him. Pressing on the brake pedal, he brought the Jag to a controlled halt. Soldiers rapidly surrounded the car and a young corporal rattled the window with his brown-stained hand, indicating that he should open it.

'Can I help you, corporal?' Riley asked, hoping he sounded friendly.

'Get out slowly and place your hands on the roof, please,' a soft, Scots-accented voice said. The corporal moved back two paces from the window, his eyes alert, darting, with the gun barrel turned towards Riley.

Riley obliged and placed his hands on the roof, palms down, and looked across at the alert eyes staring from other camouflaged faces. The corporal moved in behind Riley, moved his legs apart with his boot, ran a hand up his inner leg and over the rest of his person, then felt the contents of his pockets.

One soldier opened the car doors, searched the interior, while another looked in the boot. Three more stood behind the car, ready to stop the next vehicle to appear.

The soldier sifting through his case bawled, 'He must be a doctor.'

Another voice with a mainland accent said. 'Corp, you can get some medicine for your smelly arse while we're here.'

A light-hearted tittering followed, the tension eased and the soldiers lowered their guns. 'I'm on the way to Ballyboil hospital. I'm a surgeon there,' Riley said. The corporal relaxed and held the door open for him to get back into the car.

'What are you looking for?' Riley asked the corporal.

The corporal leant against the car with his arm resting on the open window. He said. 'Police have reported that the body of a paramilitary commander was found floating in the River Boil, about ten miles downstream from here. Apparently, he was a Belfast hard man. He didn't drown. Strangled, they said. We're doing a few checks in this locality to see if anyone known to us is floating about the county, but not dead, drowned or strangled, if you get my drift, doctor. It's nothing more sinister than that. We'll be out of here by nightfall, back to the boring barracks at Bessbrook.'

*

Riley parked up and entered the hospital, taking a detour past the private ward. Occasionally, NHS patients found themselves in that ward if others were full. That a patient recuperated in the private ward now, would only look odd to someone who knew no one should be recuperating there.

Approaching the ward, he saw the lights were on and slowed, but walked past the ward door as an auxiliary pushed a trolley around a corner. When the corridor cleared, he turned and walked back. Easing open one of the ward doors without causing the hinges to squeak, he looked through the crack. Mavis was sitting on a chair, hunched up and feeding a heavily head-bandaged patient soup from a spoon.

He smiled, plucked at the end of his knob and walked on. Perhaps he would ask Mavis to lunch with him if the Rennies quelled his dyspepsia.

*

Dotty was feeling good. Being off the brandy had really cleared her head. She was now able to consider better the problem she had with Riley.

All the evidence she had, pointed to him finagling with this nursing-sister, Mavis O'Rourke. After Riley left for the hospital, she mulled over what retribution was available to her, downed cups of tea and chain-smoked cigarettes.

Really, she had only one message to get across to him: he was hers and she intended to keep him. Whatever she did to shackle him, it would need to be profound and embarrassing enough to prevent him from straying ever again, and delivered in such a way he would never forget it.

The conclusion Dotty arrived at again was the one she'd often thought of: if pain and humiliation got the message across to that farmer, affectively persuading him never to finagle again, then similar treatment would cool Riley's heels and work the same for her.

The cook had crushed some garlic cloves with a mortar and pestle and was about to press the mulch and some rosemary into a rack of lamb, when Dotty walked into the kitchen with an empty teacup. 'Bayjasus, no, use only the rosemary. The garlic mussels did the trick and told me all I wanted to know about Riley's future movements.'

She refilled the teacup from the pot, lit another cigarette and turned to the cook. 'I meant to ask you, Bridie. Think of Boiler Street, in Ballyboil, in particular that derelict shop a few doors away from the pet shop.'

The cook dropped the mortar with a rattle on hearing Dotty's question. Looking around nervously, she said, 'Yes, missis, I, I, I think I know where you are, but.'

'What is it? It's dingy, seedy. The windows have boards covering them and confusingly it says, "Private Shop" above the door. I've seen women leave there carrying packages, trying to look incognito. Some have their heads bowed and their collars turned up, but it's unmistakeable that they wear secret smiles.'

'Oooh, t'wouldn't be wanting one of them, missis,' the cook said. She shook her head and frowned, shocked at the request for information on such a place.

'One of what, Bridie?'

'Missis, I know, I know I shouldn't know about such things. My Charlie told me, you know. It's one of those sex shops it is. One of those long things that t'wouldn't be wanting to know about is a dild…dild…do. My Charlie told me about them. Some sort of rubber knob driven by batteries they are, to be sure,' she blurted out. 'My Charlie told me about that sort of thing. My Charlie says they're things that go buzz in the night. Keeps women happy, my Charlie says they do. To be sure I, I, I didn't know what he was talking about.' Bridie absentmindedly continued to crush the garlic.

'Interesting... my thoughts were correct... I think a time is coming when you and I will take a little trip into town for a look inside this shop,' Dotty said. 'But it won't be for one of those dild... things. No, I'll be seeking an instrument of correction that'll leave painful, red wheals on a finagler's arse.'

'Sufferin' Christ, missis!' the cook said loudly, showing her distress at the idea. You couldn't get me into one of those places if the Pope walked in front of me and spring-cleaned the place with holy water.'

'Ach, we'll be okay.' Dotty was trying to soothe Bridie over her worries. 'We'll only be going there looking for an encourager, that's all. I'll be using it to focus Riley's mind on his marital responsibilities and putting an end to his finagling.'

'To be sure that might be different, but I'm not keen. You've found Doctor Dernehen's been finagling for definite, then?'

'I'm almost there...I've suspicions enough.'

'But t'woudn't it be better if you accused him face to face, rather than bother going after him with an, an instrument of correction, as you call it?'

'Riley would pawn me off, completely deny it and spin me a fanny of such outrageous proportions to cover his arse, so he would. I'll do it my way so that he never forgets I found him wanting. Now hurry and finish what you're doing, for right now we're going on a spying mission to the hospital. What we might see there today will determine when we go to the sex shop for the purchase.'

*

When Riley had finished his morning rounds, he telephoned Mavis at the private ward and arranged to meet her for lunch. Later, on his way to the canteen, she joined him. 'Everything going okay?' he asked as she came alongside.

'Mickey's quite happy there. He feels safe.'

'Good, can we have a moment alone after?'

'Getting desperate eh, doctor?' she asked and flashed him wide-eyed smile.

'When I'm around you I always feel desperate,' he replied, looking up at her. Taking a quick look around, he tweaked the end of his knob.

'Then we'd better do something about it. Let's forget lunch.' They both turned and walked down a corridor that led to the side entrance affording the easy access to the nurse's home.

*

Dotty and the cook arrived in the hospital car park around midday. They sat in the Mazda and watched the comings and goings from the hospital and the nurse's home. Bridie wore her apron and a head square covered her head. Dotty wore a deerstalker, pulling it down to the level of her glasses and looked into the distance.

'We must look a bit like Starsky and Hutch out on a surveillance job.' Dotty mentioned casually to Bridie.

'I was thinking the same thing, missis, but I'm confused. If all the doctors are wearing white coats, will we be able to recognise Doctor Dernehen if he appears?'

'He'll be the shortest person you'll ever have seen in a white coat. There's only one problem as far as I can see. If he's walking on the other side of a person who's as tall as five-foot-seven, we'll miss him,' Dotty said, sarcastically.

At five past twelve, a side door to the hospital opened. Riley stepped through, then Mavis; both stopped and stood still briefly, looking about for anyone who might recognise them, before walking quickly in the direction of the nurses' home.

Dotty nudged Bridie and said, her dander rising. 'There's the little swine. He's at his game.'

'To be sure it's him, missis. Is that the one he's been finagling with?'

'That's the one I saw touching hands with him in the courtroom. Nursing-sister Mavis O'Rourke, that's the one.'

'My word she's a big lump of a girl. What huge, sticky-out breasts. To satisfy her, Doctor Dernehen must be well-hu…'

'Enough, Bridie!

'Where's he taking her?'

'They're going across the gap between the buildings together. Now they're on a path leading towards what I suspect will be her apartment in the nurses' home. He's moving fast. His little legs can hardly keep up with hers. Do you see that the little runt is peering about nervously, looking for anyone noticing where he's going,' Dotty said with derision, while shaking her head.

'I've seen enough, Bridie. Lover boy's definitely at his game. Finagling, is it? He'll know all about finagling to be sure when I'm finished with the pint-sized twerp. He's supposed to be taking a trike ride tomorrow night with Seth Mulligan, as far as Larne, then coming back to me by bus and train. If he thinks I believe that, then I've come up the River Boil in a soapy bubble. Tomorrow night, you and I will be waiting for him to go finagling again with this Mavis creature.'

Dotty's dander was rising and Bridie looked at her, perplexed, knowing exactly where she was bound for next.

'It's all a bit of a worry to me, missis.'

They saw Mavis unlocked the patio door to her apartment, push it open, grab Riley playfully around the waist and pull him through.

Dotty drummed her fingers on the steering wheel in annoyance, her face twisting with displeasure.

'Is it to the Hall, now, missis?' Bridie asked, hopefully.

'Definitely not!' Dotty said then turned the key in the ignition. 'The brazen bitch is so sure of herself. She hasn't even locked the door behind her, but that's good for us. It indicates that when we call around with what we're now going to buy, it'll be open and we won't have to use force to get in. What I've seen today might be a bit of a worry to me, but it's going to be more of a worry for Riley. It's to the private shop, dear Bridie. I'm afraid it has to be the private shop.'

'Oh…oh, I thought as much,' Bridie wailed, 'you wouldn't be wanting me going into that hellhole with you, now would you, missis?'

'You're Starkey to my Hutch on this mission. We go in together.'

*

When he undressed in Mavis' apartment, Riley found the erection he had sported for most of the morning rock-hard, but giving him some pain. He had noted some irritation as he arose that morning, but had thought little of it.

Wearing only a slip beneath her nursing outfit, Mavis was quickly naked. He clambered on top of her and slid his hips between her raised and welcoming thighs. The missionary positioned assumed, he began nuzzling her breasts and slobbering over them in a passionate frenzy. 'Take me gently, Riley darling,' Mavis whispered as he entered her, 'I'm a little tender.'

It was only a lunch-hour quickie, but he gave it his best shot, terminating in a thundering ejaculation in which Mavis seemed to have joined him. His ejaculation had a burning quality about it, something akin to what he experienced when the Fiery Jack spread its skin-burning affects to that area of his anatomy. It was a bit of a worry.

Showered and his ardour quenched, he returned to the wards, seeing several patients during the afternoon.

*

Dotty pulled the Mazda into an in-town car park from where they could easily walk to the "Private Shop", using a route that didn't take them past the pet shop, where the staff might recognise her.

Bridie was mortified at the prospect of anyone seeing her close to the devilish place and wrapped her headsquare around her face.

'Get that thing off your face,' Dotty ordered, 'you look suspiciously like an Arab woman. You'll draw attention. Just follow me, close in behind, and you'll be all right.'

Dotty lit a cigarette. With it hanging from her bottom lip, she pulled the deerstalker down low over her glasses. With Bridie close behind her, she set out, swaggering confidently, towards the Private Shop.

'Mercifully, the street's quiet,' Bridie observed.

Dotty saw it as dingy. 'Watch your feet, there's dog crap everywhere on the pavement,' Dotty said, pointing out doggie deposits to Bridie. 'What sort of people allows their dogs to use the streets of Ballyboil as dog toilets? They should be ashamed of themselves so they should.' She skirted the deposits by moving crab-like between paving squares. 'Now remember, when we get abreast of the "Private Shop", it's a left turn, a quick push against the door and straight into the premises, no messing about, no dawdling behind.' Sparks jumped from her cigarette as she spoke.

'Yes missis,' Bridie wailed. Shuffling along, she kept pace with Dotty and followed her path.

The grubby, paint-blistered door of the private shop was now only ten paces in front of them. Bridie blurted out, 'Holy Mother of God save us.'

'Brace yourself. He won't help you here. We're going in, now, quick, left, follow me.'

Dotty's left hand shot out and pushed the door handle down. A quick push and it was open. Lurid, red-illumination leaked from the split in the curtain they found further in. Dotty pulled the shivering Bridie in behind her, walked forward a pace, parted the curtain and stepped in sideways, revealing the inside of the shop.

Bridie stepped in behind her, 'Missis, we're in the devil's pit to be sure.'

It took only a moment for their eyes to become accustomed to the dim interior. The kinky lingerie and padded briefs hanging along its walls and the securely locked, illuminated glass cases containing leathers and various pain-inflicting accessories caught Dotty's eye. Posters named the latest video releases in the blue genre.

A weedy-looking, bald-headed, pop-eyed man looked at them interestingly from behind the counter, where he unpacked a box of videos. 'What would you two fine ladies be after, then, to be sure?' he asked and stopped what he was doing.

Dotty strode up to the counter with a confident swing, her hat still low. The half-smoked cigarette she delicately removed from her bottom lip. 'We want to see a selection of your pain delivery systems,' she said.

'Missis,' Bridie sobbed behind her, 'for the love of Jasus, spare my eyes.'

The pop-eyed man bent low, removed some boxes from a shelf beneath the counter and began laying out a selection of vibrators. 'A fine selection we have and all and all. The favourite with the ladies is this large, black one. T'wouldn't for sure find the likes of this swinging between the legs of any broth of a boy, never mind the local lads from around here, now would you?'

Dotty picked up the box and curiously eyed the contents through its plastic window, never having seen one before. She mused: the women she had seen leaving the shop on other occasions had been hiding their faces. She'd be doing the same if she'd bought one of these.

'Will you be sharing it with your friend, there?' Pop-eye asked with practiced unctuousness and without a trace of a smirk.

'Will she buggery,' Bridie bawled from behind Dotty.

'That's not what I had in mind,' Dotty said, rattling her fingers on the counter. 'I'm more interested in a nice, slimline, single-tailed whip.'

*

It took until dinnertime that evening before Bridie stopped shaking. She saw the Private Shop as "Satan's den" and she repeated "Hail Marys" and crossed her breasts at every opportunity, but still she wasn't convinced she would gain absolution for entering it.

Riley arrived home with a wooden plaque etched with the words "No More Bones Please" signed, "Cedric", which he suspended from the stairs, to hang above Cedric's blanket. The cook came to the kitchen doorway to read the notice. Turning, she muttered, 'Oooooh,' before quickly returning to her duties.

Cedric was still unsteady on his feet and looked crestfallen, his jowls dribbled and hung looser. The parrots were watching from behind the barricades. A contemptible, 'Who's a pretty boy, then?' followed by a screech, greeted his lurch in their direction. Riley ordered Cedric onto his blanket, and asked the cook to give him a plate of milky porridge.

By dinnertime, the cook had regained her composure. She was able to slide the plate with half of the rack of lamb, grilled pink, beneath Riley's nose without any nervousness for him to notice. Ravenous after his lunchtime romp, he sat down and immediately began tucking into it; the new Ballyboil potatoes, mint sauce and runner beans from the garden, his jaws champed into with relish.

Dotty's head was clearer now, having been off the brandy for several days. She sat down at the table intending to keep the farce going; to prevent Riley from suspecting that she had sussed out his finagling and lead him into the taste of corrective punishment she planned for him.

She was dressed in what Riley always thought was the worst possible taste: soil-ridden trousers and floppy woollen top. To give the impression that her hands had been working earth all that afternoon, she ensured her dirty fingernails fell beneath Riley's gaze.

During the time she had spent in the garden, she had dug up a lettuce that contained a slug. She had thought of using that lettuce in the salad and extracting the slug from it in front of Riley, but the thought of doing that would have turned her stomach. Instead of sickening Riley, the slug would remind her too much of him.

'Freddy thinks we ought to have a midden for the garden,' Dotty said, rotating her plate and bringing the lamb closer.

'Whatever for?' Riley asked. 'We can get as much dung as we need from any of the local farmers.'

'I'm surprised that Farmer O'Toole didn't gift you a free load from his dunghill. Suggesting that he suited a ginormous, black tiddleypush should at least have got you a good deal on a load of mature cow crap!'

'Oh, why?' Riley asked, trying to act casual, while deftly trimming pieces of crispy fat from the edges of the lamb.

'You seem to impress your patients. The gift of the parrots is a good example.'

'No one needs to give me anything. I'm not in this profession for gifts,' Riley said, between mouthfuls.

His moustache began twitching. Another session of idiotic questioning seemed close.

Dotty took an almighty slurp from the goblet, emptying it. Leaving the table, she shuffled her slippers across the floor to the cabinet to refill the decanter. Sitting back down at the table she said, faking a slight slurring, 'Seth Mulligan is taking you on a motorcycle ride tomorrow, what time are you leaving from here?'

'He's picking me up at the front entrance of the hospital at 2 a.m. (He told her that, instead of the agreed time of 1 a.m. otherwise she might have contested his need to remain at the hospital all evening.) I'm leaving from there so I don't disturb you by leaving here at that time. Those bikes make a horrendous racket. I'll be taking the first train out of Larne in the morning, then the bus. I expect to be home by midday. Anyway, I've organised the remainder of the week off to recuperate and to be with you.'

'I'm surprised you're going at all. It seems an awful hour to set out, just to please the bikers.'

'So am I, but they were so generous with their offer of support. I didn't want to offend them. I'm certainly not going to go back on my word. Anyway, the hospital owes me some time off.'

'I enjoyed the freedom, the rip of the breeze through my hair that I felt when Seth Mulligan took Bridie and me for that spin. We ought to sell the Mazda and buy a trike. You and I would look good racing through the leafy lanes of County Boil with Cedric sitting next to me, the wind ripping the slavers from his jowls,' Dotty said, as joyously as she could muster.

Riley had already pictured the scene and still he wasn't encouraged. 'Ach, I'll let you know how I feel about that when I return tomorrow.'

'I don't suppose the parrots would like a trike ride too?' Dotty posed, desiring to sound a little sillier.

'I suppose not,' Riley said, and sighed seeing the inanity beginning. He'd have to be careful in case Dotty dragged him into unending, silly conversations again.

'They were rather nasty to Father Mack, don't you think?'

'Remind me what they said.'

'I was sure they were making aspersions about the Father's sexual proclivities,' Dotty said, taking several attempts at pronouncing proclivities. Then she gave him a sly glance, but his face was fixedly passive, concentrating on the crispy fat, giving no indication he wanted to answer her.

'Come, come. How in heaven's name would parrots know that? Father Mack is a saint. Certainly his flock thinks so,' Riley said at length.

'I don't know, but I thought it was rather rude of them. I mean Father Mack is in no way like that Father Jack in the Father Ted show on television, is he? I mean, you would never get Father Mack saying things like feck, tits and arse now would you?'

He might if he came and lived here, Riley thought.

'But there again, I suppose you think I'm a bit like their housekeeper, Mrs Doyle, a bit silly and disposable?'

'I don't think anything of the sort,' Riley replied rattily. Suddenly a sensation of burning erupted again in the same area he had felt it in at lunchtime. His meal was finished so he left the table to go and have a look.

In the bathroom, he locked the door, gingerly removed his knob, squeezed it along its length with a finger and thumb, encouraging a yellowy discharge to ooze from the urinogenital tract. Shuddering and becoming unsteady, he rested his forehead on the cold tiles of the bathroom and looked down at his knob, muttering, 'Fishhooks! Now I'm pissing feckin' fishhooks!'

The condition not only worried him it aggrieved him; it confirmed his suspicions that someone else was potting Mavis, dipping her pussy and spreading disease.

The discharge was possibly gonorrhoea and a bit of a worry. It could also be the infectious, but less-worrying, non-specific utheritis. Without a microscope to check the bugs, he wouldn't know. Anyhow, a couple of jabs of the streptomycin that he kept in the medicine cupboard fridge ought to clear up the problem in a couple of days.

The same treatment in tablet form had cleared up Constable O'Hick's problem in a week.

He stood with his head resting on the cold tiles, pondering whether he ought to tell Mavis to get treatment. It was a brief contemplation. The odious Sergeant Liptrott had been sniffing around and had probably laid her. If the sergeant hadn't infected her, then surely, for all the hassle he had caused him, the sergeant also ought to have the opportunity to acquire the infection.

Riley knew it wasn't ethical thinking, to be sure, but he thought the sergeant a worthy recipient of the pox. Not to tell Mavis anything of his condition meant he could be putting the sergeant in the same pickle: a "claptrap". Certainly, he had suffered a different form of claptrap from him.

Now he had to tell Mavis that he wouldn't be seeing her on Wednesday night or ever again. Once she became aware of her condition, exactly why he had suddenly dropped out of her life would become painfully clear, infuriatingly so.

That decision left him deflated. His relationship with Mavis, his dallying days, the daft fling, his mid-life crisis, were over; soon they'd only be remembered on the occasion of rare erections in old age.

Riley left the bathroom for the dining-room and found Dotty gathering the empty plates together for the cook. 'Perhaps the purchase of a trike and pursuing some healthier interest, as you suggested, has some merit,' he said, catching her around the waist, spinning her around, ignoring her dirty clothing, and placing a light kiss on her lips.

Dotty's face was calm, showed no surprise. She kept her mouth closed, not wanting any telltale aroma of tea to escape, not wanting him to see any tea staining on her teeth. She wondered, though, why he was displaying affection all of a sudden.

'And I think we ought to lead a healthier life from now on. Perhaps we ought to go on a cruise, get a little romance, some love and affection back into our lives. There's Viagra for women as well as men now, pink as well as blue. Perhaps we should try some. We're not too old to make love. I haven't cuddled up to you and told you that I love for some time.'

Riley kissed Dotty again on the lips, then on her forehead and left the dining-room with a purposeful stride, entered his medicine cupboard and locked the door behind him.

Dotty watched him go, unconvinced by his uncommon display of passion towards her. As for pink Viagra, he'd have to wrestle her like he did Cedric to get one of those over *her* neck!

Chapter 25

It was now Wednesday. Riley awoke at 07:30, still tired, his sleep fitful, consumed with different worries.

In the bathroom before shaving, he applied a little professional squeeze to his knob. The discharge wasn't as yellow. 'Some improvement,' he muttered. 'Perhaps it's NSU after all. I'll jab myself with strep from the new batch. That should clear it up altogether.'

He dressed, sorted out clean underwear, a shirt and some socks and put them along with some toiletries into an overnight bag. Dotty had risen with him, gone to the kitchen to put the kettle on, then had returned to the bedroom.

Standing by the door watching him rummaging in drawers, she saw exactly what he was taking; saw how fine he intended to look for his evening with Mavis.

'I'll find you a coat that's warm and waterproof; one of the gardener's duffle coats with a rubberised coating. That ought to protect you on an open-air, night-time drive, whatever the weather. I don't believe Seth will slow down because you're feeling chilled and wet,' she chided.

'I know I'll need suitable clothing,' he answered sharply and closed the zip on the bag.

'I wouldn't want you to catch your death of a cold, dearie.' Dotty trilled out the dearie. She lit a cigarette, inhaled deeply, then blew smoke rings towards him. Riley abhorred cigarette smoke, but Dotty was in the mood to annoy him. He had shown a little consideration for her the previous evening, but she realised they were just words… and his were often unfeckin'believable.

At breakfast, Riley's stomach felt leaden, not yet ready for food. He mixed the muesli with milk and tried a couple of mouthfuls; then, he pushed the bowl aside, his face sour, showing his lack of appetite as well as his uptightness. He loaded his coffee cup with sugar, then added cream.

The cook was hovering near the kitchen door, waiting for them to finish their cereal course. Noticing Doctor Dernehen push his bowl to one side, she removed his breakfast from beneath the grill. At the table, she removed the bowl and placed the breakfast plate in front of him.

It was unusual for the cook to be careless in her preparations; only a mental aberration would cause her to present to Doctor Dernehen a breakfast with a broken or under-fried egg on the plate.

Being sloppy in support of Mrs Dernehen was okay in Bridie's book. Yes, agreeing with Mrs Dernehen that finagling spouses should suffer these small irritations, would deliver him eggs that he disliked. Disrespect in plenty she had for a finagler.

She had lifted the two eggs from the frying pan early, ensuring they were runny. On the plate, the yokes had spread, surrounding an Ulster sausage, its meat bursting through the skin at one end, from where hot, fatty juices pulsed. The image revolted Riley and he called the cook back. 'Bridie, you know I don't like my eggs like this,' he said as kindly as he could manage, but his moustache twitched, showing his dissatisfaction.

Dotty was sitting opposite him, smiling wryly. Using the edge of a spoon, she was slicing her porridge into a wheel shape. Then she began spinning it around in the milk. She saw the mess on Riley's plate, but was unsympathetic. 'You've never sent runny eggs back before,' she reproached, seeing he was in a mood.

'Ach, Bridie never serves me eggs runny and broken. Those ones feckin' were,' Riley said. With his head down, he took a slurp at his coffee.

'Oh, we have got up out of the wrong side of the bed this morning. There you were, so lovey-dovey last night,' Dotty scolded and eyed him for reaction.

'Ach, no, I feckin' well haven't.' Riley retorted. Scowling, he sat with his knife and fork poised, waiting the return of his breakfast.

*

Riley arrived at the hospital at 9 a.m. He took the route that passed by the private ward on his way to his office. Walking along the corridor towards the ward, the door swung open and Mavis walked out. 'Tonight's the night. I can't wait to get shot of wee brother. A pain in the neck he is to be sure,' she said.

'What's up with him? Riley asked. 'Doesn't he know the risks you've taken to harbour him here?'

'I'm sure he does. It's just that he's so nervous. Especially after I told him the Army stopped you and what they said.'

Taking her by the arm, he led her away from the door. 'It'll all be over soon, don't worry. You know he must be ready and dressed suitably for 1 a.m., and waiting at the back door to the hospital.'

'Yes, he came in an unmarked donkey jacket, he'll wear that. I bought him a crash helmet with darkened visor from a motorbike shop in town. Wearing that lot, nobody will know it's not you, I'm sure.'

'Good, I hope he gets away with it. I'll be staying overnight in my consulting room, just to keep up the deception. My wife thinks I'm definitely off on the trip to Larne.'

Riley paused and looked thoughtful; he would have to explain. Now was an opportunity to play his "get out" card, but he'd unburden himself quickly and not be seen hanging about chatting to Mavis. 'The mention of my wife prompts me to tell you this. I think that she's very close to finding out that I've been finagling with you.'

Mavis stopped, grabbed his arm with one hand putting the other over her mouth and uttering a concerned, 'No… how has she found out?'

'I think she's detected your perfume lingering on me. That must have made her suspicious. I've caught her sniffing at me once or twice. She doesn't wear the same perfumes as you do which is why I began showering after our lovemaking. Before then, I did find myself redolent with your musk. Your perfume was irresistible, but now I must resist you.' He turned and faced her, his face downcast, a bit serious, his moustache twitching

'Does that mean you won't be seeing me again?' Mavis asked, looking sadly towards him.

'If you mean we'd better finish our relationship, then you're right. I've been taking a bit of a liberty. I'd have dashed Dorothea's happiness had she found out the truth. I realise I've been a bit of a fool, an old fool at that. Enjoyable as it has been, it has gone far enough. I will miss you, though.'

'I understand. It's been great fun. The day I have to approach you for professional advice if my bosoms sag, I'll know you'll have prior knowledge of them,' she said, lifting a breast up gently on the back of an arm. 'I just wish I could hug you here and now, one last time.'

'I enjoyed doing the things we did. You made me feel young again, gave me back my youth,' he said, looking away down the corridor, not up into her eyes. 'All good things must end, I suppose,' he said, his throat tightening, he had cared for her. 'But I'd better be off…I have some patients waiting,' he said with a struggle. 'See you in theatre some time. Please, please don't look into my eyes again. I might wilt.'

Riley walked calmly away and didn't look back. Stopping and talking with colleagues and the other hospital staff he met on his way, he was pleased that his voice had lost the squeakiness throat tightening had brought on.

In his office, he put down his overnight bag. His eyes settled on the examination bed. Yes, on there was the most comfortable place in his office to get a good night's sleep.

Eager to have company later, Mavis hastened to her ward office, telephoned Rippington Avenue RUC Station and left a message for Sergeant Liptrott.

*

Dotty walked into the kitchen as the cook was stacking the breakfast plates into the dishwasher. Bridie looked up, rattled a plate nervously and gave a little sigh. It had puzzled her all through a restless night what her duties as a lieutenant might entail. She wasn't happy and the dark rings around her eyes were proof of *her* sleepless night.

The missis hadn't told her much about what she was intending doing with the thing that she had bought in the place she saw as "Satan's" shop, but she had supposed what Missis Dernehen might do with it and that was a bit of a worry.

Dotty saw the cook's fretfulness. 'Everything is working out fine, Bridie,' she said, 'nothing at all to worry about. Now you did tell your Charlie that you were sleeping-over here tonight?'

'I did, missis, and he wasn't too pleased about me working all hours at some party for gentry that I told him of. He said, "I'd only ever been out of the marital bed for pisses and pregnancies during the whole of our marriage," he did. If, if, if it all goes wrong, I, I, I suppose you'll be able to convince my family that I haven't been out on some pornographic mission?'

'Your Charlie will be okay, so will you, you'll see. Whipping the arse of a wayward beast to assume control came easy to me when I was a vet's nurse.' Dotty's face screwed up into a ferrety frown of concentration, dead-set on sorting out her problem with Riley. 'The episode will not excite or scare me. It's all academic. It worked for another that I know of and it will work for me.

'But that's enough about tonight until tonight. We'll have a rest this afternoon until late evening. Just before 1:30 tomorrow morning, we'll set out for the hospital. Riley says the bikers are picking him up at two o'clock, so we'll be there to see him leave with them... or not as the case may be. I definitely think it's a not. Riley will be setting himself up for an all-night finagling session with that tart. I don't know where the wee runt finds the strength. I'm sure you're feeding him too well.'

'I think I'd better have a steak for *my* tea, missis. I'm going to need strength to get through the night, I'm sure.'

Chapter 26

The B-roads of County Boil are notoriously winding and narrow, with passing-places for vehicles a regular and necessary feature. Joe Reardon chose such a road for Sergeant Liptrott to spot and make the crucial decision to run over the exploding, dummy hedgehog.

The road had an added advantage for staging the planned incident: a stretch of it, connecting the fertile Boil Gully with the rest of the county, cut through moorland at the foot of Mount Boil in a series of short and dangerous chicanes. To one side of a particularly blind and tight 3in1 gradient hairpin, a bend requiring extra driver care and respect, stood Boilthwaite Farm steading.

Danger lurked on that bend for drivers travelling too fast and not having proper control of their vehicles: an adverse camber. Anyone driving shoddily or too fast would encounter steering difficulties and the vehicle would run out of road, before the driver could make adequate corrections.

On leaving the road, a high verge and thick clumps of concealing gorse would meet the vehicle. Its front-end would bounce upwards, ripping through the gorse on the route towards the top of a banking. Atop the banking, drivers would find their vehicle uncontrollable and about to descend towards a pig-dung-filled midden.

Joe Reardon had chosen the site well, the other bikers agreed, when they met up at their shebeen at 5:30 p.m. that Wednesday to receive the mission's codeword. They all thought the plan would go well when they viewed Joe's striking and eye-catching reproduction of a hedgehog. 'The explosive mix is just enough to blow a focken' great hole in the tyre,' Joe wised them up, 'and effectively cause the car to veer wildly off the road.'

About the same time, Seth parked his trike in a town centre car park and walked the short distance to the café on the corner of Rippington Avenue. Sipping a glass of Coke and puffing at a legal, hand-rolled cigarette, he watched from a window and was able to keep an eye on the comings and goings from the RUC station. The cops on the 6 p.m. until 2 a.m. shift began arriving around 5:40 p.m. for their duty parade at 5:45 p.m.

Most came in private vehicles, driving through the security gate into the yard. Sergeant Liptrott was amongst the arrivals. Shortly after 6.p.m., Seth spotted the sergeant leaving in a patrol car, the only one operational that afternoon.

Seth walked to a call box, dialled the RUC station number and spoke to the civilian telephone operator.

The Boilthwaite farmer had once reported Seth for poaching hares on his land; another time he had fired buckshot after him. Seth knew his name well. 'Paddy O'Brien here, he said, using the broad accent of the county, when the station switchboard answered. 'I'm the farmer what farms Boilthwaite Farm, you know, down towards Boil Gulley.'

'Yes, Mr O'Brien, how can I help?'

'There's a biker sitting aboard a trike that's broken down with a buckled wheel. It's just a little way from the farm gate and the rider's sitting there smoking a long, sweet-smelling cigarette what I'm thinking is illegal. He's laughing like a jackal and all. Any assistance he expects seems a long time in coming.'

'Is he still there?'

'Oy, bayjasus, I can see him well,' Seth said. 'He's sitting back with his feet up and enjoying life inside a plume of smoke, he is to be sure.'

'We'll have someone with you shortly, Mr O'Brien. Just inform us if he makes any attempt to leave and which direction he might be going.'

Seth had chosen "The Full Hog" as the codeword, deriving it from the stuffed replica and prior knowledge of the sergeant's piggish appetite. Seth then used his mobile to contact Roddy, giving him the codeword: the green light.

The civilian operator registered the call then broadcast over police-radio frequencies for a patrol car to investigate the report.

Mumping food was never far from Sergeant Liptrott's mind. His first stop after leaving the station was the pie cart, where he accepted a steak and kidney pie from the still-grateful youth in charge.

Temporarily, he had deserted his favourite snack of a hotdog roll, gluttonously piled with onions and mustard. It wasn't every day that Mavis left a message for him asking that he drop by her nurses' home apartment at 2 a.m., when he finished his shift. Hot breath yes, but hotdog, onion and mustard breath she didn't like blown into her ear.

The word "trike" in the police message was a clarion call of heart-pounding, lip-curling interest to the sergeant. Snatching up his patrol car RT handset, he bellowed gleefully into the mouthpiece, 'Put that one down as me attending,' He alone manned the patrol car. Constable O'Hicks, now an object of his hate, trudged a walking beat.

With no time to nibble at the piecrust and then savour fully the pie's stodgy gravy and minimal-meat filling, in keeping with pie cart fare, he broke off the pastry from one end of the pie in haste and sucked out the hot contents.

Throwing the pastry and the polystyrene packaging out through a window, he drove out of Market Square and raced in the direction of Boilthwaite Farm.

The sergeant had no reason to suspect that bikers were casing his progress, gaps in beech-hedge lined roads and woodland tracks along his route concealed them well. Using mobile phones, the bikers' kept in touch and relayed information on the sergeant's progress to Joe Reardon, waiting on the Boilthwaite Farm bend with the exploding hedgehog, observed only by interested black-faced sheep grazing a hillside.

Twice, during his journey, grim-faced and glowering his displeasure at the drivers of oncoming vehicles, the sergeant reversed into passing-places. Sounding bells to warn approaching drivers to pull over and allow him first passage was inappropriate for a silent, sneaky approach.

Thrice, he lined up and aimed a front wheel at a panic-stricken hedgehog, scurrying verge-wards on hearing the approaching noise. Each time his aim was good, guts splattering across the road, his rear - view mirror confirming each success, his face changing, twisting into short-lived, hideous smirks.

Joe Reardon, prompted by mobile of the sergeant's proximity, heard the car approaching, its tyres squealing. The sergeant, chortling and as happy as a pig in muck at his hit rate, had misjudged a tight bend as he was thumping the steering wheel and calling out, 'Hat trick, bang, bang, focken' bang.'

Joe walked out into the road and placed the dummy hedgehog where it would quickly take the sergeant's eye. Exiting the last bend, the practised, double-barrelled, front wheels hedgehog-sharpshooter would have enough time to adjust his aim and line up a wheel on the stationary quarry. If he had the explosive mix correct, Joe expected the deflated tyre to drag the car towards the sharply bending verge.

Joe stepped back and took cover behind a tree sagging with green crab apples.

The sergeant drove towards the last bend before the farm as fast as he dare. Feeding the steering wheel through his hands in the manner instructors on the advanced drivers' course had taught him, this time he controlled the car perfectly, into and out of the bend.

Peering out from close to the windscreen, he searched for a sighting of the trike up ahead. 'Focken' size of that,' he exploded on sighting the static shape of a hedgehog. His mind now focused on a different quarry he didn't slow and quickly closed with the target.

Screwing up his eyes, he lined up the nearside wheel, aiming to run over it, right up the middle. At the same time as the wheel made contact with the dummy, he heard a muffled, explosive crump. He knew for sure that a tyre had blown out, when the car slewed and careered towards the verge. The sergeant's sharp wrench on the steering wheel did nothing to change the speeding car's course. It slewed, slithered across and left the road. Lurching upwards, it scratched its way through high vegetation, flattening and uprooting gorse bushes.

The sergeant rocked forward into the seat belt, which jerked tight, restraining his forward momentum. His head had whipped painfully forward, then it was thrown back onto the headrest. The car cleared the gorse, approached the banking top, tilted forward and nosed downhill.

The dull yellowness of the looming midden, twenty feet below, leapt up fast to meet the car, as it slid relentlessly towards it. In flashback, the sergeant saw the variegated mass of the floating pussies of his dream. With his lips curled back, he exposed gritted teeth. He stood on the brake pedal and tugged at the unresponsive steering wheel. He was unable to stop the car's slide down the sandy earth of the banking. He was bound for the midden!

A dull whack sounded as the radiator grill smacked into the soft slurry, pushing through it as a snowplough does through snow, great dollops of dung splattering upwards to fall back onto the car. Sinking slowly, the car finally settled, dung sloshing at bumper level. 'Sufferin' fock,' the sergeant bellowed, sharp, jabbing pain racking his whiplashed neck muscles.

Sitting still in his seat, mental anguish prompted him to bellow, 'How the fock am I going to explain this to the inspector.'

Releasing the seat belt, he turned slowly and pushed his door open. The door bottom scraped over the top of the soft dung, pushing it away, like a barman's spatula over the head of foaming pint of Guinness, only for the dung to flow back and slop into the car's interior. The smell of the fish-and-bone-meal-fed pigs' droppings was evil and gassy and he gasped.

Taking a firm grip on the door top, he pulled himself up from his seat. Turning, he swung his body out through the doorway and clambered onto the roof. Sitting there amongst the dung droplets, the roof buckled under his weight. In a state of shock, his face a deathly white, he sat with both his hands holding his neck. Rubbing it did little to relieve the pain.

The roar of motorbikes pulling up on the road above, interested him enough to shift his bulk, lean back and look up. Although feeling extreme discomfort, his eyes were able to trace the flattened-foliage of the car's route down the banking.

The sound of motorbike engines died away. Seth Mulligan shoved gorse aside and appeared atop the bank. Forty or so more bearded faces pushed through behind him, roaring with laughter. Seth and his Master-at-Arms stood side by side, the remainder gathering around them, all looking down on the sergeant. 'In the shite again, eh, sergeant,' Seth Mulligan observed.

The bikers roared louder, fell about and slapped each other on the shoulders for a full minute. Then they left without offering the sergeant assistance or advice on choices of extrication.

*

Inspector Tony McShane was the senior police officer at Rippington Avenue RUC station that shift. He and Sergeant Billy Liptrott were close friends.

Attending the same Lodges, they had marched sodden alongside each other on that year's 12th of July celebrations. It had rained so heavily on the march that dogged, Loyal Orange Order members, no more than a mile into their parades through the streets of cities and towns of the province, dripped water from sad hats, suits, sashes and shoes. Halting later in front of their Lodges, the marchers found themselves bathed in bright sunlight with vapour rising like white smoke from their apparel.

Over their years of service together in the RUC, they'd done plenty to cover each other's backs. The inspector was a married man; handsome, winningly smiling, dark-headed and erect in his bearing, but behind his back constables called him the Ballyboil Bull. Finagling with as many local women as he had time to satisfy, he had often left the running of the station to the sergeant... when the sergeant deigned to attend to his police duties, rather than to his own finagling, that is.

The inspector had every confidence that the sergeant did his utmost, fairly and foully, to keep the station's numbers up. The letter Doctor Dernehen had sent to the station a couple of weeks previously, disparaging and not confirming Sergeant Liptrott's allegations with regard to the biker, Seth Mulligan, which the inspector received unopened, was proof of that.

After reading Doctor Dernehen's comments, and to ensure no excrement hit his fan, the inspector had urged the sergeant to destroy the pocket-book in which Constable O'Hicks had penned the fabricated evidence. He also persuaded the sergeant to waive all charges against the biker.

A telephone call to the station at 7 p.m. from the genuine farmer of Boilthwaite farm, reported a police patrol car stuck in his midden with a police sergeant bemoaning injury sitting on the roof. The inspector was about to leave the station for a dalliance with a wee honey, but whilst hovering close to the switchboard, where an attractive woman operator worked, he heard the message come in.

The message's content prompted him to attend the scene personally and alone; being brethren was everything. It meant forgoing the finagling with his matinee partner for the sake of the sergeant, but not without a grimace and the literal thought, 'I've got to pull that big focker out of the shite again.'

Slowing down outside Boilthwaite farm steading, the first thing the inspector noticed was a short set of skidmarks and the remains of two hedgehogs piled together on the road. Just beyond that, he saw the route the car striking them must have taken after mounting the verge and passing through the gorse patch.

Pulling up, he scratched his head and said, 'Suffering fock, the crazy focker has run over a couple of knobbing hedgies. I should be knobbing that wee honey, now, not here looking into this shambles.'

This was what the bikers wanted anyone to think, having collected up the remains of two of the sergeant's successful hits and placing them there, as if they were knobbing when he struck them.

The inspector left the car to investigate. He saw bits of whalebone bristle scattered about, but didn't associate them with the accident. On the verge, he walked through the gorse and looked down at the midden.

The farmer, on hearing the sounds of the accident, and seeing the car's final resting place and its rooftop passenger, had fetched his wife. They had stretched a ladder across from the midden's rim to the car roof and the sergeant had inched his way to safety. Now the sergeant sat miserably on a straw bale, rubbing his neck with one hand and sipping tea from a mug held in the other.

The inspector parked up his car in the farmyard and approached. 'Bayjasus, are you about to tell me what happened, Billy?' the inspector greeted the sergeant. The inspector didn't stand too close to the sergeant: dung clung to his uniform.

'Focken' tyre blew out. Took me by surprise, it did. Couldn't control the car, had no focken' chance,' the sergeant told him, keeping his eyes downcast, his head still.

'Sure you weren't hedgie hunting at the time?' the inspector teased.

'Something big stood out on the road. I tried to avoid it, couldn't and hit it. The tyre blew out, it did.'

'There's two hedgies laid splattered on the road where you took the verge. It looks like the prickly little fockers were knobbing at the time.'

'Fock off… It's no joke. It was big and I couldn't miss it. On me quick, it was.' The sergeant was in arse-saving mode.

'Were there any witnesses?'

'None that I'm aware of. I was answering a call that Mulligan was in the vicinity on a broken-down trike and smoking dope. You know how much I want to swing one on that monkey focker. The whole focken' bike club pulled up after the car settled in the crap. Roaring like focken' drains down at me, laughing their stupid focken' heads off they were… F, f, focken' hyenas the lot of them. Paddy O'Brien said he wasn't the one that reported Mulligan. Knowing that, I've been sitting here thinking it was a focken' set up. Focken' boil-headed bastards these Unlanced Boil bikers are, to be sure.'

'They planted two hedgies in their own peculiar prickles to belly stance for knobbing, just to have a go at you?'

'Something went crump. I heard it plainly. I lost the steering.'

'You'd be going too fast to get to Mulligan. Tubeless tyres have been known to lose their seal under the undue stresses of a violent skid.'

'I wasn't. My speed was safe for the conditions. As I said, I couldn't miss it and I never expected the tyre to blow.'

'Well, you're going to have to put in a neat wee report. Keep it simple and blame it on the tyre. I've never heard of knobbing hedgies causing an accident. They might have taken your eye, of course. You could be into animals and the viewing of that sort of stuff and…'

'Fock off,' the sergeant exploded. Lifting his head sharply made him wince. 'Focken' pain,' he bawled.

'The polac inspector won't believe it. So keep the hedgies out of your fairy tale. The boys at the central garage won't be too chuffed either. They'll have to clean the car out. In fact, I can say little that will cheer you up. You know the score. I have to consider that you're in shock. It's to the hospital now for a check-up and maybe an overnight stay. So get those stinking trousers off and I'll see if the farmer has an old grain sack to wrap you in.'

*

'The only ride you're getting tonight is a draughty one,' the inspector teased the sergeant. The inspector had stuck his head out of the driver's side window soon after they set off from Boilthwaite farm. Now, both front windows of the police car were fully open. The inspector wasn't kidding; he needed the throughput of fresh air. 'You're focken' minging,' he told his sergeant, as if to confirm his thoughts.

'You're focken' right,' the sergeant said in subdued tones. 'When we hit town, take me to my flat. I must shower. I can't go to the hospital smelling or dressed like this,' he pleaded, 'I'd look like a scabby focken' scarecrow and foolish with my head stuck through a hole in the bottom of a sack, and my arms sticking out of holes in its sides.'

'It's a good job you were rescued from that midden. Those are storm clouds rolling in. They mean more rain and a focken lot of it, by looks of them. You could have drowned in that pile o' pig shoite!'

'Fock off!'

The inspector swung the car around the hairpin bends, the sergeant bracing his neck in his hands, protecting it against the lateral forces.

'I saw the wee note left for you at the communications desk, lover boy. You just want to get yourself lathered over, spruced up and to lash on some gagging-for-it aftershave, ready for the wild knobbing session with Mavis,' the inspector teased.

'With my neck paining me like it is, it'll be the gentlest knobbing session I've ever focken' had,' the sergeant complained. 'I'd like her to do all the work, on top. My neck's stiffening up and I couldn't bear it wobbling about. It's focken' murder.'

He applied a two-thumb massage to the sorest spots, letting out 'Oohs' and 'aahs' as he hit the mark. 'But she doesn't like being on top, so I won't be able to support my neck on a pillow. She's so paranoid that her tits will hang low that she never does it that way with me. Lovely tits she has to be sure, though, I love them, I do. She's quite obsessed that they'll sag as she ages. She says it's all a bit of a worry.'

'You'll hardly be able to knob her properly if you've to support your neck doing it. Gentlemen take their weight on their elbows, remember?' the inspector taunted.

'Fock off! I haven't been there for days and she'll be gagging for it. She's always pleased to see me and has never complained when I've knobbed her in the past. I'll just have to lie down on her, missionary style, and rest my head between her tits. We'll melt into each other, we will.'

'She might have to come to you in a ward. I think they'll keep you in overnight for observation. You know it's RUC policy after a polac involving a personal injury. Shock can appear hours after an accident. It can make folks act funny, fall over and the likes. You could suffer physical collapse and the suspension of the body's voluntary and involuntary functions. Maybe you shouldn't knob tonight, give it a rest, but. You could go all feeble while you're on the job, lack spunk, dry up, die even.'

'Rest assured. I'll be giving it my best shot tonight, in shock or out.'

Up ahead, short legs scurried from a verge out into the road, humping a dark and round, prickly splodge across it. 'Want any more hedgies flattened to the tarmac on the way?' the inspector asked, smiling slyly.

'Fock off!'

At his apartment, the sergeant showered quickly, while the inspector waited. It wasn't until 9 p.m. that he tripped into A&E at Ballyboil hospital. The inspector left him there; he had some postponed business to attend to elsewhere.

'You definitely have symptoms of shock and a whiplash injury,' the young female intern delegated to examine the sergeant said. 'Policy is... we keep cops in for an overnight stay so we can keep an eye on them.'

The sergeant sat in a chair as the intern shone a torch into his eyes. Then she moved behind him. Pressure from her thumbs on his neck caused the sergeant to wince, but he remained silent. The intern was nice. He'd like to knob her. Maybe she was one to chat up when he was fit.

'Whiplash injury there, that's all, I'm sure. Quite common in motor vehicle accidents,' the intern said confidently. 'An X-ray just to make certain I've missed nothing, sergeant, then it's to bed for you.'

The sergeant kept on the gown they gave him in X-ray and later, an auxiliary nurse found him a bed in ward 1, on the ground floor, and fitted him with a neck support.

The auxiliary tucked him in for the night about the same time as Riley was in the canteen viewing the all-night menu. The fare available at 10 p.m. was unappetising. He carried a pot of tea and a packet of biscuits back to his office where he had a small feast.

At 10:15 p.m., he spread out some blankets on top of the plastic mattress cover of the examination bed and plumped up two of the softest pillows he could find. It was warm enough to sleep without a blanket over him.

His mobile phone had an alarm facility that he set to wake him at 07:30, enough time in the morning to wash and change; make it seem as if he had just arrived for work. With his shoes and tie off, he lay reading a medical journal.

The threatened storm arrived, wind-driven rain buffeting the window. He listened to it for a moment considering biker safety in the conditions. His eyes tired after twenty minutes and he switched the lights off. Soon, he was in a deep, untroubled sleep.

Chapter 27

Around the time Riley fell asleep at the hospital, members of the "Unlanced Boils" motorcycle club were going bananas in the Boil Arms, their usual set-off point for a rally.

The pub was heaving with both bikers and regulars. The licensee, looking out on his customers from behind the servery, saw many of the bikers dancing on his tables in studded boots. He wasn't about to chastise them for that or for the spilling of Guinness over each other's heads, to soak lengthy hair, then drip down beards to pool on his floor.

It paid the licensee to be biker-friendly and to tolerate the conduct. Large denomination notes stuffed his till. The night's takings were exceptional, but his eyes were never still and his face wore a perpetual frown. The night's bit of a worry would disappear only when the dope-toking, antic-prone bunch went their merry way.

The cops had let him be, but that didn't mean his number wasn't in their plans.

The jukebox blared out a succession of ZZ tops, AC/DC and Thin Lizzie numbers. Arms around each other, some bikers joined in with drunken accompaniments. Those disinterested in high jinks sat around tables, entertaining local floozies and some of the "ladies" accompanying them to the rally, keeping them charged up with drink, supplying them with skunk grass. The bar was thickly redolent of the smokeable drugs bikers were passing around the tables in long, well-stuffed joints.

Joe Reardon sat nursing a sore back and shoulders, at a table laden with pints of the black stuff. The pain he suffered had nothing to do with the weather; it was the prolonged back thumping his muckers subjected him to for planning the successful, hedgehog sting. It worried him greatly that by leaving-time he might not get through all of the drink bought for him.

Seth Mulligan, dressed in his leathers, was sitting alongside Tracy Mulldoony, beneath subdued lighting, on a wall seat, at a corner table. Tracy was wearing jeans, a lumberjack style shirt, open at the collar and not tucked in, and a donkey jacket. She looked as much a biker's "lady" as the other "ladies" did.

Both Tracy and Seth drank Guinness and pulled strongly on a shared joint. Seth's hand lay on Tracy's leg. Occasionally he squeezed her knee beneath the table and looked into her eyes for a response.

Tracy kept her hands still, but eyed him more intensely when he moved his hand from her knee to her inner thighs. 'What t'fock are you after, yeh randy biker bastard?' she asked in her Belfast drawl, her hot breath forcing into Seth's nearmost ear.

'Yeh're knickers are sounding like the Ballyboil creamery in full production, even in this racket, yeh Belfast bitch,' Seth replied and shuddered. Then he moved his hand up and sought out a spot where a well-placed, educated finger ought to enhance Tracy's excitement; have her gagging for a good knobbing.

Seth had spotted Tracy in the pub a couple of nights back, had bought her a drink then and encouraged her to accept a trike-ride home to Belfast. Now he was hoping for an early payment. Giving her a good knobbing against the pub wall before they left was what he had in mind.

His regular girlfriend had woman's problems and didn't feel up to the journey. In her absence, Tracy would do. She had a considerable girth that spilled over the top of her jeans and breasts that bulged out of her bra.

Seth thought her a sizeable beast of a woman and he was keen to tackle her to gain some bravery points from the membership. It was the tradition of the bike club that members treated women without fear or favour. In the club's eyes, ugly women just didn't exist. Nevertheless, the club awarded an annual prize to the member who had knobbed the ugliest one during the rally year.

Whether they were sizeable, beastly or just sizeable beasts, club policy was they were all there for knobbing. Seth would be ahead after this one, the rest were stragglers.

Tracy had said nothing to Seth about the death of her Republican Brigade Commander husband Martin, or that she had come to Ballyboil seeking his murderer. Had Seth known that, he would have treated the woman more courteously. Never would he or anyone in the club want to incur the wrath of that lot.

Tracy's enquiries on the whereabouts of Mickey O'Rourke had come to naught and she was going home. She hadn't acted suspiciously, hadn't asked many people if they'd seen anyone answering to Mickey's description. She just hung about, most days and some nights, and kept an eye on comings and goings at the hospital and the nurses' home. She had spoken to Mickey's sister, Mavis, thinking her best chance of finding the wee murdering focker, as she thought him, if he was in this area at all.

Tracy was going to murder him if she could get her hands on him: as much for Martin as for the death of the dog.

Seth's hand reached in and began undoing the fly buttons on Tracy's jeans. She shuddered. His hand was working so well that Tracy pushed it down in between her legs, closed them, squeezing it in that position, retaining it there. She shuffled her butt closer, pressed her breasts against Seth. The other hand grabbed for Seth's knob, expanding at pace between his legs and down the inside of his leathers. The thumb of her other hand she used to ensure her false

teeth were secure on her gums. Purring seductively 'Come focken' here,' she
pulled his head around with same hand, planted a wet kiss and pushed her
tongue into his mouth.

Ho, ho, here we focken' go, Seth thought. Sensing that she was gagging
for a knobbing and now, he put the joint in an ashtray. Grabbing Tracy by a
hand, he pulled her through the throng. Bikers, reading the signs as he made his
way towards the door to the car park, slapped his back repeatedly. He grinned
foolishly at the cries of 'Get those focken' knickers off the bitch, Seth boy. Give
her a brave old knobbing.'

'He had better be focken' good and hung like a focken' donkey or I'm not
focken' well coming back here,' Tracy said hoarsely, her voice unheard in the
racket.

There were few formalities in the car park. It was raining heavily and the
wind was howling but neither seemed to notice. Both urinated behind the trike,
standing up, in preparation for an uninterrupted knobbing session. Steadying
her up against the pub wall, Seth undid her jeans and pulled them down around
her ankles. After easing out one of her feet so that she could open her legs
wider, he loosed off his leathers.

The seat of Tracy's jeans was sodden and her hair lay flat when Seth tugged
her back into the pub. She looked towards the floor on the way to their seats and
not a bit upset when Seth shouted aloud to his mockers, 'The bitch was a brave
shag and I gave her a good focken' knobbing!'

*

"Unlanced Boils" bikers had no fine limits on the amounts of drink they
swallowed and the drugs they smoked or ingested; the club had never enforced
many strict rules at all. The club members had witnessed the consequences of
bikers parting with their machines at speed on a tarmac road; consequently,
they adhered to one club recommendation that they all spend a sobering half-
an-hour in the fresh air before setting off for distant rallies.

At half-past midnight that Thursday morning, under the glare of the Boil
Inn car park floodlights, bikers prepared themselves for the two-hour run to
Larne. The rain was heavy and driving.

All the bikers had drunk black coffee before leaving the pub, now many
wandered about, breathed deeply, cleansing their lungs of fug. Others urinated
openly. Others, already sprightly and soberish, fussed with their machines, eager
to set off. All had foul weather gear laid out ready to don; weather forecasters
expected heavy rain to persist throughout the night.

Tracy was standing with some "ladies" in the pub doorway. While gabbling
away with them, she wrung out water from the seat of her jeans, rubbing her
hands together and tried to stay warm.

Seth called the members together. 'Now you know I'm picking up the Doc
in the hospital car park at one o'clock. I'll go there with Tracy on the back, pick
him up and see you at the roundabout on the by-pass at the east-end of town.'

There were grunts of approval and an aside, 'Don't keep us waiting if you're going to try it doggy-fashion over Boil Bridge,' which caused them all to chortle.

'The hairy-arsed focker will be riding fock-all but trikes from now on,' floated through the rain from Tracy, her remark making her companions giggle.

At ten minutes to one, the first of the bikes kicked over. Seth led them from the car park minutes later.

Chapter 28

Mavis moved Mickey from the private ward to her apartment when it was dark enough to do so and with little chance of anyone seeing them. She hadn't seen the funny woman about since she accosted her with questions; she was taking no chances: the woman was still a bit of a worry.

The Ulster fry-up she cooked for Mickey would be good packing for the journey. She sat with him at the table, watching him clean his plate, unsure when she'd see him again. He might find a bolthole in Spain, Australia or maybe as somewhere as near as London. Others on the run from one paramilitary outfit or another seemed to successfully disappear, their nearest and dearest the only souls wise to their whereabouts.

'I haven't told you this,' Mavis said, 'but there's been an odd-looking woman, fat, jowly, a bit uncouth, hanging around, asking…'

'Bayjasus! What?' Mickey gasped and spat out a portion of sausage.

'A woman. She's been asking about you. She never said anything about the murder. Just that you owed her a greyhound…'

'It's focken' Tracy…focken' Jasus. I saw her once at a brigade funeral. Her dug got skittled by a bus or something the likes when I scarpered.' Mickey exploded, his eyes wide, looking about, 'That woman's Martin's missis, his widow. She'll rip my focken' head off if she catches hold of me.

'And that will be easy to take. If the brigade catches up with me, fock knows what they'd do. Kneecaps one day, shoulders the next, ankles the day after; they'd put a bullet in each place that moves. Then they'd whip my bollocks off before putting a bullet between my eyes and burying me in some shallow scrape in a god-forsaken bog. I knew. I knew I should have been away sooner… out of here.'

'Patience. Don't panic. You'll be out of here soon, in minutes. It's your best chance.'

'Patience! I don't have a lot of faith in faith, never mind in patience!'

Mickey was still shivering at 12:50 a.m., when Mavis placed the crash helmet over his head and tightened the strap beneath his chin. Before she pulled the visor over his eyes, she kissed him tenderly on his exposed neck then pulled up the collar of his donkey jacket. 'Best of luck dear brother, let me know where you end up. When you feel safe' she said. Both were looking into the other's eyes. Mavis, seeing the fear in Mickey's, turned to wipe a tear from hers.

Rain had fallen heavily for several hours. In the car park, water streamed towards the gutters. Mavis took Mickey by the hand and led him beneath an umbrella to the hospital's back door. At one o'clock exactly, they heard the phut-phut of the trike manoeuvring between lines of parked vehicles.

Driven rain can pound painfully on exposed flesh when one travels through it at speed. Bikers fully rigged out in leathers, gloves, crash helmets with visors, or goggles, and topped off with waterproofs remain mainly impervious.

Before setting off from the Boil Arms car park, Seth saw that Tracy had no such luxury and handed her the length of oily tarpaulin he used to cover the trike when he hadn't bothered to garage it. It was large enough to cover all of the back seats and anyone sitting on them.

Tracy sat on the centre seat, the tarpaulin up to her neck and her bag next to her. As the trike swung around and stopped, she moved the bag across, expecting the doctor coming for the hurl to Larne to take the seat closest to the hospital door.

Mickey passed through the door on his own, leaving Mavis to watch his departure from inside. Rain blew beneath the tarpaulin as he clambered aboard to sit silently. He faced the front, said no goodbyes and gave no greetings. Tracy pulled the tarpaulin around them. Folding the rough edge back as she would a cotton sheet on a bed, she covered Mickey up to crash-helmet level, as Seth moved off.

*

About the same time at Whynot Hall, Dotty and the cook rose from their slumbers and sat rubbing sleep from their eyes. They had bedded down in the sitting-room, Dotty on the couch, the cook on the chaise-longue, resting fully clothed, ready for the mission.

Dotty spoke first. 'I'll prepare the whip while you wet a pot of tea, Bridie. We'll be leaving in half an hour.'

'Okay, missis,' Bridie said half-heartedly and sniffed.

Dotty removed the wrapping from the whip. Holding it by the knobbly, bone handle and at arm's length, she flicked it, smiling gleefully each time it cracked. 'Hum, just what the doctor ordered,' she said bitterly, finding it to her liking, 'a real pain inflictor. When I'm finished with Riley, he will have scarlet wheals on his arse, running straight, parallel, close together, permanent reminders of his finagling past.'

In the kitchen, pouring tea, Dotty said to Bridie, 'There's not a lot for you to do when we enter this Mavis thingamajig's apartment, but what you do and when you do it is crucial to our success. Using this whip, I'm going to bring Riley to heel. You do understand what will happen, yes?'

'I think so, missis, but if it's going inflict pain where I expect, won't there be a lot of noise and hollering?'

'I've sorted that one. Now listen...'

Chapter 29

Using secondary roads for the first part of their journey, the bikers headed west and joined Ulster's A31 at Moneymore. From there, they travelled north towards the A6, arterial road. Joining that, they turned left towards Toomebridge, Randallstown and Belfast. On the A6, the rain, blowing in from the west, eased slightly. Seth stepped on the gas.

By the time they'd joined the A6, Tracy had become quite intrigued with the shortish, silent figure sitting next to her. Wearing the skidlid, and a black visor that hid his face, she couldn't tell what he looked like facially. He had sat stock-still, except when the trike encountered potholes and they had both shot up from their seats.

He might be more communicative if she warmed him up, Tracy thought. All he did was shiver. She was sure if they sat closer, they'd feel as snug as bugs in a rug. She needed warmth: the arse of her jeans was still sodden. Belfast was still a distance way and it was dead boring stuck on the back seat of a trike, in the dark, with nothing to do. Giving him a touching-up beneath the tarpaulin was one thought. That might be out of the question, though: Seth had said he was a doctor, but she didn't believe them all to be saints.

Mickey had jumped on board the trike not knowing he would have a travelling companion until Tracy moved the tarpaulin, allowing him to get beneath it. As the trike raced out of the car park onto the by-pass, he turned his head once to the right.

What he saw was a brain stunner: Tracy! A quicker thinker would have leapt off the trike, even while it was moving. Instead, he became immediately frozen, sphincter-clenching petrified, throat-tightened speechless. Was he reliving a "gotcha" as seen on a TV show? A focken' stitch up. Was he to be the quarry in a Hillshanks brigade hunt, the easy coconut on the rickety shy? Was he there for shooting, like a plastic duck in a slow-moving shooting gallery? Were these bikers brigade members' mates and taking him to his death? Just what was Martin's widow doing sharing the journey? What was she up to? How did he land with this?

Mickey had so many questions, but could think of no satisfactory answers. Nobody had told him he would have company. Surely, Tracy can't know who's sitting next to her! Surely not! She won't take any interest in me! Did she notice me at that funeral? What if she did and recognises me now? What am I to do to get out of this pickle?

Mickey was still mind searching when his luck took another twist. Tracy's left hand moved from beneath the tarpaulin, clawed its way around his back and tugged on his shoulder, pulling him towards her. With a little gasp of annoyance, he shrugged the hand away. Still he faced the front. Tracy was having none of it. Gripping him with one hand, she pulled his collar down with the other. 'It's focken' cold in here, Doc, lets cuddle in, warm ourselves up,' she said close to his crash-helmet. 'I can see yeh are shivering like fock, need a hot chick next to yeh.' Tracy began to sidle closer, her seat creaking with her weight.

Tracy's action chilled Mickey, stiffened his back and brought the cheeks of his backside snapping together. No way was he getting close to Tracy; never, she would kill him...strangle him for strangling Martin, Tracy would.

Her breath smelled strong. Sour like that greyhound's did when it leapt onto his back in that yard, but it would be nothing to the strength of her hatred. His shivers turned to hiccup-like convulsions, his full body lurching involuntarily, spasmodically. Feeling again the greyhound's nose, cold and wet, pressing on his neck, like cold steel, prompting a teeth-jolting jerk.

The rain blew into them in sheets as Seth took a bend in the road a mile from the bridge where the A6 crossed the River Bann.

Chapter 30

Dotty said her goodbyes to a very sleepy Cedric. His eyes were droopy and he showed little interest. The parrots were anything but sleepy. Quite alert and attentive, they were having a late-night feed of tropical fruits. 'So you want pain,' followed by a long, drawn out fiendish screech, Dotty heard as she carried the whip into the hallway. 'Behave, girls,' she said crossly, having heard everything.

She set the alarms on the Hall's windows and doors and locked up.

The rain showed no signs of easing, but Dotty and Bridie were dressed adequately for a jaunt in rough weather. Dotty had successfully hunted out waterproof jackets, leggings and sou'westers from outhouses. Importantly, they were all Army-surplus camouflage gear.

'Dressed like this, we look more like poachers heading for Loch Neagh when salmon are running,' Bridie fancied. She rustled loudly, getting her waterproofed bulk through the front passenger door of the Mazda.

'You'll have to tread silently when we reach our target area,' Dotty reminded her. 'No loose talk, no sniffing, no noise, tiptoes all the way, all of the time.'

The journey to the hospital was uneventful. Dotty drove around the car park when she arrived and found a favourable spot, allowing unobstructed observation between two other parked cars to the patio-door entrance to Mavis' apartment. 'The bikers will be here shortly if my Riley has not been sparing with the truth,' she told Bridie, held up the whip to the light and called it by the action it would soon take, 'Fettler.'

'May the Good Lord forgive me for tonight, for I know not what I do,' Bridie wailed.

'The Good Lord will forgive you okay. You're about to save an adulterer from further folly. I'll bless you if you follow my instructions and don't foul up,' Dotty said. Close up to the windscreen her breath condensed on the glass, fogging it. She wiped it with a tissue and occasionally flicked the wiper.

Chapter 31

To Sergeant Liptrott, time had passed slowly since a nurse had gently laid sheets over him. Most of that time, he had lain nursing an erection, thinking over the quandary: when should he appear at Mavis' apartment? He had no idea what her movements were that day. Certainly, she wasn't at work that night. She had a telephone in her apartment, but he wasn't about to give the game away to other hospital staff and call her there. If he left the precincts of the hospital before he was expected, and Mavis wasn't home, then he'd get a soaking for nothing and have to hang around, wet.

His neck would stiffen up worse, feel tighter, give him more pain, but she would be there for definite to greet him at two o'clock. She had said so. The promise of a knobbing session was just that to Mavis and she wouldn't miss out. He was frustrated, but he made his mind up not to go to her before then.

Often an official visitor to the hospital to take statements from accident and assault victims, the sergeant knew his way around the corridors. As 2 a.m. approached, he eased himself out of the bed. In one corner of the ward, another patient, prepped for an operation later that morning, snored loudly between bouts of restlessness.

The sergeant reached the back door of the hospital and pushed it open. Wearing his surgical collar, he guessed he'd look foolish and inadequate in Mavis' eyes. Without it now, his neck creased him, the pain making him wince each time he took a step. To try to prevent more spasms, he leant forward and held his head steady between two hands. In that manner, he set out to cover the fifty yards to Mavis' patio door entrance.

*

'There he goes, the dirty little scoundrel,' Dotty erupted, her face set grim. She cleaned the windscreen inside and flicked the wiper for a better look.

'Are you sure, missis,' Bridie ventured, sick to the pit of her stomach that the worst was about to happen.

'It's him alright. It's two o'clock already. There are no bikers presenting themselves and I can't hear any on their way. That means there's no trike ride in the rain for him. There's no one else I know working at the hospital who's as little as Riley. Look at him go, he must be on a promise right enough. Look at those wee, dainty steps. That's as fast as he dare go in the direction of the tart's apartment. He has left it late, though; he could have been in there hours ago.'

*

'Focken' thing,' the sergeant erupted. Two steps into his journey and he knew he couldn't hold his head steady and at the same time prevent the gown's tightness around his ankles from hampering his progress.

Stooping and taking hold of the hem of the gown with one hand, he dragged it up to knee height and held it there. His chin he cushioned in his other hand, preventing his neck from rocking. Using short, rapid steps, he hugged a wall and made his way as best he could along the path connecting the two buildings, towards the patio door, which he saw standing ajar as he neared. 'Thank fock for that. She's home,' he mouthed silently then breathed in deeply.

Slipping inside, he straightened up and closed the door a touch. Through the bedroom door, he saw the dim light of a low-energy lamp: all the light he required. Anything worth embracing on the bed, he could find by touch.

*

'He's in,' Dotty said and grabbed Bridie by the arm. 'You're up for it, now, aren't you? I can't afford a let-down now.'

'Aye... aye, I suppose so. Let's get it done, but it's all a bit of a worry.'

Dotty pulled on a pair of prophylactic gloves before she left the car. 'Don't want to leave any telltale prints about, now do we?' You do the same,' she instructed Bridie and handed her a pair.

Rain pattered onto their waterproofs as she tugged the reluctant Bridie all the way up to the patio door. On the move, their wellingtons had whacked against their legs. The whip had whooped and cracked through the air as Dotty practised slashes with it.

Silently, Dotty eased the patio door open and ushered Bridie in to stand alongside her. Dotty pointed towards an inner door from where only a dim light shone and rock music sounded. 'The bedroom door,' she whispered and placed her hand on Bridie's arm. Together, taking small steps, they silently crept forward.

*

The sergeant saw Mavis lying naked on the bed, her arms already reaching out for him. She said huskily, 'Come quickly, I'm hot for you.' Gently, he began to remove the gown up over his head. His neck pained him plenty, too much to attempt any of the usual preliminaries they enjoyed. 'Won't be getting my six or my nine tonight,' he mumbled, 'Can't give you the full treatment. Focken' neck's a bit of a worry,' he said, throwing the gown to one side.

'Come on anyway, hurry,' Mavis answered, disappointedly, 'I'll ask you what happened to it later, after the knobbing and it had better be good.'

The sergeant clambered onto the bed, straddled Mavis and rested his brow between her breasts, taking his weight on one elbow. Thrusting his other hand down between his legs, he took hold of his erect knob and entered her, as he had done so often before. Wasn't her pussy always there for him, juicy, easily accessible? Each time, with a mind of its own, it gripped his knob, favouring it with muscular contractions: wonderful feelings that made Mavis different from any other woman he had ever knobbed.

The devious doctor, he had a period of being in favour; often, he had watched his comings and goings to and from Mavis' apartment. Hadn't he to skulk lonely and demented with jealousy in the car park?

Now he was there by request. Injured as he was, he would make the best of it, do it better than the doctor had. Slowly, his buttocks rose and fell, Mavis taking the weight of his belly, squealing with delight, grunting passionately and begging, 'Billy, give it me long and strong.'

The sergeant moaned, sometimes in pain, sometimes looking for sympathy, sometimes with short-lived pleasure. Nothing else could he add to his thrusting. Like red-hot needles piercing flesh, jagged pangs of pain jolted his neck on any skew-whiff or rash movement. With his head low, he nuzzled into Mavis' breasts and moved his brow back and forth in a straight line between them.

*

At the open bedroom door, the light was poor but Dotty saw the bed, the vague outline of legs spread-eagled, legs in between, the missionary-positioned bodies in motion. She held Bridie by the arm and gently nudged her towards one side of the bed.

Walking birdlike, Wellington boot soles quietly placed, Bridie made her way to the position where she would perform her function. Dotty was pensive, moved slowly, followed behind Bridie and reached her spot. Their waterproofs' faint rustling went unheard by the lovebirds, drowned out by their grunting, moaning and the raucous guitar sounds of the rock music.

Dotty stood looking towards Bridie over the sergeant's slender buttocks. Lifting gently then lowering, his cheeks squeezing together on each insertion, waxing then waning: vertical smiles of pleasure.

Dotty was in position and signalled Bridie, still of a dither, to ready herself. As she raised the whip, Bridie lifted one wellington-clad foot and accidentally kicked the heel of the other with it. Losing her balance, she fell forward and turned through ninety degrees. Stretching out her right arm, she pursed her lips and breathed in deeply as her sou'wester skewed and covered her eyes.

Unbalanced, her elbow thudded onto the small of the sergeant's back. Reeling backwards and attempting to right herself, her elbow followed a juddering path over vertebrae to the nape of the sergeant's neck; where the missis said she had to place it anyway, and for her to keep all her weight pressed there.

The bony hinge found the uppermost vertebra and stopped, pinning the sergeant. With her weight on that point, her other hand reached out, flailing, seeking another support. Her fingers found and clawed at the sergeant's buttocks. Digging them in deep, she wrenched open a cheek and recovered her equilibrium.

Dotty was standing with the whip raised, her face a picture of astonishment; her plan was disassembling in front of her eyes. Bridie had wobbled awkwardly and now held, in a vice-like grip, half of the area chosen to receive the lashes.

But there in the half-open buttocks, Dotty quickly saw other possibilities. Grabbing hold of the other cheek, she pulled that wide, too, revealing a new target: an area of anatomy that would cause the recipient immense amounts of pain, if she were to use all of her strength and force into that orifice the knobbly end of the whip.

Dotty recalled that the farmer's wife had meted out a different punishment to win back her finagling husband. This alternative form of retribution should have similar results and, she assumed, would generate within herself, the joyous feeling she had expected.

Lining up the whip's knobbly handle with the centre of the target, Dotty flexed her biceps and pushed. Quickly, it disappeared deep into the sergeant's lurching anus. With her face contorted into a malicious grin, she twisted it around, like a mortar crushing into the sides of a pestle.

The sergeant's latest agonising experience registered on the intruders' ears as snuffles, snorts and long but effectively-stifled, bull-like roars of anguish. Stuck securely between Mavis' breasts, his head was hardly moving.

Not until well after Dotty had signalled to Bridie that they should leave and she had lifted her elbow, was there anything like an audible bellow of distress, earsplitting, long, and repeated. The sergeant's newfound sounds joined with the shrill cries of alarm issuing from Mavis, as the knobbly handle rocketed from the sergeant's anus to clatter against a wall.

*

The rattle of the whip hitting the wall galvanised Dotty and Bridie to exit hastily. The rustling of the waterproofs encasing their fast-moving bodies was just audible in the gaps between the sergeant's roars of anguish.

Out into the car park and into the rain Dotty raced, the heavier Bridie struggling to go the pace, lagging and gasping behind her. The engine was running by the time Bridie lurched into the car and it was on the move before she closed her door.

'Amazingly, the car clock only says ten past two. It seemed we were in there for hours,' Dotty said. She left the car lights off until she cleared the car park. The roads were quiet; the by-pass deserted.

Dotty lit a cigarette and inhaled deeply, finding it soothing.

'Do you think Doctor Dernehen will call the cops, missis?' Bridie asked, her breathing settled.

'Not a chance, but I can't wait to hear how he talks his way out of this one. I've heard plenty of his bum stories. Mind you, his recent ones have gone in one ear and out the other. The one he returns home with tomorrow might have a ring of truth to it. When he attempts to explain the tenderness that he's bound to be feeling in his nether regions, I will be listening avidly. How he embellishes this tale could better any that he has ever told. He was doing some roaring when we left. His voice sounded quite distorted. Indeed, they weren't the roars of passion. No, they were not roars of passion... or sounds suggesting he was enjoying the experience... or that he might ever consider going back there for more.'

'No missis, but how am I ever to look him in the eye again? It's all a bit of a worry.'

Chapter 32

Tracy was having none of it. This little doctor fella wasn't going to repel her advances. His crash helmet was black, shiny, streaming with rain and glistening in the headlights of passing vehicles. She felt for the end of the visor and flipped it up. The rain blasted into the gap, stinging Mickey's eyes. She would see what he looked like, then slag him off for being so standoffish.

Mickey wrestled his arms out from beneath the tarpaulin, took hold of the visor and pulled it back down.

She let go of his shoulder, lifted her arm and hooked it around his neck, locking the crook of her arm between the helmet and his shoulders. She wrestled and twisted Mickey's head, like Martin had often done to her when he played that repulsive game of Dutch ovens. The beast had made a habit of it, forcing her head beneath the sheets after he had farted.

Dragging Mickey down, she held him close, his head resting on her lap, face downwards. Easing her grip a touch, she turned his head to search for the strap on the crash helmet and tugged at the buckle.

Mickey rearranged both his arms and pushed Tracy away, forcing her arms apart, loosening her grip on him. Breathing out deeply, the gush of air whistled through gaps to the side of the visor. Rocking, he moved away from Tracy, closer now to the side of the trike frame. The seating arrangements were insecure, like those of a rough-public-house toilet. Sliding sideways, he overbalanced.

Seth was concentrating on the approaching bridge when he felt the violent movements going on behind him. The trike had begun swaying and the steering wheel was kicking in his hands. His glance back over his shoulder happened the split second he lost control of the machine.

As Mickey rocked, Tracy had lurched across and pounced. Seeking another grip on his neck, she forced both their heads and shoulders to hang out over the mudguard, spray zipping up on them.

The opposite back wheel and the front wheel lifted from the road and the engine roared. Seth turned his head quickly, took his foot off the accelerator pedal and fought the trike's obstinacy as it teetered on one wheel, worryingly skewing away from its course.

Moving his weight in the direction of the lift, Seth twisted the steering wheel the other way, bringing the front wheel back down onto the road. Then the rear wheel landed, bouncing the frame upwards on the springs. In his panic to bring the trike under control, Seth over-steered, causing the rear of the trike to swerve, the back tyres skidding, having poor adhesion on the rain-lashed road surface.

The trike's nearside rear swung in between two steel, H-beam supports on the left hand side of the bridge. The countering swing out from between them never came. The rear wheel smacked into an approaching support, as did Mickey's crash-helmeted head. As the trike careered on, a raised edge dragged him from the trike by the neck, along with Tracy, her arm still crooked around it.

Chapter 33

The sound of the whip hitting the wall was dying in the sergeant's head as he slid his body off the end of the bed. His feet hit the floor and he stood there, bent over the mattress, whimpering, with his head resting on the sheet. His hand crept slowly towards his buttocks, not knowing what to touch or whether to.

Mavis threw her legs from the bed onto the floor and dashed, hand raised, for a switch, her body wraith-like in the dimness.

A ceiling light illuminated the bedroom and she moved quickly to the sergeant, placed an arm around him, resting her breasts on his back. 'I think we've been attacked, Billy!' she shrieked. 'I'm sure I heard something going on, someone in the room.' She saw the whip lying on the floor through widening eyes. She moved her eyes from it and looked through the bedroom door. The patio door stood ajar, enough room to allow two people through together. 'What? Jasus! Did someone do what I think they've done, Billy?'

'For the love of fock, Mavis, aye, it feels as if my hole's been reamed out, but. I'll get some focker for this, you wait and see.'

Mavis stepped behind the sergeant, kneeled and went to part his buttocks. 'Be focken' careful,' he roared, 'it's focken' nippin' back there. It's more painful than my focken neck, so it is.'

'Ugh, who could have wanted to do this to you?' Mavis asked and gulped, 'there's no signs of any whipping.' Gingerly she parted his buttocks and viewed the area with a nursing-sister's eye. 'Whoever's done this shoved the whip handle up your hole. There's a drop of blood oozing out of it. A bit of internal bleeding, or maybe a pile has burst.'

'I've never had piles in my focken' life. I think you've a jealous lover, that's what t'fock this is all about. I'm the sufferer because of it.'

'Couldn't be.'

'The old, Devious Doctor, I know he's been sniffing around,' he said mockingly.

'Doctor Dernehen. Impossible. It couldn't be him.'

'Are you sure about that?'

'Very sure. This will need to be looked at. An infection there will give you much more pain. Maybe a doctor will have to use a stitch. That'll be painful too. You're not having much luck, are you?'

'Sufferin' fock. You're not about to raise a doctor to look at this tonight, are you?'

'I'll ask Doctor Dernehen to look at it later today. In the meantime I'll clean around it.'

'He's going to have a right good laugh at this. I wouldn't want it to get around the station. Laughing focken' stock, I'd be.'

'Maybe so, but Doctor Dernehen's the best. You'll have to make up a story that you sat or fell on something…Tell me, why were you wearing an X-ray gown? I've just noticed it laid there.'

'Another focken' tragedy. I'm sure those focken meathead, bastard bikers set me up to have an accident. I've been lying in a ward for focken' hours. The accident unit put me in for observation. RUC rules. Shock, they reckoned. I've wricked my focken neck, and all. I came here from the ward. Would there be anything else you want to know?' he asked irritably. 'And if you have another lover, I don't suppose it's a biker?'

'I only know one, and then only casually, nothing serious!' Mavis replied, sheepishly.

Chapter 34

Robbie Manson had turned twenty-one years of age a month back. Three weeks later, he passed the HGV test on his first attempt.

He was dead chuffed. Soon he'd join the ranks of macho truckers, making up convoys, yacking trucker-talk over the CB airways and warning good buddies of smokies on their tails. The tales of truck stops, the evening stopovers, the strippers, the wild drinking sessions, how to fiddle the tachograph, tips on uncoupling the engine governor if he were desperate to make up time and how to avoid the Traffic Commissioners, made him yearn for his turn on the open road.

Until that night, he had fought his frustrations. His employers, O'Grady Transport, had restricted his driving to moving tractor units around their yard on the outskirts of Toomebridge. It seemed to Robbie that his boss was at last appreciating his driving skills and had loosed him onto the road alone, to collect a trailer of hanging beef from an abattoir and return it to the yard.

Later that day, an experienced driver would take the load to London for the Monday morning opening of Smithfield's meat market.

Nobody bothered to tell Robbie that hanging beef was a hazardous cargo, catching out many drivers who allowed the load to swing.

Robbie's foot was flat to the boards, but the engine governor kept his speed down to 60 mph. To drive safely in the road conditions, Robbie should have slowed down, but he would like to have driven even faster.

Half-way across the bridge, the windblown rain seriously affecting his visibility, even with the wipers lashing water away on fast speed, the truck headlights picked out the trike. Two people had just fallen off it, he was sure, and he could see the trike driver wrestling with the steering wheel, turning it this way and that, trying to bring the machine under control. The driver hadn't a hope and it veered into his lane. Robbie's eyes were only for the trike, fifty yards away, closing fast and making right for him.

Braking savagely, he threw his steering wheel over, doing everything in a rookie driver's ken to avoid the trike. The end of the trailer slewed and aquaplaned on locked wheels, its momentum pulling the tractor unit at an angle into the oncoming lane. The hanging meat moved, the weight-in-motion altering the trailer's equilibrium, toppling it onto the bridge parapet.

There was another explosion of sound. The snapping and grinding of metal and escaping compressed air, announced the tractor unit parting company with the trailer. The trailer scraped along the parapet, wobbled before straightening, its offside wheels running over the already dead bodies of Tracy and Mickey, laid together, arms entwined, in a grotesque embrace.

Then it hit a major pillar, where it thudded to a halt, its back doors bursting open.

The jolt of the tractor unit's catastrophic uncoupling savagely threw Robbie forward, bending him double over the steering wheel, which had caught him on the abdomen. The tractor unit careered on, uncontrolled.

Seth, miraculously, for he saw little through fogged-up goggles, passed by the swerving tractor unit and the toppled trailer. The trike was snaking as it passed by, but its undulations decreased steadily, Seth steering out of the skid. With the trike's course straightened, he steered into the correct lane and stopped.

The leading bikers ploughed on, striking the slowing tractor unit. The ones to the rear braked, before skidding into the carnage littering the road in front of them.

Robbie pushed himself backwards and instinctively stood on the brake pedal. The tractor unit juddered to a halt, its headlights now illuminating a scarier scene.

Robbie picked up his mobile phone and punched in 999, his hands shaking, his teeth chattering. Already he was learning of some aspects to trucking worrying to drivers.

Police and Fire Brigade vehicles and ambulances raced to the bridge from Toomebridge and Randallstown, approaching the accident scene in torrential rain. At first sight, the emergency services thought the carnage the worst ever seen on the roads of the province.

On closer inspection, many of the inert bundles first thought as bodies were, in fact, sides of beef jettisoned out the trailer's back door when it had abruptly halted.

A doctor attending the scene of the accident pronounced dead the horribly mangled bodies of one male and one female, found close to the bridge wall.

After police had attended, reported the accident details and photographed the scene, an undertaker transported the corpses to Toomebridge mortuary.

At the time of the accident, the bikers were travelling nose to tail. The leaders fared worse than their following muckers did. Joe Reardon braked early when he saw Seth having difficulties, as did Roddy O'Dowd. Both hit the tractor unit glancing blows, which threw them from their bikes. Both catapulted into the air to land on their crash helmets, which no doubt saved their lives, but did nothing to prevent broken collarbones.

Injuries to other bikers, caused mainly by skidding when braking and taking preventative action, varied from broken legs, wrists and fingers, to cuts and bruises and the badly-skinned back of one the "ladies", travelling without protective leathers. Her injuries were such that, later that morning, an ambulance transferred her to Ballyboil hospital, which housed the only specialist skin-graft unit west of Belfast.

Chapter 35

Into the darkness of that windy, rains-wept morning, stepped Mavis, umbrella in hand, poor protection in the conditions for herself and the slow-moving sergeant. Each short step the sergeant took heaped further agonies on his violated body. Five minutes passed before they, sodden by now, reached the hospital's back door. Mavis found a wheelchair, which speeded the increasingly complaining sergeant back to the ward.

With his head hanging over the two pillows supporting his neck and lying face downwards, Mavis tucked him into the bed, fitted his surgical collar and saw him resting comfortably. Then she left him. Her priority now was to search for a suitable instrument on which the sergeant might possibly have an accident. Her thoughts had turned to the shower he would have later that morning.

*

At 09:00, that morning, Cynthia arrived for work. She thought it strange to find the door leading to her office and Doctor Dernehen's consulting room locked. Thinking it a mistake by a cleaner, she sought out Security and took possession of a spare key.

Both her office and the consulting room were in darkness when she opened up. Immediately it was obvious that not all was okay.

Hearing a voice calling, she hastily snapped on a light and entered the consulting room.

The room looked empty, but drawn curtains concealed the examination bed. Approaching it warily, she pulled the curtains wide. Doctor Dernehen lay on his back, on the bed. From his ankles up to his armpits, layer upon layer of orthopaedic tape bound him to the bed. When ripped from limbs, that super-sticky tape made children cry and strong men wince. Quite plainly, the doctor was unable to move, could never have made his escape.

'What in heaven's name has happened, doctor?' Cynthia cried, her voice rising, showing her concern.

'Get a sharp knife, then I'll tell you,' he said, turning his head and waggling a finger. He was unable to move much else.

Riley's trousers and shirt were ruined. He kept them on, but later that morning he sent Cynthia into town for replacements.

Dressed in his white coat, sitting in a chair and rubbing some circulation into his limbs, moments after all the tape had been removed, he explained: 'I fell asleep last night after setting the alarm facility on my mobile to wake me at twelve-thirty. I was due to take a ride to Larne with a motorcycle club.

'They were calling for me here at one o'clock. The alarm sounded, I woke up, but I couldn't move, couldn't get up, as you saw. Quite a shock it was to be sure. A bit of a worry to find myself in the dark and strapped in like that with an alarm ringing.' Riley's thoughts turned to Mavis. Only she knew he was sleeping over in his consulting room.

'For the love of Jasus, how horrible,' Cynthia said, holding a hand to her mouth. 'You've no idea who might have been responsible?'

'None. I never felt anyone applying the tape. Maybe someone trying to prevent me from taking the ride, but I don't know. I won't know if the bikers called for me until I see one of the club members. I don't feel harmed, but it was quite an odd experience, claustrophobic. April Fool's Day hasn't been postponed this year until now, has it?'

'It's a serious assault as far as I'm concerned. I'd call the police if I were you.'

'I'll let it ride for an hour or two. Nobody has stolen anything, as far as I can tell. In that time, I might get a clearer picture as to why it happened to me and who's responsible. Spotting a couple of young interns, writhing about, devastated with laughter, might just pinpoint the culprits. It looks more a student-like prank than anything else I can think of. I'm sure I got up to similar tricks when I was at university.'

*

Mavis had thought that a drain plunger, sitting upright on its sucker, was a piece of equipment a cleaner might accidentally leave in a shower. If fallen upon arse first, it would possess enough potential to cause similar injuries to those afflicting the sergeant.

The sergeant made his weary way to the shower room immediately after eating his breakfast, uttering a succession of ouches on each short step he took. Within a minute, the reverberations of someone slipping and landing solidly, reached the ears of nurses attending a desk in the corridor outside the ward.

The sergeant didn't mind his neck pain flaring or the indignity of another female prising open his buttocks to assess his injuries; he was just pleased that he now had a less embarrassing reason for having them.

Mavis supervised the nurses assisting the sergeant back onto the bed, where once again he lay face down. Mavis dried him off and instructed a nurse to telephone for Doctor Dernehen.

The telephone rang in Cynthia's office as she was speaking to the doctor. She answered it, listened and said, 'Sister O'Rourke asks if you'd mind popping by Ward 1, doctor. Apparently, a police sergeant has suffered an accident in a hospital shower and he needs attention rather urgently.'

'Drat,' the doctor said. 'I'd arranged to have the day off. Shouldn't be here by rights, but I'll take a look.'

Riley was in full flight along the corridor leading to the ward. Taking short, fast steps, his feet were flying out to the sides, his toes pointing skywards. He was showing no signs whatsoever that he had suffered any ordeal when Mavis stopped him.

Riley read the concern in her eyes. She laid a hand on his arm and led him away from the desk and the vicinity of any potential eavesdroppers. Breathlessly she said, 'Before you ask, it was me. I knew you'd need a reason for not taking the trike ride. The bikers might turn nasty. They're a dangerous lot to cross. I just couldn't let that happen. Now you have an alibi. I'll see to it that the bikers learn of your ordeal. I tied you good and tight, I had to do it like that. Sleeping like a top, you were. Nothing hurts, no?'

'No. Nothing. Cynthia found me. She'll make a statement to the cops if I ask her. She thinks I should report it.'

'Oh good… Now about Billy… er, Sergeant Liptrott has had an unfortunate accident in a shower. Now don't laugh when I tell you…'

Ballyboil hospital's emergency unit received a telephone message that an ambulance was on its way, carrying an injured female for admittance to the skin-graft unit. About the same time, Riley arrived at the foot of the sergeant's bed, wearing a hard-to-hide smile. The doctor's bleeper sounded. He pivoted on one foot and left the ward for the desk, picked up a telephone handset, pressed some numbers and listened.

He returned to the ward and said to the assembly of giggling nurses, gathering around as if for a grand unveiling, 'I'm going to be quite busy shortly, so show me the rest of this damaged arsehole!'

*

At 9 a.m. that morning, Dotty was slightly concerned that the cops might be seeking the perpetrators of an indecent assault at a nurse's home, which prompted her to switch on the sitting-room television set for Ulster TV's news update. She stood watching the adverts finish, an elbow in the palm of a hand, smoke curling from the cigarette held between fingers of the other.

As the programme began, the bridge over the River Bann at Toomebridge loomed into the screen. 'Horrendous accident on the bridge over the River Bann, the main story of the morning,' boomed the unseen announcer. 'Our cameraman, on the scene soon after the occurrence, has picked out the main features. A trailer lies toppled onto the bridge parapet, smashed motorcycles lie on their sides in twisted poses. Some sides of prime Irish beef lie together as in a mass grave. Other carcasses dotting the road look like cadavers on a Hollywood-epic battlefield.' The bouffant-haired announcer appeared on the screen, looking pleased with his account. 'Police at Toomebridge state that several motorcyclists, on their way to a rally on the mainland, collided with an articulated lorry,' he continued, 'the accident happened around 2 a.m. as heavy rain fell.'

The picture changed to a television reporter standing facing a wet and bedraggled Seth Mulligan. Answering a question unheard by viewers, Seth was saying, 'All I can remember is the trailer and tractor unit aquaplaning from the other lane. I avoided it on my trike by steering around it. Unfortunately some of my muckers didn't and were injured.'

'As the lorry driver is reported to have said,' the interviewer asked Seth, 'did the two persons found dead at the scene fall from your trike?'

Dotty saw Seth brow furrow, saw him clamming up, heard him give a safe answer: 'I didn't see them. I don't know them. I know nothing at all about them. I've told the cops they were hitching a lift. I swerved to avoid the truck. I was on the other side of the road when the lorry skidded and swerved. It must have skittled them.'

'The whole array of emergency services attended the scene,' the announcer continued. 'Ambulances transferred the injured to various hospitals in the region. Police at Toomebridge seek witnesses and anyone who can assist with the identities of the man and a woman confirmed dead at the scene. Anyone wishing further information should contact Toomebridge RUC station on this telephone number.'

Dotty gasped. She didn't believe Seth's account. She recalled from her tour of country lanes with him that there were no seatbelts on the trike. There probably should have been; she was sure the law required them and that Seth had lied on camera, as he would have to, as he would have done to the cops… to save his arse. There were three seats on the trike and if Riley had made that journey, he too could possibly have been among the dead. How lucky was that?

Chapter 36

Mustard-keen Jessica Dodds was the junior reporter on the Toomebridge Clarion. She relished the opportunity to escape the typing-up of uninteresting words onto a computer screen in a stuffy office. When nothing occurred in the area to whet reader appetites, the editor expected her to write-up dreary, topical accounts. It could be anything from Paddy with his prize onion and his damned local-dung-enriched plot to detailing the jam recipes sent in by the League of Wives and Mothers.

The accident on the bridge over the River Bahn afforded the chance to escape the drudgery that wasn't stretching this "Little Miss Dynamite's" talents for sniffing out real stories… scoops.

A report of the incident awaited her when she arrived for work that morning. A computer, set up to receive overnight reports from a news agency, had churned it out. She ripped off the printed sheet and took off, before any senior reporter got their hands on it.

Jessica drove to the scene, but by 9 a.m. no involved vehicles remained and traffic flowed freely in both directions. It dawned on Jessica that she needed to become acquainted with and friendly towards a member of the police or the emergency services: a person willing to notify her, day or night, for a small inducement, perhaps, of similar occurrences. Only then, could she obtain the scoops and pen dramatic, moving accounts of the most-newsworthy incidents.

The Toomebridge Clarion headlines would shout: Our Readership Clamours for Jessica. Circulation would soar and all because of her descriptive, literary skills.

At Toombridge RUC station, the desk sergeant provided only meagre details. 'My hands are tied until the coroner allows the release of more details,' he said. With the solemness of an undertaker, he told her the number of persons killed and the locations of the hospitals where ambulances had taken the injured. That amounted to his contribution: revealing no cause, blaming no one, giving away no snippets of interest. It was hardly what Jessica required to write her revealing report.

The young constable just leaving the station as she left, weighed down with wet weather gear, she thought a better source, if he would fall for a smile of encouragement and a spot of chat. She followed him outside. The shred of information he stuttered out, after she had gigglingly convinced him that she had spotted him at a Saturday night disco, offered definite possibilities.

He ushered Jessica to the rear of a van he was about to drive away and parted with the little he knew: a night shift cop, spouting earlier that morning in the canteen, was once a member of a church congregation in Ballyboil. He had thought he recognised one of the mangled dead as being the husband of the niece of the minister of that church. He thought the dead woman too large to be the niece and he knew that the couple were living in the former manse, Whynot Hall.

A quick scan at an Ordinance Survey Map provided Jessica with the location of the Hall, about an hour's drive away.

*

Dotty had allowed Bridie to take off the remainder of the day. After breakfast, dressed in the same wet weather gear, she pedalled her bicycle away towards her home in her village, still shaking her head.

The successful outcome of their mission led Dotty to believe that Riley would require no food for a day or two. She smiled smugly, thinking his little bottom would need time to recuperate and repair, maybe in a sling, certainly in cold, Dettol-laced baths.

The parrots screeching in unison on hearing or detecting in some way the approach of a strange vehicle, was an ability of theirs that Dotty had only recently noticed. Their crescendo of noise began as the credits rolled on a TV soap she was watching about a city hospital, which ended at 11 a.m.

She switched off the set and entered the hallway, fully expecting to see a vehicle pull up that she didn't recognise. Dotty wondered how in heaven's name the parrots heard the Fiat Cinquecento that appeared from between the trees lining the drive, headlights blazing. It was raining hard and the wind was gusting so much that she couldn't hear the car's engine. The 'shush,' she said to the parrots seemed lost, too, for it had little affect on them.

A floral-design umbrella appeared from the driver's door and snapped open. It was in danger of turning inside out until Jessica, beefy thighs flashing white beneath her leather mini-skirt, her raincoat flying open, eased out of the car and arranged it closer to her head. She peered from beneath the umbrella, looked up the steps to where she saw Dotty standing, 'Ah,' she uttered, and took to the steps. 'Would you be the minister's niece?' she blurted out from halfway up.

'I might be. Who's asking?' Dotty asked, standing, hands on hips, somewhat bemused.

Taking the answer as a yes, Jessica said, 'I'm a reporter from the Toomebridge Clarion. Is your husband at home?' In the shelter of the porch, she lowered her umbrella.

'I'm expecting him shortly,' Dotty stalled, 'why do you ask?'

'You've no idea where he is right now?'

The question startled Dotty. She had no idea where Riley was. She knew where he was at 2 a.m., but no idea at all where he was right then. She suspected he might be bathing his sorrows, among other things, but where at, she didn't know. Was he still in Sister O'Rourke's apartment? Was he in his office at the hospital? Was he at this moment receiving treatment from another doctor? She could only be sure that he wasn't reporting the incident to Sergeant Liptrott.

Wherever he was at that moment, she only expected his subdued reappearance at the Hall to come later that afternoon, and armed with some unbelievable fanny of his trip on a trike and the nether injury he suffered on landing heavily on a pointed object, after lurching into space when a trike wheel dipped deep into a pothole.

What could she tell this inquisitive girl?

'Right now, no.'

'I'm sorry that it's me that brings you this news, but a man answering your husband's description was killed in a trike accident on the bridge over the River Bann...'

'Ridiculous!' Dotty roared.

'...at Toomebridge...in the early hours.'

'How would you know what he looks like?' Dotty asked, shocked at the suggestion.

Jessica recoiled at the outburst. Breaking bad news had its drawbacks.

Nevertheless, she raced on, sniffing an interesting leader unfolding. 'This morning,' she stuttered, 'this morning a...a...at Toomebridge RUC station, I, I, I talked to a contact who told me a body had been identified as that of the man married to a minister's niece. And...and that they lived at Whynot Hall.'

Dotty gasped, clutched at her breasts, reeled and held onto the doorframe, her thoughts running riot. This just couldn't be true. Someone must have mistakenly identified the body as that of Riley. Certainly, he was supposed to take a ride on Seth's trike...but it couldn't be him. He wasn't there...just couldn't be...he was in nursing-sister O'Rourke's apartment at Ballyboil hospital nursing home, finagling, when the accident happened...wasn't he? But if that wasn't Riley in the nursing-sister's apartment...just whose backside was it she had infringed? Could it possibly have been someone else's?

'You all right?' Jessica asked, her voice rising, showing concern at Dotty's shocked expression. She stepped forward and steadied Dotty.

'You've shaken me... though I don't believe what you say can be true.'

Time to get some substance for a storyline sorted out, thought Jessica. 'You're upset. I'll run you over to Toomebridge mortuary. Now, if you like. You can make a positive identification there. If it's not your husband, then you'll be able to shed your worries. I'll fetch you back here afterwards.'

Dotty thought that was exactly what she should do. Better to go with this girl now. Less traumatic than waiting for the cops to come and ask her to do the same thing...whenever they decided to get their fingers out.

Never had she rung up a hospital requesting knowledge of her husband's whereabouts or when he was due to leave for home. She wasn't about to do that now. After all, he was supposed to be taking today off. Telephonists listening in to conversations were renowned tittle-tattlers. Knowledge of her seeking the whereabouts of Doctor Dernehen on his day off would be on the lips of all hospital personnel and start rumour spreading.

Beneath Jessica's umbrella, Dotty walked disconsolately down the steps to the Fiat.

On their way, Jessica used her mobile and telephoned ahead to Toomebridge RUC station, explaining she was transporting a Mrs Dernehen, a person who might be able to identify one of the bodies, to the mortuary.

They, and a cop driving a police car, arrived at the mortuary, just as the stiff, sombre and displeased attendant was about to leave for his lunch break. 'Make it quick,' he said snappily.

Two cadavers lay covered-over on stainless-steel tables, in the basic surroundings of the mortuary, its floor recently hosed down, redolent of disinfectant.

'Prepare yourself, it's not a pretty sight,' the attendant said gravely, having encountered many reactions from viewers of the corpses he had laid out on the "slab". 'The head's flattened. The truck ran over it. It's still squashed and inside the helmet.'

On his guidance, Dotty stood close to the covered head, her face whitening, her legs quivering, knees weakening. Jessica stood back, feeling similarly affected.

The attendant whipped back the cover.

The sight was a bit of a worry. Dotty turned her head away quickly and retched onto the floor. The cadaver's head was unrecognisable. A mixture of bits, blood, bone, skin and brain, oozed from cracks in the crushed helmet. Only the thin hairline of a moustache, a portion of top lip and teeth protruding through a narrow aperture in the crushed fibreglass, gave any indication that it might be Riley. Sighting the cadaver's naked neck and shoulders hadn't helper her recognise it.

Dotty recovered, but kept a hand up to her mouth. Hesitantly, she said, 'I'm not sure,' and moved towards the door, wanting to get well away before she retched again, into the fresh air, leaving the sight and the smells behind.

'Are there any body marks you know of? That would help if you do, Mrs Dernehen.' the cop called after her.

'No, there's none I can think of,' she said. She was almost at the door when she stopped suddenly, a thought striking her. Turning back to the table, she flexed a finger and said to the attendant, 'Pull the cover right back, let me have a look at his knob.'

The attendant and the cop each raised an eyebrow and looked shocked at the unexpected request, but the attendant duly obliged.

Dotty swallowed hard. What she saw reminded her of walking out with Riley on Mount Boil, her first encounter with his "wheeker". 'That's not my Riley,' she said, turning her head away. The lower part of the naked body was unscathed, apart from some wicked cuts below the knee.

'How are you so sure?' asked the constable.

'My Riley is well-hung. That there's an earplug!'

This is an interesting story, but *my* editor won't print it, thought Jessica.

*

Before they reached the outskirts of Ballyboil on the return journey to the Hall, Dotty had convinced Jessica there were no grounds for including her name in any story that she might be encouraged to write for her newspaper. 'Go out and dig some more,' she encouraged, 'you've the knack, the balls to ferret out a real tale, find the names of the real victims.'

She fed her some blarney: 'It took courage to act on the information you received and initiative to find me, before the cops have their act together.'

On Ballyboil bypass, Dotty asked Jessica to drive past the hospital. She wasn't about to change her mind and ask the questions on Riley's whereabouts or say anything that would give the girl reporter another lead. She just wanted to see Riley's Jaguar parked there, something to reassure her following the trauma of the mortuary.

The car was there, in its parking place out front. Dotty said nothing to Jessica about the car, gave nothing away. 'Drive on,' she said, 'take me home. I need a cigarette.'

*

Squalls were a feature of the late afternoon, prohibiting gardening activities at the Hall. Dotty sat in the sitting-room, reflecting, sipping tea, chain-smoking… enjoying the silence, her own company.

The hallway clock was striking 4 p.m. when she heard the sound of a car above the patter of rain blowing against a window. The parrots hadn't detected the car as strange and remained silent. Someone she knew was calling. She reached the hallway door to see Riley, already out of the Jaguar.

Dotty took a deep breath, shuddered and then exhaled just as deeply as she looked down at him. Her jaw had dropped, was askew. Her arms were hanging listlessly down by her side, hands low, much like those of a heavyweight boxer relaxing in a neutral corner following the delivery of a haymaker to the point of an opponent's chin.

This was Riley leaving the canvas, refreshed; how had he dodged the blow? He was mounting the steps jauntily, a spring in his heels, leaping up them two at a time, without any obvious signs of having any painful condition, whatsoever. Seeing him act so fit was a canvas-calling blow to her chin, staggering her, surely prohibiting her recovery under a count to ten.

'Well, have I had a day of it today?' Riley's face beamed as he greeted Dotty, gripping her arms at biceps level, squeezing them and kissing her gently on a cheek.

'It was rough on the trike last night, was it?' Dotty spoke with a controlled voice, not understanding his jauntiness, not understanding much at all, but noting he wore a different shirt and trousers than what he had packed into his overnight bag.

'Didn't get that far,' Riley replied, most casually, as he eased past her and into the hallway.

'Why, what happened? Why didn't you go with Seth? Dotty asked, trying to sound as casual as he did.

'I never made the trip. I was hanging around and just about to head for the side door of the hospital to meet with him, when an ambulance brought in a police sergeant. He was suffering a horrific and embarrassing injury.'

Riley did his rounds of the hallway menagerie, rubbing Cedric's ears, sticking a finger through the grills of the parrot's cage, stroking the sides of offered heads. 'The parrots are vying for my attention now. Look, they both like their ears rubbed,' he said, his face screwed up with delight.

Dotty swallowed hard; wondered why Riley was acting so cool. 'A police sergeant suffering a horrific, embarrassing injury; what might that be? Couldn't be…could it? Was this another of Riley's fannies? What was she to make of it? 'Sounds serious,' she probed, coyly. 'It must have been to keep you from your trike ride. You were so keen. Surely there was another doctor available and capable of sorting out the sergeant?'

'They could have called on someone else to deal with it, I know. I was Johnny-on-the-spot, so to speak. All I needed to do was change clothes. Quite apologetic from the word go the A&E nightshift staff were, to have collared me. I've spent most of the morning in theatre attempting to rectify the sergeant's embarrassment. I'll have to apologise to the bikers for not being there when they called.'

They entered the sitting-room. Riley chose the chaise-longue, stretching out, hands behind his head, relaxing, Dotty the couch.

'I took interest in the case and couldn't let it go by me, immediately the young Chinese intern began explaining the nature of the sergeant's injuries.

"Sorry to trouble you, Doctor Dernehen," she said, "but an ambulance has brought in a Sergeant Liptrott. He has a horrendous anal injury, consistent with that of a male rape. We have also admitted a woman with a problem quite similar to that which the sergeant suffers. The ambulance crew found her in the same location as the sergeant and brought them into A&E together. Her problem, though slightly less tragic, is only an inch away in bodily terms from that of the sergeant's injury."

'Couldn't believe it, when I found out it was him. It was hard hiding my smirks and smothering my sniggers. I felt quite unprofessional, but couldn't help myself.

I went directly to A&E. The sergeant's roars of pain were easily audible as I entered. Much like those of a bear suffering an aching tooth and a sore head, they were. Feck only knows how a bear with a sore arse sounds. I peeked through the cubicle curtains. Slavers were running from the sergeant's contorted mouth in greater quantities than I've ever seen Cedric spray, when *he* suffered a painful arse.

'The Chinese intern was by my side. She told me that she was a bit naïve on the subject of rectal injury and that when the sergeant came in, he was continually repeating the words, "Voodoo Vibrator…"'

'Feckin' what?' Dotty cried out, as much in disgust as the worry of which direction Riley's story was about to take.

'I've not ever encountered one personally, but I believe they're readily available from that Adult Shop in town,' Riley answered, not taken from his stride. 'A&E staff comes across these titillation tools more often than I do. I've heard them tittering together that some hapless soul has attended to have a vibrator removed, still buzzing, apparently, from deep within an orifice.

'Then the sergeant went on to say… "That's the last time I'll ask daft questions. Fock me; I'll never utter those words again." The intern thought we'd a right one on our hands and asked me if I also thought so.

'The sergeant must have been in great pain to sound so nonsensical Out of his head.' Dotty felt she had to make comment.

'He was indeed. The pain wasn't going to go away quickly, either. Because he had treated me so shabbily and made me suffer the indignity of a court appearance, I instructed the intern to slip an icepack into his crevice. I could have given the silly bugger a shot of morphine to shut him up for a while, but I refrained. It wasn't professional, I know, but I was going to hang on for as long as I could before examining him. I then took a leisurely cup of coffee with the intern.

'Over the coffee, I asked her exactly what had happened to the sergeant. She told me he had just begun night duty when the assault occurred. The police inspector who followed the ambulance to the hospital was embarrassed that it had happened to one of their lot, and didn't want any gossip getting around.

'I asked her how the woman was, to be told she was extremely tired and resting in a ladies' ward, sleeping deeply and serenely, with one hell of a smile on her face. The intern told me she had talked to her and that her story, though extremely strange, fitted in with the sergeant's injury.

'The intern wrote it down for me in the form of a report, which I read later. It began: My husband has gone to work abroad and didn't want me to go astray looking for sex with other men while he was away. His fear was great and he went to considerable lengths to have me comply with his wishes, and considered that only a vibrator or something of that nature would calm the eruptions of nymphomania to which I am prone.

'In an Adult Shop, in Ballyboil, where this type of article is freely available, the shopkeeper there offered him an extra-special device. It was black, over-sized and the box it came in described it as a Voodoo Voice-Activated Vibrator. The price was two hundred pounds and, my husband, knowing I enjoyed kinky sex, bought one without hesitation.

'He didn't have a lot of time before leaving for the airport and only gave me brief details of how to use it to achieve sexual contentment. His instructions were for me to take it from the box, fit the batteries and say to it in a distinct voice, 'Fuck me.' That instruction programmed the vibrator to switch on, to find my receptive orifice, and to enter it without assistance.

'I tried it tonight and it worked perfectly when I instructed it, but a problem soon became apparent. My husband had forgotten to tell me what vocal instruction switched off the damned thing. I lay thrashing around on my bed, shouting *stop*, but the thing kept ramming away, causing multiple orgasms, until I was too weak to pull it from my vagina. It nearly drove me crazy. I thought a knobbing-to-death was on the cards. The batteries were long-life and would last for weeks. It was certainly doing the job for which my husband bought it.

'As I got into my car to drive to the hospital, my hollering and frenzied jerking rendered my watching neighbours hysterical. On the way, I had more orgasms. My head was rolling from side to side and my tongue was lolling from my head. I opened the car window and screamed, "I'm coming again, I'm coming again," like you do when the knobbing is great. My head was out the window when I saw the police car pull in front of me. I braked and stopped behind it.

'The sergeant left his vehicle and spoke to me through my open window, asking if I was okay. An amicable and charming man he was and I knew he liked the look of me when his lips rolled back, like a stallion snickering as it approaches a mare in heat. "No, I'm feckin' well not," I screeched at him. "This Voodoo Voice-Activated Vibrator is knobbing me to death."

'I lifted the release lever and edged the seat back. Then I lifted my skirt. The sergeant saw the vibrator jerking crazily and he heard the buzz. Leaning into the car, he placed both hands between my legs, gripping the vibrator firmly, but even he didn't have the strength to budge it. He pulled his head back, scratched it and said, "Fuck me." That's when *his* problems began.'

Dotty's mind was in a quandary. How could all this be? Riley's tale was clearly a fanny. She had come to expect them from him, though elements of the truth garnished this tale: the injury, pain and suffering of the sergeant. Hadn't her assault with the whip, though in the end she had used it differently, been on Riley? Now he was telling her of an injury to a sergeant; an injury in the exact location that she had expected *him* to be suffering on his arrival home.

'Later I went to the cubicle. I pulled sharply on the curtains encircling the patient. They opened with a swish. The police inspector had returned and was sitting there drinking tea from the plastic cup he was holding in one hand. In the other hand, he was holding a cup with a straw, with which he was moistening the sergeant's lips. I thought that quite touching.

'My entrance seemed to have shocked the inspector for he dribbled hot tea down his chin. Rising from the stool, he wiped some remnants of a Kitkat from his tunic. The sergeant was lying face down so the inspector moved his stool and placed the plastic cup on it.

'The inspector then stuck the straw into the sergeant's mouth. Then he left, but not before I had teased him that the sergeant might need something harder to bite on when I began my examination of his brutalised area.

'I whipped the covering sheet from the sergeant's back, fitted prophylactics and removed the icepack. The sergeant groaned so I walked to the front of the stretcher to see better his pain-ravaged face. It was then that I noticed an injury to the sergeant's neck, consistent with an assault with a hard implement.

'I recall once seeing a similar injury. A contestant had savagely thrust an elbow downwards onto the nape of the patient's neck. It happened at The Queens Hall in Belfast and was the result of a kidology-gone-out-the-window professional wrestling move at a show there.'

Dotty swallowed hard. Riley's tale continued to reveal too much déjà vu for her liking. A brandy would have gone nicely with what she was hearing, but the decanter was full of cold tea.

'"This should not hurt too much," I told him. He was frightened. His eyes were those of a maddened horse, large, brown and bulging. I retreated to his nether end where I yanked the bruised cheeks apart, exposing his injured orifice. He howled blue murder.

'"Mercy me," I mouthed, while peering closely, my eyes evaluating the injury. The injuries were consistent with the woman's unusual tale. Then I said to him, and I know *you've* heard the description from me before, "The last time I saw anything of this nature, I was examining the anus of my St Bernard dog, following a feast it had of boiled bone. The dog had crunched, swallowed too much of it, was unable to digest it properly, and the anus had turned itself inside out in its struggle to defecate." He bawled even louder, when I said to him, "Your anus looks just like a portion of king prawns marinating in a Tandoori sauce. Would you like a photograph?"

'Then, I let out several knowledgeable hums and some ahas. When I let go of his cheeks, it allowed them to clap together. That brought forth another pained utterance.

'I eased the straw from his lips, removed the plastic cup from the stool and sat facing the sergeant. He seemed happier with his face pointing downwards. Perhaps he didn't want to look at me. Having him in that position, I was unable to ascertain whether he was pleased to see me again or not.

'His injury needed delicate surgery, for sure. I thought some nobbly instrument must have caused it as it was rammed in forcefully by a powerful arm, with more damage arising as it exited at speed, with a plop and a loudish holler, no doubt. I gave him a nonsense prognosis. I thought he deserved one. "You will require a small amount of skin grafting to help repair a deep, rectal fissure. It will not heal quickly or perfectly if we leave it agape."

'I had seen from his notes that he was a gentile and while examining him I noticed a considerable amount of prepuce. "But have no fear," I said to him, "you have an ample foreskin, which, hand held, will have flip-flopped on many occasions over your bobby's helmet. You don't really need it. A circumcision in the circumstances would provide enough skin to use as a graft and satisfactorily repair the anal lesion. Your ability to pass a pain-free stool in the future will rely on the quality of my repair. However, being a cop, you'll have a distinct advantage over others of your ilk. In fact, I believe it a much-sought-after quality and you will be the envy of the RUC. For each time you thrust a hand behind your back to wipe, you will feel both a bit of a prick and a complete arsehole."'

'He must have thought that a bit of a worry, Riley?'

'I didn't bother asking him, Dotty. You know how cops tell lies?'

'Yes Riley, liars are a bit of a worry. If the sergeant had fallen as he showered, on the upright end of a plunger, say, wouldn't he have received a similar injury?'

'Hmmmmmmmmmmmmmmmm,'

.

Printed in Great Britain
by Amazon